Sign up for our newsletter to hear
about new and upcoming releases.

www.ylva-publishing.com

OTHER BOOKS BY ROSLYN SINCLAIR

The X Ingredient
The Lily and the Crown

The Carlisle series
Truth and Measure
Above All Things

THE CARLISLE SERIES: BOOK 2

ABOVE *ALL* THINGS

Roslyn Sinclair

ACKNOWLEDGMENTS

This series is a labor of love that could never have been completed without the invaluable help of my friends and colleagues at Ylva Publishing. I would particularly like to thank Astrid Ohletz, Sandra Gerth, and most of all my editor, the peerless Lee Winter, who whipped the series into shape.

The greatest thanks must go to my wife, whose patience and keen eye for detail helped me see what the story needed to become. I couldn't have done it without her.

DEDICATION

The *Carlisle Series* is dedicated to the readers who have given me so much support and joy over the years. You all mean more to me than you'll ever know.

CHAPTER 1

"What do you consider your professional strengths?"

The question sent a shiver up Jules Moretti's spine. No matter how many job interviews she sat through, the fears of inadequacy—the surety that you just weren't what they were looking for—never went away. Not completely.

And she had to nail this interview. She really did. There were a lot fewer options than she'd expected when she'd begun the search.

"Well," the slender, dark-haired woman in front of her replied, "as my résumé says, I've worked for two families in the past ten years—it really gave me a chance to bond with their children. Before that, I worked in a day care all through high school, where I got to know many of the kids over time. So I'd have to say that my real strength is"—she gave a self-deprecating laugh—"endurance."

"Definitely seems useful. Essential, even." Jules looked back down at her list of questions. "Um, how would you handle a crying baby?"

The woman, whose name was Zahra, folded her hands in her lap and gave a modest smile. "Well, since I'm starting my master's in child psychology, I keep up-to-date on all the latest studies and models—"

"You mean the latest trends?"

Jules turned a swift glare onto Vivian Carlisle, who sat next to her on the love seat in the den opposite from their candidate. Even now, it took a bit of gumption to glare at Vivian. Nobody just glared at the editor-in-chief of *Du Jour*, the world's most influential fashion magazine.

But nobody else was Vivian's girlfriend either, much less a girlfriend who'd been tearing her hair out about finding a nanny.

Vivian had better not screw this up. They'd conducted two other interviews so far, and both of the applicants had taken jobs elsewhere. Finding a top-tier nanny in Manhattan was no joke. Jules could never have imagined the competition.

Zahra didn't seem rattled by Vivian's rude question, though. Instead, she gave Vivian a serene smile. "I wouldn't call them 'trends' so much as 'evolutions of thought,' but I certainly understand why that might seem frustrating. It's like, why can't we just pick an approach and stick to it?"

"Exactly."

That was the strongest display of enthusiasm from Vivian so far. Jules dared to hope. Zahra was a perfect candidate, and she'd be a real get for them.

Vivian was just over five months pregnant. They should have had somebody locked down by now. The best nannies planned months ahead when they were transitioning from their current jobs. Zahra's current charge was turning five in June, and his parents had decided it was time to hire a Parisian au pair instead. Never mind that Zahra was fluent in French, Arabic, and Spanish. She also had a minor in computer science and had played piano in the Columbia University Orchestra.

With all her might, Jules willed Vivian to hear her thoughts: *don't drive this one off.*

"Crying means that your needs aren't being met," Zahra said. "If the baby's hungry? I feed her. If she's sleepy? I rock her and sing to her, if she's into it. When your child is brand-new to the world, it's essential to make her feel like she'll get what she needs. Her future development depends on it."

"No pressure, huh?" Jules said. "Ha, ha."

Vivian's glare, coupled with Zahra's polite smile, told Jules that the joke hadn't landed.

The rest of the interview went more smoothly. Zahra seemed impressed by Jules's description of how the house would be set up for the baby and with how specific Vivian was about what Zahra's duties would be. How very, very specific. And particular. In fact, Vivian's particularity seemed to woo Zahra instead of scare her like it did *Du Jour* employees.

"It's really helpful to know exactly what a parent is looking for," Zahra said as she rose to her feet.

Jules glanced at Vivian with a rueful smile. "Vivian's pretty good at knowing exactly what she wants from an employee."

Vivian looked decidedly unapologetic.

Zahra flashed Jules a grin that showed off her perfect teeth. "Well, as her assistant, you probably appreciate the benefits of that."

Jules opened her mouth to say "It's a mixed blessing" when the truth caught up with her. She wasn't Vivian's assistant anymore. She'd been fired a week ago by Mark Tavio, chairman of the Koening publishing group and Vivian's asshole boss.

So now it would look weird to outsiders that she was helping out with this whole nanny process.

Sweat broke out under her arms. What should she say? She didn't want to lie. Not exactly. But she and Vivian hadn't discussed this. They didn't have a cover story. Now that she was thinking about it, that was so stupid. Why hadn't they worked something out?

Now Vivian's face had closed off, inscrutable, as she gazed at Jules while Zahra waited expectantly. She was letting Jules take the lead.

Jules prided herself in thinking on her feet, but all she could manage to say now was, "It took a while, but there are definitely benefits to clarity."

"For sure." Zahra slung her Parker Clay tote over her shoulder. "It was very nice to meet both of you. Ms. Carlisle, thank you for your time."

"Of course. Julia, will you walk Zahra to the door?"

Vivian's tone was cooler than it had been before. It made Jules frown as she led Zahra to the front door. What was Vivian's problem? Jules was only being professional.

She took Zahra's business card, waved goodbye, and then turned back to the house. Time to find out what Vivian's attitude was about.

When she returned to the den, Vivian was perched on the edge of the loveseat, hands folded her in her lap and clearly ready for a conversation with a capital C.

Might as well beat her to the punch. Jules slid a hand through her thick, dark hair as she approached. "We should have prepped in advance."

"Prepped what, exactly?"

Jules sat next to Vivian on the love seat. Normally, she'd reach out for Vivian to settle against her, but that didn't seem to be on the menu right now. "Our cover story about our relationship. Sorry I was clumsy earlier. I'll—"

"Our cover story."

Vivian's tone was as flat as a Kansas highway. Her eyes hadn't warmed up one jot either. What was her problem?

"Well, yes," Jules said. "I can't exactly snuggle up to you and give you a big kiss."

"What a shame," Vivian said. "That's exactly the sort of gesture I love. Julia, I agree there's something we need to discuss, but I wouldn't have called it a cover story."

Zahra's business card crumpled in Jules's palm. "What would you call it?"

"I know we're in an unusual situation," Vivian said tightly, "but I've never been interested in living a lie."

"I didn't *lie*," Jules protested. "I didn't say I'm your assistant."

That was so weak, and Vivian didn't let her get away with it. "No, but you let her think it. You're not my assistant, you're my girlfriend. I'm not saying it's a problem right now, but if we hire her, I'm not interested in pretending to be something we're not."

Even in a fraught moment, hearing the words *you're my girlfriend* from Vivian Carlisle's lips sent an uncontrollable thrill through Jules. Only a month ago, that would have seemed completely impossible. Was Jules to be blamed for wanting to protect their fledgling relationship?

"So what do you want her to think?" Jules asked. "Vivian, it's still too early to come out in public. You just got divorced, and I just stopped working for you. Plus, we haven't been together for long."

"I'm not talking about taking you to the Met benefit," Vivian said in exasperation. "Good domestic help is known for being discreet, and if Zahra is as qualified as she seems, she's not going to blab to Page Six if we hire her. You don't have to tiptoe around our relationship in my house, of all places."

Put like that, Jules's caution did seem extreme. The thought of being out to anyone, including the nanny, still made her blush. Ordinarily, it wouldn't have bothered her at all.

4

Ordinarily didn't include your lover being pregnant, freshly divorced, and—oh yeah—the most powerful person in the fashion industry. To say nothing of that person being your former boss.

People would talk so much shit about both Jules and Vivian for this. Jules would be alternately a victim and a gold digger while Vivian would be alternately a predator and a sucker. Nobody would see it as a relationship of equals who were going into it with clear eyes and level heads.

Yeah. Jules definitely felt level-headed about Vivian Carlisle, all right.

She bit her lip as she looked at Vivian, taking in her bright blue eyes and short, blonde hair; her sharp, elegant features and her faultless poise. A slouchy cream sweater played down the slightly rounded shape of her stomach. Today, on a relaxed Sunday afternoon, she still looked more chic than most women dressed to the nines. Behind her eyes ran a mind that could see every situation from every angle without breaking a sweat. And beneath her casually elegant clothes hid a woman who was incredible in bed.

The most primitive part of Jules's brain snarled, *Of course I want everyone to know she's mine.*

The slightly more evolved part reminded Jules that Vivian might not feel the same way. Vivian might not, for example, get a mushy feeling in her chest at the thought of Jules. Vivian might not see a brunette woman in a crowd and feel her heart skip a beat, wondering if it was Jules.

Vivian might not love Jules back.

Oh, she cared for Jules. She'd made that clear. But how far did caring go? So far, it extended to wanting to have Jules around, wanting to have sex a lot, and talking and spending time together in a way that Vivian didn't with anybody else. But she hadn't used the word *love* or anything like it and showed no indication of doing so.

"It was just a reflex, I guess," Jules muttered instead of saying any of that. "I wasn't thinking about it. We've both got a lot of other things going on right now, right?" She held up her hands and began to count on her fingers. "You having a baby, tying up your divorce, fending off Mark, plus me starting a new job, and…"

Thankfully, a rueful smile crossed Vivian's face. "I take your point. The divorce is in the rearview mirror, though."

No kidding. Vivian's cheating ex-husband, Robert Kirk, had been eager to finish the divorce process. Which would have been fine, if not for the fact that he was just as eager—no, more eager—to sign away all rights to his own daughter, leaving Vivian with sole custody.

That was just how Vivian had wanted it, but Jules couldn't help thinking it was kind of a shame, even if Robert was an asshole. The baby was going to grow up knowing that her dad hadn't wanted her.

I'll make up for it, Jules thought before she could catch herself.

"Yes," she said instead, scooting in closer to Vivian. "He's history, and you're all mine."

Vivian's snort belied her relaxing body language, the way she leaned toward Jules. "The possessiveness comes out, does it?"

"You know it does." Jules slid a hand through Vivian's hair. "Wanna make out before we call Zahra?"

Vivian's fingertips were already tracing over Jules's blouse buttons. "Think this one will say yes?"

"Do you?"

"I do." Vivian's eyes cut a swathe into Jules's own. "I'm pretty good at seeing when someone wants to say yes to me."

Heat suffused Jules until her scalp prickled. She made a low, breathless sound.

Vivian dropped her hand down to Jules's knee and slid it forward until it cupped the inside of Jules's thigh, burning through her pants. "Would you like to do more than make out, Julia?"

"Yes, Vivian," Jules whispered, leaning forward for a kiss. "Oh yes."

CHAPTER 2

A FEW DAYS LATER FIRST thing Friday morning, Jules finally got a look at the office space that her new boss, Simon Carvalho, had commandeered. It was the headquarters for Adrian & Jo—the upscale online consignment store he'd left *Du Jour* to found. Even though Jules had been thrown into working with Simon thanks to being fired, she was still excited. It was cool to be in on the ground floor.

Not that she was doing anything thrilling. Currently, her duties were similar to what they'd been while working for Vivian at *Du Jour*. Simon had promised her a quick path to advancement, though. She'd be more than an assistant soon.

How soon remained to be seen.

The space itself was nothing special. *Du Jour*'s office was an exquisite place, laid out in cream and glass, the walls covered with original work from the hottest artists. It occupied a prime place in the Koening Building in Midtown. Adrian & Jo had humbler beginnings: standard, crappy office tile. Bare walls. Cubicles dotting the landscape. Simon was renting half a floor in Murray Hill. Not the most fashionable part of town.

It was definitely a letdown after *Du Jour*, but Jules supposed she'd been spoiled in that regard.

Adrian & Jo would move up in the world. You had to start somewhere.

At least it wasn't an open-office plan. Simon had imitated Vivian, who said it was a basic human right not to have to look at people in all directions. It was her one mercy to the underlings.

Jules looked around the empty office, put her hands on her hips, and exhaled. There was plenty to take care of. And taking care of things was her specialty. She whipped out her cell phone with the ease of a career gunslinger and got to work.

After a few days of being at loose ends, it was like putting on a comfortable pair of shoes. You needed those when you hit the ground running. She'd never had to pester tech support at *Du Jour* or the phone service provider or office furniture rental stores. But it was all about having soft skills, right?

She was carving out a professional space for herself to make up for the one she'd just lost. It was separate from her relationship with Vivian too. Something just for Jules.

The experts said that kind of thing was healthy in a relationship. Separate interests and careers and all. If Jules repeated that to herself enough, she might believe it.

To Jules's pleased surprise, Simon called her at six thirty p.m. and told her to wait at the office. He arrived fifteen minutes later, looking exhausted, and gave her a wry smile.

"I was busy wrapping up *Du Jour* business all day," he said. "I'm so glad Vivian wasn't there. I just thought I'd stop by and see what—"

He glanced around the reception area and saw Jules's iMac humming along atop her neatly organized desk. Then he looked into his office and saw the same thing.

"Wow," he said.

"I called in our IT guy," Jules said. "I think he likes me."

"Do I smell coffee?"

"I got a Keurig."

"Did you *vacuum*?"

"Dusted too."

"Do you want my job?"

Jules laughed. So did Simon.

"Give me another ten years," she said. "At least. Then maybe."

"Ah-h-h." Simon stretched, pressing at the small of his back. "I kid, I kid. I'm not giving up this gig."

Then he took a deep breath and exhaled it slowly. He looked a little apprehensive.

"You'll be great," Jules said. "This whole thing will be great. I've been sending emails," she added, "and I got some replies. It sounds like a lot of people are excited about what we're doing. A high-end online designer consignment store is groundbreaking."

"I know." Simon raised an eyebrow, impressed. "I got copied on a lot of those replies. You've been a busy little bee."

Jules shrugged. Better not to say that keeping busy was the best remedy for missing Vivian.

"Well." Simon rubbed his hands together as he headed into his office.

Jules followed him, watching with amusement as he sat down in his chair and straightened his shoulders.

Then he lifted his chin.

"Julia," he began.

"Oh no," Jules said, already giggling.

Simon prissily placed his hands on the top of the desk and then looked at Jules over the rim of his glasses. "I'll want my La Colombe coffee here in five minutes. No. Three."

"Oh...stop..." Jules said, and leaned back against the wall, holding her stomach as she laughed.

"And then I'll want to hear from Testino yesterday. Literally. Now hurry up and reverse the Earth's rotation—"

"Yes, Simon," Jules managed as she tried to control herself. "I'll get Allie on that right away."

"Oh God," Simon said and broke character as he lowered his head to his desk, laughing. "Allie. We left her with *Allie.*"

Thinking of Allie, the hapless intern Jules had hired right before getting fired herself, only made Jules grin. "Maybe not for much longer." The thought sobered her. "If Allie can't do the job on her own, she's toast."

"Out of your hands, I'm afraid," Simon said, sitting up again.

"I know, but I feel kind of responsible," Jules said. "I mean, I hi—I recommended Allie in the first place. And Vivian told me she might have to fire her if—"

She realized just a moment too late what she'd just confessed. When Simon looked at her with wide eyes, she knew he'd realized it too.

"And when did Vivian say this?" Simon inquired neutrally.

Jules took a deep breath and tried to sound casual, which didn't really go well with taking a deep breath, so she wasn't surprised when it didn't work. "Yesterday."

"So you're still talking to her."

"Yes," Jules said, refusing to break eye contact or back down. She wasn't about to lie about it. Not to Simon. It wasn't a crime to communicate with your former boss.

"You know," Simon said, leaning back in his chair, "I'm actually not as surprised as I probably should be." He never took his eyes off Jules's face.

Try not to sweat. "You said she'd miss me. You knew all along that she—"

"Needs you?" Simon said bluntly.

Jules turned pink. "I guess so. But…but I won't let it interfere with my job, Simon. I work for you now, not her. It's just"—she waved her hand helplessly—"we're sort of—"

Simon's lips quirked. "Friends?"

"Yes," Jules said, a little ashamed. It didn't feel good to deny what Vivian meant to her. But if she couldn't explain their relationship to the nanny, she sure as hell wasn't going to try it with Simon. Not yet.

"I wonder if it's easier to be friends with Vivian outside of work," he mused, then smiled ruefully. "You'll have to let me know. I don't think I'll get the chance to find out for myself."

Jules bit her lip, wishing she could say otherwise. But Simon had wounded Vivian. Worse, he'd caught her unawares, and that was what she'd never forgive. The best Jules could tell Simon was that Vivian had decided he might still be useful, and she was pretty sure she shouldn't say that at all.

"Anyway, what are you doing tomorrow afternoon?" Simon asked. "I'm attending a little get-together with Jack and Lazaro. Should be fun. Lots of alcohol. Be nice if you could come too."

"I'd love to." Jules bit her lip. "But I might already have plans."

"Oh?" Simon raised both eyebrows. "Anything particularly exciting that justifies missing an opportunity to make new connections?"

Jules squirmed. "It kind of falls under the rubric of, uh, the subject we were just discussing."

"The sub—" Simon blinked. "Vivian?"

Jules blushed. "She wants to take me out to lunch for my birthday."

"Your birthday was last week."

"I remember, seeing as how it was the day I got fired," Jules said dryly. "It's kind of a belated thing."

It was also kind of a fictional thing. Vivian and Jules were meeting for a belated birthday celebration, it was true. But they weren't going out anywhere. Jules had been very clear that her idea of the perfect celebration would involve more private activities.

They'd had a *pre*birthday celebration for Jules already, one that involved their first time having sex. It had also involved an email from the magazine *Modernity* inviting Jules to submit a lifestyle article, courtesy of Vivian's influence.

Jules was still on the fence about that particular gift, to say the least. She'd been relieved when Vivian had said she wanted to give Jules something more traditional this time.

Simon sighed, and his thoughtful expression vanished into a resigned why-do-I-even-bother look. "I'll think of you when I'm sucking down gin fizzes and ogling male models."

The statement was benign enough. Simon's voice had no suspicion or accusation in it.

Jules still had the feeling she wasn't off the hook just yet.

CHAPTER 3

WHEN JULES CALLED THAT NIGHT, Vivian picked up on the first ring. It was a total ego stroke, but Jules knew that if she made any waiting-by-the-phone jokes, the conversation would be over before it could even begin. And she hadn't heard Vivian's voice all day long, so that option wasn't on the table.

You're such a goner, Moretti.

"How's it going?" she asked.

"It went," Vivian said, and hearing her voice made Jules feel weightless, buoyant, and giddy. "I'm glad the day is over."

"What happened?" Jules asked in concern.

"Nothing out of the ordinary." Vivian sighed. "Just another Saturday when I didn't have a second to myself until now."

"Oh." Jules bit her lip. "Should I call back later? Or—" It was almost ten o'clock. "Or just wait till tomorrow?"

"No. Tell me about your day. Is setting up an office as thrilling as it sounds?"

"Oh yeah. I got a lot of work done. I ordered a coffee maker."

"And here I was afraid your talents would be wasted."

Like Jules had been using them to their highest potential at *Du Jour*? "Nope. In full bloom."

"So I see."

And then Jules got an idea. A wonderful, magnificent, potentially impossible idea. "I mean, I am multitalented."

She'd tried to sound innocent—bland, even—but something in her voice must have tipped Vivian off because the moment of silence went on a little too long.

And Vivian sounded suspicious when she replied, "I suppose so."

"I've missed you," Jules said.

Vivian cleared her throat. "Well," she said, "you'll see me tomorrow."

"I haven't seen you since Wednesday."

"I came by your apartment on Thursday."

"Not what I meant."

"Julia…"

"I meant I haven't seen some of my favorite parts of you since Wednesday."

"Julia!" Now Vivian sounded almost scandalized.

Jules grinned. "Well, it's true."

"You'll—like I said. Tomorrow."

"Not soon enough," Jules said.

Vivian's breath caught again.

"Have you missed me too?"

"I, uh…" Vivian said, then admitted, "Yes."

"Any particular parts of me?"

"This conversation took a classy turn."

"Sorry." Jules laughed. "I didn't know phone sex was about class."

"We are not having phone—we're not doing that."

"No?" Jules made sure her disappointment came through loud and clear.

Vivian coughed. "No."

"Even if I do all the talking?"

"No."

Jules felt her face flushing and her nipples going tight beneath her pajama top. "Even if I tell you all the things I want to do to you tomorrow?"

"Who says," Vivian replied, "that you're going to do all the work?"

Jules gasped. She could practically see Vivian smirking on the other end of the line. She rallied quickly. "But it's my birthday party, isn't it?"

"I'm pretty sure we already had that particular kind of party," Vivian said archly.

"That was the prebirthday party. This is the post."

"Who do you think you are," Vivian asked, "Kim Kardashian?"

Jules ignored her and barged onward. "So, anyway, as birthday girl, I think I should get to do whatever I want. And what *I* want is to do *you*."

13

"I…" Vivian's voice trailed off. Then she said, "Yes?"

Jules grinned. The night was looking up. "Yeah. Don't get me wrong: everything you do to me feels great. But what really gets me going is pinning you down and having my way."

"Oh?" Vivian said faintly.

"And you like it too, don't you? I like doing. You like being done to. Don't you?"

"Yes," Vivian admitted.

"How's that make you feel?" Jules said, her face flushing hotter than ever. "All you have to do is just *be*, and you'll drive me crazy. Does that make you happy?"

"Yes," Vivian repeated—gulped, really.

"Good." Jules smiled. "So…you'll let me, won't you?"

Vivian's voice dropped down into a low rasping register as she asked, "Let you what?"

Jules closed her eyes and swallowed hard. "Strip you off, lay you down, and fuck you."

"Oh," Vivian said after a few seconds, "well."

"And take it slowly," Jules whispered. "No more of that quickie stuff. We'll take it so slowly. Just the way you like it. I like it too."

"Y-you do?"

"Oh yes," Jules said. "Licking you up and down. And whatever else you want. Don't you know I like doing that?"

"I might have had a clue," Vivian croaked.

"Will you let me do that?"

Jules could practically see Vivian discarding a dozen clever responses before giving in and saying, "Yes."

"Good," Jules breathed. "I can't wait." She paused. "Can you wait?"

"I don't have much choice, do I?" Vivian said in a strained voice.

"Yes, you do. You know you do."

"Don't," Vivian warned.

"Why not?" Jules said. "What would be wrong with…it?"

"With what? If you want me to do it, you can say it."

"Touch yourself, then," Jules said, and she blushed at her own audacity, telling Vivian Carlisle to masturbate.

"You'd like that, would you?" Vivian murmured. "Listening to that?"

It was Jules's turn to make a croaking noise. "Yes," she managed.

"That's a shame," Vivian said, "because while I've done my fair share of that, this time it won't satisfy me. I want your touch, Julia, not my own."

Jules's mouth opened, but nothing came out. And yet more nothing. Then she managed a squeak.

"Good night, Julia," Vivian purred. She ended the call.

Jules stared at her phone and then fell back down against her pillow with a wail, cursing the woman she loved with all of her heart.

Vivian was the most powerful woman in the fashion industry. It made sense that she gave extravagant presents without a second thought. And now that Jules wasn't working for her, she'd clearly decided it was fine to do just that.

Jules tried not to feel self-conscious about opening three beautifully wrapped boxes that contained a Bottega Veneta bag, Stella McCartney ankle boots, and a bottle of Amouage perfume. Put together, they amounted to almost two months of her new salary.

She spritzed the perfume on her wrist. She smelled strong notes of incense and amber. Not something she'd have bought for herself—hefty price tag aside—but it was already growing on her. A new perfume was a risky gift. Of course Vivian had gone for it.

Jules sniffed her wrist. "This is really nice. How did you know I'd like it?"

Vivian smiled at her. They were on the sofa in the living room, Vivian with one bare foot tucked beneath her, Jules with a lapful of wrapping paper. "It suits you, doesn't it?"

"Yeah. I wouldn't have thought so. It's...heavier than what I usually wear." Jules sniffed again.

"Like everything in fashion, perfume either has intelligence or it doesn't. You deserve something smarter than a one-note floral. Give me your arm." Vivian held out a commanding hand.

Jules obeyed, extending her arm so Vivian could smell her wrist. At the brush of Vivian's nose on her skin—and seconds later her mouth—Jules got goose bumps. As Vivian had no doubt intended.

"I'm starting to think you have an agenda," she breathed.

15

"See? It's making you more intelligent already." Vivian kissed her wrist again.

"Ha, ha." Jules used the opportunity to stroke Vivian's cheek, which turned pink beneath her touch.

Vivian's breath caught. "Behave yourself."

"Me?" Jules withdrew her hand from Vivian's grasp and put the stopper back on the perfume bottle. "I'm just packing up all these lovely presents."

Vivian cleared her throat. "There might be one more."

Jules looked at her quickly and saw that her cheeks were even pinker.

"*Really*," she said.

Vivian nodded.

Hell yeah. Whatever this was, Jules was one hundred percent here for it. "Gee, why isn't it here with all the other stuff?"

"You're infuriating," Vivian said very calmly for someone blushing.

"Glad to hear it," Jules said, aroused and more than a bit curious. It had to be naughty underwear, but what would Vivian have bought for her? If she knew what Jules would like perfume-wise, did she have similar insight into teddies and chemises?

Whatever she'd bought, she knew Jules would want to wear it for her. That was beyond question. Jules was already anticipating putting on something skimpy and filmy, only to take it off again slowly before Vivian's burning gaze.

Then Vivian shifted on the sofa, looking uncomfortable. "Nnngh."

"Are you okay?"

"Yes," Vivian said, rising to her feet, "but I think I'd better go upstairs." Now her pink cheeks didn't so much suggest arousal as embarrassment. "Just give me a few minutes and then feel free to come on up."

"Oh. Okay. I'll be up soon," Jules said, delicately not pressing for further information. Vivian had once said that pregnancy was a degrading experience. She wouldn't appreciate being asked about the particulars of whatever symptoms degraded her at any given moment.

"Fine," Vivian said and headed quickly out of the room.

While she waited, Jules looked at the Amouage bottle she'd placed back in its velvet-lined box. It was a big bottle, not the usual hope-you-like-it smaller size. Vivian had known it would suit Jules.

Unspoken was: *I know you well enough for that.*

A shiver ran up and down Jules's spine. To be known, to be seen by Vivian was both thrilling and scary. What if Vivian saw something Jules wasn't yet ready for? Like how deeply she'd fallen?

One day at a time. Jules took a deep breath and let it go. *That's what relationships are about, right?*

It had been long enough. Jules headed upstairs.

She knocked on Vivian's door, but there was no answer. Anxiety of a different kind curled in her stomach. Was Vivian okay?

Jules dared to open the bedroom door uninvited. From the doorway, she called, "Vivian?"

"I'll be out in a moment," Vivian called back from behind her bathroom door. "You can come in."

Relieved that Vivian hadn't passed out or anything, Jules shut the door behind her and sat on the gigantic bed, trying not to bounce up and down in anticipation of naughty underwear and stripteases. Vivian apparently wasn't feeling well, after all. And that was the most important thing. Jules had to be considerate and thoughtful. Because Vivian might not even feel like—

Vivian opened the door and emerged from the bathroom in a rustle of champagne-colored silk and gold lace.

She was wearing the gown she'd worn on New Year's Eve. The night Jules had realized how far she'd fallen for Vivian when faced with all of her beauty and grace.

Jules's eyes widened. Her heart stopped. She couldn't breathe. Her skin heated as if with a fever. It was official: Vivian Carlisle was a medical condition.

Vivian folded her hands placidly and cocked her head to the side, her eyes bright with amusement, which was par for the course whenever Jules looked like a drooling idiot. But how else was Jules supposed to look with Vivian standing right in front of her and wearing...*that?*

The gown fit her differently now, of course. The waist of the dress looked tighter, for one thing. And her breasts were bigger than they'd been on New Year's. And she obviously wasn't wearing any kind of bra. And *oh, oh, oh.*

"Um, uh," Jules said and held out both her hands, frantically beckoning Vivian to the bed. Her knees might not hold her up if she tried to stand.

Vivian chuckled and glided forward.

"You've already worn your New Year's outfit for me," she said. "Turnabout's fair play."

This was turnabout with interest. Jules's head spun as she remembered how Vivian had moved in that dress on New Year's Eve. How everyone in the ballroom had stared at her. And how Jules had been so completely certain that she'd never, ever be allowed to touch so much as Vivian's hand.

She stood up. And without a word, she took Vivian's face in her hands and kissed her very slowly, very gently, as if it were their first kiss all over again.

Vivian grabbed her shoulders and pressed closer but seemed content to let Jules take her time with their kisses. Days. It had been days since they'd—

"You have quite a few fantasies to fulfill." Vivian breathed the words against her mouth.

She'd have to get more specific. Jules had more than *quite a few* fantasies. "I-I do?"

"Of course. The fantasies you told me about with me wearing this dress."

Jules bent down to kiss Vivian's throat. Oh Jesus, she was wearing the same perfume. She'd even tousled her short hair the same way. Had she done it on purpose, or was Vivian just being *Vivian*, uncannily able to do the perfect thing with the perfect outfit every single time?

"What fantasies were those? Tell me." Jules nipped Vivian's throat.

Vivian hissed.

"Tell me," Jules repeated.

"Let me see." Vivian tilted her head to the side and shivered when Jules cupped her breast. "Oh. You said…something about taking me on my back in the coatroom."

Jules rubbed her thumb, and Vivian's nipple went pebble hard.

"*Oh,*" Vivian moaned.

"That was actually your fantasy," Jules pointed out, her head starting to spin. She slid her free hand down Vivian's back and stroked her ass.

Vivian shuddered again.

"You had another one." Jules kissed Vivian's shoulder. "Remember?"

"I—"

"You fantasized about me pushing you down on the bed while you were still wearing the dress and still in your shoes." Jules kissed her again, deeper this time, until they were both panting. "And about how wet you'd be."

She bit gently at the side of Vivian's throat.

Vivian groaned, sliding her hands up and down Jules's back. Jules felt her getting weak in the knees, felt her breath becoming uneven, and recognized the other signs that meant Vivian was losing the ability to do anything but let Jules fuck her.

"Are you wet yet?" Jules whispered.

"Julia," Vivian said, then whimpered, "*Julia*," when Jules began to kiss downward along the edge of her bodice, nuzzling at the rise of her breasts.

Jules bit her nipple through the silk and lace, and Vivian gasped, scrabbling at Jules's back with her fingernails and rubbing her nose in Jules's hair.

With shaking knees, Jules sat back down on the edge of the bed. When Vivian made to join her, Jules held her still so that she could lean forward and bury her face in Vivian's breasts again, could reach around and cup her ass.

Vivian swayed forward even as her head fell back, and she had to put her hands on Jules's shoulders for balance.

"You said you'd beg me to do whatever I wanted to you," Jules said. She stroked up until she found the gown's zipper between Vivian's shoulder blades and carefully slid it down. The hiss of the zipper, almost indecent by itself, made her feel faint.

She didn't want Vivian to take the dress off yet, though, so she left the zipper at half-mast and tugged at one of the gown's spaghetti straps. "Here, let's…"

Vivian wriggled, shrugged, and eased the strap down until she'd slipped her arm through it and exposed one of her breasts, flushed pink and with its nipple tight and hard.

Jules leaned in and kissed and licked and pulled with her teeth until Vivian said, "Please," and "please," and "*oh*."

Dizzy with heat, Jules paused just long enough to pull off her own shirt before tugging Vivian down to the bed. She laid her flat and leaned down, kissing her again, then again, over and over. She reached beneath the skirt—Vivian trembled eagerly—to find the soft, smooth skin she loved, then trailed her fingers higher up until she realized Vivian wasn't wearing any underwear at all.

"Oh," Jules whispered. She moved her fingers. "Yeah, you're wet."

Vivian trembled, looking up at Jules with dazed eyes.

Jules moved her fingers down and away to stroke the inside of Vivian's thigh.

"Oh no, please."

"Please what?" Jules whispered, nibbling her throat again.

"Please," Vivian managed. She arched her hips. "I need, I need—"

"Need what?" Jules remembered Vivian being high-handed on the phone last night. She smiled against her skin. "My mouth? You want my mouth on you?" She stroked Vivian's thigh again. "Want me to eat you right up?"

"God!" Vivian gasped and squeezed her eyes shut.

Jules pinched her nipple.

"Oh! Hurry... Don't make me wait..."

"It's my birthday party," Jules whispered, and something in her voice—maybe the promise of torment—made Vivian moan and tremble again. "And I get to do what I want."

"Oh no," Vivian whimpered, but it was the opposite of a protest.

"And I want it slow. Nice and slow."

"No," Vivian repeated, which might have worked better if her nipples hadn't gone even harder and if Jules hadn't felt her moisture beginning to drip down the inside of her thigh. "I need—"

"I've got what you need."

Jules proved it, making love to Vivian slowly, peeling the gown off her inch by inch. And the more Vivian begged for Jules to do it faster and harder, the more thrilled she was when Jules refused to comply.

By the time they were both naked, the gown was probably ruined and Vivian had lost the ability to speak in recognizable words.

Jules finally gave in to her own desires and stopped the torture. She fingered Vivian so slowly, so gently, that when Vivian began to shudder and sob and clench all around Jules's fingers, it seemed to echo inside Jules as well.

Vivian moaned when she was done and melted back against the mattress, trembling. The sight of her flushed and delighted made Jules's vision swim.

"Jesus *Christ*, Julia."

Jules, sticky and breathless and so turned on that she might actually die, tried to come up with something to say. All she managed was, "I love doing this. I—"

Vivian opened her glassy eyes and looked at her. Before Jules could say anything else—before she could admit to loving Vivian even more than sex—Vivian stroked her own hand up Jules's thigh.

To her own surprise, Jules gasped. "No. Not yet."

Vivian blinked and said hoarsely, "No?"

"Not yet," Jules repeated and swallowed hard. There was something else she wanted even more. "Let's get you cleaned up."

Vivian blinked again. "What?" And then, when Jules bent her head and began lapping hungrily between her legs, she cried out.

"Can't get enough of you." Jules's cheeks, hair, and even her ears were getting sticky. She kissed, licked, sucked, all while Vivian writhed and grabbed at the pillows, too breathless now to beg or plead. "Wish I could do this to you all the time."

"Please," Vivian wailed and came again with a cry that ended on a sob. Her thighs quivered.

Jules pulled away, licking her lips, and waited for Vivian to pry her eyes open.

After a moment, she did, and her breathing began to slow again. Vivian trembled, covered her eyes with her hand, uncovered them again, and swallowed hard. "Um-m." Then she managed to say, "Come here."

Jules did, lying down next to her, looking into her eyes. *Get it under control,* she ordered herself. *Make the moment last.*

Vivian, of course, was interested in doing no such thing. Instead, she touched Jules's chin, urged her in for a kiss, and tasted herself on Jules's lips.

"Well," she said throatily when they parted.

Her voice made Jules shiver; Vivian was always at her most mischievous when she'd just been sated and was ready to turn the tables.

"Enjoyed that, did you?" Vivian asked.

Jules might have been able to come up with something smart-assed had Vivian not trailed her fingertips up the inside of Jules's thigh. So she just gasped, "Yeah."

"Did you get what you wanted?" Vivian's eyes glinted. "'Having your way with me?' Wasn't that how you put it? Did you get to do that?"

She slid her middle finger inside Jules, who almost came on the spot.

Vivian's lips curved into a pleased little smile. "Well, did you?"

"You tell me," Jules panted. "You were there, weren't you?"

Vivian pressed her thumb against Jules's clit.

Jules whimpered. "Oh God."

"Yes," Vivian murmured. "I was there."

"A couple of times." Jules grinned, suddenly elated. She loved Vivian so much in that moment that it hurt. It actually took the edge off her arousal for a second. She beamed, combed her sweaty hair off her forehead, and kissed Vivian's nose.

Vivian, of course, looked surprised. Then her eyes narrowed in clear suspicion, as if wondering what Jules had up her sleeve this time.

Absolutely nothing, as it happened. Jules chuckled. "Are you going to get me off or what?"

"You do laugh at the strangest times," Vivian said and took her revenge by sliding another finger inside Jules.

Jules stopped giggling at once and bit her lip too slowly to stifle a moan.

It was Vivian's turn to chuckle. "So what would get you off?"

Jules decided to go for it. She kissed Vivian's forehead, then her temple, and murmured, "Last night, you said you've touched yourself. More than once."

Vivian hissed, and her fingers went still.

"Tell me what you think about." Jules cupped Vivian's breast again, plucking at her nipple. "Tell me."

Vivian could have played with her a little more. Taunted her a little more. She didn't. Just whispered, "You."

"Jesus." Jules rested her forehead against Vivian's.

Vivian's breath puffed against Jules's lips as she said, "Would you like to hear about the first time I did it?"

"Yes," Jules whimpered but forestalled Vivian by kissing her because she couldn't help herself.

When she pulled away again, Vivian flexed her fingers.

Jules trembled. And trembled harder when Vivian began to whisper.

"When you kissed my cheek." Her voice, that purr, raced up and down Jules's every nerve. "The first night we had dinner here."

"Oh, my God." Jules gasped.

"I was so surprised at my reaction." Vivian turned her head and kissed Jules's throat. "That night, I tried to go to sleep." She bit down lightly. "I couldn't."

"Vivian." Jules dug her nails into her own palms as she tried not to come, her mind on fire. "Please."

"I thought about New Year's Eve. How much you wanted me. And how soft your mouth was." Vivian licked where she'd bitten and began to thrust with her fingers.

Jules's hips arched forward helplessly.

"And I wondered what I would have done if you hadn't gone home. If you'd come into the room and slipped into bed with me and began to kiss me, touch me..."

"Jesus," Jules sobbed again, grinding down onto Vivian's fingers.

"What would I do?" Vivian murmured. "Would I be angry? Would I tell you to leave? Or would I..." She parted her legs.

Jules groaned and buried her face in the soft, salty curve of Vivian's throat.

"I wondered. And I did this. Exactly this." Vivian began to brush her thumb over Jules's clit again—very, very lightly. "Exactly what I'm doing to you now. Which is when I discovered that I do like it slow. And gentle."

"Going to come," Jules panted against her skin. "Going to...going..."

"But you like it rougher," Vivian said, "don't you?" And she pressed down firmly with her thumb.

"Christ!" Jules wailed into Vivian's shoulder and thrust her hips once, twice before freezing in place because she couldn't move anymore. Pleasure locked up her muscles, and Vivian didn't stop moving her thumb, and...

She almost fainted. The world definitely got blurry and gray, and she couldn't exactly remember the seconds between Vivian lifting her thumb away and sliding her fingers out.

"I think," Vivian said—gasped, rather—"that we made an even bigger mess than before you cleaned me up."

"Did...did you really do that? Touch yourself? After I kissed you?" Or had Vivian just thought Jules would like the idea?

"Oh yes," Vivian said. "I really did."

"Wow." Jules could almost hear Vivian rolling her eyes at that. She nestled in close and waited to get control of her own mind back.

Yeah. Fat chance of that now.

"Thought you didn't like talking dirty," she added and, for want of something better to do with her hands, stroked Vivian's gently rounded belly.

Vivian harrumphed but didn't sound truly upset as she said, "Many of my former rules don't seem to apply to you. That's the least of them."

Jules grinned as her delight returned.

"Besides," Vivian added, "apparently I'm good at it."

"Oh yeah," Jules said fervently.

"Yes," Vivian said, having needed no affirmation. "I like doing things I'm good at."

"You don't say." Jules propped herself up on one elbow and squinted at the clock on the nightstand. It was almost three.

As if reading her mind, Vivian rubbed her thumb idly against Jules's arm. "I have to leave for the MOMA exhibit premiere at five."

That meant Vivian's personal stylist would arrive at four on the dot. Jules held back a sigh as she combed her fingertips through Vivian's sweaty hair. "I remember. Hank Willis Thomas, right?"

"Yes. His mixed-media collection. It should be stunning. I was thinking Simon could reach out to…"

Silence fell so hard that Jules felt its weight land on her shoulders. She bit her lip. "Tomorrow is his last day, right?"

"We're not talking about that." All of the post-sex relaxation had drained from Vivian's body, leaving her as tense as a pulled wire against Jules. "It was just a slip of the tongue. Put it down to pregnancy brain."

"Okay."

"I can't believe—" Vivian began, then swallowed and repeated, "We're not talking about it." She stared up at the ceiling and refused to turn her head a single degree in Jules's direction.

Her anger made sense. Simon had been at Vivian's side for years, always faithful, always steady, always there. Always competent. He'd outlasted all of her husbands. He'd weathered her moods and catered to her whims and—from what Jules had gathered—very, very occasionally called her on her bullshit. He'd been the closest thing she had to a real friend. And he'd had enough.

Jules couldn't blame him, really. Since he'd been at *Du Jour* for so long, he knew how easily Vivian discarded people when they couldn't get the job done. Jules had seen the same thing enough times that it had made her sure Vivian was going to throw her to the curb too. So Simon hadn't wanted to take the risk that Vivian's favor would last. The prospect of striking out on his own had been much more attractive.

No, Jules couldn't blame Simon for wanting out. But now, looking at Vivian's blank face and tightly pressed lips, Jules could hate him a little for it. Just a little.

She wondered if Vivian was actually about to cry. She wasn't sure she'd be able to handle that because what did you do when Vivian Carlisle wept? Maybe take shelter since it must be a sign of the end-times.

But Vivian didn't weep. She just swallowed hard and didn't say anything else.

There had to be something Jules could say. But before she could think of it, something else saved her.

Vivian gasped and pressed a hand to her belly. "Ah!"

A rush of panic, cold and immediate. Jules tried to stay calm in the face of it. "What's the matter?"

"She kicked." Vivian grunted as if that wasn't the most mind-blowing thing to come out of her mouth all day.

Jules stared at her. Then she stared at Vivian's belly as she ran the calculations. Just past five months. Yeah, it was time for that. "Can I...?"

Vivian took Jules's hand in her own and placed it over her belly.

Jules held her breath. For a moment, she was afraid the show was over, but then she felt it: a faint, unmistakable thump against her palm.

"Wow," she breathed. "Is this the first time it's happened?"

"It happened last night," Vivian admitted. "I was going to tell you earlier, but you distracted me."

Jules rubbed a gentle thumb against Vivian's belly. "What does it feel like?"

"Hard to describe. Not really like a kick. It's almost like a...twitch." For the briefest of moments, anxiety crossed Vivian's face. "That's normal, right?"

A minute later, they were both looking at Jules's phone as Jules scrolled through WebMD.com.

"Normal," Jules said in relief. "Looks like it can feel like all kinds of things."

Vivian exhaled. "Good."

"We should still check in with Dr. Viswanathan, though. Keep her updated." Sita Viswanathan was Vivian's obstetrician.

"And what cover story are we giving her?" Vivian asked dryly.

Jules gave her a quick look, but the question seemed rhetorical as Vivian continued. "I hope she doesn't get on me again about my diet. I can't be expected to cut out red meat *entirely*. Seriously, I think…"

It went in one ear and out the other. Jules tried to listen to Vivian, but it was a lot easier to worry about the future and everything it might bring—or worse, what it might not bring.

She rested her hand against Vivian's belly again. *One day at a time,* she reminded herself. *One day at a time.*

CHAPTER 4

JULES SAT BACK ON HER sofa with a deep exhalation. Her laptop, perched on her knees, taunted her. *Hit Send. Just hit it, you coward.*

There was no reason to be cowardly. Jules had worked her ass off on this. She'd finished her article on the influence of Old Hollywood style on this season's fashions for *Modernity*, a prestigious lifestyle magazine that had solicited a piece from her.

Solicited it thanks to Vivian's influence, anyway. Jules was still undecided about that one. It would have felt both foolish and ungracious to reject Vivian's gift to her. She hadn't asked for it, and publishing was all about having connections. Everyone knew that.

Besides, there was no guarantee that the article would be accepted. Vivian had just made sure *Modernity* would extend her the offer. If Jules wrote a subpar piece, they wouldn't take it. If they accepted her work, that meant it was worthy of acceptance. Right?

So this better not be subpar. Jules had written the article, shown it to Simon, rewritten, shown it to Vivian, *really* rewritten, and this was as good as it was going to get.

Her heart pounding, she hit Send and watched her work fly off into the ether, hopefully to a receptive audience. There. It was done. Nothing to do now but wait.

All of a sudden, Jules understood why Vivian hated waiting for anything.

———

The next week helped with the waiting, as busy as it was. Jules was on the hop from morning until night, helping with the launch of Adrian & Jo.

Simon had hired her as a jane-of-all-trades. Not only was she setting up the office and sending emails, she connected delivery trucks with warehouses, wrote press releases, and skimmed résumés for interns to serve as fashion consultants who would meet with customers via chat windows.

It left her with zero leisure. That week, there was no time to have dinner with Vivian, who was also working around-the-clock. Jules would leave her apartment at six thirty a.m. and stagger back at nine p.m. if she was lucky. If the stars aligned, she and Vivian managed a phone call. Otherwise, they texted in what few spare minutes they had until one or both of them pleaded exhaustion for the night.

Jules loved the exhilaration of her new job, but she loved Vivian more. Missing her really sucked. Her previous relationship had ended because she was too committed to her job. Maybe, though, it had also ended because her heart hadn't ached when she thought about Aaron, her ex-boyfriend. She hadn't longed for him when they were apart. That seemed relevant.

Did Vivian feel the same way? Jules didn't quite have the courage to ask.

This weekend, she told herself on Thursday night as she set her phone on the nightstand for the final time. *I'll see her on Sunday. And this isn't forever. We'll have more time when things are less crazy.*

Then, the next morning, Jules got an email that made her yearn for the garden-variety craziness of her job.

Dear Ms. Moretti:

On behalf of the editorial staff at Modernity, *I am pleased to accept your article "From Hepburn to Halston" for publication in our June issue. The article will appear on both the website and in the print version of our magazine. The publishing agreement is attached. Please complete, sign, and return it to me as soon as possible.*

Jules clutched her collar as a wave of joy threatened to knock her down. *Modernity* had accepted her work. They'd liked it. They were going to publish it. Jules was going to have an article in freaking *Modernity.*

And there was a publishing agreement! They were going to pay her! She'd almost forgotten about that part. It would probably be more than she'd gotten from *Salon* but still not enough to go crazy with. Maybe she could use it to update her spring wardrobe a bit. Or she could finally indulge the English major in her and buy the Riccardi Press edition of *Sonnets from the Portuguese* at Bauman Rare Books.

She was so excited that she almost didn't notice the next paragraph.

I found your article interesting. It's fortunate that Vivian Carlisle brought you to our attention.

Regards,
Carter Mathson
Features Editor
Modernity *Magazine*

It sucked Jules's excitement out of her as if she'd been a rug beneath a particularly enthusiastic vacuum.

Interesting? Everyone knew that that meant *not interesting at all* with a side of *I can't find anything nicer to say.*

And the last sentence. The one about Vivian. Carter Mathson might as well have written *Vivian Carlisle made us publish you.*

The warmth in Jules's belly was gone, replaced with nausea. *You're overreacting,* she told herself. *He might not really have meant that. What's he supposed to do, exclaim over your genius? And Vivian did bring you to* Modernity's *attention. It's just a statement of fact.*

Yeah. If Jules told herself that often enough, it might become the truth.

She tried to remind herself that both Simon and Vivian had given their stamps of approval. Both had exacting tastes. Neither of them was shy when it came to criticism. They wouldn't have let her submit subpar work. So maybe Mathson hadn't been insulting Jules's writing per se.

Just the way it had gotten to him. Thanks to Vivian.

Her temples throbbed with the beginnings of a headache. Jules rubbed them with a groan.

This was why she'd felt weird about Vivian's gift. On some level, she'd known this would happen. Vivian held enormous power in both the fashion and publishing industries, even with Mark Tavio's interference. If she wanted *Modernity* to publish Jules's article, it was going to happen. Jules had been naïve to think otherwise.

She couldn't let it happen again. It was too humiliating. Although Vivian's intentions had been good, Jules couldn't ride through life on her coattails.

She re-read Mathson's email. For a second, she thought about declining his offer. It would be the principled thing to do.

Principles were one thing. Stupidity was another. The people who read Jules's article would have no idea what had gone on behind the scenes. Let them be the judges. If *Modernity's* readers liked her article, then she could move forward on her own merits. Didn't most people get their start through having connections?

This experience could still be a thrilling one. It didn't have to feel… tainted.

Jules opened up the publication offer. Time to swallow down the bad taste in her mouth, sign it, then think about how to explain her feelings to Vivian.

For someone who aspired to a writing career, it sure was hard to find the words sometimes.

CHAPTER 5

By the time she showed up at Vivian's on Sunday, Jules still hadn't found those words. She was starting to feel ridiculous. They'd talked on the phone a couple of times, and she hadn't said anything about it. And here she was in person, still not sure how to begin.

"You've barely touched your salad," Vivian pointed out.

Jules looked down at the salmon salad with its savory fish, crisp greens, and perfectly judged portion of dressing that Ellen, Vivian's cook, had prepared before leaving. It did seem like a waste. "I haven't had much of an appetite lately. I tend not to eat as much when I'm stressed."

"I imagine you've been very busy this week at work."

An indefinable note in Vivian's voice put Jules on alert. "Yes. I've told you about it, right?"

"Not much," Vivian said. "You've been reticent."

She was right—everything else aside, Jules didn't like to blab too much about her new job. It was a sensitive topic. She should have remembered that Vivian didn't shy away from those and would call her on it eventually. "Um, I didn't know if you'd want to talk about it."

Vivian narrowed her eyes. "Why wouldn't I want to talk about it?"

"Because you're mad at Simon," Jules said. She might as well get it over with. "And I didn't think you'd want to hear about him."

"I'm not mad at Simon," Vivian said coldly. "What an idea."

Oh great. Vivian was in a mood and was going to play it like that tonight. Jules knew there was a reason she'd been nervous.

Jules muffled a heavy sigh. "Yes, I've been busy. So has he. You know, trying to get everything together and off the ground."

"Yes," Vivian said, her voice flat. "I know."

Vivian did know. Huh. All else aside, this was a good chance to ask her about something Jules had often wondered about. Plus it would turn the conversation away from Simon—*bonus*.

"I know you know," she said. "I sometimes think about what it was like when you started at *Du Jour*. How you had to adjust, and the changes you made."

Vivian lifted one shoulder in a bored half shrug. "You'll find out soon enough. You're going through all of that yourself." Then she popped a bite of salad into her mouth.

"But it's different. You were taking over something from somebody else and running it in a totally different way."

It was true. Vivian had been the editor of Koening's youth fashion publication, *Jeune Du Jour*, when *Du Jour's* numbers were plummeting. Back then, Mark Tavio had been able to see her as an asset. She'd swept in, toppled the previous editor, and revived Koening's flagship publication with a speed and effectiveness that had astonished the entire industry. And she hadn't slowed down since.

What was Mark Tavio's problem anyway? Had he forgotten what a powerhouse Vivian was? Didn't the magazine turn a profit?

"Was it difficult," Jules asked, "when everyone had to adjust?"

Now Vivian looked thoughtful. "I seem to recall firing a lot of people. It settled down after that." She tapped her fingers against her lips and scowled. "Heady times."

It was easy to see what she was thinking about. Jules asked, "Work's been rough this week, hasn't it?"

Vivian glanced at her quickly. "It's always rough."

"Extra rough, though? More than you said on the phone?"

Vivian pursed her lips. "People believe they can see the writing on the wall. They think I don't hear the whispers or know what they say behind my back or listen to the gossip about who will inevitably replace me when Mark lowers the boom."

Jules licked her lips nervously. "Who do they think it is?"

Vivian shrugged. "Beatrice LaSalla is the current favorite," she said, referring to the editor in chief of *Du Jour Italia*. "But the gossip changes every day. I'm sure there's a betting pool."

At least Monique Leung was out of the running. The former editor in chief of *Du Jour China* had once offered Jules a job, angering Vivian like nothing else could have. But Monique was starting her own fashion label and seemed uninterested in taking on another mammoth task.

"Do you think Mark's going to make a move?" Jules asked.

"I'm sure he's planning on it, but he's taking his time. First he fired you. In a few days it will be someone else. And then someone else again. He'll want to draw it out. Save me for last."

Jules shuddered.

Vivian simply took a calm sip of ice water. "Try not to worry about it."

"Are you serious?"

"I'll take care of it," Vivian said, obviously attempting to close the subject.

No dice. "I know you will." Jules prayed that was true. "But I can't help worrying. I'm not there to help you."

"You could never help me with this."

She'd probably meant to make Jules feel better in her own Vivian-ish way. It didn't work. Instead, Jules felt reminded yet again of how powerless she was and always had been.

"Yeah," she muttered. "I know I'm not exactly influential."

Vivian sighed. "Your time will come. Be patient and work your way up the ladder."

Well. Jules was never going to get a better opening than that.

She braced herself and rose from the kitchen table, taking Vivian's empty plate and her own half-full one to the sink. "You mean with the occasional assist?"

"Pardon?"

Jules scraped her remaining food into the sink's garbage disposal, sure that this was a metaphor for how the conversation was about to go. "I need to talk to you about my *Modernity* article."

"What about it? You told me they accepted it."

When Jules turned around, she saw Vivian looking genuinely puzzled. She sighed, leaned back against the sink, and crossed her arms. "Yeah. But I didn't tell you what they said."

So she did. It didn't take long, but Vivian's face had enough time to darken with anger.

Nevertheless, when she spoke again, her voice was even. "That doesn't seem so bad."

"*Interesting*," Jules said.

Vivian's jaw clenched. "People in publishing are often in a hurry, Julia. He might not have had time to write reams of praise. Don't read too much into it."

"He specifically pointed out that you'd pushed me in front of him. We both know what he was saying. C'mon, don't try to bullshit it."

"Fine," Vivian snapped. "The cliché is true: it's not what you know, it's who you know. If a features editor thinks he works in a meritocracy, he's in for a rude awakening." She snorted. "I'm picturing a twenty-eight-year-old with a master of fine arts and outsized beard. What do you think?"

Jules couldn't hold back a chuckle. "Don't forget the scarf and vape pen."

"I couldn't if I tried."

Vivian's little smile could distract Jules all the way out of this conversation if she let it. She couldn't let it.

Instead, she sat back down at the kitchen table and took Vivian's hand in hers. "I appreciate what you did. But let me take it from here, okay?"

The smile left Vivian's face, and she made to pull her hand away.

Jules held on. "No, come on. How would you feel in my shoes?"

"I wouldn't wear your shoes, for one thing. As to your question, I'd seize the opportunity I was given, take down names, and bide my time."

Vivian's voice could have lasered through the walls of Fort Knox. Her gaze was even more intense. It shouldn't have been hot.

Jules still fought not to squirm in her seat. "Good advice. Anyway, that's all I had to say. I want to knock your socks off on my own merits, remember? I always have."

The words actually made Vivian's eyes soften. "Yes, you have."

Jules's stomach warmed. Maybe Vivian was remembering before they'd gotten together, when Jules had worked to get published in *Salon* without asking for Vivian's help. At the time, Vivian had felt insulted. Only later had she understood that Jules was trying to impress her, to bring something of her own to the table.

The combination of Vivian's soft eyes and hard words was now doing a real number on Jules. It had been a whole week since they'd been intimate.

Easy to forget that at the end of a long, exhausting day, but they were here now.

She smiled hopefully at Vivian. "Want me to knock your socks off in another way?"

Vivian turned pink, making Jules's heart soar. But then she looked apologetic. "I haven't felt well today. I really don't think—"

Damn. Jules practically tripped over herself to say, "Oh right. Sure. No problem." The last thing she needed was to look desperate. "Is anything wrong?"

"Nothing dreadful. Just exhaustion, discomfort, various symptoms I'm not going to tell you about, and a general malaise." She grimaced. "It really wasn't a good week."

"You know, you can tell me about that on the phone," Jules suggested, "or when you're texting me. You don't have to stew over it. It's not like I mind hearing it."

"But I mind talking about it," Vivian said, then amended, "every day. It would wear me out. It's easier face-to-face."

Jules looked at their entwined hands. True. There was something to be said for being in the same space. "Makes sense."

Vivian released Jules's hand, stretched in her chair, and winced as she patted her belly. She definitely looked a little bigger than she had last week. Now that they weren't seeing each other every day, the changes in Vivian's body became more dramatically visible. *Weird.*

"She didn't give me any rest last night," Vivian muttered.

"Maybe she'll calm down tonight."

"I live in hope," Vivian said. "I guess it's better to have her doing high kicks than the alternative."

"Look, take care of yourself, okay?" Jules said. "Is Allie making you eat lunch?"

"Allie couldn't make water ripple if she threw a rock in it," Vivian said. "But every day, my food appears from a menu I'm pretty sure she didn't make up, and I eat it."

"I left her a few lists," Jules said sheepishly.

"I'm shocked and amazed." Vivian looked pleased. "The dressed kale salad from the Picnic Basket is especially good."

"I'll let her know." Jules grinned. "If you don't feel like sex, wanna hang out in the den? I can snuggle up and look at my phone while you review the latest mock-ups."

"That sounds disgustingly domestic," Vivian said. "Why not?"

"Yeah. And maybe we can get together before next Sunday," Jules added hopefully. This once-a-week thing sucked. They had to come up with a better plan.

"We'll see," Vivian said. "You're working late most nights now, aren't you?"

Jules nodded unhappily.

Vivian didn't look pleased anymore. More like resigned. "So it begins." She tilted her head to the side and regarded Jules thoughtfully. "You wondered, didn't you," she said, "why I was late for dates with my husband? You wondered why I couldn't just keep those simple, straightforward promises."

Jules swallowed hard and nodded.

Now Vivian almost looked sad. "You're about to find out."

CHAPTER 6

Vivian's words troubled Jules more than she would ever have admitted. Admitted to Vivian, anyway.

She'd left Vivian that night with a kiss, trying hard not to wish for more. And she'd gone home and stared at the ceiling—since meeting Vivian and working at *Du Jour*, she'd started doing that a lot—and pondered.

She had to keep her priorities straight. There had to be room for compromise. Because God knew Jules wasn't the only guilty one; Vivian was busy too, as busy as always, and under more stress to boot. They could let work drive them apart if they weren't careful.

Or…if they didn't care enough. If Vivian decided their relationship wasn't as important as her career—or Jules did.

No. Not even an option. Jules wouldn't let this go for anything, wouldn't let go of what she and Vivian had, whatever the hell it was.

Would she?

Jules thought about writing freelance and publishing more articles, about winning Pulitzer Prizes and everything else. And as always, whenever she thought about those things, she indulged in those daydreams, felt a tug of desire, the pull of ambition.

Her childhood dreams were within reach. She didn't want to give them up. She didn't think she could.

But she couldn't give up Vivian either: Vivian, whom she loved more than she'd ever loved Aaron.

Jules didn't want to give up dinners at the Carlisle house either or the baby or any other part of the strange domestic world she'd been sucked into willy-nilly ever since Christmas. Before then, even.

How were you supposed to manage it? How were you supposed to juggle? Who the heck was Jules supposed to ask for advice—Vivian herself? Or Simon? *Yeah, right.*

She wondered unhappily why there were no normal people in her life anymore. Thanks to her frenetic career, she'd lost touch with friends from high school and college. Social media meant they shared shallow connections, but that wasn't the same. Jules couldn't reach out to a former friend who'd just posted baby pictures and say, "Congratulations! Got time for a chat about my torrid affair with my former boss?"

The closest thing she had to a friend her own age was Allie, the intern Jules had hired before getting canned. She tried to imagine telling Allie about any of this. Allie could explain Einstein's theory of general relativity without breaking a sweat but also got confused about which side of her MetroCard to swipe at the subway turnstile. Every day.

The idea of talking to Allie was laughable—and inappropriate besides. She still worked for Vivian, and Jules couldn't put her in that position. So who else was there?

Who indeed?

"I'm not surprised you're so busy, honey," her mother said the next evening. "It's a new job. You're going to have to pull some late shifts."

Jules closed her eyes, reaching for patience. "I don't have a problem with working late. I got used to that at *Du Jour*. But there's got to be a little time for me, doesn't there? For my life?"

"Well, of course there does. I don't want you turning into some kind of robot. Nobody wants that."

"So how do I do it?" Jules said in frustration. "Dad's a lawyer. You're always working overtime at the insurance agency. How do you make time for each other?"

"You just make the time," her mother said, which was the least helpful advice Jules had ever heard in her life. "You make choices. You make sacrifices. And you have to work out what's most important to you."

"I know that," Jules said impatiently. "I mean, that's easy to say. But it's harder when there's...um...something fun I want to do but I can't because

I'm at work until ten thirty every night and then I'm so tired when I get home, I collapse. Almost every night."

"Well, you've got to pay your dues," her mom said. "Isn't that what you're always telling us? Although, when you were at that magazine, your father and I always said you—"

Jules suppressed the urge to howl.

Perhaps her mother sensed her distress because she finished with, "Well, never mind that. You're young. You don't have a family. You're not even dating anybody right now—are you?" she added hopefully. "Is that what's bringing this on?"

"No, I'm not dating anybody," Jules hedged, wondering if there really was a hell and how much time she was buying herself in it. She and Vivian weren't dating exactly, were they? They didn't go on actual dates or anything. "Sorry, Mom. I'm just asking."

"Oh." Her mother sounded disappointed. "Well, what I meant to say was, you have less to juggle now. So it's easier for you to concentrate on work until something better comes along."

Like a world-famous fashion editor with a kid on the way. "I know," Jules said helplessly. "I just—"

"And you'll know when it happens," her mother added, "when the right one shows up. It wasn't Aaron, was it?"

"No," Jules said, closing her eyes. "No, it wasn't."

"Right," her mother said. "I know my little girl. You're smart. You've got your head together. When the right man shows up, you'll figure out what's most important. So will he, if he's worth anything." Then her mom cleared her throat. "Or the right girl. You know."

Jules suppressed a heavy sigh. Her parents theoretically supported her bisexuality, but they weren't about to march in pride parades anytime soon. "Yeah."

"Just think about what you want when the time comes," her mother said. "Do you want the awards and the money or do you want friends and family? I know they say you don't have to pick, but you do."

"Yeah," Jules said again. "I know."

Then to her horror, her mother said, "You know who you should think about? Your old boss. That woman."

Jules couldn't remember the last time her mother had actually deigned to say Vivian's name, not since sometime after Jules told them she'd been fired, when they'd barely been able to contain their delight that she was away from Vivian's influence.

"A string of failed marriages," her mother continued. "And now she's pregnant, and—"

"No," Jules said at once. "Leave Vivian out of this."

"Well, aren't you touchy? Hit a little close to home, did I?"

Closer than she could possibly know. "Just quit it, Mom. I don't want to talk about Vivian."

"Okay, honey." Now her mom sounded soothing, which was worse. "That's all I've got to say anyway."

She would have said a lot more if she'd known the truth. "Well, thanks for all the help."

"There's no need to give me attitude. Just remember, when you meet the one, it'll all fall into place."

"Yeah," Jules said. "I bet it'll get really easy then."

"Jules," her mother said sharply.

"Sorry," Jules sighed. "I'm just tired. I'd better go. It's late."

"You take care of yourself," her mother said. "Don't work too hard. And don't worry too much. Okay?"

Talk about easier said than done. Jules finished the phone call with the usual pleasantries and growled with irritation when she ended the call.

Barely five minutes later, her phone rang again. Vivian.

Jules picked up at once. "Hey there. How's it going?"

"Hello, Julia," Vivian said. The sound of her voice lifted Jules's spirits right away. "Things are—well, I had to go to a party tonight. Do you remember that odious little man who works for Michael Kors? Pierre what's-his-name?"

"Vaguely." Jules laughed and made herself more comfortable on the couch. It'd be longer than a fifteen-minute chat tonight, obviously.

In fact, it was almost an hour. Jules should have been sleepy by the time they were winding up.

She wasn't, though. Instead, she'd drawn her knees up to her chest on the couch and had wrapped one arm tightly around them, holding herself together. Her toes were curling inside her fluffy socks. Her heartbeat shook in her ears.

The more she'd listened to Vivian's voice tonight, the more naturally their conversation had flowed, the more certain Jules became that it was time to step out on a limb. It felt right. That didn't mean it felt easy.

This might be a dumb decision. Probably was. But her mother's words rang in her head: *when you meet the one, it'll all fall into place.*

And Vivian had shown Jules again and again that if you didn't take risks to get what you wanted, you'd never get anything but disappointment.

And it didn't have to be a big dramatic deal or anything.

And if Jules didn't say it, she just might explode.

Her palms sweated. Her mouth felt dry. Courage seemed a long way off, so she'd have to do this while she was scared out of her mind.

The moment came when Vivian said, "Well, I'd better go."

"Me too." Jules closed her eyes. She didn't pray anymore but sent a general *please* out into the universe's direction anyway. "Goodnight. I, um, I love you."

There was a moment of silence. And then another one. It felt like it lasted for years.

Had she made a mistake? *Dammit.* That was the trouble with stepping out on limbs. Sometimes they broke and you plummeted toward the ground. Jules might be in for the hardest landing ever.

She didn't regret it per se. Even if Vivian rejected her, Jules had still spoken what was in her heart. It would just be so much better if Vivian—

"Well," Vivian said faintly. "Yes."

Jules blinked, not at all sure what to make of that.

"Good night," Vivian added. Her voice was softer than usual.

"Yeah," Jules said. "N-night."

And then she quickly pressed the disconnect icon with a shaking finger before she could say something that would screw everything up, assuming she hadn't just done exactly that. And then she went to bed and stared at the ceiling yet again.

Well…she'd said it. She'd started staking a claim for what was important in her life, for what mattered the most.

And Vivian had said yes, whatever that meant in the grand scheme of things. In a certain tone of voice.

Jules sorted through her mental catalogue of Vivian's intonations. She hadn't said yes in the brisk tone she used at the office or the considering tone she used after coming to a decision. She certainly hadn't said it with anything like the ecstasy she showed in bed.

But she'd still said yes, not no. So it had gone okay. Nothing to freak out about. Yeah. Sure.

Jules kept looking at the ceiling until her eyes closed and she finally went to sleep, exhausted by her own thoughts.

Her phone's insistent bleeping woke her up what seemed like four seconds later.

Jules opened her eyes with a gasp, rolled over, and squinted at the phone display. It was three thirty in the morning. And Vivian was calling.

Emergency? Still more than half asleep, Jules answered right away. "Hello? What's the matter?"

"Did you mean it?" Vivian demanded.

"Huh?" Then Jules woke up just a little more. "Oh, my God," she said and mashed her face into her pillow.

"Well, did you?" Vivian said. "I've been lying awake for hours—"

"I haven't," Jules said, lifting her face back up. "You woke me up. *Again*." Although maybe that was a good thing. Having this conversation in broad daylight would have terrified her. It was easier when she was groggy and pissed off. "Of course I meant it."

"Oh," Vivian said.

"I wouldn't have said it if I didn't."

"Sometimes people—the word *love* gets tossed around like—"

"Oh, my God," Jules said again. "Did you really not know? Come on."

"Well," Vivian said.

"Give me some fucking credit." Jules rubbed her hand against her forehead. *Unbelievable*. And there were only three hours before she had to get up again.

"There's no need for—"

"Vivian?"

"What?"

"Don't call me at three thirty in the morning unless you are dying."

"I—ah."

"And don't die," Jules added, deciding that was necessary advice since Vivian apparently needed an instruction manual for everything.

"I—" Vivian said. She sounded a little strangled. "I—"

"We're gonna make this work." Jules rested her head back against her lovely, soft pillow. "Can I go back to sleep now?"

"I—" Vivian said again, then finished, "—guess so."

"Thanks." Jules disconnected and dropped the phone back on her nightstand. She had the feeling that they hadn't quite finished something, but she'd work it out in the morning. Later in the morning. Besides, Vivian needed the rest too. She was sleeping for two now, and…

Jules rolled over and went back to sleep. For some reason, it was much easier this time.

CHAPTER 7

SLEEP WAS NOTORIOUS FOR INTRODUCING temporary amnesia. Jules was actually on the subway and headed to work before remembering that she'd told Vivian she loved her the night before.

It made Jules close her eyes as she tried to recall the conversation they'd had afterward. It was difficult. She'd been kind of out of it.

But Jules still felt good about what she'd said. She'd told Vivian the truth, even if Vivian had been strangely shocked. Really strangely.

For God's sake, what did she think Jules felt? Did she think Jules would have gone through all this if her feelings hadn't been serious?

Jules had honestly thought her confession would be more of a formality at this point. A terrifying one, yes, in the moment. Something that exposed her vulnerable underbelly and made it easier than ever for Vivian to break her heart. But she hadn't thought Vivian would be *surprised.*

Vivian hadn't broken her heart, though. She'd called Jules back to make sure it was real. That had to mean something. It meant it *mattered,* at least.

Wondering what Vivian was thinking had rarely gotten Jules anywhere. It would just send her mind spinning all over the place. She vowed to put Vivian out of her head at least temporarily when she arrived at work.

But that plan went out the window as soon as she brought Simon his coffee and he greeted her with a frown as he held out a square cream-colored envelope. It had her name on it, written in exquisite calligraphy.

"I got one too." He held up an invitation on heavy paper.

Jules recognized it immediately. She'd been the one to order it from the stationers.

"Apparently, we're both invited to her little shindig in a couple of weeks," he said.

Vivian's "little shindig" was really a secretive, exclusive gathering she'd begun to plan months ago. Even Jules hadn't known what it was for. Sixty of the most elite people in publishing had been invited to a rooftop party for dinner prepared by the Michelin-starred chef Hélène Darroze. And now Jules and Simon were invited as well.

Jules didn't have to fake her surprise. It was shocking that Vivian had invited Simon after what he'd done—even more shocking that she'd invited Jules. Not to mention sending the invitation to Jules's job, where, of course, Simon would be sure to see it.

Her heart was racing. What did this mean? They'd just talked about how it was too early to come out. What was Vivian thinking by inviting Jules to a social event like this? And why hadn't she told Jules about it before springing this on her in front of Simon?

"What's she plotting?" Simon asked, echoing Jules's thoughts.

"I don't know," Jules said, glad she could be honest. "She told me to organize the party last month, but she never told me why she's throwing it or what it's for. I don't even know who's coming since Mark fired me before the guest list was finalized."

"Great," Simon said. "Now I'm paranoid. I was already invited, of course, but that was before..." His voice trailed off. Then he gave Jules the sharp look she'd expected. "And why, one wonders, are *you* invited?"

Yeah, honesty was great. Maybe this was why Vivian hadn't told Jules about the invitation in advance. "I have no idea. This is the first I've heard about it."

"Fantastic. Jules, I now designate you my official food taster. If you try my salad and fall over dead, I'll fund a scholarship in your name or something."

"We might not get to sit together," Jules pointed out, deciding that Simon was almost certainly joking. "Then I can't taste anything for you."

"Fair enough," he said, then added, "I hope we get to sit together."

"I've never felt more appreciated."

Jules was able to wait all of one hour before she was out of Simon's presence and could text Vivian.

Just got the party invitation. COUPLE OF QUESTIONS

She knew Vivian was run off her feet with things to do, so it must have been a really eye-catching text; Vivian responded only five minutes later.

Make them quick.

Ok one why am I invited??

Why wouldn't you be?

Was that a trick question? Jules replied:

I'm not your assistant anymore. Won't people wonder why I'm there?

Not for long.

Jules stared down at the text bubble. *Not for long?* What in the world did that mean? Her first crazed thought was that, following Jules's grand declaration last night, Vivian had decided to out them in front of high society.

Then her brain gave her a pointed reminder that the invitations would have been sent days ago. Still, though. Was Vivian thinking to introduce their relationship to the public?

She couldn't be. Even Vivian wouldn't take such a huge step without consulting Jules. Right? She wouldn't, right?

Had Vivian read her mind? Because, within another moment, she texted Jules again:

This isn't about us, Julia. I need you to be there for other reasons.

The hell? What other reasons? Jules wasn't coordinating the catering anymore.

Like what?

Just trust me and be discreet. We can talk later tonight. I have to go.

Dammit. Jules typed back just two letters:

Ok

Talk soon.

Soon. Yeah, right. The next few hours were going to feel very long indeed.

What was Vivian up to now?

———————————

"Poisoning Simon," Vivian said with a sniff as they spoke on the phone that evening. "Where does he come up with these things?"

"So now you're not mad at him anymore?" Jules asked as she sat back on her sofa and propped her feet up on the coffee table. They ached after another long day.

"I never said I was mad at him in the first place," Vivian said coolly. "In fact, I'm pretty sure I've said I don't care at all."

Jules could push at this sore spot, or she could abandon it temporarily and get to what she really wanted to know. No contest.

"Fine," she said. "So can you please tell me why I'm invited?"

A moment of silence. Then Vivian said, "You're not going to like this, but no."

"At least you knew I wouldn't like it," Jules growled.

"It's better for you not to know. I'm asking for your trust on this."

Last night, Jules had told Vivian she loved her. How could she not trust her? It wasn't so much to ask. So Vivian was throwing a mysterious party. She'd probably schemed a lot worse over the years, and everything had turned out okay so far.

Jules looked at her feet, out of their wedges and encased in fuzzy socks. A heavy sigh escaped her. "All right. You've got it. And you're really not going to spill the beans?"

"Not a single bean. But wear your pin," Vivian added, sounding suddenly inspired, "the one I gave you at the end of London Fashion Week."

The pin, a fabulous gold-plated snake with malachite eyes by Stephen Webster, was the first gift Vivian had ever given her. Simon had told her it was worth thousands of dollars. Jules had wanted to faint when she learned its value. She'd never actually worn it.

"Okay," Jules said slowly. "I'll wear the pin."

"But not the jumpsuit from New Year's Eve. Nothing that revealing."

Jules laughed. "I thought you liked me in that jumpsuit."

"That jumpsuit is no longer for public consumption. That jumpsuit is for me."

"Fine. We'll save it for special occasions. Really special ones."

"Such as?"

"Such as you just got crowned queen of the universe or something."

"That would be special," Vivian allowed. "Well, give me time."

"If anybody can do it." Jules laughed again. "So, what should I wear?"

"The invitation specified," Vivian said. "The dress code is black tie."

"I know that." Jules rolled her eyes. "Anything specific in mind? I need time to start looking if I'm going to find something I can actually afford."

Luckily, she now had an in with discounted high-end designer wear, thanks to Adrian & Jo. She wasn't about to mention that to Vivian, though. And there was no guarantee a formal gown in her size would show up, much less one she liked. She needed options.

"I'll send you something. And before you object," Vivian said, raising her voice before Jules could do just that, "this is not me giving you a gift. Think of it as a uniform. I've invited you, and it's only fair that I provide you with what you need—yes, *need*—to wear. This is top-tier, Julia, and that's how you have to show up. Trust me, you'll thank me when you're not in last season's cast-offs."

Trust me again. Jules took in a deep breath. "Okay. Do I get to pick it?"

"Already done. You'll like it."

Like Jules had liked the perfume. Yet again, Vivian knowing Jules from top to bottom. She still couldn't stop a little thrill from running up her spine. Impossible to do when Vivian Carlisle was choosing fancy dress for you. "What does it look like?"

"You'll see." Vivian's voice was warmer now. "You'll fit in perfectly."

Jules doubted that. This gathering was for the cream of the crop, and she was far from that, no matter what she wore. "You like me in formal wear?"

"I like you best," Vivian said, "in nothing at all."

Jules's breath paused. Heat filled her cheeks. "Oh." She gulped. "Well, that's…thanks."

"Are you sitting comfortably?" Vivian inquired.

Oh boy. This sounded good. Jules's curiosity was vanishing with embarrassing swiftness into sheer lust. "Y-yes."

"Because I need you to be comfortable," Vivian said, then added, "and flexible, at least for the next few minutes."

Jules's eyes widened. "Are we going to…over the phone?"

"Oh yes," Vivian said mildly. "I assume you don't have any objections."

"No, none at all," Jules managed. The top of her head was spinning off into space. "None at all!"

"Seeing as how I denied you on Sunday," Vivian cooed, "and after you'd waited so patiently all week."

"Not patiently," Jules said, jumping to her feet and stumbling toward her bed where she'd be a lot more comfortable. And flexible. She almost tripped. "Just because I had to."

Vivian wanted to do this. Vivian was going to be *awesome* at this.

Jules yanked her pajama bottoms off along with her underwear and socks and tossed them all onto the floor. She had no idea what was making Vivian so accommodating tonight, but she wasn't about to push her luck and ask.

Instead she said, "Have you ever had phone sex?"

"No." Vivian sounded amused. "I think this is the part where I'm supposed to ask you what you're wearing, though."

"Just a T-shirt," Jules said and confessed, "I pretty much just ripped off my pants."

Vivian's breath caught.

Jules bared her teeth in what was a pretty savage smile. "You like that idea?"

"Lose the shirt," Vivian said, her voice hoarse. She cleared her throat. "Get naked. Right now."

"Say please."

"Oh no," Vivian said. "You'll be the one begging tonight. Not me."

Jules damn near fainted at that, but she also set the phone down just long enough to pull off her shirt. Yes, Vivian was definitely going to be awesome at this.

"Okay," she whispered when she picked up the phone again. "I'm all naked and on the bed."

"Good," Vivian murmured. "You should never be anywhere else or in any other condition."

A groan almost escaped before Jules muffled it. She couldn't help it. Once Vivian let her voice drop down low like that—

"You should always be naked," Vivian continued. "Always on the bed. Always with your legs spread. Always wet and ready." She paused. "Are you?"

"Getting there," Jules croaked. She was getting slick and swollen without even a touch.

Legs spread, Vivian had said. Jules could do that. She spread them so wide her thighs burned, and even that felt good.

"For me?" Vivian asked. "You're wet because of me?"

"Nobody but you," Jules said, her fingers twitching as she stroked them up and down her thigh. "Promise. Really. Should I touch myself n—"

"No. Not yet. Be patient."

"I can't. Not around you. Every time I see you, I can't wait."

"But you make me wait," Vivian said softly. "You make me wait, and then you make me scream."

Jules thought about what Vivian sounded like when she screamed. How her throat worked, her cheeks went red, and her eyes closed in ecstasy. Jules whimpered helplessly.

"Do you like that?" Vivian continued. "I think you do. I think you enjoy knowing the effect you have on me. Knowing that no one else has ever done to me what you do."

"Really? Like...like what?"

"Well, let's see," Vivian said. "You already know that nobody else has made me come by eating me before."

Jules whimpered again.

"So that's not a surprise. Hmm. Do you know that nobody else has ever made me scream? Or...beg?"

"B-beg?"

"Oh yes," Vivian said. "I have never begged anyone else to touch me or lick me or fuck me or any of that. Anyone but you. But with you, I can't..." Her voice trailed off, then she resumed, saying hoarsely, "I can't seem to stop myself."

"I love it when you beg," Jules whispered. "But you don't have to. I'll give you anything you want."

Vivian gasped.

"I'll touch you and lick you and fuck you until you can't even move anymore."

"Julia," Vivian choked.

"And then I'll do it again. And again. You don't have to beg, Vivian." Jules took a shuddering breath. "I could do you all day long—still wouldn't be enough. Wish I was with you right now, doing all those things to you right now."

"Julia—!"

"Are you naked too?"

"Close enough," Vivian managed. "I wish...I wish you were here too."

"You do?" Jules panted. In that moment, she really did want it more than anything—wanted to be with Vivian, who wanted her there too, because nobody had ever made Vivian feel like Jules did—

"Yes. Let me tell you." Vivian paused. "Let me tell you what I wish you were doing to me right now."

"Oh," Jules said. "Jesus, yes. Tell me."

"Touch yourself first," Vivian whispered. "But slowly. Don't come."

That was a tall order for sure. Jules gritted her teeth and brushed her fingers against herself, against her labia, and groaned. "Okay."

"Are you doing it?"

"Yes." Jules swallowed. "Are you?"

"Not yet," Vivian said.

"How naked are you?"

"Underwear off," Vivian replied. "Skirt up." She paused. "Heels on."

"Oh God," Jules said and had to move her hand away and grab her thigh before it was too late. "Tell me now. Tell me—"

"Your mouth," Vivian said. "I want your mouth. Between my legs. Now."

"Yeah? No foreplay? You want it right now?"

"Yes," Vivian said, her voice strained. "I can't wait. You've been teasing me for hours."

"H-have I?"

"Oh yes. All day long. A low-cut blouse, a short skirt, and every chance you got, you flaunted yourself."

"I totally would," Jules admitted. If she'd thought for one second she could get away with it at work. In fact—"Are we at *Du Jour*?"

"Yes," Vivian said. "You started in the elevator, of course. You knew there were cameras and we couldn't—you whispered to me."

"What did I say?"

"You tell me," Vivian said. "You tell me what you said in the elevator."

Jules had wanted to say a *lot* of things to Vivian in the elevator. "I said, 'Vivian, I'm going to fuck you cross-eyed. It's all I'm going to think about today. And every time I look at you—'"

"Ah."

"'—every time you see me looking at you, you're going to know that I'm thinking about it. All the time.' That's what I said. And then, after work—"

"Y-yes?"

"We're not going home. I'm locking the door to your office and closing the blinds."

"You—you'd—"

Jules had her eyes closed as she tried to remember the layout of Vivian's office. It was difficult under the circumstances. "You're on that sofa in the corner where you've got more room. And this is why I've got my head between your legs and you're pulling on my hair."

"Yes," Vivian whimpered. That whimper would undo Jules every time. "Y-yes, that's…that's why we're here…"

"I've spread you wide. You taste so good. And I know you like it slow, but I can't do it slow, not now."

Vivian groaned.

"I'm going at it fast because…"—Jules's mind raced—"because we could get caught any minute. We don't know if everybody's gone home. We should have waited, but I couldn't. I just made you pull up your skirt and—"

"And I did," Vivian panted. "I did…"

"You did," Jules moaned and slid a finger inside herself, dying to rub her clit, knowing that she'd come in a heartbeat if she did. "You've got your leg over my shoulder. Now tell me what you want."

"I-I, um," Vivian said and then rallied. "I want your fingers inside me. T-two, I think." Jules heard her gulp. "I want your tongue up…higher."

"On your clit?"

"Yes."

"Are you touching yourself now?"

"Yes." Vivian whimpered.

"Oh God. Tell me what you're doing. Do you have two fingers in?"

"J-just barely."

"Feel good?"

"Not enough…"

"No?" Jules said. "You want me to give you more?"

"Yes."

"Then I'll just have to unbutton your shirt."

"Oh," Vivian moaned.

"And take off your bra." Jules closed her eyes, imagining Vivian's perfect, perfectly sensitive breasts. Remembering how gorgeous they'd felt against her lips and tongue that first night and how she'd sent Vivian through the ceiling just by nuzzling them. "I'll use my mouth. Just the way you love it."

"Oh…God…"

"I suck you and bite you. Hard. But then I make it softer. Then I just lick."

"And the other one—you use your fingers."

That had driven Vivian nuts too. Made Jules feel a thousand feet tall. "Yeah. And you've got your hand covering your mouth. You can't keep quiet. You never can."

"Not with you," Vivian admitted.

The confession almost brought Jules to the edge. "Are you close?"

"Yes, but I'm trying not to—"

"So am I. Jesus." Jules flicked her thumb over her clit, and her hips jolted as she almost came. The close call, the risk, thrilled her even more. "Do you know what you look like right now?"

"What…what do I…"

53

"Where are you really? On your bed?"

"Yes."

"Where I ate you the first time? Where I fucked you in your dress? That bed?"

"Yes…"

Jules pulled her finger out and slid two back in, hard. She moaned helplessly, but she didn't come. Barely. "What did you do with the dress, anyway? Do you still have it?"

"Yes, but it's ruined."

"No. We tore one of the straps and you got wet in it and it smells like you. It's perfect. Will you let me have it?"

Vivian huffed out a chuckle. "Make it worth my while."

"Trade you for the jumpsuit," Jules offered, not really kidding. Hell, she'd probably trade an arm for the right to keep that dress in her closet forever.

"Well," Vivian gasped. "Good start… Keep going."

"I—okay," Jules said, trying to think beyond the throb between her thighs. "Let me tell you what you look like right now. You're on your bed, and your blouse is off, isn't it? Because you were too hot to keep it on?"

"Yes…"

"And your skirt is hiked up around your hips and your legs are spread and you're still in your heels."

"One heel," Vivian managed. "I, um, the other one—"

"Got kicked off," Jules breathed. "And you've got a hand between your legs. And I'm watching you."

"Y-you…you're…"

"I'm standing in the room. At the foot of the bed." Jules's eyes closed yet again as she pictured it: Vivian's skirt (that pinstriped one that Jules really liked) bunched up around her hips; her legs in black stockings; one foot in one of those burgundy Manolos; and from the other ankle, the one without the shoe, dangled her black lace underwear. And those elegant fingers buried inside the most beautiful thing of all.

"I'm watching you," Jules repeated in a whisper.

"Watching—oh, don't *look*…"

"No? Why not?" Jules said relentlessly. "I told you I wanted to watch you do this. From the start."

"Don't..." Vivian sounded delirious. "Don't, oh..."

"I'm going to watch," Jules said, and curled her fingers. *Fuck,* that felt incredible. "I'm watching you. Do what I tell you to do."

Vivian cried out softly.

Just that idea made the lights flash brighter in her head. The idea that in bed, if nowhere else, Vivian would do what Jules wanted because nobody else made her feel like Jules did. "Do what I tell you so I can see. Take your fingers out, nice and slow."

When Vivian groaned, Jules added, "Are they out? Are you empty?"

"Y-yes—"

God. *God.* "Now slide one back in. Your middle finger. Slowly."

"Oh...slowly..." Vivian's voice was the threadiest whisper now. Her mouth would be open while she reached for breath with her eyes closed, her chest heaving for air. If she was close enough, she would be shaking.

"Is it in?" Jules choked.

Vivian's whimper was confirmation enough.

"Move it in and out, just a little bit. Right around the entrance. You love that. Remember, I'm watching you."

"Yes, I remember," Vivian said breathlessly. "I remember I said that you were going to beg...not me."

And just like that, the tables turned. "I-I am?"

"I'll do what you want," Vivian whispered. "I'll do anything you want."

"Uh, um—"

"But I'm not like you. You have to beg me to do it." Vivian's voice suddenly dropped into a low growl of command. "Now. Beg me."

Jules's whole heartbeat seemed to have migrated down to her clit. She swallowed harshly. "Vivian, please touch yourself. Please fuck yourself."

"How? Tell me how you want me to do it."

"Whatever it takes," Jules said, giving up, unable to prolong this for a single second longer. "Make yourself come. Do whatever it takes. Now."

"Say..."

"Please," Jules begged. "Please make yourself come. Please let me hear you, Vivian, please."

"Ah—yes, I'll—Oh..."

"Please, Vivian—"

"Oh!" Vivian cried, her voice low and raw enough that Jules knew she wasn't faking it, wasn't playacting even a little.

And just the sound of it, of those breathless noises that Jules loved, was enough to make Jules ram in her fingers and rub with her palm and arch into her hand until she was coming so hard that her whole palm got soaked.

"Oh God, yes. Oh…" Vivian finished, her voice dwindling down into a whimpering whine. "*Oh*."

"F-f-fuck," Jules managed. Yeah. Vivian had been more than awesome at this. "Was that good?"

There was a pause while Vivian gulped to get her own air back. "Yes," she rasped. "Yes. It was good."

"Sounded good," Jules said, exhaling slowly. "That was amazing. You're amazing."

"Am I?" Vivian sounded terribly pleased with herself. "Well. Now it's your turn."

Whoops. Jules squirmed. "I kind of already took my turn."

"What?"

"I couldn't wait," Jules admitted. "I got off when you did."

"I didn't hear you," Vivian said, sounding outraged. "You were supposed to—"

Jules bit her bottom lip. Too bad she wasn't biting Vivian's. "Guess I still don't know how to be patient."

"Evidently not," Vivian huffed. "How selfish."

"I know," Jules said sheepishly. "It was really nice of you, though."

"I wanted to hear you."

"Sorry. We'll just have to do it again sometime. Or in person, where you can see me too," she added hopefully.

"I might have a headache."

"You might," Jules laughed. She reached for a nearby box of tissues so she could wipe off her fingers. "I feel pretty good right now, though. Don't you?"

"I guess." Vivian sighed. "I've certainly felt worse."

Jules could just picture her dragging a martyred, sticky hand across her forehead. She laughed again helplessly.

"Really, is there anything that doesn't make you giggle?"

"I don't know," Jules said, holding on to her stomach, knowing that her giddiness was making everything seem a lot funnier than it really was. "Thank you. Seriously. That was great."

"Oh, well," Vivian said lightly, "I'm glad you enjoyed it."

"When can we get together in person?"

"Are you free on Sunday afternoon?"

"Yeah," Jules said. Apparently, that was turning into their default time. Well, it was better than not having a default time, but still. "What time?"

"Come for dinner again."

Jules perked up. By dinnertime, Vivian might have revived a little. "Promise you won't have a headache?"

"I'll make no such promise."

Yeah, that had been too much to hope for. "Six thirty okay? And I'll call you tomorrow night?"

"Six thirty is fine, but tomorrow I've got a dinner that will run late," Vivian said. "I'll call you."

"Okay. Sounds good." Then Jules yawned audibly.

"Coming prematurely, rolling over, and going to sleep," Vivian mused. "I think I married a few men like you."

"Vivian!"

Vivian snickered.

"That was mean!"

"I'm sorry," she said. "I guess I wanted to step out of character for a second."

"Yes," Jules said, deciding to imitate Vivian's snooty tones. "Well, I can't keep my eyes open. I'd better go." She paused. "And I have to wash my hands."

Vivian harrumphed, but it was really a laugh. "Don't let me keep you from your well-earned rest. Sleep well."

Like the night before, her voice was unwontedly soft. It gave Jules the courage to say, "Okay. You too. Good night. I love you."

"I—yes," Vivian said, and now she sounded breathless. "Good night." Then she disconnected.

Jules blinked and then frowned briefly at the ceiling, processing that.

Vivian didn't seem inclined to return the three magic words, but she obviously didn't mind hearing them. In fact, judging by the way she'd felt compelled to call Jules at ridiculous o'clock the night before, the words were pretty damn important to her.

Well, Jules could relate. They were important to her too, though it wasn't the *best* feeling in the world to tell someone you loved them and for them not to say it back.

The real test would be when Jules could finally say the words face-to-face. If she could get the guts to do it. Looking Vivian Carlisle dead in the eye and saying, "I love you…" How were you supposed to pull off something like that?

Better than the men Vivian had married, Jules hoped. She'd figure it out. In the meantime, she followed their example by rolling over, turning off the lamp, and falling fast asleep. Washing her hands could wait.

CHAPTER 8

VIVIAN HAD SAID SHE'D ARRANGE for Jules to have a gown for her mysterious party. Jules should have expected that it would arrive soon at her apartment. Two days later, to be exact, at ten p.m. on the dot.

What she couldn't have expected was the method of delivery.

"I'm so excited!" Allie said breathlessly, perched on the edge of Jules's sofa as Jules inspected the dress box. "When Vivian told me to get this dress for you, I asked if I could deliver it personally instead of sending it."

Jules looked up from the box, her eyes widening. Vivian had told Allie about getting an expensive dress for Jules so Jules could go to her secretive party? So much for discretion. "Uh, what did she say when you asked her that?"

Allie gave Jules a blank look. "She said yes."

Jules held back a smile. Beneath Allie's cloud of curly red hair was a very unusual mind, one that excelled at high-level physics and virtually nothing else. "Gotcha."

"Open it!" Allie clapped her hands. "I've been dying to see it in person. It looks amazing in the photos."

High-end designer gowns usually did. Jules was long since used to seeing and handling the finest fashion had to offer. Nevertheless, she could afford to buy few top-tier items brand-new, and definitely not a Zuhair Murad evening gown.

Even she couldn't hold back a shiver of excitement as she opened the box and then removed the top layer of tissue.

Then she frowned at what she saw inside.

You'll like it, Vivian had said.

At first glance, Jules wasn't entirely sure that was true. The folded dress looked very... That is, it was really...

"Metallic is so chic." Allie propped her elbows on her knees, then her chin in her hands, eyes sparkling. "C'mon, take it out."

"On it." Jules very carefully lifted the gown out of the tissue-lined box. As she stood holding the gown by the cap sleeves, it rose from the box in a ripple of bronze and burgundy.

"Will you need help getting it on?"

Hopefully not. Jules wouldn't have anyone here to help her when she got ready to go to the party. "Let me try it on my own."

She bid a quick retreat to her bedroom, where she slipped into the gown with a few grunts and wriggles. The zipper went up the back, but Jules managed to pull it up herself after bending over in a couple of unlikely directions. Then she straightened up and looked at herself in the full-length mirror that she'd hooked over the back of her bedroom door.

It was a gorgeous dress. There was no denying that. It required altering, and Jules would need shapewear and just the right bra, but once she took care of that, it would fit like a glove.

A sweetheart neckline accented the rise of her breasts without pushing them up and out too much. The cap sleeves were just enough to cover her shoulders, beginning right at the line of her clavicle and drawing attention to her throat. The gown cinched at her natural waist and then flowed down to the floor in narrow pleats that made the fabric shimmer as she moved. A slit ran up her left thigh, stopping short of her hip. It would be visible only if she deliberately stuck her leg through it.

The skirt wasn't what caught Jules's eye, though. Most of the dress's top was a shining shade of burgundy, but two swaths of bronze-accented fabric crossed over her breasts. It was flattering, but not in a sexual way. More than anything, it looked like...

Armor.

Jules put her hands on her hips in puzzlement. Yes, it was a terrific dress; Vivian wouldn't have picked anything else. But why *this* specific dress? It wasn't Jules's style at all, and she didn't feel at home in it. It was impossible to stop a surge of disappointment and, on top of that, apprehension at how to tell Vivian.

"Could you get it on?" Allie called from the other side of the door. "Need any help?"

"No." Jules sighed. "Here I come."

She opened her bedroom door and stepped into the living room. The gown rustled around her ankles as she walked. She stopped a few feet away from the sofa so Allie could get a good look at her from head to toe. Surely Allie would see this didn't work for her. Maybe she'd even agree to take a picture that Jules could send to Vivian as evidence.

"Oh, Jules," Allie said.

"I know." Jules plucked at the skirt. "It's not—"

"It's so *you*!"

What? Jules looked quickly at Allie, who was now leaning back against the sofa, a hand against her breast and a transported look on her face.

"It is?" Jules asked.

"Oh yes! It works, even though it's not your usual look. It makes you seem so—powerful!"

"You think so?" Jules glanced back toward the mirror on her bedroom door. Should she double-check? "I'm not sure."

Allie shook her head so hard that her red hair swung over her shoulders. "No, trust me. It's perfect. The front almost looks like a breastplate. You remind me of the women in that superhero movie. You know, the ones who own the website that sells everything."

"The ones who..." Jules closed her eyes as she figured it out. "You mean the Amazons, don't you?"

"Yes! That's them! And it's *shiny*. Oh, Jules, say you love it. You look fantastic."

Could Allie be right? Jules marched back to her bedroom door, which she'd left open, so she could stand in front of the mirror and look at the dress with fresh eyes.

Huh. Now that Allie mentioned it, Jules did look pretty badass. The dress even brought out a gleam of determination in her dark eyes.

Allie appeared in the mirror behind her. "See what I mean? I wouldn't get in your way, that's for sure."

Which was, of course, exactly the look Vivian wanted for Jules. Something powerful. Just like with the Amouage perfume, she'd seen more in Jules than Jules could see in herself.

Trust me, she'd said.

"Vivian knows you really well," Allie murmured.

That snapped Jules back to reality in a hurry. She met Allie's eyes in the mirror, but Allie's expression had no guile or cunning. Only genuine enthusiasm.

Jules's mouth still felt dry as she said, "She's a perceptive person."

"For sure. Like this morning, I told her that Harris Reed's PR department told *me* that the samples were in shipment right then, and she said, 'That means they haven't even packed them up yet.' And you know what?" Allie crossed her arms. "She was right."

Jules didn't bother hiding her grin. "She usually is."

"Like about this dress." Allie stepped backward. "You're lucky you get to go to the party. It's so fancy. I can't even pronounce most of the wines."

"Just say you love the smokey overtones. That usually works." Jules traced her fingertips across the neckline. Yeah, this was definitely growing on her. "Speaking of wine, you want a glass? I promise it's a label we can pronounce."

"I'd love that! It's so nice to see you again. I miss you around the office, especially the way you know how to do things."

Jules laughed. "I miss you too."

"And I miss Simon. He was funny. Uh…I don't say any of that in front of Vivian, though."

Other than waxing poetic about Kepler's laws of planetary motion, that was probably the smartest thing Allie had ever done. "Good idea."

"I can pour the wine while you get changed."

"Oh, thanks. Could you get the zipper started for me?"

"Sure thing!" Allie carefully began to draw it down Jules's back. "Are you going to be able to get out of this by yourself afterward?"

Hopefully not. Hopefully *afterward* would involve Vivian unzipping Jules instead, after the party was over, its mystery solved. Vivian whispering in Jules's ear about how beautiful the dress made her look. How powerful.

"No worries," Jules said, a dreamy note in her voice. "I'm sure I'll think of something."

CHAPTER 9

JULES HAD PLANNED TO THANK Vivian for the dress when they next spoke, but there was no time for gratitude. Nor was there playfulness. By the time Vivian called, it was almost eleven, and her voice was brusque, her words clipped and short as she said hello and inquired after Jules's well-being as if about to be led off to a firing squad.

"What happened?" Jules asked.

"Mark fired Jocelyn this morning," Vivian said.

"Oh no," Jules said, grimacing. Jocelyn was head of accessories at *Du Jour*. Or had been. "You've been expecting that kind of thing, right?"

"Jocelyn wasn't," Vivian said. "I had to put up with histrionics until the moment security escorted her out. At least Mark spared you that indignity."

Jules shivered, indeed glad she'd avoided that particular abject humiliation.

"She's mounting a wrongful dismissal suit. She might get some kind of quiet settlement."

It hadn't occurred to Jules to do anything like that. She didn't think she had the energy or spite for it, and she certainly didn't want to draw more of Mark's attention to her relationship with Vivian. "I hope it works out for her."

"It's put me in an embarrassing position. I overheard Amanda wondering if the next editor in chief would want new office furniture or would keep mine as a memento."

"What?" Jules said incredulously.

"So I lost two employees today," Vivian said. "Extremely irritating."

"What are you going to do?"

"Promote Paul to Accessories and hire a new bookings editor," Vivian said. "Human Resources is even more annoyed with me than usual."

"That's not what I—"

"Beyond that? We'll see," Vivian continued. "I'm playing it by ear."

"Did anything good happen?" Jules asked hesitantly.

"Allie did something right."

"She did?" Jules smiled. "That's great. What?"

"I don't remember," Vivian said. "I just remember observing it in surprise and moving on."

"Oh, uh…" Jules said, and decided it was time to stop talking about work. "Well, she did a good job dropping my gown off last night and giving her opinion. It was nice to see her. And I love the dress."

There was a pause, and when Vivian spoke again, her voice was warmer. "I knew you would. I thought of you when I saw it in the collection preview."

A squeal of delight tried to make it out of Jules's mouth. She stopped it just in time but couldn't prevent a happy little wriggle in her seat. *Keep it cool, Moretti. You're not in high school.*

"I should have had Allie take a picture for you," she said. "I didn't think of it until after she left."

"Good. I don't want to see the dress on you until you arrive at the party. Surprise me."

Vivian had said the same thing about the red jumpsuit Jules had worn on New Year's Eve. Jules had worried that it wouldn't look appropriate at the formal ball; Vivian had insisted she take a risk and refused to give her stamp of approval ahead of time.

"You like the reveal, don't you?" Jules realized. "That moment in the movies when the woman comes down the stairs and everyone sees her in the dress for the first time."

"And you don't?" Vivian returned. "You didn't have much of a poker face when I did exactly that on New Year's Eve in *my* dress. I wondered if you were about to rush me then and there."

Oh man. Jules cringed in retroactive embarrassment. She really had been obvious, huh? "Um, anyway, how's the baby? Doing any handstands lately?"

"She'll have a future in the Olympics." Vivian sighed. "I'll be able to tell you more about her Friday night."

Vivian's next checkup with Dr. Viswanathan was on Friday afternoon. Jules wouldn't be tagging along, now that she was working for Simon. "That's right. I wish I could go with you."

"Yes, well," Vivian said, "I'm not taking Allie. I'll tell you that."

That meant Vivian would pick and choose the advice she wished to listen to. Jules said, "Well, she might be useful."

"I'm not taking Allie," Vivian repeated. "Call and talk to that receptionist who likes you if you want a spy."

"I'm pretty sure there are laws against that."

"Oh, well," Vivian said. "If it really gives you a thrill, you can always call and schedule my cesarean section."

Surely Jules had misheard. "I can what?"

"Schedule my C-section," Vivian repeated impatiently. "July is already filling up, and I'm due by the middle of it. Hold on, let me open my calendar—"

"Are you kidding?"

"Why would I be kidding? Ah, here we go. I'm due on July 16, didn't the doctor say? Something like that. Anyway, why don't you call and pencil me in—"

"Pencil you—"

"Let's say the weekend of the twelfth. I'm still fairly open then."

"Vivian, don't you think you should talk to Dr. Viswanathan first?"

"I can't imagine why she'd object. Isn't it my choice? Why should I have to receive permission for how to give birth to my child?"

Vivian excelled at asking questions for which there was no right answer. Jules sidestepped this one as best she could. "Why do you want a C-section in the first place?"

"Why wouldn't I?" Vivian said.

Jules blinked. "A lot of reasons? It's more painful—"

"I have every intention of being unconscious."

"Riskier—"

"Isn't Dr. Viswanathan the best in the business?"

"Messier—"

"Doctors and nurses are paid to clean up after themselves."

"And it has a longer recovery time. Much longer than vaginal birth. You'll be out of commission for a while."

"Nonsense." Vivian sniffed. "Most of it's mind over matter."

"Vivian, they cut a great big hole in you," Jules felt obliged to point out. "Then they have to sew it up afterward. Why do you want to do something so risky and painful when you don't have to? Can I point out that I don't *love* the idea of you unnecessarily under anesthesia?"

There was a brief moment of silence. That was exactly the amount of time it took to remember that women in the fashion industry underwent unnecessary procedures all the time. Jules didn't know for sure, but the rumor was that Vivian had had a chin tuck a couple of years ago.

Her face heated again. "Um, so…"

"I can schedule it," Vivian said, her voice even. "I know exactly when it's coming and what will be done. No surprises."

"Oh," Jules said.

"I've had enough surprises concerning this child. I want to know that one fine morning I'll go to the hospital, undergo a routine surgical procedure, and exit the hospital at a predetermined time with a healthy baby in tow."

"Well—" Jules began.

But Vivian had a full head of steam now. "I get my blood pressure, blood sugar, and a dozen other things checked every time I go to that office. I've had two ultrasounds, and I'll have one more. Why would I need to be rubber-stamped?"

"Just talk to the doctor, okay?" Jules pleaded. "Be open to what she has to say. The visit doesn't have to be a big deal. Think of it like—you're just going in for routine maintenance. You're getting your fluids checked."

This time, the moment of silence lasted considerably longer.

"What I mean is—" Jules began, turning red.

"These pearls just fall out of your mouth, don't they?" Vivian asked.

"I'm just trying to say—"

"My *fluids*?"

"Well, they'll check your blood again and probably swab your mouth for glucose, and of course they'll get you to—"

"Stop," Vivian said. "Stop right now."

Jules pressed her hand over her mouth to stop a snort of laughter. "Okay, okay. But you know what I mean."

"Tragically, I do. On that note, it's time for bed. Tomorrow won't be any easier than today was."

"Okay," Jules said, trying not to sound worried. "Get some rest. I'll talk to you tomorrow."

"Yes." Vivian paused. "Until tomorrow, then. Good night."

"Good night."

Jules padded toward her bathroom to get ready for bed. But just as she was starting to floss, her phone rang again. Vivian.

Was everything okay? Had something happened with the baby in the last few minutes? Jules scrambled to answer. "Hello? What's wrong?"

"Well?" Vivian said.

Jules looked at her phone screen in confusion.

Vivian said, again, *"Well?"*

"Uh," Jules said, then realized. "I-I love you?"

"Thank you," Vivian said, clearly exasperated, before disconnecting again.

Of all the—! Jules growled as she strung the dental floss between her teeth, considering and discarding the idea of calling Vivian back within moments. She didn't have the energy.

Vivian was weird. Jules was sleepy. She'd press the issue later.

Somehow.

CHAPTER 10

"Interviews?" Jules said.

"Interviews," Simon repeated. "It's time to get our name on everyone's lips for real."

He rubbed his hands, looking around at the office space Jules was painstakingly putting together. Now a modest crew inhabited the cubicles: an office admin, an IT specialist, an inventory coordinator, and the sales manager. Unlike *Du Jour*, they didn't have a whole building dedicated to their business that could host accounting, human resources, legal, and other services. All of that had to be outsourced. Many staff members worked remotely for lack of a larger office space.

Adrian & Jo had rented three warehouses: one in Staten Island, one just outside of Dallas, and one in Fullerton, California. If the venture was successful, Simon wanted to add another one in the Midwest. The multiple locations made it easier for their customers—no, clients, Simon called them—to ship and purchase secondhand goods from all over the country.

Those weren't the glamorous details of the business, though, and Simon had decided it was time to focus on those. Luckily, he had Jules in mind. Jules, who had been handling nothing but the less glamorous details, was chomping at the bit.

"Who am I interviewing?" she asked.

"Designers. We'll put the interviews on the site and on our social media as well as in press kits to send to journalists. It gives us more legitimacy."

With an effort, Jules kept her face neutral. This seemed like an...iffy idea. Adrian & Jo was an online consignment store, and normally, high-end designers wouldn't touch that sort of thing with a ten-foot pole.

As if reading her mind, Simon said, "I've got a few connections other people don't, Jules. And a lot of people owe me favors. It's time to call them in. We're a cut above the competition, and our clients need to see that."

Still seemed iffy. After all, in striking out on his own, Simon had made a formidable enemy. He had connections, but Vivian was the most powerful person in fashion, and she was furious at him. There might be a few scrappy, iconoclastic designers who'd be willing to brave her wrath. However, the most prestigious brands wouldn't be so eager. Why should they come afoul of Vivian Carlisle? Especially just to associate themselves with a fancy secondhand store?

Well…that wasn't quite fair. Simon had put a lot of effort into pitching Adrian & Jo to everyone as an opportunity for further brand exposure. Every item on the website would also include a link to the designer's latest runway shows. "Connecting past with present," Simon had said. "Building that buzz and showing clients that the designer is about more than that particular handbag they're about to buy."

His optimism was admirable. Jules couldn't help bracing for impact anyway.

"Got it," was all she said. "Leave it to me. Are there any designers you want me to prioritize, or can I figure that out on my own?"

She fully expected the second option. But Simon got a canny gleam in his eye that showed he wasn't totally delusional after all.

"Actually," he said, "I was thinking you could start with Monique Leung."

Monique Leung, the glamorous soon-to-be-former editor of *Du Jour China* and designer of her own fashion line. Monique Leung, who'd met Jules in London and offered her a job. Monique Leung, who'd aroused Vivian's jealousy like no one else had ever done.

Since getting fired from *Du Jour*, Jules hadn't given Monique any thought. There was little reason for their paths to cross again. Except now Simon had pulled one out of thin air.

It was easy enough to schedule the interview through Monique's personal assistant, Randall, whom Jules had met in London. Simon had chosen well. Out of every designer on the planet, Monique would care least about offending Vivian. Vivian already hated her and Monique had her own power base, so why worry about it?

Randall seemed pleased to reconnect with her and ended their text chain with:

We'll have to hang out soon. Monique says she's glad to hear from you btw

Great! I'm looking forward to it too

Jules pressed Send, looked at her lie, and bit her lower lip. How was she going to explain this to Vivian?

───────────

Based on Vivian's reaction, she'd done it clumsily.

"I see," Vivian said, her voice frost laden. "Monique again. Well."

Jules, perched as usual on her couch, pulled her knees up to her chest and hugged them. "It's not *again*, Vivian. C'mon. I just wanted to tell you because…" *Because you'd find out anyway, and it'd be even worse if I hadn't.*

"Because you knew there was no point in hiding it," Vivian said accurately. "And you didn't *want* to tell me."

Fair enough. "Okay, no I didn't, but I *had* to tell you. I know you don't like Monique, and I didn't want you to get the wrong idea."

"What idea would that be?"

So Vivian was going to play it that way? "Well, you did accuse her of wanting to seduce me a few months ago. She didn't. Besides, I looked her up, and she's gotten back together with her ex-girlfriend."

"That on-again, off-again affair? They'll break up in six months."

"Do you really think I'm going to cheat on you with Monique?" Jules asked incredulously.

"No, but I don't trust her as far as I can throw her when it comes to you. She tried to hire you away from *Du Jour* right under my nose."

"I don't work at *Du Jour* anymore anyway."

"You know it was more than that."

Vivian wasn't referring to Monique's intentions now. She was talking about her own reaction to it all, which had been disproportionate to losing a mere employee.

"Yeah," Jules said quietly. "I know it was."

"I won't put up with that. Not with you."

The possessive growl in Vivian's voice was an undeniable thrill. Better not to keep going down that road, though. Vivian could become positively unreasonable.

"I don't want to leave Adrian & Jo any more than I wanted to leave you. I-I like what I'm doing here." Even now, saying that felt like treason.

A moment of silence followed. Then Vivian said, "I know. It suits you. And I'm glad you've got an assignment that involves your brain for once. How long has it been since you've written anything?"

"Nothing since my *Modernity* article." And Jules wasn't anxious to open that can of worms with Vivian again either. "I haven't had time to look for anything else."

Vivian made a displeased-sounding noise. "I certainly hope you find the time. We can talk it through this Sunday."

That was Vivian trying to be helpful, Jules knew, but the last thing she wanted to talk about on Sunday was her stalled writing career. Their time together was too precious to spend like that. They talked all week; weekends were for the physical, doing things together they couldn't do over the phone or via text. Like sex.

Or other things.

"You know what I was thinking we could do on Sunday?" Jules asked. "Just watch a movie."

"A movie?" Vivian sounded as if she'd never heard the word before.

"Sure. Why not? We haven't done that before, and I bet it'd be fun to watch a movie with you."

"You're the first person in history to say so."

"Sunday night. We'll stream a slasher film. You'll be crawling in my lap by the end, begging me to protect you." Jules thought for a moment. "Then we'll have sex on the couch."

"I make no promises on that front," Vivian said. "But all right. We'll watch a movie."

Was Jules imagining a slightly wistful note in her voice? Maybe not. Maybe Vivian, like Jules, longed for the humble gestures of everyday romance. "Great! What do you want to watch?"

"You decide. See if you can guess what I'll like."

Uh-oh. "Don't I even get a hint?"

"No," Vivian said. "Now, good night. Don't count on a phone call tomorrow," she added. "I'll text you instead."

Oh, right. Vivian had a party to go to. Jules couldn't remember what it was, which was weird after spending two years fully immersed in Vivian's schedule. It'd probably run late, and Vivian would be craving pure peace and quiet, even from Jules's voice. "Okay. Take care. Simon's going to a reception anyway, and I've got to be there."

"I remember. Well. Good night," Vivian repeated.

"Good night," Jules said, and let the pause drag out. "Oh, are you waiting for something?" she added in mock surprise.

"I don't know," Vivian said, and something about the tone of her voice—wistful, almost apprehensive—flipped Jules's brain upside-down. "Am I?"

"I love you," Jules said at once, suddenly wishing more than anything that Vivian was in the room with her so she could show, not tell. "Um, *je t'aime*? *Te quiero*? Uh..." She racked her brains. What was the German for—

"Don't hurt yourself," Vivian said, now sounding amused instead of apprehensive. "I'll see you on Sunday."

"But—well, yes," Jules said, "but—"

"Good night," Vivian said softly.

"But—" Jules said again, although it was too late. Vivian had ended the call.

Maybe she should call Vivian back this time. By now, Vivian must know Jules wanted to hear the words too. But she wasn't saying them.

Why wasn't she? What was going on?

Vivian undoubtedly had her reasons. Jules didn't want to hear them, not right now. She flopped back down on the couch and glared at the living room wall instead of her bedroom ceiling, just for a change of scenery.

CHAPTER 11

J ULES TRIED TO BE IN a good mood at the reception the next afternoon. She wasn't going to let Vivian's inability to say a very simple thing ruin an opportunity to network. Vivian would never let such a petty concern distract *her*, after all.

It turned out to be a pretty good opportunity. The reception was for a gallery opening where the latest artists, musicians, and fashion designers collided to rub elbows and pretend to admire each other's work. Vivian rarely attended such events, so even if Jules didn't know Vivian's plans, she didn't worry about her showing up. Simon could circulate without that possibility hanging over his head.

Theoretically, Jules was there to play the part of Simon's assistant: taking notes, getting him from points A to B, making sure he wasn't stuck with annoying people for too long. All familiar territory.

But she was more than a mere assistant now, and Simon made sure she knew it. Several of New York's darlings were there, not just other artists but writers and even a couple of big-name designers. To Jules's surprise, they treated Simon with the utmost courtesy. Nobody made the sign of the cross at him or fled the presence of someone who'd offended Vivian Carlisle.

In fact, Luis Ribera, a Chilean designer whose newest collection was making waves, made conversation with Simon that sounded downright normal, including discussion of his line showing up on Adrian & Jo, an idea that seemed not to displease him.

Jules stared in astonishment. Luis was one of Vivian's discoveries, someone whose career she'd pushed to the top. He'd been unfailingly loyal to her. And yet here he was. In fact, the conversation ended with him agreeing to an interview with Jules for a press packet.

"A great opportunity for everyone," he said with a smile at Simon. "I can see why Vivian's lending it her support. She always knows which way the wind blows before the wind itself does."

What? Jules fought not to rock backward on her feet in shock. Her heels were too high and she'd collapse.

Simon betrayed no such surprise. "That's Vivian," he agreed. "We'll be in touch. So good to see you, Luis."

After Luis had given his farewells, Simon turned to Jules. "Could you manage not to look like a lightning bolt just struck you?"

"Vivian's support?" Jules hissed. "What's he talking about? She's so mad—" *That she refuses to even talk about you.* Jules barely managed not to say the words.

"Of course." Simon's voice carried the patience of ages. "But she can't let anyone know that, can she? She can't let anyone know I caught her by surprise. What would that do to her all-knowing image?"

Put like that, it seemed so obvious. "Um—"

"So she'll make like she knew all along and pretend that the venture has her full support," Simon concluded. "A pleasant fiction that benefits us all. I'm not stupid, Jules. I know you thought sending you after those designers was a fool's errand, but you'll find it's the exact opposite. They all think they've got Vivian's blessing."

Jules's breath escaped her in a long exhale that was almost a whistle. "Wow. So—"

"I think 'checkmate' is the word you're looking for." Simon gave Jules a small smile that rivaled Vivian's best canny look. "For now, anyway."

At least he put the conditional on it. Vivian could wait to strike in a different way. Revenge was best served cold and all that. Simon clearly knew it and was playing his own long game in return.

Jules could only hope not to get caught in the crossfire. Vivian would want to keep her out of that.

Wouldn't she?

"I should have figured that out," she admitted. "I can't believe I didn't."

"Well, you're still young."

Jules glared. Not something she loved hearing. "Ha, ha."

Simon glanced at his watch. "I think I've had enough ass kissing for one night. You got any plans?"

"Nope," Jules said. It was seven thirty. The afternoon reception had run late, and she hadn't even noticed the time. "All yours tonight."

"Excellent," he said, stepping away long enough to bid good night to an artist and then taking Jules's arm as they headed into the cooling evening air.

Simon hailed a cab and gallantly held the door open for Jules before sliding in behind her. "Alfredo's Trattoria on Eighth," he told the driver, and added to Jules, "I miss *Du Jour's* town cars."

"They'll come," Jules said reassuringly. "We're on our way. Everyone wanted to talk to you tonight." And now she knew why.

Simon nodded. "We've been able to offer some attractive advertising packages, we've lined up a couple of big names for content, and the subscriber base is already bigger than projected. It's coming together. I'm glad to get out of there, though."

"You didn't enjoy the reception?"

"I admit I'm happy to do less of it than I used to. Putting together something of my own is more satisfying."

"Yeah, back to that. I just thought of something. If we don't have to worry about blowback, then why'd you start me off interviewing Monique Leung instead of a more established designer who's not scared to talk to us?"

"Monique's been very helpful to me. More than you know, probably. I owe her. Besides...you already knew her." Simon adjusted his cufflinks. Sterling silver from Tiffany & Co. Jules had ordered them herself. "She made you an offer you couldn't refuse yet somehow did, I hear. At London Fashion Week."

Jules's heart stuttered. *Calm down,* she told herself. *You can think of a reason why.* "Um, I just didn't feel—"

"You know, you looked like hell that whole week," Simon said.

"Gee, thanks."

"Except that last morning," Simon added thoughtfully. "I noticed the difference. Remarkable, considering you were recovering from food poisoning but had all your pep back."

"Er. Yeah. I guess...I guess I'd just been feeling a little run-down."

That was one way of putting it. Vivian had been spending a lot of time with Stan Oppenheimer, a handsome, highly placed Koening executive. She'd looked delighted after every secretive meeting they'd had. Meanwhile, Jules had been eaten up with jealousy, grief, and fury at her own stupidity. She'd felt run-down, all right: run down by a truck.

Then on that incredible night, Vivian had reassured Jules she'd had nothing to worry about. No wonder Simon had noticed the difference later.

Jules added, "But you know, I do remember feeling better that morning."

"I was worried about you," Simon said. "I'd been wondering if Vivian made you sleep chained to the wall or something."

Jules forced a laugh. "Oh no," she said. "No, no."

"Apparently not," Simon said. Then he added, "Hey. Whatever happened to that cute pin you had on in the airport?"

Jules's heartbeat began to pick up, working at a faster rate than her brain could manage. What the hell was going on? "Uh, the pin?"

"Oh, you know, the Stephen Webster snake," Simon said. "The one Vivian really liked but apparently gave to you."

Then he turned and looked her dead in the eye. His face was—not cold exactly, but intent. Serious. As serious as she'd ever seen him.

"I-I put it in the bank," Jules said softly. "In a safe-deposit box."

Simon nodded, waiting expectantly.

Jules licked her lips. "I don't want to lose it," she whispered. "I'd hate for anything to happen to it."

"I'm sure." Simon looked away from her, peering through the windshield. "This restaurant has pretty good wine."

Jules felt frozen for the rest of the cab ride. They didn't speak again, but she knew what was coming.

Simon had figured it out. Or he'd already known and was deciding to bring it up now. Or he was just guessing but had guessed just enough.

The cab pulled up in front of a small, unprepossessing Italian restaurant, the kind that had been in Manhattan for decades while hipster bars came and went. Simon paid the driver and got out, rounding the cab to open Jules's door for her.

In the interval, the driver met Jules's eyes through the rearview mirror and said, "You are busted. For what, I don't know."

"Yeah," Jules said.

76

"Your husband?"

"No," Jules said at once, just as Simon opened her door. She practically fell out of the cab in her haste to exit.

"Welcome to Alfredo's," Simon said. They both looked up at the blinking neon sign for a moment and then Simon silently led her inside.

The interior wasn't exactly five-star. Maybe not even three. But it smelled heavenly. Too bad Jules had lost her appetite.

A hostess led them to a plastic booth. Simon ordered two glasses of the house red. Now that, Jules could get behind. She didn't want to get too drunk, though—who knew what she'd say?—and she hadn't had more at the reception than a few bites of various hors d'oeuvres, so she decided to go easy.

It was going to be tough. She could really use a drink.

Simon swirled the wine in the glass, sniffed, sipped, then nodded appreciatively. Jules didn't know why, since this wasn't exactly the kind of place where the sommelier hung around until the customer approved the vintage, but whatever gave Simon a kick. She carefully sipped her own instead of chugging it as she wanted.

Simon opened his menu. "The clam linguine here is excellent."

"Oh," Jules said. "You, um, go ahead. I'm actually not hungry." Nearly nauseated, actually.

"We'll split an entrée," Simon announced and waved the menus at the nearest server. "One order of clam linguine, two plates."

"You want to share, it's five bucks extra," the waitress said, and popped her bubble gum.

"Fine." Simon sighed. When the waitress left, he added, "I wonder why they do that. It's the same amount of food. Criminal, really."

"Us splitting a meal drives down her tip," Jules pointed out, glad to latch on to another topic. Maybe she could keep this one going all night somehow. "I waitressed in college. Trust me, you want her on your side."

"Well," Simon said and gave Jules a half smile. "When you and Vivian go out to dinner, you'll just have to be extra sweet to the waitress."

Dammit. Jules smiled mirthlessly right back at him. "I don't think I'll be going out to dinner with Vivian anytime soon."

"No?"

"No," Jules said. "Simon, come on—"

"She's a charming dinner companion," Simon said. "You wouldn't think so, but she is. She can be very, very charming when she wants."

"Yes," Jules said and gripped her wineglass more tightly. "Yes, she can."

"Jules, I've been watching it happen for months," Simon said, his voice low and utterly serious. "Maybe I didn't understand what I was seeing at first—not completely—Well, I was kind of preoccupied." He snorted again. "I should have put it together long ago. But I have now. Her rage when Mark fired you was probably the tip-off. When I thought about it later, I remembered Vivian doesn't do rage." He shook his head. "I want to ask you if you're crazy, but the answer's pretty obvious."

Well, here it came, then. There was no use hoping that, by some act of God, they weren't going to have this conversation.

Jules swallowed hard. "What do you want me to say?" she whispered. "I know it's a stupid idea."

"That's a comfort," Simon said. "Jules, can't you see what's really happening here?"

"Yes. Yes, I can." Jules looked Simon in the eye. Now was the moment to prove how serious she was. "Simon, I know it's nuts. I've known all along, and so has she."

"Vivian's judgment isn't sound right now, Jules," Simon said firmly. "Not about things like this. You of all people should know that."

"What's that supposed to mean?"

"You know what," Simon said. "Vivian needs you. I've said that all along, even when I didn't know the whole truth. Drowning people grab the first thing they can find to save themselves. Sound judgment doesn't have to enter into it."

"I don't—" Jules's eyes widened. Simon couldn't possibly mean what she thought he meant. "I don't understand. What are you trying to say?"

"I'm sorry," Simon said. "I know it's a hard thing to hear. It's a hard thing to say. But after Robert left her and she learned she was pregnant, I watched her grab onto you—"

"Wait." Jules's hands began to shake so much that she had to set down her wineglass. "No, that's not—"

"Like she realized she didn't have a friend in the world right when she needed one," Simon finished. "Jules, I'm not saying she doesn't care about you. She obviously cares. She feels as if she can't get by without you, apparently." He shrugged and sighed. "Maybe that's what love is. I wouldn't know. It's been a while."

"You think she's with me because I'm the only person around?" Jules couldn't believe how much that hurt. What was next? An actual slap to the cheek? "That's not true. You don't know what's going on. You don't have any idea—"

"I don't?"

"No!" Jules said at once. But...maybe that wasn't true.

Maybe he did.

Jules remembered with a sickening lurch in her stomach how Vivian had approached her in London only after Jules had walked out on her. Had she been afraid that Jules had finally had enough of her, that she was finally going to leave and had to be stopped by whatever means necessary? She remembered how Vivian liked it when Jules said she loved her—how she seemed to need to hear it—but how she never said it back. ⁻

Maybe she panics when you're more than ten feet away.

Simon himself had said that months ago, long before Jules and Vivian had begun their...whatever they had. He'd been referring to how Vivian kept Jules close while her life turned upside down.

Was that it? Was that why Vivian was so willing to stick out her neck? For need, not love?

How many times had Jules thought about this very thing before she and Vivian had gotten together? How many times had she reflected that Vivian had no friends, nobody to turn to? How many times had her own parents told her it was bizarre that Vivian should rely on her, a lowly assistant, so much?

No. Come on. This was ridiculous. Jules tried to remember the other stuff, the good stuff, like talking on the phone, laughing together in bed, wearing sexy clothes. Like the gown Vivian had worn on New Year's Eve the night she'd realized Jules would do anything for her because—

Thinking wasn't helping. Jules took a deep breath and tried again. "She..." But she didn't know what to say. "Simon..." Because what could she say?

Well, how about, "Simon, she's not stupid. She knows what's at stake for her." *Everything.* "You really think she would do this if I was just...convenient?"

"I don't know," Simon said to Jules's surprise. "I don't know her nearly as well as I thought I did, apparently. Jules, listen to me. I'm not saying anything's wrong with you. I'm not saying that at all."

"No?" And goddamn it, there went the first tear, streaking hotly down her cheek.

Simon sighed and offered her a paper napkin. "Is that Diorshow mascara?"

"Yes," Jules mumbled, dabbing at her cheek.

"The black shade's not right for you. Try the brown. But what I'm saying is, there's nothing wrong with you. You're a fine person. Truth to tell, you've become one of my favorite people." He offered her a sad smile. "Vivian has every reason in the world to care about you. I'm just not sure she's doing it for the right ones."

"Oh," Jules managed and swallowed hard, trying frantically to shore up her dignity. It was quite the effort. "Jesus, Simon."

"Jules, I'm not telling you this for my health or yours," Simon said quietly. "If you get caught—if Mark Tavio gets wind or, hell, the press—"

"Oh God. Stop. Please," Jules said.

"Stop?" Simon sounded incredulous. "You think they'd stop if you told them to?"

"We're being discreet," Jules said and added pleadingly, "Aren't we? Simon, you haven't heard talk, have you?"

"No," Simon admitted, and Jules relaxed for a moment. "No talk, no gossip. Yet." He took a deep breath. "Jules, I've got to put this on the table. Adrian & Jo is new. We can't afford a scandal."

Jules stared at him.

He stared right back as he said, "I've worked very hard, and I've waited a long time. If a scandal breaks—"

"No such thing as bad publicity." Jules reached for a new napkin and blew her nose.

"As a writer, you should spend more time on Twitter," Simon said, an edge in his voice for the first time. "Did the #MeToo movement escape you completely? You were Vivian's assistant. Rightly or wrongly, she'd be called out as a predator."

That thought—that truth—put a cold lump in the center of Jules's stomach. Vivian herself had said as much, although she hadn't been referring to her public image at the time. She'd been worried about *being* a predator, about Jules feeling forced into something.

Jules never had been forced, but that wasn't Simon's concern right now. She yanked herself back to the present. "And you've been associated with her for years."

"So everyone would think I knew about it," Simon agreed. "In fact, how convenient that I got you a job, isn't it? What if Vivian's been doing this for years? Maybe I've been covering for her. That's what they'll all wonder."

"I'd deny..." Jules's voice petered out. Who'd believe her if she denied anything? Besides, a whole troop of lawyers would probably descend on her and forbid her to say anything at all.

Simon's raised eyebrows agreed with all of that. "Where the revenue goes, the shareholders follow." He tilted his head to the side. "It could go either way. But odds are that it'd go more one way than the other."

Jules's heart was making a damn good effort to beat right out of her chest. Why couldn't she go back in time to this morning and somehow prevent this conversation from happening?

"That's why this *is* my business," Simon said, "aside from the fact that I am your friend as well as your boss, and if you make me fire you when we could be having a fabulous time together, I will hate you forever." He played with the saltshaker, not meeting her eyes while she struggled for breath. "Believe it or not, I'm not trying to tell you what to do. I'm not telling you Vivian doesn't care about you. I'm not making you pick sides. I'm just letting you know...what you need to know. So you can make an informed decision. Whatever you decide."

Suddenly, the waitress appeared out of nowhere and put a big steaming platter of clam linguine between them along with two plates and two sets of utensils.

"Anything else for you, doll?" she asked Simon.

"No, thank you," Simon said. "This looks great."

The waitress nodded and walked away while Jules looked at the cream-covered noodles and wondered if she'd ever be able to eat again.

"I will admit..." Simon began, then paused.

Jules looked at him but didn't prompt him. She barely managed not to say "shut up."

Simon continued anyway. "I will admit that she was gracious—as gracious as she knows how to be—about letting me spirit you away when Mark fired you. I remember finding it remarkable what she said at the time"—Simon lifted his chin in the air—"'I'll at least trust you to look out for her.' Believe it or not, that's what I'm trying to do."

"I need to go." Jules shoved her arms into her jacket sleeves and picked up her handbag.

Simon opened his mouth.

"I'm not mad at you," she said.

Simon looked disbelieving.

Yeah, fair. But the tears were bad enough. Why should Simon get to know how badly he'd hurt her? "I know you're just trying to look out for me, but it's fine. It really is."

"Jules—"

"I can take care of myself." The words were coming too quickly. Why couldn't Jules take a deep breath and slow them down? Why were her eyes getting hot again? "Don't worry about me. I've got this. It's fine. It's—it's totally fine."

"*Jules.* I want you to be happy," Simon said. "Hell, I want it for myself too. Just remember that Vivian's got her limits. If something goes wrong, there's only so much she can—or will—do to protect you, and the same goes for me."

"Enjoy the linguine." Jules staggered to her feet and hurried out of the restaurant without another word. She thought she heard Simon say her name as she left but didn't stop to make sure.

Now she just had to figure out where to go. Striking out down the street toward the nearest subway stop, Jules decided she should just go home. Go home, drink a little more—or a lot more—or watch TV, or write, or do *anything* but—

Her phone was at her ear before she quite realized what she was doing. She had stopped dead in the street, and Vivian was on the other end saying, "Julia? Why are you calling?"

Vivian didn't sound delighted to hear from her. The opposite, in fact, as if Jules was intruding on her time.

Jules's hand clenched on her purse strap. The leather edges dug into her palms. "Um... Hi. Sorry to bother y— How was the party?"

"It was fine," Vivian said, sounding annoyed. "And I'm exhausted. As I told you I'd be."

"Yeah," Jules said. "You...you did say that."

"Is something wrong?"

How did Jules even begin to answer that? "Um—"

"What is it?" Vivian demanded. "For God's sake, out with it. Are you in the hospital or something?"

"No," Jules said.

"Did somebody die?"

"No—"

"Did you get fired?"

"Not yet," Jules rasped.

"What's that?"

Jules cleared her throat. She blinked because she was almost crying again. "I said no. I shouldn't have..." She closed her eyes and moved to stand by the side of the nearest shop window out of the foot traffic. "I have to know something. It's not going to wait until tomorrow. I'm sorry."

"What are you talking about?" Vivian said.

"I was just talking to...and..." Jules took a deep breath and let it out.

Okay. Vivian liked it when people got to the point. And it was long past time for Jules to speak her own mind and to ask for what she wanted.

"I need to know," she said. "Do you love me?"

The ensuing silence stretched on. And on. And on.

"Oh," Jules finally said, wondering if an asteroid would miraculously hit her. It seemed preferable to being here in this moment when Vivian had answered with her silence. *"Oh."*

"Why are you asking?" Vivian said.

Not all the paper napkins in the world would save Jules's mascara now. "Holy shit," she choked out, wiping her hand over her cheek, getting more smudges on her fingertips.

"Where are you?"

Like it *mattered*? "Nowhere. I'm going home." Either that or she'd crawl under the nearest rock. Or buy a one-way train ticket back to Philadelphia. That could work too.

"No, you're not. Come here."

"The hell I will!" Thank God she was in New York. Nobody on the street glanced her way as she yelled it.

Vivian's voice rose in return. "Have you been drinking?"

One glass didn't count. Everyone knew that. "I'm sober, trust me. Enough to understand what it means when somebody can't answer a simple question."

"Get over here," Vivian barked, "unless you want me knocking down your door instead. I'm not having this conversation over the phone."

The call ended.

Jules stared down at the phone through blurry eyes, shaking even harder than she had in the restaurant. How dare Vivian be so high-handed? Jules should call her back at once and give her a piece of her mind. Except, no, Jules shouldn't do that. Jules should run as far from all this as she could and never call or text Vivian's number for the rest of her life.

Her phone rang again. It was Vivian—again.

Even as Jules's rational self was howling at her not to pick up, she did. *"What?"*

"In case you were wondering, this is not negotiable," Vivian said. "I mean it. Get...get over here now." Then she disconnected again.

Now. The word made all the difference because Vivian's voice had wobbled, nearly broken on it.

Jules found herself sticking out a hand to flag a passing taxi. Okay. Vivian didn't want to have this conversation over the phone? Maybe she had a point. Some things it was better, more satisfying, to hash out in person.

With all the rage trembling on her tongue, Jules just hoped she wouldn't say something she'd regret.

CHAPTER 12

Vivian answered the door before Jules could even ring the bell.

Then everything was a blur of motion as Vivian moved faster than a pregnant woman in her forties had a right to. She yanked Jules inside by her elbow so that Jules nearly stumbled and fell. And then, never losing her grip, she dragged Jules toward the kitchen. What for? Maybe she was planning to bake Jules a nice apple pie after breaking her heart.

Jules glanced at the doorway to the den as Vivian tugged her past it. "What about—"

"Not there," Vivian snapped.

Absurdly, in a moment like this, Jules could only think to ask, "Why not?"

"The den is for happy memories. The kitchen is better for this."

That was enough to make Jules yank her arm free. Just as well, since they'd arrived in the kitchen anyway. All the lights were on, bright and white, making Jules feel like a suspect in an interrogation room.

Vivian rounded on her. Her lips pinched with displeasure, and they got even more pinched when she saw the evidence of Jules's tears. Jules had done her best to wipe off her streaky makeup in the cab, but she couldn't get rid of her red eyes or cheeks.

"What happened?" Vivian asked flatly. "Why are you calling me in a flood of tears and asking me if I love you?"

Jules took a deep breath. She was in the middle of a very weird feeling, one in which nothing around her seemed real while everything also stood out in sharp relief. "Why aren't *you* able to answer the question? I just—"

But Vivian pressed on. "This hasn't come out of nowhere, Julia. This isn't some random question you're asking out of the blue. Why. Are. You. Crying?"

"I'm not anymore," Jules snapped. Then humiliatingly, she sniffled. Dammit.

"Julia," Vivian said.

Jules had to tell her. Someone had learned the truth about them. Vivian needed to know about that. "Simon," she said.

Vivian's eyes darkened.

"We were talking, and he told me he's figured it out." She swallowed. "I think he's been putting the pieces together for a while."

Vivian's jaw tightened. "And is he planning to tell anyone? Go to the press? Call Mark?"

"No!" Jules wiped her eyes. Please God, let this be the last time she had to do that. "He wouldn't do that. He just wanted to talk to me about it."

"Why?" Vivian growled. "If he's not going to tattle, why is he sticking his nose in our business?"

"That's not the reason I'm so—"

"Tell me!"

Jules straightened her shoulders, shocked at the vehemence in Vivian's voice, at the fury in her eyes. "He just wanted to talk to me," she repeated. "He just wanted to make sure everything was…okay."

She left out the part about Simon firing her if the affair became public. It didn't seem necessary, and it did seem like the kind of thing that would push Vivian over the edge into a frothing rage.

"Okay?" Vivian said. "He wanted to make sure everything was 'okay'? Does he think I'm putting a knife to your throat or something? Forcing you into this?"

"No! He's just worried about what might happen if… Uh, he doesn't want us to get in trouble."

"And that made you cry?" Vivian said, narrowing her eyes. "Simon's touching concern for our mutual well-being made you cry?"

"No." Jules took yet another deep breath. Time to stop beating around the bush. Vivian had told her again and again to speak her mind.

"He said," she began, trying not to let her voice shake, "that he was worried that you just need me instead of caring about me, you know, as a person. Of course I told him that was ridiculous, that you wouldn't take all these risks if you didn't care, but…"

Vivian's eyes had widened.

Jules swallowed harshly. "He said that you just needed someone to be there for you because things were so tough. He said I was the only one who was there, that I was convenient."

Now Vivian's jaw was hanging open.

Jules grabbed her own arms as if she were standing outside in a blizzard and kept going. "I tell you I love you, and you don't say it back, and I don't know why. Maybe you think it's stupid or something, but if you said it, I'd believe you. It's not such a big deal, is it? It's—"

"You'd...*believe* me?" Vivian said slowly, repeating after Jules again, astonishment still in her eyes. "It's not a 'big deal'?"

"Yes!" Why the hell was this so hard to understand? Even if Vivian thought it was a meaningless gesture—which Vivian didn't. "You like it when I say it to you. You called me in the middle of the night to make sure I meant it the first time. But you never say it back!"

"You believe I don't care about you?" Vivian said. The shock on her face had resolved, flattened into something expressionless, except for her burning eyes.

"I *know* you care about me," Jules said through gritted teeth. "You said you did. Back in London."

"Yes," Vivian said. "Yes, I did say that."

"It's just a stupid word. I mean, three stupid words. Why is this freaking you out?" Jules flung her arms wide. "I'll say them to you anytime you want. I can say them till the cows come home. Hey, look at this, it's easy—"

"Stupid—?"

"I love you. There, see? Want me to do it again? I can do it. I can do a lot of tricks. I can hold my breath underwater for more than a minute."

"You're being totally ridiculous." Vivian's face was pale now.

"No, I'm not." Jules set her jaw. "It's not ridiculous to love somebody and tell them so and want them to tell you back. There is absolutely nothing wrong with that."

"Or what?" Vivian said.

Jules stared at her.

"Or what?" Vivian repeated harshly. "Is this an ultimatum? If I don't make some kind of grand declaration, you walk?"

"Grand declaration?" Jules said incredulously. "Saying 'Hey, I love you' to somebody in your own house is a grand declaration?" She took a step forward.

Vivian stood her ground, her jaw twitching, her eyes flashing with fury. "At least tell me why you won't say it. Can you at least tell me that?"

"I've tried," Vivian said.

Jules's shoulders went rigidly straight. Vivian didn't say anything else. They looked at each other.

"I've tried," Vivian repeated through her teeth. "Several times."

Jules might be about to choke. Vivian had *tried* to say it? Like you might say you *tried* to go on a horrible diet or you *tried* to enjoy yourself at a boring party? "What does that even mean?"

"I can't do it over the phone," Vivian said.

"I— Huh?"

"I'm not saying it over the phone," Vivian said. "Not the first time. That's not the sort of—I told you it shouldn't be casual because people—"

Jules couldn't believe this. "Are you telling me I did it wrong?"

"I wouldn't presume. How could I? It's so easy for you. Those words are so *stupid*."

"That's not what I meant, and you know it!"

"I'm not going to say it over the phone," Vivian repeated. "I need to say something like that in person."

There was a pause.

"Well?" Jules said, spreading her arms again. "Here I am!"

"Forget it," Vivian snapped. "Not when I'm this mad."

Jules's arms immediately dropped back down. "*You're* mad?"

"I can't believe you called me up and asked me that. Have you gone through the last few months with your eyes shut?" Vivian hissed. "How can you possibly not know—"

Her voice broke. She looked away as she swallowed harshly.

"Know *what*?" Jules demanded.

At her sharp tone, Vivian looked back at her. She set her jaw. "How can you not know what you mean to me? One conversation with Simon and you go to pieces?"

"That's not fair! I just told you why I felt that way!"

"You sure did." Vivian raised the pitch of her voice. "'Vivian, Simon said something that made me doubt everything you've ever done or said—'"

"Hey!"

"'—and I left my brain in another handbag this morning, so would you please kiss me and make it all better?'"

"I'm upset," Jules yelled, not caring that she was raising her voice this time. "You told me to tell you when I get upset. Remember?"

"And what's all this about me needing you just because you were there?"

"Didn't you?" Jules said. "What about Christmas? We hadn't had a lot of deep conversations when you called me to London out of nowhere..."

I've never cared for yellow.

The words rang in Jules's memory for some reason. Vivian had said that to her months ago, an idle observation while looking over an editorial spread. Except that Vivian never made idle observations with employees. Jules had even thought so at the time. Did that count as deep conversation for Vivian—even the tiniest reveal of her preferences to someone so beneath her?

"Had we?" Jules finished weakly.

Vivian set her jaw but then conceded harshly. "Not a lot, no."

Whew. "So what was that about?" Jules pressed.

"I—" Vivian inhaled sharply through her nose and then exhaled slowly. "You were there for one of the worst moments of my life. Several of them, in fact. And I never for one moment worried that you'd tattle, although you had a lot to gain by doing so."

What would Jules have had to gain except being ashamed of herself? "Of course I wouldn't tattle!"

"And afterward you did everything I needed, everything I asked without complaint, without asking for anything in return. I noticed this. I told you I noticed this. Have you forgotten?"

"No," Jules said, her mouth dry. "No, I haven't."

"How many people in your position would have done the same?" Vivian asked. "I'll tell you: few. And of those, almost none would have had your resourcefulness or your intelligence, which I seem to dimly remember."

Jules opened her mouth, not entirely sure what would come out of it.

Vivian held up her hand. "No, no. You wanted me to say this, didn't you?"

"I don't know what you're saying," Jules said, beyond frustrated. "Because it's really starting to sound like you're saying you needed me because I was there!"

"I did!" Vivian shouted. It was the first time she'd raised her voice all night. It was the first time she'd raised her voice to Jules ever. "I needed you because you were there, and *you were there because I needed you.* At times like that, you learn who your real friends are. I saw what kind of person you were. Are you actually blaming me for finding that attractive? Should we have had a deep conversation where I explained this to you in detail?"

Adrenaline pounded so hard through Jules's body that she shook with it. It seemed that Simon was wrong about a few key things, but this wasn't enough.

"Maybe we should have," she said. "Maybe then we wouldn't be talking about it now instead."

"Only because you can't put two and two together." Vivian's bottom lip trembled before she bit it, quickly. "I can't believe you're saying all this."

"Well, I'm sorry," Jules said, clenching her hands into fists and sounding anything but sorry. "I'm sorry you can't believe that I want you to say you love me."

"Well, I can't believe it," Vivian snapped. "You should already know."

The ground must have shifted beneath Jules's feet. It explained why she rocked backward on her heels. Mere words couldn't have done that. "I—"

But Vivian wasn't done. She took a step forward, her blue eyes throwing sparks. "Maybe this is just how we're different, Julia. I care about actions, and you care about words. It must be a writer thing."

Jules was still wrestling with *You should already know.* That was a declaration, right? Vivian had admitted to loving Jules, right? In her way? "What do you—"

"But I trust your words anyway when I could choose to focus a lot more on what you do."

Jules's thoughts stopped their spiral at that. "What I do?"

"You tell me every night that you love me." The snarl in Vivian's voice made the hairs on Jules's arms stand up. "All while you're working for the man who stuck a knife in my back and preparing for a nice little chat with the woman who tried to steal you from me."

She took another step forward, and Jules instinctively took a step back. She bumped into the kitchen island. "Vivian, we've talked a million times about—"

"It would be so easy for me to be suspicious, but I'm not. And do you know why? Because when you say you love me, I believe you. Meanwhile, here I am, not killing Simon's little venture in its infancy."

Simon had talked about that very thing. "Of course you're not," Jules said defensively. "It'd show he took you by surprise. What does that have to do with anything?"

Vivian's eyes widened. "Took me by surprise? What are you talking about?"

Jules's head was spinning. As ever, Vivian's mind was two steps ahead of everyone else's, and it was an impossible race to catch up. "If...if you punished him, it'd show everyone that you didn't know what he was up to. You wouldn't look like you were in control."

"That's what you think it's about?" Vivian stepped forward yet again until her belly pressed against Jules's. The soft rise of it wasn't enough to prevent her from leaning in and putting her hands on the countertop to either side of Jules, pinning her in.

Jules's hands found their way to Vivian's shoulders, rubbing against the soft cotton of her blouse quite of their own accord.

Their faces were close enough that when Vivian whispered, her breath brushed against Jules's lips. "I wouldn't seem *in control*? If I punished Simon, everyone in the industry would see firsthand what happens when you cross me. Revenge isn't best served cold. I like it piping hot."

It made no sense at all that Jules's hands were sliding up until her fingertips brushed Vivian's throat. "Then why didn't you?"

Fast as lightning, Vivian's hands moved from the countertop to grab Jules's hips, cupping them as though she wanted to hold Jules there with her forever. "Because it was an opportunity for you. Because it meant something *to you*. I wanted to end him, and I didn't, I didn't, because—"

In lieu of finishing her sentence, she leaned in and kissed Jules hard. Their collision would have sent Jules to her knees if not for Vivian's body holding her in place against the counter.

"Vivian," she gasped when let up for air.

"On the counter." Vivian squeezed Jules's hips, her thumbs digging into the soft dip of the pelvis. "Sit on the counter. Now."

"We should keep talking!" They really should. Jules had no idea why she was hoisting herself onto the counter instead.

91

"Weren't you listening?" Vivian's words were cool; the high color in her face looked anything but. "I like showing, not telling. Pull these down."

She plucked at the burgundy silk of Jules's tights, which had provided an extra layer against an early April evening. They felt suffocating now.

Maybe that was why Jules kicked off her shoes, raised her ass, and began wriggling the tights down her legs. It was a comfort thing. It had nothing to do with the rising ache between her legs. "We should... I need to hear..."

Vivian grabbed the tights before Jules could slide them over her ankles. "Stop there."

The silk of the tights kept Jules from spreading her legs, from moving, held her at Vivian's mercy.

"Do you know what *I* need to hear?" Vivian asked, her voice hot in Jules's ear.

"Wh-what?"

Vivian leaned in, and her hand slipped beneath Jules's skirt. Jules's hips arched forward without her brain's conscious input.

Vivian's palm slid unerringly between the waistband of Jules's panties and her belly. Her fingers found Jules's lips, spread them, and pressed down.

Jules cried out as her hips bucked forward.

"Yes," Vivian rasped. "That's what I need to hear. Take off your shirt and bra. Now."

The blouse seemed to take forever to go over her head, but Jules wrestled it off and tossed it to the side, uncaring where it fell. Bra next. It was a nice bra, lacy and expensive, and Vivian didn't give it a second look. She didn't look at anything except Jules's eyes.

"Hold up your breasts," she said. "Offer them to me."

Fuck. Jules's vision actually went blurry at the edges. She cupped her breasts. They were pretty great breasts, soft handfuls for an offering.

"Good girl." Vivian leaned in farther, opening her mouth and sucking on the left one.

"Oh God," Jules moaned, fighting to keep her hands where they were instead of grabbing Vivian's head.

Vivian's mouth was hot and hungry, her tongue agile as it flicked over Jules's nipple while her hand continued to press rhythmically between Jules's legs.

Jules's hips lifted to meet her touch. Her back arched forward toward Vivian's mouth.

Vivian released her breast with a groan. Her breath blew against Jules's nipple as she said, "You're getting wet for me. You're swelling against my fingers."

"Vivian!" Why couldn't Jules spread her legs wider? Why couldn't she give Vivian more room to—

One of Vivian's fingers slid between her lips, crooked, and pushed up into the soaked space waiting for it.

Jules actually shrieked. Her panties held Vivian's hand against her, her tights kept her legs tied, all of it creating pressure that seemed to drive Vivian as deeply inside as possible, that pressed the heel of Vivian's hand against her clit.

Vivian curled her finger forward, rubbing roughly against Jules's G-spot.

Jules rocked forward with a sob.

"Hold still," Vivian said. "I'm giving you another."

"Please." Jules licked her lips, reached for air. "I need… Let me take off my tights…"

"No." Vivian pulled her finger out and traced it upward, rubbing it over Jules's clit enough to show Jules definitively how wet she was. "You're right where I want you."

What would Jules look like if someone saw her now? Her legs spread as wide as they could go while being bound by her tights, torso bare, holding up her breasts while she pushed her hips forward and begged shamelessly for more?

She groaned loudly and tried to spread wider, unable to do so.

It didn't matter. Vivian still had enough room to slide two fingers inside Jules, filling her up while she leaned in again.

At that, Jules let it happen. She tossed her head back, gave in to the hot mouth on her breasts, and rode Vivian's fingers while her cries rang off the kitchen walls. Her hips rocked as Vivian fucked her, ruthlessly raising her higher and higher.

"Mine," Vivian gasped against her. "All mine."

"Yes," Jules said, and then again, "*Yes,*" as she began to come. She leaned back on her hands, feeling the air on her wet breasts and the deep clench inside her as she cried out. How could anything feel this good? How was it possible to feel this good and survive it?

Through it all, Vivian murmured words like *do it* and *that's right* and *good girl*. Impossibly, they only made Jules come harder until her vision swam.

"Enough," she finally moaned, sinking back on her elbows. "Oh God."

Vivian slowly withdrew her fingers. They seemed to shake a little. Maybe that was just Jules's imagination; her brain had turned to mush.

Jules, closing her eyes, felt something at her mouth. Vivian's fingertips, covered with Jules's own come. Without thinking about it, she obediently opened her mouth and tasted herself, salty and sharp.

"There now." Vivian sounded breathless as she pulled her fingers back. "There now."

"Jesus," Jules said weakly. "Vivian, you wrecked me."

"That was the idea."

With a groan, Jules managed to sit up and take in the sight before her. Vivian's face was flushed. Her lips were wet as if she'd been licking them.

Time for Jules to press her own lips to them. Jules reached for Vivian, still short of breath but ready to lose it all over again for a kiss.

Vivian put her hands on Jules's chest, holding her still. Then she leaned in to take the kiss herself. She didn't try to devour Jules this time, but her kiss was firm, reminding Jules in no uncertain terms who was in charge of this encounter.

"What can I do for you?" Jules whispered when their mouths parted. "What do you want?"

She imagined going on her knees, her shirt still off while she pulled down Vivian's pants, leaning forward into the glorious warmth and wet until she made Vivian just as incoherent as Jules had been moments ago.

"I want to go upstairs," Vivian said.

With difficulty, Jules swam out of her fantasies. "Huh?"

"With you," Vivian clarified. "It's been a long, exhausting day, and I want to put this foolishness behind us."

Jules looked down at herself, at her bare breasts and spread legs. It was starting to feel less sexy and more awkward. She wasn't ready to put this behind them yet. Had Vivian thought sex in the kitchen would magically solve everything?

Vivian's fingers—the dry ones—touched Jules's cheek.

"This conversation isn't over, Julia," she said. "Trust me on that."

Her eyes were softer now. And more tired.

Jules felt that. An evening of being put through the wringer could do that to a girl.

"All right, then," she said. "Lead the way."

Vivian's bathroom had a whirlpool tub that could easily fit both her and Jules, and she was very particular about water temperature, bath salts, candles, music, and the overall atmosphere. She didn't have time to take many long baths, but "When you do, Julia," she said, "it should be an *experience.*"

So Jules browsed Vivian's bookshelves while Vivian performed arcane bath-time rites behind closed doors, turning water off and on again. As she was picking up a copy of *The Beautiful Fall*, she heard her phone beep.

It was Simon. He'd texted.

Are you ok?

Jules fought down a surge of irritation along with the urge to reply "No thanks to you." Instead, she responded with: *Yeah, I'm ok*

Can we talk?

Jules glanced at the bathroom door. Vivian had only been in there for a minute or so. Worth the risk. She called Simon.

"I thought I'd give you some time to cool down," Simon said without preface.

"Good idea," Jules agreed. Thank God he hadn't called, say, fifteen minutes ago.

"You know what?" Simon said. "I felt terrible. I can't believe you made me feel terrible."

"It's all right," Jules said, meaning it. It was easy to forgive people when you'd just had the orgasm of a lifetime. "*I* don't feel terrible anymore. You're off the hook."

Simon sighed. "Do I even need to ask where you are?"

"Probably not," Jules admitted.

"She's not *there*, is she?"

Jules looked at the bathroom door again. "Not right this second, but we don't have long. Anyway, we, uh…talked it out." Jules's face heated at the memory. "Good talk. It was a good talk."

"Great," Simon said. "Up charges the white knight, the fair maiden says, 'No, thanks, pal,' and shacks up with the dragon. I'm never trying to help anyone again."

Jules laughed. "That's what you were doing, huh?"

"I have no idea what I was doing."

"Why are you so sure I'm the fair maiden in this picture?"

"No," Simon said at once. "We're not going there. We are not even joking about it."

Jules laughed again.

"Christ. There are things I never want to know. Why did I call you?"

"Simon, really," Jules said, becoming serious, "it's okay. We're just doing the best we can. We're trying to figure it out. We don't want anything bad to happen to anybody."

Well, that wasn't totally true. Vivian wanted bad things to happen to Simon, but she wasn't going to make them happen because she cared more about Jules's happiness than revenge.

Jules grinned from ear to ear. Good thing Simon couldn't see that.

"If you say so," Simon said. "Just remember what I said."

The thing about Adrian & Jo being taken down by scandal? Jules would prefer not to remember that. "Yeah, sure. By the way, I have a question."

"Yes?" Simon sounded suspicious.

"What kind of movies does she like?"

"You're going to watch movies with Vivian?" Simon said.

"Simon, just tell me," Jules pleaded. If he didn't know, nobody would.

"You're going to—okay." Jules could practically see Simon rolling his eyes up to the ceiling and praying for strength. "She'll tell you she likes Truffaut and Bergman and whatever thing won the most recent Palme d'Or. She's lying. She thinks they're boring. I have no idea what she really likes, if she likes anything. We've never shared a single tub of popcorn. True story."

"Great," Jules said, rolling her eyes. "Thanks."

"Good luck," Simon said. "Glad it's not me."

"Yeah, me too," Jules said. "So we're…we're good, right?"

"Until you do something idiotic, we're fabulous," Simon said. "Don't do something idiotic. More idiotic. Please." He paused. "Look, I'm sorry, but I just have to tell you one more time. What you're doing is idiotic."

"I think you've made that clear." Jules started to tense up again. "I'm not asking you to approve or anything." Although she longed for him to approve. Or at least one other person to approve.

"Good," Simon said. "I don't."

So much for that. Jules held back a heavy sigh.

He continued. "But except for what I told you, it's none of my business. I'll keep out of it if I possibly can, Jules. I care about you, I care about her, and I'm keeping out of it."

"Simon, I care about you too," Jules said, and to her surprise, she felt her throat getting thick. "I don't want to make trouble for you or the business. I swear."

"I know."

"I'll try not to do anything stupid. Stupider."

"Glad to hear it. Please don't ask me any more questions about movies or anything else. I don't want to be involved again. I mean it."

"Right," Jules mumbled. So much for Simon's approval. Apparently, they were going to pretend together that nothing at all was going on. Maybe it was for the best. "I'll see you Monday morning."

"I'm counting on it," Simon said and ended the call.

Well, that brought down the mood. Jules tossed her phone onto the mattress.

Get over it, she told herself. Jules could handle Simon's disapproval. She could, if necessary, handle more than that.

Of course, it would be great if she didn't have to.

The bathroom door opened and Vivian stepped through it. She'd changed from her day clothes into a white lace-trimmed silk robe that draped attractively over her. At the end of a long day, only getting ready to take a bath, she still looked like a million bucks.

And Jules, who'd just come so hard her teeth rattled, felt a spark of interest all over again. She whistled. "Wow."

Vivian smirked. "The water is exactly one hundred degrees, the candle is hemlock pine, and I hope you like Mahler. Come on. Why are you still dressed?"

"I'm not entirely," Jules pointed out. She touched the waistband of her skirt. "I'm just wearing this and my underwear."

A contemplative look crossed Vivian's face. "Undress in the bathroom. The mirror's bigger in there. I'll watch you while I'm in the tub."

Oh yeah. The spark was back, all right. Licking her lips, Jules followed Vivian into the bathroom.

Not a bad way to end the evening, all things considered.

CHAPTER 13

MONIQUE LEUNG WAS JUST AS stunning over Zoom as she was in person. Vivian wouldn't appreciate knowing that, although she'd like the part where Monique was in Beijing instead of New York.

"Congratulations on your new job," Monique said with a warm smile. "How are you liking it?"

Jules tried not to look too much like an eager beaver. Like Vivian, Monique gave off a vibe that made people try to impress her. You just couldn't *look* like you were trying, since that was the least impressive thing ever.

"It's exhausting, but I love it," she said. "We've stocked enough inventory to open the website tomorrow. Our social media's been on blast, and there's a ton of interest."

"Yes, I've seen it. I'm given to understand two of my pieces will feature on the splash page?"

"Already set," Jules promised. "The black leather jacket with studs and the mosaic-print cocktail dress."

"Excellent. Thank you." Monique propped her chin on the back of her hand. She wore an enormous turquoise cocktail ring. "Sounds like you're off to a good start. My faith wasn't misplaced."

"Your faith?" Jules asked, but she realized what Monique meant before the second word left her mouth.

Monique confirmed her suspicions. "Yes. I've known about Simon's plan for a while. He reached out to me as a potential sponsor."

Jules would go to her grave before she told Vivian that. "We, um, certainly appreciate your support."

A canny smile crossed Monique's face. She tucked a lock of dark hair behind one ear. "Mm. Not to rub salt in the wound, but I hear Simon's new venture came as a surprise to you. After an unpleasant event, no less."

"Uh…" Jules was in no hurry to talk about Mark Tavio firing her. "Yes, but it's been a great opportunity. I'm grateful to Simon for it."

"He's looking out for you." Monique's look turned serious again. "The pieces are moving on the board, and you're well out of the game."

Was it too cold in the office? That could explain why Jules had goose bumps. Monique could only be referring to Mark Tavio's vendetta against Vivian. "Have you heard anything?"

"Nothing specific, but it's not looking good. I'm on my way out of that mess, thankfully. And you should stay out of it too. That's my last piece of advice on the matter."

If only Monique knew that staying out of it wasn't an option. Being in a relationship with Vivian made it impossible.

It's not looking good. Was Tavio getting ready to move against Vivian yet again? Vivian hadn't said anything about that to Jules. Maybe she didn't know. Jules's stomach twisted at the thought, and she had to stop herself from ending the interview to call Vivian right away.

That also wasn't an option. Not if Jules wanted to keep her current job. If Tavio was moving against Vivian—and he probably was—it was unlikely to be during the next twenty minutes.

Jules cleared her throat. "Right. Let's start the interview. You mentioned getting out. When's your last day at *Du Jour China*, and what are your immediate plans afterward?"

"I'm out of *Du Jour China* next month, and then I hit the ground running. First thing is a private showing in Paris…"

Jules referred to her notes a lot for the rest of the interview. It was the only thing that allowed her to focus, reminding her of the questions she wanted to ask and the facts she needed to verify.

She'd been busy with her new job and Vivian hadn't said anything lately, so it had been easy to forget about the danger Tavio posed. Now it would be all she could think about all day.

But when she called Vivian as soon as the interview was over, Vivian didn't seem nearly as worried as Jules was.

"Are you really surprised?" Vivian sighed. "I'm not. In fact, the only thing that surprises me is that Monique was so overt. She said she wanted to warn you? How touching."

Vivian couldn't distract Jules with her jealousy. Not now. "C'mon, this is serious."

"I know. I'm well aware that everything Monique told you is true."

Jules dug her fingertips into the wood veneer of her desk. "You haven't been talking about it lately. I didn't know anything new was in the works. Is Mark—"

"Julia, please," Vivian cut in firmly. "You'll have to trust that I know about the storm clouds. Now I have to go back to work and save Versace from themselves. I'll speak to you tonight. Goodbye."

"Good—" But Vivian had already disconnected, of course. Jules stuck her tongue out at the phone. Then she turned back to the screen that showed the copy she'd transcribed from Monique.

"Did your computer murder someone, or did the interview go that badly?"

Jules looked up from her monitor to see Simon heading for her desk with a Gucci messenger bag slung over his shoulder. "Uh, no. It went great, actually. I'm just about to start putting the copy together. Nothing's wrong."

The doubtful purse of Simon's lips said it all. "Okay. Send it my way as soon as you're done so I can review it for the press packets. And choose two quotes for the splash page and send them to our website gurus. Got your Luis Ribera interview scheduled yet?"

At the rate Jules was going, she was going to need an assistant too. Maybe Allie was ready for a change of scene. "Yes. It's tomorrow."

"Good job, Moretti. If anyone needs me, I don't care about them. I've got a million phone calls." He gave her another glance as he headed into his office. "Don't forget to take your lunch break today, okay?"

Jules smiled as his office door closed behind him. She'd long since realized—and felt a little guilty about it—that her new job was a lot more fun than her old one. Part of it was the excitement of the new venture, part of it was her increased level of responsibility, but part of it was also undeniably her relationship with Simon, which was far more relaxed and friendly than it had ever been with Vivian.

She missed Vivian like crazy, though. Sure, it was healthier, more well-adjusted, whatever, to have a life apart from your lover. And sure, Jules was taking to her new position like a fish to water.

But…it would be nice to see Vivian more often than once a week, no matter how busy they both were. That wasn't asking too much of the universe, was it?

It was with relief, then, that she answered Vivian's call that night at ten thirty, skipping the greeting entirely as she said, "Okay, so what's going on with Mark Tavio?"

There was a pause, and then Vivian gave another sigh, even heavier than this morning. "Look. What if I told you that you're going to know everything in time, that I don't want you to worry about it, and that, for God's sake, I don't want to talk about this right now?"

Ordinarily, Jules would have pushed. The exhausted note in Vivian's voice stopped her. She could imagine all too well the slump of Vivian's shoulders and the weariness in her eyes.

"Okay," she said quietly. "I trust you."

Relief permeated Vivian's voice. "Thank you. Let's move on. Dr. Viswanathan has graciously allowed me to get a C-section on July 12. Eight thirty in the morning at Columbia University Medical Center."

Talk about a sudden change of subject. Jules immediately opened her calendar app. "So she had no concerns about the operation?"

"She listened to all of my reasons for wanting it," Vivian replied.

Jules glowered, even though Vivian wasn't there to see her. "That's not the same thing."

"It's scheduled, Julia. She wouldn't have done that if she thought the risk was too great."

Jules remembered Dr. Viswanathan's no-nonsense attitude. Vivian must really have laid it on thick to get this. "I guess not. And everything else checked out okay?"

"Everything else is fine. I wish—" Then Vivian stopped.

Jules waited for her to continue, and when she didn't, she said, "I wish I'd been there too."

Vivian cleared her throat. "Well, you'll be there for the important part. Or—maybe I shouldn't assume."

"You mean the birth?" Jules sat up straight on the couch where she'd been reclining. "You're joking. Of course I'll be there. Will they let me in the operating room?"

"They better," Vivian said, obviously trying to sound firm. Instead, the relief came through in her voice once more. "Unless they put me under general anesthesia, which I don't want."

Neither did Jules. When Vivian had first mentioned wanting a C-section, Jules had had nightmarish visions of her being put under and not coming back up. Apparently, epidurals were more common.

"You don't get squeamish, do you?" Vivian asked.

"No," lied Jules, who always had to close her eyes during surgery scenes on TV shows or movies. She could get it together for the real thing. Surely.

Then she yawned. She wanted to talk to Vivian forever, but it had been such a long day that she was dragging. Tomorrow promised to be no better.

"Go to bed." The order was stern, but Vivian's tone was affectionate.

"I will if you will." Jules dragged a hand over her forehead as if that would jolt her back into wakefulness. "You've got to be way more tired than I am. We're still on for Sunday, right?"

"Oh yes. Have you picked out that movie yet?"

That made Jules grin. "I have, actually. I thought of it just before I went to sleep last night."

"That sounds intriguing. And?"

Jules threw Vivian's words right back at her. "What if I told you that you're going to know everything in time?"

Vivian made a disgusted sound. "Very clever."

"You'll like it," Jules promised. "I really think I've figured it out."

"All right." Somehow Vivian managed to sound as doubtful as if Jules had said she could realign the Hubble Telescope. "Impress me."

Violins and horns started swelling, the words *To Catch a Thief* appeared on the screen in bold pink letters, and Jules barely—just barely—heard Vivian give a soft sigh on the couch next to her.

She bit her lip to keep a smug smile off her face. She'd chosen well. And for the next couple of hours, Jules watched Vivian out of the corner of her eye, seeing her enthralled by Cary Grant and Grace Kelly on the French Riviera surrounded by luxury and saying their lines in smooth, cultured tones that Vivian had obviously worked hard to emulate.

Vivian had told Jules about how she'd longed to escape her humdrum origins, get to New York, get the power and the money and the fancy house and everything else. How did a girl growing up poor in Toledo, Ohio, develop such a burning desire? What had Vivian sought in coming to New York?

So while browsing Netflix, Jules had homed in on the old classic films: slick features done in black-and-white and featuring the stars of decades past—Spencer Tracy, Bette Davis, Clark Gable, Greta Garbo. Movies where women swanned around banquets dripping diamonds from their necks and wrists while their satin gowns glowed in the candlelight. Where actors said the iconic lines that everybody knew and tilted their heads just right.

Vivian was into classic things. And head tilts.

So Grace and Cary it was. And it had worked.

When the movie was over, Vivian turned to face Jules on the couch. She raised an eyebrow. "So how much psychoanalysis did you attempt before you picked this?"

Well, Vivian had seen through her from day one, so why should today be any different? Jules lied, "Who said it was about you? I like the movie too. I wanted to watch it."

"Hmm. Regardless, good pick," Vivian said, blessedly letting it go.

"Huh. You know what you need?" Jules said softly, looking into Vivian's eyes and reaching out to rest a hand on her knee.

"I'm sure you're about to tell me," Vivian said and swallowed hard. Then she shivered when Jules rubbed a thumb against her knee.

Jules grinned. "You need to do what Cary Grant did and admit you can't do everything on your own."

Vivian pinched the bridge of her own nose. "Good grief."

"Face it, you need a woman's help. You're not a lone wolf—"

"That's enough, Grace," Vivian said, reaching out and tugging Jules in for a kiss.

104

When they parted, she didn't pull back, and Jules happily settled in next to her, sliding an arm around her shoulders so they could get comfortable.

"So," Jules said, "you liked the movie?"

"You tell me," Vivian said, and without meeting Jules's eyes, she slid her hand beneath Jules's shirt. "Does this feel like a lack of enthusiasm?"

"Mm." Jules said, and kissed Vivian's temple. "I don't know yet. Keep going so I can decide."

"Here?"

Jules chuckled breathlessly. "Anywhere's good." She kissed Vivian's cheek. "Anywhere, anytime." She thought about the bedroom, even though she really didn't want to move. "Maybe we should—"

"I love you very much," Vivian said quietly.

Jules's heart stopped. The words rang through her head for a moment, and she wondered if she'd imagined them. Then she pulled back just enough to look at Vivian's face and knew she hadn't. Vivian was regarding her seriously. And watchfully. Waiting for her to react.

So naturally, Jules said, like a dummy, "Yeah?"

"Yes." Vivian nodded as if to finalize the matter.

"Oh. Well." Jules swallowed. "Wow."

Vivian smiled faintly. "Mm-hmm." Then she wrinkled her nose. "Are you crying?"

"No!" Jules said instantly, dashing a hand across her eyes. "I just, um… I got dust in my… There was pepper in the food tonight, I think—"

Vivian reached over to the table beside the sofa where a box of Kleenex sat. She plucked out a tissue and gave it to Jules, who sniffled and dabbed at her eyes. She felt completely ridiculous, but she was also glowing so hard that she felt like a nuclear reactor.

"Thanks," she said thickly, and gave Vivian what was probably a wobbly smile.

"You're welcome." Now Vivian looked amused.

"And, um, you know, I…"

Vivian pressed her lips together as if to stop a smile but was not entirely successful. "Yes? You what?"

"Well," Jules said sheepishly. She looked down at the Kleenex and fiddled with it. "I do. Love you. I mean…a lot."

"Well, I'm glad we got that worked out." The softness in Vivian's eyes belied the archly spoken words.

"What else do you want to work out?" Jules asked, trying to sound smooth again but ruining it when she hiccupped.

"Mm." Vivian put Jules's hand back on her knee. "Now, there's a question."

Oh hell yes. "Are you tired tonight?" Jules murmured.

"Always, but not *that* tired. How does the bedroom sound?"

"It sounds amazing." Jules positively hopped off the couch.

Vivian watched enviously as she struggled to move off the couch, only without the hopping part.

Jules offered a hand, and Vivian glared at her. "Not until that's absolutely necessary," she growled and levered herself up before rising slowly to her feet. "And I don't appreciate the concern."

"Sorry," Jules said as she traced a fingertip up and down Vivian's arm. "I hope what's about to happen in your bedroom won't bother you too much. I'm going to be pretty thoughtful and considerate."

Vivian raised her eyebrows again, but it was no more than the truth. Jules was going to treat Vivian very, very well tonight, leave her with no cause to complain.

Not that she ever did, but tonight Jules was really planning to overdo it.

Maybe Vivian saw it in her eyes. She swallowed hard and looked eager before she could entirely master herself. *Ha.*

"Lead the way," Jules said and licked her lips.

Vivian rolled her eyes. And did.

CHAPTER 14

THE NEXT THURSDAY MORNING, THE day of Vivian's mysterious party, Jules took the liberty of stopping by her bank to make a little withdrawal. She'd been meaning to do it all week, but the launch of Adrian & Jo's website had run her off her feet. Business was booming, and while that was great, it didn't leave her a lot of time for personal errands.

She got the Stephen Webster snake brooch from the safe deposit box and spent the rest of the day carrying it around in her handbag and guarding it with her life.

Simon noticed this. "It's a lovely pin, Jules, but I'm not sure you need to carry your handbag with you when you go to the water cooler."

"I know," Jules said sheepishly. She could have explained how special the pin was, but Simon wouldn't want to hear it. Which was too bad because he was the only person she could have told at all.

"I think it's the buildup," she added. "This is the first time I'm wearing it out, and I know the party is a gigantic deal, but I still don't know why."

All she knew was that Vivian was up to something and was pulling out all the stops. It undoubtedly had something to do with those meetings she'd had with Stan Oppenheimer months ago or maybe something to do with Mark Tavio or maybe both—Jules wasn't so dumb that she couldn't put those things together. She just had no way of knowing exactly how they combined or what Vivian was planning.

"So she's never said anything?" Simon asked.

"Silent as the grave. I have no idea what's happening. I mean, I have a few guesses…"

"So do I," Simon admitted. "Well, we'll find out tonight." He took a deep breath and exhaled. "Why does she still make me nervous?"

Jules laughed, but privately she felt the same way. Sure, Vivian had always been secretive. And sometimes it was fine to have secrets. She'd asked Jules to trust her, and Jules was okay with that. The suspense was killing her, though.

By that night, neither Jules nor Simon had shed their case of the nerves. Jules hadn't spoken to Vivian the night before—she'd had to stay even later than usual at Adrian & Jo. There had been no final opportunity to try to worm something out of her.

So now on Thursday night (and that was another thing: it was weird to throw an evening party on a work night), Jules and Simon found themselves sharing a cab.

"Thanks for the lift," Jules said as the cab pulled away from her apartment. "I know it's out of your way."

Simon looked admiringly over Jules's burgundy-and-bronze gown. "I wasn't about to let you take that work of art on the subway. Zuhair Murad knocked it out of the park this year."

No way Simon had really thought Jules would take the subway. Vivian would have never allowed it and in fact had been a bit peeved that Simon had offered a ride before she could pay for Jules's Uber. Simon just wanted sympathetic company on the way, and given how Vivian currently felt about him, Jules didn't blame him a bit.

The gown's long skirt felt heavenly as Jules smoothed her hand over it. "It's pretty great, huh?" Hopefully, Simon wouldn't ask how she'd gotten it.

"Definitely." His eyes widened. "Wait, where's your pin?"

"*What?*" Horrified, sure that the pin had fallen off her gown, Jules looked down to see it shining near her shoulder exactly where she'd fastened it.

She glared at Simon, who smirked back. "Don't do that."

"Sorry," he said, not looking sorry at all. "But you do look lovely, darling."

"Thanks. So do you."

"I know."

The cab rolled through the streets of Manhattan up from the Lower East Side to Midtown. Jules hadn't been to Midtown since getting fired from *Du Jour*, and as they drove past all the familiar buildings, she felt a brief pang. Yes, it was way too touristy and expensive and overall a pain in the ass, but the energy was undeniable.

In fact, their path took them past the Koening Building. Both Jules and Simon looked at it as they passed. A low exhalation escaped Simon's chest, but he said nothing.

Finally, the cab approached their destination. Simon leaned forward to peer through the windshield of the cab. "Well, brace yourself."

"Here goes nothing," Jules agreed.

"She can't do anything too awful, can she?" Simon asked hopefully. "She's not going to announce that she now controls all of capitalism and is closing down Adrian & Jo, right?"

"I wouldn't put it past her, but I doubt it." Jules patted his arm again. "Simon, I don't think it has anything to do with you. This was in the works before you quit."

Simon did not look reassured.

"Oh, come on," Jules added and stuck her chin in the air. "Man up."

Simon glared. "Just for that, you can open your own car door," he said as the cab pulled up to the curb.

The party was in a roof garden atop an art gallery. Jules had known that Vivian would disdain anything so plebeian as a normal restaurant, and besides, not a lot of well-known restaurants were keen to dethrone their famous chefs in order to make way for somebody else's cook of choice. The gallery, however, had a kitchen that it frequently rented out for such events (Jules suspected the place made more money from hosting parties than it did from selling art) and which Hélène Darroze had pronounced adequate for her needs.

The whole event had an almost intimate air for a gathering of the New York elite. There were no movie stars here, no celebrities, and yet, surrounded by the millionaires and billionaires who played the city like a grand piano, Jules felt more out of place than if she'd been sitting next to Chris Hemsworth.

She tried to ignore the feeling as she and Simon arrived arm in arm where a polite maître-d' informed everyone of their seats as they entered.

"Simon Carvalho and Julia Moretti," Simon told him.

"Ah, yes, Mr. Carvalho," the maître-d' said, not even looking at a seating chart or anything else. He obviously had it all memorized. "You will be at table four between Helga Schumann and Rudolph Bryson."

Simon drooped visibly, and Jules tried not to grin. Rudolph Bryson was an eighty-five-year-old investor and, by all accounts, rapidly going senile. Helga Schumann was an unpleasant woman who'd been rude to Jules on Christmas Day at the Ritz. Jules didn't envy Simon sitting with either of them. Vivian still had him in the doghouse for sure.

"She's not sitting with me?" Simon asked pleadingly, tilting his head toward Jules.

"No, sir," the maître-d' said. "Ms. Moretti is sitting at table one between Vivian Carlisle and Tilda Barnhardt."

For a moment, Simon and Jules stood frozen together, too stunned to move.

"I'm where?" Jules squeaked.

"At table one, Miss," the maître-d' repeated patiently. "Your place card will be waiting at your seat."

"Um…" Jules said.

"Thank you," Simon said and quickly steered them both away from the door, where people had begun to line up behind them. They stopped by a large potted tree, not quite hiding behind it but almost. "Breathe," he ordered.

"I'm breathing," Jules gulped. "It's not weird. Right?"

"Right." Simon patted her arm and glanced around the garden.

"I mean, I sat with her at the main table at Christmas. And she took me to that New Year's ball. So people know that she takes me places."

"Uh-huh."

"And just because she's throwing the party, this isn't a big deal. I mean, the press isn't even here…"

Security was keeping the media at bay tonight, and paparazzi usually weren't too interested in a bunch of old men in tuxes anyway. Vivian hadn't exactly gone out of her way to publicize the event either. It was definitely private invitation only. So surely—

"I said breathe," Simon said, and Jules did. "Pull yourself together. If it isn't a big deal, then don't act like it is or it becomes one. Man up," he added with a small smile. "At least you're not with Rudolph and Helga. Now, let's be polite and greet our hostess."

"Right," Jules said, nodding hard, feeling her hoop earrings bobbing with her. "Right."

They maneuvered their way from behind the tree and into the thick of the party, nodding and smiling as they went. Jules tried to look relaxed, to smile, but it was hard because she kept imagining that people were staring at her as she walked by, wondering what the hell she was doing there. There were only a few other people her age present, and they were all children of the establishment, all heirs to fortunes and empires.

Or they were the trophy wives of powerful older men. Jules shied away from that thought at once. That wasn't her. She belonged to neither group. She—

"Good evening, Vivian," Simon said.

Jules jerked herself back into the moment and was so glad she did because she was directly in the path of Vivian Carlisle—who looked like a goddess.

Her gown was Iris van Herpen. Jules recognized it right away. They'd spoken of the van Herpen collection during London Fashion Week as something that *worked* even when the odds were against it—just like Vivian and Jules did as a couple. Fashion both sublime and impossible.

On Vivian, it was just sublime. The gown was clearly an altered version of one of the outré runway looks toned down to be wearable in public. The original had featured floor-length feather-shaped sleeves, along with cutouts that exposed the model's slender waist. It had also been a shade of gold softly trimmed in silver.

Vivian had swapped out the silver. Now she swept through the party as a golden blaze edged with black, a sun dazzling the viewer from the depths of space. The gown's neckline plunged to emphasize her cleavage. The floor-length skirt had been altered to accommodate the increased roundness of her belly, which she was clearly showing off instead of minimizing. And a slit ran up the left side of the skirt to expose a leg whose perfect contours Jules knew by heart.

Jules could barely breathe. Her heartbeat did double duty to make up for it. After years of working in fashion, viewing hundreds of runways and photoshoots and closets, she'd never seen anything so magnificent.

It was the fight of a lifetime not to fall to her knees and swear fealty. And then do other things.

Then Vivian broke the spell. "Simon," she said, tilting her head and giving him the polite, empty I-probably-hate-you smile that she turned on almost everyone at these events.

Jules tumbled back into the present moment as Simon's arm stiffened in her own. She briefly pitied him before Vivian turned to face Jules and the smile became—almost imperceptibly—genuine.

And then, just as on Christmas Day, she leaned in and kissed the air to the side of Jules's cheeks. She was wearing a new perfume tonight that smelled of sandalwood and myrrh.

Jules had put on the Amouage perfume that Vivian gave her for her birthday. Near her ear, Vivian's breath caught, so clearly she'd noticed it.

She had full command of herself, however, when she pulled back. "Julia. Don't you look nice tonight."

Only Vivian could make *nice* sound like *good enough to eat*. Jules's knees were barely holding her up. Why were they in public? Why weren't they in a private corner where they could—

The arrival of a man stopped her spiraling fantasies. While Jules struggled for equilibrium, Stan Oppenheimer came to stand at Vivian's side.

Stan Oppenheimer, the handsome Koening executive whom Jules had once believed Vivian was having an affair with. She'd never hated anybody so much back then. It must have put Vivian's jealousy over Monique in the shade.

"Julia, I don't think you and Mr. Oppenheimer have been formally introduced," Vivian said. "Stan, this is my former assistant, Julia Moretti. She'll be joining our table this evening. You already know Simon, of course."

"A pleasure, Julia." Mr. Oppenheimer took Jules's hand in a firm, warm grip and gave her a charming smile.

Jules managed to smile back, even though she still had the instinctive desire to slap him, which wouldn't have been fair, considering. She was relieved when he let go of her to shake Simon's hand instead.

"Simon," he said. "Good to see you again. How's the new business going?"

"Swimmingly," Simon said, glancing back and forth between Oppenheimer and Vivian. His arm was still tense. Jules had the feeling that if she tried to disengage her own from it, she'd sprain something. "I'm very pleased with our progress."

"Wonderful," Vivian murmured, and there were definitely daggers in her eyes now.

"Well, you were a great loss to Koening," Mr. Oppenheimer said, apparently oblivious to the dangerous undercurrents. Or he didn't care. "But who knows? Maybe we'll be able to woo you back someday."

"Who knows?" Simon agreed tightly. "Thank you."

"Ah," Vivian said, glancing at somebody over Simon's shoulder. She smiled and waved. "Kiyoshi, darling."

Simon and Jules took the hint. Simon bowed his head and said, "It's lovely to see you both. Enjoy the party."

Vivian ignored him completely.

"You too," Mr. Oppenheimer said. "Julia, looks like I'll see you again in a few minutes." He smiled, and Jules gratefully let Simon lead her away.

"What do you think Tahiti's like?" Simon mused. "How fast can we get there?"

"Oh, Simon," Jules said, though she had to admit it sounded tempting. Away from Vivian's glory, she could collect herself. It was easier to remember that a purpose lay behind this party, and it couldn't be anything benign.

"It'll be great. We'll rent a bungalow. I'll wear a grass skirt, and you can play the ukulele."

"That's Hawaii," Jules said, "but I'm game."

"Really?"

"Yeah. After dinner."

"Damn," Simon said.

Just then, the dinner gong rang. Jules glanced down at Simon's watch and saw that it was eight p.m. on the dot. Of course a Vivian Carlisle fête would never start a minute late or early.

Simon released Jules, who flexed her arm until she could feel it again. Then, trying very, very hard to be inconspicuous, she almost crept to the head table, where people were already seating themselves.

Vivian wasn't there yet, but a man held out Jules's chair for her as she sat down. Geoffrey Barnhardt, she recalled from the Christmas Day luncheon.

113

"A pleasure, Julia," he said. "You remember my wife, Tilda, of course?"

"Oh yes," Jules said, trying to sound breezy as she moved her head to say hello to the woman on her left.

And as she did, she found herself staring at Mark Tavio, sitting across the table with his wife.

With murder in his eyes.

Jules froze and swallowed hard. "M-Mr. Tavio," she managed.

He just stared back at her with a narrowed gaze. His wife was studying the flowers on the table with great concentration. A minimalist arrangement of orchids, just as Vivian had specified.

Each place was set with three wineglasses: two empty ones for red and white and champagne coupes that…were already filled in clear anticipation of a toast.

Uh-oh.

Jules felt a hand on her left elbow and nearly jumped. But it was only Tilda Barnhardt, looking at her with a kind smile as if she realized how terrified Jules suddenly was. "My dear," she said, "how lovely to see you here tonight."

"Th-thank you, Mrs. Barnhardt," Jules said, and tried to smile. "It's good to see you again. How are you?"

"Marvelous," Mrs. Barnhardt replied. "And you? I understand you've abandoned us."

Her eyes twinkled and there was no hint of malice in her voice, but Jules was still mortified.

"Uh," she said, refusing to look anywhere near Mark, "I had a wonderful, er, opportunity to…"

"So I heard." Mrs. Barnhardt playfully tapped Jules's arm with her fingertips before turning to smile at Mark. And now there was a little malice with her twinkle as she said, "Mark, however could you let her get away? Vivian's a book on how gifted she is. And you know that doesn't happen often."

Mark gave Mrs. Barnhardt a very tight-lipped smile.

Mrs. Tavio pursed her lips and moved her gaze from the orchids to the flatware.

Okay, so tonight was about screwing Mark over. Not such a surprise, on reflection. No doubt Jules was about to find out the particulars soon.

In the meantime, she just had to keep smiling and acting as if she went to parties like this every night and be very glad that she hadn't had a hand in whatever was going on. She had a feeling it was pretty dirty because if it was about Mark and screwing him over, Vivian wouldn't settle for anything clean.

Then as if summoned by Jules's musings, Vivian appeared on the arm of Stan Oppenheimer. She smiled benevolently down at the table; the Barnhardts beamed back up at her.

Jules didn't dare even look at Mark to check his reaction.

"Well," Vivian said as Stan let go of her arm, "no reason not to kick the evening off with a toast. Mark, would you do the honors, or should we?"

"Go to hell," Mark said through his teeth as if straining the words through them into a bitter cup. "Go to hell, you scheming bitch."

Jules nearly gasped, but Vivian didn't seem particularly perturbed. Neither did anybody else, although Mr. Oppenheimer said, "Simmer down, Mark. You want to get out of this with your dignity, don't you?"

"At the very least, pretend that it was all your idea," Vivian said, the corners of her mouth lifting in her cruelest smile.

"Oh, for God's sake, Mark, just say something," Mrs. Tavio said, her voice hoarse. She placed her hands in her lap and raised a vacant smile. "Get it over with."

Mark's face darkened with fury, but Vivian said, "Excellent." She clapped her hands, and the guests raised their eyes expectantly. "Good evening, my dear friends. Thank you so much for finding the time to attend our little soirée tonight."

A light scattering of applause.

"Thank you. Thank you," Vivian repeated. She was positively glowing with demonic joy. "Well, I'm sure many of you are curious as to why we're all here on this lovely night, getting ready to enjoy some wonderful fare at the hands of Hélène Darroze."

More applause and cheers of anticipation.

"But before we begin, Mark Tavio would like to make an announcement. And then a toast, didn't you say, Mark?"

Without another word, Vivian sat down smoothly in her seat. Jules hoped she wasn't planning on getting up again anytime soon because it wouldn't look half as graceful.

Stan Oppenheimer also sat down and began to clap. Soon the other guests, looking interested and apprehensive by turns, followed suit.

Jules caught Simon's eye. He raised his eyebrows at her, but she could only shrug weakly. Too bad they hadn't made a run for Tahiti when they'd had the chance.

Mark rose to his feet, smiled tightly, and took a short bow.

"Ladies and gentlemen—my friends—good evening," he said. "I have some exciting news for everyone! Some of you will be surprised. Well, you shouldn't be." His smile became more jocular. He might have been playing the part of somebody's kindly old grandpa. "It's no secret that I'm closing in on seventy-five, is it?"

"You carry it well!" somebody called from the far end of the garden. There was appreciative laughter.

Mark forced a chuckle. His right hand clenched briefly.

"Well, thank you, Reggie," he said, "but there comes a time in a man's life when he just wants the simple things. You know—playing with the grandkids, tending the garden, wintering in the Maldives."

More laughter, although comprehension was beginning to dawn on people's faces.

"So it is with both pleasure and regret that I announce tonight that I will be stepping down as chairman and CEO of the Koening Group, effective next month."

Murmuring broke out all over the roof.

Jules exchanged another glance with Simon and saw that, like her, he hadn't exactly been expecting it but he wasn't surprised either.

Mark raised a hand, shaking his head genially. He really was pulling this off pretty well. "No, no, my mind's made up," he said. "I've long had a dream of paradise: the prospect of a long, peaceful retirement."

Hesitant laughter all around.

"Mary and I already have plans to travel the world with nary a board meeting in sight. I'm confident that Koening will continue to move forward toward the vision I laid out for it when I took over...more years ago than I like to think about." He chuckled again. "Ladies and gentlemen, it is my pleasure to introduce to you the new CEO of the Koening Group: Geoffrey Barnhardt, taking over from our UK operation."

Geoffrey stood up to enthusiastic applause, then sat down again.

116

Jules wondered if the tic at Mark's forehead was visible from any of the other tables.

"And," Mark continued, "the new chairman, Stan Oppenheimer."

Mr. Oppenheimer stood up to more slightly surprised applause, then reseated himself.

Vivian reached over and patted his arm with a smile.

So it had been a mutual power grab. Jules didn't know squat about this kind of thing, but she was pretty sure neither Barnhardt nor Oppenheimer alone would have had the power to take down Mark. Barnhardt had worked on it from London, and Oppenheimer had kept a closer eye on things in New York.

And who had brought them together? Whose idea had it been in the first place? Not that she knew for sure—not yet—but Jules was pretty certain that she wouldn't need to look any farther than the woman on her right.

Vivian had her head tilted to the side and was gazing angelically across the crowd as she joined in the applause for Oppenheimer and Barnhardt. And of course for the demise of Mark Tavio.

The demise and public humiliation. Mark was being gracious because it was better than admitting that they'd taken him completely by surprise. He'd even come to a party to celebrate his own defeat before his peers and friends.

Vivian wasn't just twisting the knife. She'd stabbed Mark with it while it was still white-hot from the forge.

Suddenly, Jules flashed back to the night that Vivian had taken her on the kitchen counter. *If I punished Simon,* Vivian had said, *everyone in the industry would see firsthand what happens when you cross me.*

That was why the party was on a Thursday. Vivian wanted everybody talking about it at work the next morning around the water coolers and coffee makers. She wanted it to make the rounds right away.

Mark, still smiling, made to sit down.

"Oh no, Mark," Vivian trilled. "Don't forget you promised us a toast!"

"Hear, hear," Mr. Barnhardt said and began to clap.

So did everyone else, with calls of encouragement.

Jules was astonished that Mark didn't leap over the table to throttle Vivian where she sat. For a split second, he looked as if he was seriously considering it, but then he gritted his teeth, took his champagne glass, and raised it high.

Everyone else picked up their own glasses. Vivian's, of course, contained mineral water.

"My friends," Mark said, sounding only a little bit strangled, "to the future of Koening!"

"The future," everyone chorused and took a drink.

Jules barely tasted hers. Which was a shame because Vivian turned to her and whispered, "Clicquot La Grande Dame, Julia. Savor it for me."

It was bizarrely difficult to savor anything. Mark Tavio's defeat was an unqualified triumph; there was no denying that. Finally, he was even more humiliated than Jules had been when he'd fired her. That part of tonight tasted better than any champagne.

There were other parts, though. They mainly involved Vivian making a huge decision while keeping Jules in the dark. Telling Jules to trust her and stay out of the way.

Jules had because she'd never imagined the end result would be anything like this. And now—what was she doing at table one watching the chief of a multibillion-dollar corporation going down in flames as if she belonged here? Why wasn't she spending a nice quiet Thursday night in her pajamas?

Mark sat down, and Jules prepared herself for the most awkward first course in history. But then Stan Oppenheimer stood.

"There's one more announcement," he said, "which I have been authorized to make on behalf of the lovely and multitalented Vivian Carlisle, who is apparently too shy—"

That got a real laugh out of the crowd. Vivian smiled and made an oh-*you* gesture with her hand at Oppenheimer.

"Koening is in a time of great transition and, as Mark said, exciting change," Oppenheimer continued, even though Mark had said no such thing. "But change always brings startling adjustments. Therefore, it is with no small regret that I announce to you tonight that Vivian Carlisle will be stepping down from her position as editor in chief of *Du Jour* magazine."

The words were barely out of his mouth before the room exploded. It seemed that Jules hadn't been alone in half expecting Mark's destruction, but nobody had expected this at all.

As for Jules, she felt as if someone had just slammed her head into a wall. Vivian? Stepping down from *Du Jour*, her life's blood? Vivian retiring?

And she'd said nothing at all about it to Jules?

Jules looked over at Simon, who also looked like he was about to pass out cold. Then she looked back at Vivian, who was smiling and nodding beatifically while everyone stared at her in shock.

"But," Mr. Oppenheimer said, raising his hand for silence, "it is with unmitigated pleasure that I announce that she will remain with Koening in a new and different capacity, one which we have created especially for her: vice president in charge of the American division of our lifestyle magazines."

More murmuring as people's eyes widened once again in comprehension.

Jules, for her part, wondered how she was still upright in her chair.

"For nearly two decades, Vivian has transformed both *Du Jour* and the fashion industry," Mr. Oppenheimer continued. "She is a visionary. Many would say a genius. I would hardly disagree."

He grinned. The guests laughed.

"She will now bring this incredible vision to bear in an executive role within Koening. I, for one, am confident that she's up to the job. Ladies and gentlemen: to Vivian Carlisle."

"Vivian Carlisle," everyone chorused and drank again.

Jules clinked her glass with Tilda Barnhardt as if in a dream and turned back to Vivian, who did not, of course, toast herself. But she did look back at Jules with a gleam of utter satisfaction.

"Oh, my God," Jules muttered through her teeth, trying to smile like she was expected to. "What—How—"

"We'll talk later," Vivian said calmly as the clapping died down.

"Enjoy your dinner, everyone," Mr. Oppenheimer said and took his seat to one final round of applause.

The next thing Jules knew, a waiter was pouring her a glass of Puligny-Montrachet Chardonnay. The first course was a smoked eel tartlet with Szechuan pepper, one of Hélène's specialties.

This couldn't really be happening.

The Tavios left directly after the first course, waving briefly at the crowd and ducking out. Apparently, it was more painful to keep up appearances than it was to retreat without a word.

Well, Mark was a billionaire. He'd handle it. Jules was on to a new crisis now.

"S-so, Vivian," she stammered as the waiters brought out trays of sorbet to cleanse the palate for the next course and began to pour the red wine. "Tell us a little more about this new job of yours. Or, well, tell me—I'm sure everybody else is already in the know."

Like Jules should have been. But she still managed a smile.

"Mm," Vivian said, looking pleased as she sipped her water. "Well, it's quite simple, really. And quite complicated."

The Barnhardts and Mr. Oppenheimer chuckled. Without the Tavios at the table, the atmosphere had become positively congenial as the conspirators congratulated themselves on their success.

"Geoffrey, Tilda, and Stan have agreed to create this new position in which I am in charge, as Stan said, of publications oriented around fashion and lifestyle: *Herself, Lovely Home*, and so on. They're all still stuck in the print-is-king model. I'm going to drag them into the digital age if it kills them."

That was probably literal.

"I can't wait," Mrs. Barnhardt said. She turned to Jules. "My daughter Angelica is flying in from London to be part of the editorial staff. You two should get to know each other—share war stories."

"Oh," Jules said, trying hard for enthusiasm, "I'd like that."

"Yes," Vivian said, taking control of the conversation once more, a skill that came easily to her. "You see, Julia, what I've noticed for years is that our women's magazines lack that certain unity, that uniformity of what Stan calls—accurately, I think—vision."

She turned to smile at Mr. Oppenheimer, who raised his wineglass in return.

"*Herself* has stagnated for five years now," Vivian continued. "*Lovely Home*'s missing a prime opportunity to appeal to millennials and Gen Z. Everyone talks about how they're not buying houses, but nobody talks about how they're fantasizing about it on Zillow. It's time to clear out the deadwood. Bring in fresh blood. I know I'm mixing my metaphors."

"Wow," Jules said. "That's, uh—"

"Magnificent," Mr. Barnhardt proclaimed. "As are you, Vivian. As is everyone at this table." He smiled benignly at Jules. "Including you, I understand. But no doubt you feel a little overwhelmed by all this, yes?"

Jules nodded wordlessly. No point in denying it.

"Don't worry," Mr. Barnhardt said. "So do we."

They all laughed. Jules managed to laugh too.

The discussion for the rest of the dinner was more or less over Jules's head as Vivian, the Barnhardts, and Stan Oppenheimer chatted excitedly about their plans. Jules listened in, following along as best she could and trying to learn what was going on, but there was only so much she could contribute to a conversation about trimming down the budget for *The Sporting Life*.

"Speaking of trimming budgets," Mr. Barnhardt said and looked at Vivian pointedly.

Vivian waved her hand with a little laugh. "I promise not to do too much damage, Geoffrey. I'll hire people who are likelier to pinch pennies than I am if they can work up to standard." She turned her sparkling eyes on Jules. "I think I can persuade them to do that, don't you, Julia?"

"For sure," Jules said. She swallowed and glanced briefly down at Vivian's rounded belly. "But if you don't mind my asking—"

"Oh, we'll cross that bridge when we come to it," Vivian said carelessly as if she hadn't just upended her own life and, by extension, Jules's. "It's true the timing isn't ideal, but I understand that a generous maternity leave isn't off the table."

"Take as much time as you want," Mr. Oppenheimer said. "Koening'll be waiting when you get back."

"We hope," added Mr. Barnhardt. Everyone chuckled.

Beneath the tablecloth, Jules felt Vivian nudge her foot with her own. She froze. Had she done something wrong, said something amiss? Was Vivian telling her to shut up?

But then all of a sudden, Vivian's foot didn't have a shoe on it anymore and it was rubbing gently up and down Jules's ankle.

Footsie. Vivian was playing footsie with her. And she was in that golden dress and she smelled of sandalwood and her eyes were sparkling, and Jules really, really wished she was less susceptible because she was trying to be indignant, confused, and indignantly confused. But that was going to be tough when Vivian was giving off her very best fuck-me vibe like there was no tomorrow.

Dammit.

Over dessert, when the Barnhardts and Mr. Oppenheimer were briefly engaged in chatting with each other, Vivian quickly leaned in and, without getting improperly close, murmured in Jules's ear, "Come over tonight." She rubbed her foot again.

Jules gulped.

"I should wait. I can't."

Jules tried not to blush at that.

"Can you come? Will you mind if I keep you up just a little late tonight?"

"Uh," Jules said, breaking out in a sweat. "I—"

At that moment, Mrs. Barnhardt turned to Jules with a smile, and Vivian leaned back. Mrs. Barnhardt gestured at Jules's shoulder.

"My dear," she said, "I've been meaning to tell you all night—that's a really lovely pin."

CHAPTER 15

VIVIAN LEFT THE PARTY AT nine thirty. Twenty minutes later, Jules could wait no longer and gathered her things.

"Leaving so quickly, Julia?" Mr. Barnhardt said in what seemed to be genuine surprise.

"I really have to get going," Jules said, shaking his hand. "I have to be at work tomorrow morning, and it'll, um, take me a while to get home." Especially since she was stopping by somebody else's house on the way. "I enjoyed it so much. It was lovely to see you all again."

"And you as well," Mrs. Barnhardt said graciously. "Vivian has such good things to say about you."

Jules's cheeks scalded.

Seeing this, Mrs. Barnhardt smiled. Then she leaned in to speak softly to Jules. "Of course, we were all horrified by what Mark did to you. What a low blow. It was Vivian's idea to seat you here with him. Didn't it send a beautiful message? I hope you enjoyed the look on his face. I know I did."

"Y-yes," Jules said and tried to smile again. "In fact, it's a little overwhelming. What a night, huh?" She laughed shakily. "I hope you all enjoy the rest of the evening."

Stan Oppenheimer raised his wineglass. "I'm sure we will. Good evening, Julia."

Jules hurried out of the party, barely remembering to wave at Simon on her way out. He was deep in conversation with an obviously tipsy Mrs. Schumann, while at his other side, Rudolph Bryson appeared to have fallen asleep.

Simon sent her an envious glare as she fled.

Too bad for him. Jules hailed a cab as she emerged out of the gallery and into the street. Paranoid once again, she took off her pin and put it in her handbag. Then she used the rest of the ride to Vivian's house to work out what she was going to say.

As it happened, she didn't get the chance to say anything.

She paid the driver, left the cab, mounted the front steps, and was yet again greeted by Vivian yanking open the door and hauling her inside.

Only this time, Vivian didn't drag her into the kitchen so they could yell at each other. She slammed the door shut, and Jules barely had time to hear the lock click back into place before Vivian cupped Jules's face in her hands and kissed her soundly. She was already gasping.

Jules wondered if she was going to get out of this alive.

"You're beautiful," Vivian groaned. The raw need in her voice made Jules's head spin. So did the golden silk of her gown, like and unlike the dress on New Year's Eve in the way it moved and hung on her body.

"Like a rose," Vivian continued dreamily, smiling against Jules's mouth, stroking over the burgundy fabric at Jules's shoulder. "Petals and thorns. I want them both."

She actually sounded drunk. Well, if anything could intoxicate Vivian, it'd be masterminding a hostile takeover.

No wonder she'd looked postcoital after her meetings with Stan Oppenheimer. No wonder she'd laughed when Jules told her so.

"Come upstairs," Vivian said between kisses.

Jules had the vague feeling that there were questions she had meant to ask or accusations she had meant to levy. But the fact was, Vivian still smelled like sandalwood and myrrh and her skin was as soft as ever and she was all over Jules, begging for sex, and maybe, Jules decided fuzzily, questions could wait. She kicked off her shoes and followed an already barefoot Vivian up the stairs.

They almost didn't make it a couple of times. On the landing, Vivian stopped to take another kiss, which ended with Jules's back against the wall while one kiss turned into four. The same thing happened in the hallway to Vivian's room. But they stumbled on, and before Jules quite realized it, Vivian was pushing her back down onto the mattress of her bed.

Tonight varied from their normal routine in the bedroom. Vivian didn't seem inclined to lie back and enjoy it like she usually did. Tonight she was more like the Vivian who'd ravished Jules on the kitchen counter.

Mostly she wanted to kiss, which meant that she wrapped her arms around Jules's waist. Jules's hands raked through Vivian's hair as they lay in a pile of crumpling silk, burgundy against gold.

Jules moaned into Vivian's mouth, and Vivian shuddered at the sound of it, kissing her even harder. It almost bruised, it almost hurt—but only almost, just enough to keep Jules anchored in the moment, wrapped up in the scent of sandalwood and the feel of Vivian's hair in her hands.

Was this how Vivian felt when Jules pressed her down on the bed and devoured her? Like she was the most desired thing in the world?

Because that was exactly how Jules felt right now, and she moaned again, trying to get closer. Vivian clutched her tight and growled. They paused just long enough for Jules to take off her earrings, and then Vivian was at her neck, kissing and nuzzling and sighing while Jules slid one hand down, grabbed Vivian's skirt, and began to slide it up her legs.

Vivian moaned and cupped Jules between her legs. "I want, I want— with my mouth—"

Jules gasped.

"But I don't see *how*," Vivian finished with a frustrated growl. "I'm not comfortable lying on my stomach, and there's no way I'm getting on my knees."

She wrestled with the zipper on the back of Jules's dress, and Jules sat up just enough so they could shuck the gown down around her waist. Jules pulled off her bra, and Vivian bent and took a nipple in her mouth.

Jules groaned, the sound echoing in the room.

"You'll just have to sit on my face," Vivian said. Her words, uttered in a brisk no-nonsense tone, sent Jules's train of thought right off the rails and into the chasm below. "Get this thing off."

The work of art Allie had so admired got tossed down on the floor like a dirty dishrag. Vivian wedged a pillow under Jules's head and got comfortable as Jules discarded her slip and panties with shaking hands.

"Keep the stockings," Vivian ordered hoarsely, stroking Jules's thigh-highs. "Now straddle me."

Jules did, throwing one leg over Vivian and hovered over her chest, keeping her weight on her knees, feeling drunk herself now. Vivian had this *look* on her face, like she couldn't wait, like this was going to be the most incredible thing she'd ever done in her life. Like Jules always felt when making love to her.

"You smell incredible," Vivian breathed and slid her hands up the backs of Jules's thighs until she was cupping her ass.

Jules whimpered.

"Move up. Don't you dare suffocate me."

Jules scooted up and then lunged forward until she could grab the headboard to support herself while Vivian—

"I'm going to ruin my makeup," Vivian said, then grabbed Jules's hips and went for it.

She'd only gone down on Jules once so far, but apparently, she'd been thinking about it since then because she moved her tongue as if she'd been planning a well-ordered campaign for ages.

Jules wailed and bucked, trying to balance on her knees and not fall. It was hard since all she really wanted to do was gyrate and grind against those lips and that tongue and even those teeth.

Vivian's tongue skipped and slid nimbly over her labia, up inside her and then out again. It teased her clit and moved away again and again until all Jules could think about was the movement of that wicked mouth that was driving her insane.

It was embarrassingly short. Again. Jules knew that Vivian probably didn't want to spend hours eating her or anything, but it seemed like no time until Vivian's tongue was swirling around Jules's clit so hard and fast, so hungrily, that Jules was squirming and sobbing and coming while lights flashed behind her eyelids.

And then all of a sudden, her clit was so hot and sensitive that she had to arch away, gasping.

Vivian's mouth chased after her with bereft little moans. But Jules wasn't like Vivian, who could come an absurd number of times in a row whenever she felt like it. She had to lift a shaking leg up and over so she could collapse next to Vivian on the mattress.

Jules covered her eyes. "Oh wow. Vivian. Jesus. Wow."

"Mm."

Jules opened her eyes and turned to see Vivian licking her lips. Her shiny lips. On her slick and shiny face. She'd ruined her makeup, all right, and looked exactly like the cat who had stolen the cream.

"I take it that was a success," Vivian said.

"God," Jules said, forgetting about whatever it was she'd worried about earlier. "That was amazing. You're incredible." She rolled over, threw an arm across Vivian, and kissed her, tasting herself.

Vivian kissed back enthusiastically, sliding her fingers through Jules's hair, which was falling out of its stylish updo, one held together by surprisingly few pins. Vivian plucked at a pin, pulled it out, and smiled as a lock of hair fell down over Jules's left ear.

"Take it down," she murmured. "Take down your hair for me."

With a groan, Jules sat up and obeyed. She pulled out three more pins and shook her head, and her hair cascaded down around her shoulders.

Vivian looked utterly enchanted. She'd never seemed so relaxed, so open, so happy—at least not that Jules had seen.

Time to make her happier. "So," Jules said, "your turn, right?"

Jules's turn too. Jules's turn to eat her right up.

But Vivian said, to her surprise, "Not tonight. I've had plenty, thanks."

Oh. Well. Jules tried not to be disappointed. There would be more chances. Plenty more. They had time.

Vivian beckoned. When Jules lay next to her, Vivian rolled onto her side and combed her fingers through Jules's loose hair. "Wasn't that wonderful?"

"Oh yeah," Jules said fervently, and then she realized that Vivian hadn't been talking about the sex. Her feelings abruptly took a one-eighty turn as her misgivings suddenly returned in full force. She watched Vivian's eyes shine while she thought about the coup and her new job and all the other stuff she hadn't seen fit to mention to Jules.

"It was everything I knew it would be," Vivian said, still petting Jules's hair, oblivious to her sudden distress. "I told you, didn't I? That things would improve for us."

"Yeah," Jules said, and swallowed. "You did. How long has this been in the works?"

"Oh, forever," Vivian said airily. "I had the idea when I saw Geoffrey at the Christmas Day luncheon, actually. He's always hated Mark, and

suddenly it all came together. I enlisted Tilda, which guaranteed success."
She chuckled. "We all had lunch a few days later. I agreed—"

"At the sushi place," Jules said. "When I told you that you couldn't have
sushi."

Vivian looked astonished. "That's right. You remember?"

"I remember a lot of things," Jules said. It was part of what made her
good at her job.

"Well," Vivian said, evidently impressed, "anyway, I agreed when we got
back that I'd get in touch with Stan. I did. He was more than agreeable."
She chuckled. "He's always been agreeable. Geoffrey and I will manage
him easily. But he's good-looking and has charisma—I don't know if you've
noticed, but Mark's lacking on both counts—and PR will love him."

"But..." Jules whispered. Where to begin? "You're giving up *Du Jour*."

"Oh no." Vivian shook her head. "Weren't you listening? Everything I
did for *Du Jour*, every innovation I made, everything I did to make sales
skyrocket... I'll do more of that. Everywhere." Her eyes gleamed. "I'm not
losing a magazine. I'm gaining eight."

"Oh," Jules said faintly. "But...what about fashion? Isn't that what you
really love?"

"I really do," Vivian said. "I really love a lot of things, Julia. Why would
my new job give me *less* influence in the fashion industry?"

"I just meant—"

"You don't need to edit a fashion magazine to love fashion or influence
it," Vivian said firmly. "Everyone in fashion has even more reason to listen
to me now. Oh, I'll still be attending fashion weeks, Julia. In the front row,
just like always."

"Makes sense," Jules said feebly.

Vivian moved her hand out of Jules's hair and began to stroke her bare
arm. "My contract's written in stone. No loopholes. Nobody can touch
me now." She raised her eyebrows. "And the obscene pay raise doesn't hurt
anything. Plus there are the shares."

"Um, yeah. Shares."

Vivian bared her teeth in a terrifying grin. "It's tasteless, isn't it? I don't
care. I know it's not the most important thing, and I'll never say it again,
but I don't care tonight. We're going to be filthy rich."

We.

"Oh," Jules repeated. "I always thought, you know, that you were already pretty rich. Not that I cared."

"Yes, yes." Vivian shrugged impatiently. "I know." The look in her eyes suddenly became serious, and Jules's heart began to pound. "I do know that, Julia."

"Oh," Jules gulped. "Good. It's just, I don't think I'd do so well at being, you know: kept."

Now Vivian looked exasperated. "I know. Didn't I just say so? You're nobody's pet, Julia. I wouldn't love you if you were."

At the magic word, Jules's brain went blank, right on schedule.

"But the fact is, I've got money, and I'm going to have more money. And you're part of my life. However you handle that—handle it."

Jules went stiff, and her jaw tensed.

Vivian raised an eyebrow. "Truth hurts?"

"Kind of," Jules growled.

Vivian sighed. "I knew it was tasteless. Listen, it really doesn't matter. We've been handling it so far, haven't we? Nothing has to change."

But everything had changed. The money wasn't even the worst of it. Vivian obviously liked having it—probably because of Toledo, Ohio—but it wasn't her main motivation.

No, Vivian's life was about her work. And now she had new work. A lot of new work. Running nine magazines instead of one. With her level of commitment and attention to detail right before having a kid—what was she thinking?

"Stay the night," Vivian said. The look in her eyes had become tender again. And hopeful.

Which was when Jules realized that she wasn't going to say anything. Not tonight. Whatever the long-term implications, Vivian was basking in her victory and wanted to share it. Jules just didn't have the heart to ruin her evening. How often did Vivian open up like this? They could have a discussion later.

So all Jules said was, "I want to, but I have to be at work at eight tomorrow. And I didn't bring a change of clothes or anything." She looked at the clock by the bed. It was almost eleven. Hardly insanely late, but she still felt exhausted. And the bed sure was nice.

Vivian cleared her throat. "I have a few things here that will fit you."

Jules gave her a quick look.

Vivian returned it with equanimity, but her cheeks had gone a little pink.

"Do you?" Jules said, unable to stop a small smile.

"Don't look so pleased with yourself. It's only practical. Look in the guest bedroom closet."

"I will. Tomorrow." Jules rose from the bed and patted down her hair.

Vivian watched appreciatively and Jules blushed, remembering that she was only wearing thigh-highs.

Then Vivian sat up with a groan. "This dress is even less comfortable than it looks."

It had to be super uncomfortable, then. The silk skirt was rumpled and crinkled, and some of the gown's most delicate details looked distressed beyond repair.

Jules winced. Iris van Herpen didn't make a dress that cost less than twenty thousand dollars, and no way would Vivian have gotten the cheapest model.

"Pajamas'll feel better." She bent down and pecked Vivian on the cheek. When she pulled away, Vivian's eyes were glowing again.

"It really was wonderful, wasn't it?" she said. Before Jules could fumble for a response, she added, "I'm so glad you were there, Julia. It wouldn't have been right if you hadn't seen it too."

Hopefully, Jules's smile didn't look too fake. "Yeah. Let me help you get undressed. What time are you leaving in the morning?"

"No later than seven," Vivian said. "I'll have plenty to do tomorrow, believe me. There's the press, for one thing, when the announcement breaks. At least Allie's good at handling them."

Jules blinked. "She is?"

"Oh yes. She's still not sure how the phones work, so she winds up redirecting calls all over the building. I think the last person to field questions about my pregnancy was Craig in accounting."

"That's—" Jules shook her head rapidly to clear it. "Well. That's really—"

"Yes, isn't it?" Vivian rose to her feet and slid the gown's side zipper down with no need of help from Jules. "You take the guest shower. I'll take this one. I don't think I could make it through a bath."

"Sure," Jules said. A shower didn't sound like a bad idea. Nor did sleep. Nor did anything else that would let Jules put off fretting for a little while longer.

It might be jumping the gun to fret anyway. It would be better to wait and see what was going to happen, wouldn't it? Maybe Vivian's schedule wouldn't change as drastically as Jules feared. Maybe Vivian would be able to handle it without too many problems.

Maybe Vivian would magically realize in the middle of the night that you were supposed to tell your significant other when you were thinking about rearranging your life completely. Then Jules wouldn't have to find an opportune time to tell her so.

Yeah. Maybe all that would happen.

Jules wasn't holding her breath, though.

CHAPTER 16

VIVIAN'S STUNT WAS INDEED THE talk of the water coolers and coffee makers the next morning, afternoon, and, as Jules discovered, the bars after work.

Jules sat at a booth in the Black Sheep with Keisha and Jerry, two fellow *Du Jour* refugees brought over by Simon. They sipped cocktails while Jules spilled every detail of the dinner the night before. The three of them hadn't spent much time together until Jules had juicy intel. It figured they hadn't invited Jules out because of her dazzling organizational skills.

"Wow, she's got balls," Keisha said, shaking her head. "And she sat at Mark's table? She made him give a toast?"

"Yes and yes," Jules repeated.

"What was that like?" Jerry asked eagerly. "Sitting at her table, I mean, with Mark Tavio right there. Wasn't that…awkward?"

"Understatement of the year," Jules said. "He left after the first course, though." Thank God. "It was…intense."

"Probably felt good, though," Keisha said, "after the shit he pulled with you, I mean."

Jules dipped her head in acknowledgment and took a long pull from her beer bottle.

"Tell us about the new guy. What's Oppenheimer like?" Jerry asked.

"Besides ungodly hot," Keisha added, and winked at Jules, who smiled back weakly.

It *was* almost like having friends again. Jerry and Keisha were pros too, driven and focused. They understood what it was like to make sacrifices.

And to Jules's relief, they all worked in different departments. Jerry ran marketing, Keisha was on the creative directing team, and Jules wasn't interested in going after either of their jobs. So they could hang out without needing to watch their backs too much or to call a truce.

Jules wondered tiredly if every job was like this or if she was just lucky.

Before she could answer Jerry's question, her phone rang. "Sorry," she said as she pulled it out of her bag.

Keisha and Jerry just shrugged. Of course Jules had to take calls at a moment's notice—nothing rude about it to them.

Thank God they weren't interested, since Vivian's name was on the display.

Jules should go outside to talk, but it was a lousy evening, drizzly and cool. So when she answered the phone at the table, she felt very daring—speaking with Vivian in front of other people, bold as brass. "Hello?"

"What are you doing?" Vivian asked.

"I'm having a drink with some"—okay, maybe not friends—"people from work. What's up?"

"Sorry, but tonight's a no-go." Vivian sighed. "It's chaos around here, and I can't get away. I should have predicted as much."

"Oh," Jules said in disappointment. "Then when can we get together?"

"Tomorrow's out too. I've had that afternoon scheduled for ages, and if I don't get some work done in the morning... Maybe Sunday?"

"Yeah, Sunday should—"

"Good," Vivian said. "I have to go. I'll call you later. Er...love you." The words seemed to stumble out of her mouth.

At least she'd said them. Jules put down her phone a little more viciously than she'd meant to. When she looked up, Jerry and Keisha were looking at her curiously. She tried to smile. "Sorry."

"No worries," Jerry said, and glanced around the bar. "It's filling up in here, isn't it?"

"I'm starving," Keisha announced, "and this place has amazing wings."

"Oh man. I'm dying for some wings. Jules?"

"Sure," Jules said and managed to smile again. "I'm wide open tonight."

Jules didn't hear from Vivian all day Saturday. She texted her at nine o'clock but got no reply. In a huff, she turned the volume way up on the action movie she was watching in her pajamas. Too bad Keisha and Jerry didn't seem like the type to go out clubbing on Saturday night.

The sad thing was, there were tons of parties going on everywhere that Jules would be welcome at, especially after the events of Thursday. She didn't want to go to any of them, though. She wanted to sit at home and stew.

Thankfully, when she woke on Sunday morning, she had a text from Vivian. It read:

Still on for dinner tonight?

Jules blew her breath through her lips. Finally. She replied:

Yeah, is 6 ok?

7. See you then.

Thank God Jules hadn't asked for seven in the first place. Then Vivian might have said eight.

She dared to arrive early, and Vivian remotely opened the door for her, texting:

Come to my office.

Jules hadn't been inside Vivian's office yet. She couldn't help being curious. She climbed the stairs to the second floor and walked down the hallway to the only open door.

Vivian's home office was as meticulously organized as her work one, if smaller. There were no unsightly stacks of papers, no battered file cabinets. Just tasteful midcentury furniture, soothing lighting, a live edge desk, and Vivian. She was bent over a printout of a spreadsheet, her brow furrowed in concentration as she made notations.

"Hi," Jules said pointedly.

"Yes?" Vivian glanced up briefly. "Oh. Hello, Julia. How are you?"

"Hungry," Jules said. "I think Ellen left our dinner in the oven. I smelled it on the way up."

"Oh." Vivian blinked and looked at the clock on the wall. Her eyes widened. "That's right, I said seven. Just let me—"

"The food is in the oven," Jules repeated, trying to be patient. "I'm starving."

Vivian opened her mouth.

"And I've missed you," Jules added.

Vivian's mouth snapped shut, and she sighed as a resigned smile teased her lips. She stood up with a slight grunt, and Jules, relieved, leaned in for a brief kiss.

"Hi," she repeated.

"Hello," Vivian replied against her lips and kissed her again.

Jules briefly rested a hand on Vivian's belly. "How's things? We haven't even talked on the phone in a couple of days." Which hadn't happened in a long time. Even after Mark fired Jules, they'd made a point of talking every day.

"Fine, of course." Vivian patted Jules on the elbow. "And yourself?"

"I'm okay," Jules said, deciding that would do for now because it definitely wasn't the time to start a discussion. She could smell the roast duck from here too.

Apparently, Vivian could as well. She tilted her head toward the door. "Dinner, you say?"

"Yeah," Jules said, and slid her arm around Vivian's waist as they headed through the door. She felt good against Jules's side: warm, solid, soft. She was wearing her usual perfume today, though, for which Jules was profoundly grateful. It made it easier not to pounce on her before dinner.

Vivian drew her arm away as they approached the staircase. Jules let go of Vivian's waist and tried not to look like she was keeping an eye on Vivian as they headed down the stairs. Against her will, she fretted about Vivian living on the second floor when she was getting bigger and bigger.

Vivian, however, would not appreciate the concern, so Jules kept her mouth shut and tried to enjoy the meal. The duck was excellent. So was everything else, and Jules had to concentrate not to stuff her face. Vivian's personal chef, Ellen, had a magic touch.

She knew they had to talk, but she didn't know where to begin. When she'd swallowed her third mouthful, she began, "So how's—"

At the same time, Vivian said, "I started packing up my offi—"

They fell silent and looked at each other. After a moment, Vivian chuckled. So did Jules.

"Go on," Jules said. "Packed up your office? Where are you moving to?"

"Top floor," Vivian said with obvious relish. "I'm having it completely redone. My decorator sent me sketches today. I'll show you after dinner."

"Uh, sounds great. Who's going to take over your old place? Who's the new editor of *Du Jour*?"

"The board's considering a few candidates. I'll be pushing for Beatrice LaSalla from *Du Jour Italia*." Her lips twitched. "I'm sure Mark will be pleased. She was his original pick to replace me too."

"Will the board listen to you?"

"They'll have little choice." Now Vivian's smile looked like a shark's. "I'm on it now. Besides, I don't think there will be any objections to Beatrice. She hasn't stepped on too many toes."

Meaning she hadn't stepped on Vivian's, which was all that mattered. "Got it."

"Now, if only I could decide what to do with Allie."

"Allie?" Jules brought her water glass to her mouth. "What do you have to decide about Allie?"

"Whether to leave her at *Du Jour* or bring her with me," Vivian said blandly. Her eyes sparkled as Jules, who had been in the middle of swallowing water, almost choked.

"*Allie?*" Jules shook her head hard as she mopped her mouth with a napkin. "Why the hell would you bring her?"

"Don't you like Allie? You recommended her for the internship, didn't you?"

"Ha-ha," Jules said. "Sure, I like Allie, but she's not exactly..." There had to be a diplomatic way to put this.

Vivian waited.

"...good at anything," Jules finished. So much for diplomacy.

"No, no," Vivian said. "It isn't that she's not good, Julia. It's that she's bad. Completely bad. I've never seen this level of ineptitude before, and that's really saying something." A strange look crossed her face, and it took Jules a moment to realize that Vivian was impressed. "It takes real dedication to fail so utterly that your failure turns one hundred and eighty degrees into something like success. Now, that's talent. I'd be remiss if I didn't nurture it."

"You're kidding."

"You're gone," Vivian pointed out, her eyes sparkling with mirth. "If I can't have the best, I refuse to settle for anything less than the worst."

"You're totally kidding," Jules said flatly.

Vivian waved her hand carelessly. "Of course I am. I wouldn't let her within a mile of my new job. I'd transfer her to Products if I wasn't afraid she'd manage to kill herself with a tube of concealer."

"That's pretty thoughtful of you," Jules said with a laugh. "She must have grown on you."

"I admit nothing," Vivian said. "I will, however, send her to Art. If she's good at—buttresses, or whatever she came up with for the Charleston shoot, she can help with set design."

"Wow," Jules said. "I bet she'll be...uh—"

"An unmitigated disaster, yes."

"Oh God," Jules said, unable to help another laugh. Poor, sweet Allie deserved better than this. "I need to give her a call. Meet her for a drink or something."

"How's your weekend been?"

"Kind of dull," Jules said, trying not to remember how she'd sulked around her apartment in sweatpants all day.

"Mm." Vivian put down her fork and stretched. "I wish I could say the same. This is the first quiet moment I've had."

"Let's enjoy it, then."

Vivian blushed. "Not right after dinner. In fact, I'm not feeling very amorous tonight."

"I didn't mean that, actually." Jules took her hand. "I just, you know, want to hang out. Catch up."

"Oh." For just a moment, Vivian looked disappointed. "Well, then. How was work on Friday?" Her eyes gleamed. "Did anybody mention—"

"Your coup? Yeah, a few people." Jules squeezed Vivian's hand before she let it go. "Everybody was asking me about it. I didn't get a chance to talk to Simon, but he looked like he was about to stroke out at the party."

Vivian chortled.

"I definitely got a lot more popular. Everybody wanted to know what it was like to sit with Mark."

"Did you tell them it was transcendent?"

"I told them it was awkward," Jules said.

Vivian looked at her in surprise.

"I was so shocked. Vivian, why didn't you tell me?"

Might as well get it out now. There was no sense in delaying the conversation, and they were likelier to be civil after a good meal.

But to Jules's irritation, Vivian only waved her hand again. "I didn't tell anyone. Nobody who wasn't directly involved knew until the board meeting on Thursday afternoon." Her lips curved in her most diabolical smile. "It was better that way. Trust me."

"It's not just that," Jules said. *Rational and calm. Be those things.* "I don't mean getting rid of Mark. I mean your new job."

"Well, that was part of getting rid of Mark," Vivian said dryly. "How could I have told you about the job without telling you about the plan? Or would you have believed Mark was going to give me a promotion?"

"Okay, point," Jules conceded, though it hurt. "I get why you didn't tell anyone, but Vivian…I'm not just anyone."

Vivian looked at her in silence. Then she sat back in her chair and folded her arms, clearly gearing up for battle. It was undoubtedly the kind of battle her ex-husbands would have led.

"This is a good thing for us," she said. "Unequivocally good. Or would it have been better for me to get thrown out in disgrace?"

"It wouldn't have, of course. Vivian, I'm really glad Mark's gone and you're safe. It's just such a huge change. Especially now."

Comprehension flashed in Vivian's eyes, replacing the annoyance. She rested a hand on her belly. "I know the timing's bad, but you can only work with what you're given. And it was obviously in the nick of time, wasn't it?"

"Obviously, but—"

"Don't worry so much," Vivian said, her voice gentle. "I'll look after myself, Julia."

Jules almost laughed. Of all people, Vivian didn't have to say she was going to look after herself. "I know that. It's part of the problem. You're not a solo operator here. This is going to affect both our lives." When Vivian opened her mouth, Jules added, "I'm not saying you shouldn't have done it. Just that you should have told me. I'd have told you if I was getting a new job that was going to make me really busy."

"You're always busy, and so am I."

"You'll be busier now," Jules said. "How can you not be?"

"At first, yes," Vivian admitted. "There's so much to arrange." She smirked. "The infrastructure needs to be reworked so that the right people know they're answering to me now. There's been panic all over the building. Gretchen knows her days are numbered."

Gretchen edited *Herself*, which had apparently been stagnating for five years. Jules fought down a surge of pity. It wasn't the time to get into Vivian's planned reforms. Instead, it was time to bite the bullet. "So it seems like you're going to have a lot less time for things. Like yourself. And me." She paused. "Us."

Vivian's eyes widened. Unease flittered across her face for the barest of seconds. But her voice was perfectly reassuring when she repeated, "At first. Once things settle into place, it won't be so bad."

"Vivian, you're going to be running nine magazines instead of one and making huge changes," Jules pointed out. "You said so yourself."

"I won't be *editing* nine magazines. Not with that level of attention to detail."

"Okay," Jules said, letting her doubt bleed into her voice. "If you're sure."

"I'm sure," Vivian said firmly, as if speaking firmly would make it true. "Give it a chance, Julia. It will settle down. We'll have time." She gave Jules a small smile. "Like we do right now."

Good point. They hadn't had Friday or Saturday, but they had tonight, and it wouldn't last forever.

Jules nodded. "Right."

Vivian looked relieved.

Okay. Jules would give Vivian the benefit of the doubt. Sure, she'd be busier for a while. But Jules didn't want to turn into her ex-boyfriend Aaron—or Vivian's ex-husbands—by refusing to understand the demands of the job. This was a big deal, and Vivian was obviously over the moon about it.

If Vivian said she'd make time for her private life, for *them*, then Jules had no choice but to believe her until Vivian proved otherwise.

"Just don't do that again, okay?" she said. "Not if it'll affect both of us. Bring me into it. I'll do the same if—well, I can't imagine anything *similar* happening to me, but I'll do the same if a big change happens."

Vivian looked mulish, but she said, "I guess that's reasonable."

Thank God for that. "I'm proud of you," Jules said sincerely. "I'm proud to be with you. I can't think of anyone else who could have pulled off what you did."

It was the truth. Vivian wasn't the kind of person to lie back and accept her fate. She was a fighter, and she'd vanquished a more powerful enemy. You had to respect that.

"Neither can I." Vivian's tone was light and careless, but her eyes filled with pleasure at Jules's words. "I'm glad you noticed."

"Oh, I noticed." Jules scooted her chair a little closer to Vivian's. "I notice a lot of things about you, you know."

Vivian blushed. She was beautiful when she blushed.

Well, well, well.

"You said you weren't feeling amorous," Jules murmured. "I'd hate to push you."

She leaned forward and put her hand on Vivian's knee hopefully.

Vivian blushed harder. It was a lot more appealing than her Machiavelli impersonation. Then she cleared her throat. "What happened to wanting to catch up?"

"Oh. Well," Jules said sheepishly. She'd misread that one. And she could see how it was a little crass. After all, they hadn't talked for days. She made to remove her hand.

Vivian grabbed it and put it right back on her knee, glaring at Jules.

"You fraud," Jules said in delight.

"It's like you don't know me at all," Vivian said. "Honestly."

"Well," Jules repeated, "you are full of surprises, you know."

Vivian shivered, but then glanced down at her belly and muttered, "It's getting more awkward now. You know, on Thursday we had to—"

Still smiling angelically, Jules said, "Why do you think I have to approach from the front?"

Vivian's eyes widened. The corners of her mouth twitched. "Oh my, my."

"You just let me do all the work tonight." Jules rubbed her thumb against Vivian's knee.

"What a wonderful idea," Vivian said, sounding almost breathless. "The den?"

"Actually," Jules said, "think we can make it to the guest room on the second floor?"

"What? Why that room?"

"Bedposts," Jules said.

Vivian blinked. "Bedposts?"

"Have a little faith," Jules said, imitating Vivian's archest tone.

Five minutes later, Vivian was clinging to a bedpost to support herself while Jules stood behind her and licked and nuzzled the nape of her neck.

Jules had never lingered around this particular part of Vivian before. Apparently, she should have. Vivian was already gasping and she didn't even have her top off yet.

Jules remedied that, pulling back long enough to tug Vivian's shirt over her head.

Vivian cooperated, although she squirmed in protest until Jules bent back down and began kissing her neck, her shoulders. Then she sighed and tilted her head, grabbing the bedpost again.

Her bra clasped in the front. *Fantastic.* Jules reached around, popped it open, then licked her fingers and began playing with Vivian's nipples, trying to time it with her kisses.

She pressed in as close as she could until they were standing back to front, melded together. It was the closest she'd ever been to Vivian. "We're a good fit," she said and nibbled Vivian's earlobe.

"Yes," Vivian said vaguely. "Yes, we are."

A perfect fit, even. Suddenly, Jules's misgivings returned when she hadn't quite expected it. Didn't—couldn't—Vivian see how good this was? That it wasn't worth giving up, that it was worth sacrificing for? Before she knew it, she'd bitten Vivian's neck again, only harder than she'd intended, hard enough to leave a mark.

Vivian said, "Oh!"

Jules reared back in immediate guilt—what the hell had that been about?—and said, "Sorry."

"Again," Vivian gasped.

Jules gasped too. And then she bent to the other side of Vivian's neck—perfect symmetry—and did it again.

Vivian wriggled, grinding her ass back into Jules's hips as she gave an appreciative little moan.

"You like it rough sometimes after all?" Jules said hoarsely. "Just a little bit?"

"Apparently," Vivian said, and Jules nipped her again for that little bit of sass. This time, Vivian actually cooed in delight. "Oh, that's...mm." She moved her ass again, and the rub of her made Jules throb. "Do you like it too?"

"God," Jules said and circled her hips against Vivian, bending down to suck and bite at the curve of her shoulder.

Vivian gasped.

"I like everyth—I love you." It was suddenly very, very important to make Vivian understand that. "You make me crazy. I want to make you feel so good all the time."

"You do," Vivian said. The whimper in her voice told Jules more than the words; it told her that Vivian was already starting to get lost in it. "Oh yes, you do." She shivered again. "I love you too. Please."

Jules moved her hands off Vivian's belly and slid them down between their bodies, cupping and squeezing her ass until Vivian shivered, relented, and stood with her legs farther apart.

After hiking up Vivian's skirt, Jules slid one hand under it, biting her lip when she found the damp satin. "Oh God, I love it when you're already wet," she moaned softly.

"Easy to please, then," Vivian muttered and shifted her hips hopefully. Jules rubbed her knuckles against the satin, and Vivian bucked backward. "More."

"You want me to take these off?" Jules asked. "You want me to slide them down?"

Vivian nodded quickly.

"No," Jules said and cupped Vivian through her underwear, rocking her hand back and forth while Vivian moved her hips so that Jules rubbed her from clit to slit, to ass and back again through the satin. She leaned forward and blew lightly against Vivian's nape and then nibbled again.

Vivian practically fell forward against the bedpost, clutching it for dear life. She whimpered again, and at the sound of it, Jules had to let go of her just long enough to unzip her own jeans. She wedged her hand inside beneath the underwear until she could rub her fingers against her wetness. She jerked forward into her own touch.

Then she pulled her hand out, her fingertips wet, and reached around to rub them gently against Vivian's mouth.

Vivian gasped, startled, but then licked them eagerly, drew Jules's fingertips into her mouth, and sucked on them.

"Oh God!" Jules said. "Oh God, Vivian!"

Vivian panted against Jules's finger. "Inside me. Inside me."

Jules yanked her hand from Vivian's mouth, reached down again, and tugged down her underwear while she shifted and wriggled cooperatively. And then, very gently, Jules slid her middle finger, the same one Vivian had just sucked, deep inside.

This new angle meant that her palm rubbed firmly against Vivian's perineum instead of her clit. Vivian seemed to realize this too as she moaned and then ground against Jules's hand.

Jules groaned against her shoulder and began to move her finger. There, that rough spot, against her knuckle, there—

Vivian cried out, "Please!"

"Fuck," Jules gasped. "It's harder to get at your clit from here. You want to help me?" She chuckled breathlessly. "Think you can hold yourself up with one hand?"

"Oh," Vivian said. "I—yes." She removed one hand from the bedpost and reached down, circumnavigating her own belly until she was touching herself, her fingers only centimeters from Jules's inside her.

Vivian shuddered, gasped, moved her fingers, and set the pace from slow to quick while Jules followed her lead. After a few moments, she began to sob.

There was nobody to hear them, so Jules didn't know why she suddenly put her free hand over Vivian's mouth and whispered, "Sh-h."

The reason didn't matter. Vivian cried out, her breath hot against Jules's hand, getting even wetter around Jules's fingers.

Her tongue darted out, licking Jules's palm, flicking against the salt there. And she came, pulsing around Jules, her sobs reduced to quick, gasping sighs.

Then she went weak, and her head tilted backward against Jules's shoulder.

Jules let go of her mouth and nuzzled at her temple, her hair. She slid her finger out, licked it, and rubbed it against Vivian's mouth again.

"Oh God," Vivian panted against it. "You"—she gulped for air—"are incredible."

Jules didn't bother replying. Instead, she shoved her jeans and underwear down around her thighs, pulled Vivian's hips back, and ground against her ass, sliding slickly against that warm flesh, hissing into Vivian's throat as she came.

"Mm," Vivian said happily as Jules's frantic gyrations slowed to a stop. "Delightful."

"Yeah," Jules gasped as she loosened her grip. "You're pretty incredible yourself."

Vivian gave a dreamy sigh and let go of the bedpost, leaning back against Jules once more. Trusting Jules to hold her up. To support her.

Jules silently vowed to do it and hoped it was a promise she could keep.

CHAPTER 17

THE NEXT WEEK, VIVIAN CALLED Jules all of twice. Their conversations were always brief, and Vivian usually sounded tired. Jules attempted to phone Vivian on the nights she didn't call and always ended up with voicemail, except for one night when Vivian said in a harassed tone that she was putting together some numbers and she'd call Jules when she was free to talk.

"But I might not be free to—" Jules began.

"Good night," Vivian said in an absent tone and ended the call.

Jules threw the phone across the room, but only because she knew it would land on the bed. Vivian didn't call back later.

Jules was not invited to dinner that Sunday night. Vivian was having dinner with Stan Oppenheimer and Beatrice LaSalla. Jules sulked into her ramen noodles, got pissed off at herself for sulking, and went to bed early.

The next night, though, Vivian finally called. She was nearly chortling with excitement: her new office was being set up close to Mark's old digs (which were now Stan Oppenheimer's new digs).

"It's going to be lovely, Julia," she said. "An incredible view. You'll have to come by and see it."

"I'd love to," Jules said, wondering how they were going to pull that one off. Inspired, she suddenly said, "Maybe really late at night."

"What? Ah."

"You can give me a private tour. You know."

"Julia," Vivian said, and Jules could practically see her rolling her eyes.

"You have a locking door, right?"

"Complete with security cameras."

"Oh," Jules said, deflating.

"Well, never mind," Vivian said. "You're adept at imagining things, aren't you?"

"I'm adept at a lot of stuff."

"I'll never look at a bedpost the same way again," Vivian admitted. "Changing the subject, I'm starting to think that there's an infinite supply of cardboard boxes and they're all showing up in my new office."

The Adrian & Jo offices were constantly filled with packages and mail. Jules sometimes unpacked boxes in her sleep. "Yeah. Moving sucks. Especially in New York."

"Not when you pay hefty men to move for you," Vivian said. "But, yes, it's time-consuming, especially when you're moving houses instead of offices."

Jules rolled her eyes. Of course Vivian assumed anybody could afford a professional moving service. "Agreed."

"I wish you'd find somewhere new, though," Vivian added. "I don't like your building."

"It's pretty safe here," Jules said in surprise. "The neighborhood's cool."

"I didn't say the neighborhood. I said the building. It looks like it's one step away from falling down around your head."

"The building is completely fine," Jules said, eyeing the crack in the wall that ran nearly from the floor to the ceiling. She was pretty sure it was bigger now than when she'd moved in. "Besides, my parents own my unit, and all I have to pay is utilities and part of the property tax. And there's a great bagel place just a few doors down."

"Well, God forbid you leave the bagel place. It's probably the only one in New York City."

"Honey, I'm fine here," Jules laughed.

Silence fell.

Jules realized what she'd just said. Her face heated up. "Um…I meant—"

"'Honey' is okay, if you have to," Vivian said as if submitting to a fate worse than death. "I guess it could be worse. But use it sparingly."

Relieved, Jules grinned. She really hadn't meant to say it. She just liked endearments and nicknames, even if they weren't original ones. "I'll try not to wear it out, pumpkin."

"There's that famous wit of yours."

Jules couldn't stop giggling. "You know you love it, cupcake."

"There is a limit, *dear*," Vivian said.

"Uh-oh. 'Dear' means I'm in big trouble, right?"

"Bright girl."

These moments are worth waiting for, Jules thought. *They're worth everything.* "I'm glad you think so, Cary."

"'Cary'?"

"Sure. You be Cary Grant and I'll be Grace Kelly, and it'll be this awesome inside joke—"

"Oh, my God," Vivian said. "Good night already."

"Good night," Jules said, deciding not to push her luck any further. "I love you."

"Yes. Good night." The call ended.

Jules still wore a smile, but it dimmed a little at what Vivian hadn't said. Maybe she'd annoyed Vivian too much to say the words. It would have been nice to hear them, though, after last week. Not that Jules could make her say them or anything.

Her phone rang. Vivian again.

"Hello?" Jules said.

Vivian cleared her throat. "I love you too. Good night again."

Then she ended the call before she could hear Jules laugh aloud in delight.

Just as well.

Jules went to bed with a smile on her face and let it sustain her through the following hectic Tuesday. But that night, Vivian did not call, and, as usual, Jules got sent to her voicemail when she tried it herself. She sent a text but got no reply until the following morning.

Jules glared at her screen while she brushed her teeth. Okay. They were going to have a talk about this. Yes, Vivian was busy, but she'd sworn up and down to make time for Jules. That meant swapping at least a couple of texts a day, right?

Maybe they had different standards about what "making time" meant. They should probably hammer out what those were.

In the meantime, she could find some chill about it. A lot of couples didn't see each other or even talk every day. It was good to have some space. Moreover, it was pathetic to sit by the phone. If Vivian was going to spend her evenings on things and people other than Jules, why shouldn't Jules return the favor?

Tomorrow she'd make a call during lunch.

***

"Drinks tonight? Ooh, I'd love to!" Allie said.

"Let's say eight thirty," Jules suggested. "Simon's going to dinner with a couple of writers, so he won't need me hanging around the office tonight."

"Great!" Allie chirped, and at eight thirty, Jules arrived at Federico's. It was the bar where Simon had guessed the truth about Vivian's pregnancy and made Jules spit her bright orange cocktail everywhere.

That night seemed like years ago. It was incredible to think it had only been in December.

Allie waited for Jules at a high-top table. She was scribbling something on a cocktail napkin.

"Hi, Allie. What's that?" Jules asked as she slung her purse strap over the back of the chair.

"It's a limerick," Allie said absently. "I just need to tweak the equation."

"Equation? In a limerick?"

"Sure. It's a math limerick. I write them to relax. Oh, there we are!" Allie wrote something else, put down her pen, and held the cocktail napkin out with a triumphant smile.

Jules stared at a row of mathematical symbols. This was calculus, if she remembered her AP high school class correctly.

"Get it?" Allie prompted. "It goes, 'The integral y-cubed xy, from five to the square root of pi'—"

Jules nodded along, wide-eyed as Allie finished the poem and then handed the napkin back. "Uh, wow, that's…cool."

Allie gave a modest shrug. "I do them for physics too when I'm really inspired." Then she clapped a hand over her mouth. "Gosh, my manners! Hi, Jules. How are you?"

"Glad to see you," Jules replied with a grin, hoisting herself onto her tall stool. "Looks like you're okay too."

"Oh yeah. I've never been here before," Allie said, looking around with wide eyes. "It's really nice."

"Sure is," Jules said. "Whatever you do, don't get the sunburst martini."

"The what?"

"Trust me." Jules looked at the menu and decided that, since Simon wasn't buying, she'd avoid the pricey mixed drinks altogether. "I'll just have a glass of wine."

"Then I will too."

They ordered two glasses of white, then Allie looked across the table at Jules with her usual perky expression. "How have you been? Do you still like your new job? Is it exciting?"

"I do like it," Jules said. "I'm meeting lots of new people, doing some cool interviews, and—"

"Ooh, are you the one putting the quotes on the website? I check it every day. I've already bought a pair of Tom Ford sunglasses, and I want some sandals too."

"Aw-w." Jules smiled. "That's awesome."

"I told someone at *Du Jour* about it, and they said the site sounded dangerous." Allie frowned and shook her head. "I said I was sure you and Simon would protect their data."

"I don't think that's what they meant by..." Jules gave up. "Never mind. Thanks for using the site. I appreciate it."

"You must be so busy," Allie said. "Do you have time to write anything?"

At that moment, a server dropped off two glasses of ice water. That was fitting, since Jules felt like she'd just had one thrown in her face.

"Need some time?" the server asked.

"No," Jules muttered, looking at the drinks menu like she was trying to decode it. "Just the Pike Road Pinot Gris, please."

"Me too," Allie said.

As the server left, Jules tried to think about how to answer Allie's question or how to avoid it. The truth was, she hadn't written a word in weeks. Vivian and Simon, usually the ones to prod her, had both been too busy to ask her about it.

She hadn't been able to write since the embarrassment of *Modernity*. Vivian had forced the magazine to publish her article, and word was likely to get around. Who was to say that Jules's name wasn't tarnished in publishing circles? How could she trust that anything she submitted would be accepted because it was worthy?

It wasn't exactly a big boost to her confidence, and it sucked her inspiration dry. The closest she could come was writing up the designer interviews for the press kits.

"No," she said in answer to Allie's question, her mouth dry. "It's been crazy. I-I haven't had time to look for opportunities. I don't know who's looking for anything to publish."

Not a lie, she told herself. *That's, like, at least ninety-four percent the truth.*

Allie said, "Oh, that's too bad. I hope it lightens up soon. I've really liked all your articles."

It was past time to change the subject. "Thanks. Hey, what about you? How have you been?"

"Oh, Vivian just gave me a promotion!" Allie beamed. "Isn't that great? I'm going to the art department. I'll be the assistant to the design director!" She frowned. "Well, I'm not sure that's a promotion, actually. But I can help design sets until my internship is over this May."

"Congratulations," Jules said, and their wine arrived just in time for them to toast each other. "To a new bullet point on your résumé."

"Yeah," Allie said and added, "Vivian really misses you."

Jules almost did a second spit-take in Federico's but avoided it at the last minute.

"Well," she mumbled and took a very careful sip of her wine, "I guess it's an adjustment for her."

"At least you still get to see her at dinner and stuff."

Jules blinked, froze, and stared at Allie

Allie looked back, and her smile faltered a little at whatever she saw on Jules's face.

"Um," Jules said, "how...how did—"

"Oh!" Allie said, and her eyes widened. "Should I not have said anything? It's just that, you remember, sometimes Ellen calls to check up on the schedule and everything to see when Vivian will get home."

"Ellen?" Jules said, horrified. "Vivian's cook?"

"Sure. She likes me. One time, I told her about my grandma's special recipe for jellied chicken, and she couldn't stop laughing. I asked if she'd make it for Vivian sometime, and she said she was definitely tempted." Allie flipped her hair back, looking proud of herself. "I'm sure it's full of protein and it'd be very good for her."

Jellied chicken? Thank God they hadn't gotten any appetizers, or Jules's stomach would be staging a revolt right now.

"So she likes me," Allie said. Then she tilted her head to the side. "That's, uh…That's how I know. About you having all those dinners with Vivian. She hasn't told anybody else. I won't tell either."

Jules's spine stiffened, and she looked into Allie's large, brown eyes. They were full of understanding and kindness, and suddenly Jules remembered the day she'd been fired, when Allie had tried to make her feel better.

"Oh," she said.

"Yeah," Allie replied. "I mean, it's just dinner, right?"

It's not just dinner, she meant.

This was the Allie who solved physics problems, wasn't it? The one who took the data and solved the equation that most people wouldn't understand. This was a hell of a time for her to apply that gift somewhere outside of a lab or textbook.

"So what's there to tell?" Allie added.

Jules swallowed hard. "Nothing, I guess."

"Right," Allie said, nodding. Then she added gently, "Everybody has a right to be happy, Jules. That's what I've always thought."

"I think so too," Jules said, her throat suddenly thick.

Allie's forehead crinkled in a frown. "I mean, unless you're a mass murderer or something. Like Hitler."

"Yeah, we'll make an exception for him." Jules looked down at her cocktail napkin and traced a fingertip over the even grooves at its edges. "Thanks, Allie."

"No problem." Allie looked around the bar again with bright, interested eyes. "Wow. Why do you think they used so much red in here? I think it's clashing with my hair."

CHAPTER 18

Jules needed a sign from the universe.

The next afternoon during a rare quiet moment at her desk, she looked moodily at her laptop screen. She'd opened Google Docs and started a new page. Now it mocked her.

Just jot down some ideas, she told herself. *Something. Anything.* But nothing came to mind.

She had to get over this paralysis. Yes, Vivian had done Jules a disservice in trying to help. She'd also been well-intentioned, and there was nothing to be done about it now. Jules could only move forward. She didn't want the highlight of her career to be interviews with fashion designers for web copy.

Ironically, what had lit the original fire under her ass months ago was wanting to impress Vivian. She'd wanted to prove she had talent beyond keeping to a daily schedule. Then it had become more. Once she'd started, it had felt so good to use that part of her brain again. She'd loved writing in college and had fallen out of practice.

Dammit. Jules flopped back in her chair and growled at the laptop. She could tell herself all she wanted that it was because she was busy. And she was—there never seemed to be enough hours in a day—but she wasn't even trying. It wasn't about the hours; it was about the stupid voice in her head telling her that nobody would take her seriously.

Yeah, a sign would be great. A flash from the heavens to tell her that she wasn't a pretender after all. Her confidence was sucked dry.

Come on. One passive-aggressive email and you lose your courage? How insecure are you?

Right. Yeah. She should listen to *that* little voice instead and then write something. Anything. It didn't have to be brilliant. Just words that, if you squinted at them, formed a sequence of some kind.

"Looking for something to do?"

Jules looked up to see Simon approaching her desk. She resisted the impulse to slam her laptop shut as if she'd been doing something wrong. "Uh, yeah, always. I think I've finally got the truck company on a regular delivery schedule."

"Good, good. Changing the subject, I have an invitation for you. Nonobligatory in this case. Maxwell Walker is an absurdly wealthy investment banker who's started a rock band as a vanity project, and he's hosting a concert at the Cutting Room. He's expressed some interest in A&J as a potential investment opportunity."

What could Jules possibly contribute to that? This better not be a gross ask. She didn't want to walk out on this job.

Simon must have read her mind because he said quickly, "This isn't me asking you to wear a low-cut top. If anything, *I'd* be the one to—" He coughed. "Not that it's about that."

Well, well. Simon's cheeks had gone red.

Jules leaned forward with a grin. "Can I see his picture?"

"You can Google it," Simon said with dignity.

"Trust me, I will. So when is this concert that's only about investment opportunities?"

"Starts eight p.m. next Friday. And that's enough out of you, smartass."

Jules and Vivian never got together on Fridays. She tried to imagine inviting Vivian to a rock concert where Simon was planning to flirt with an investment banker and Jules was playing wingman. It was easier to imagine inviting Vivian to fly to the moon.

"Sounds good," she said, opening her calendar app. "I haven't been to a concert in forever."

"I have the sinking feeling he's more handsome than talented. Oh well. The drinks should be on point. Speaking of drinks, how were yours with Allie last night? Did she get lost on the way to the restroom, or did she launch the next space shuttle?"

"A little bit of both." Jules laughed. "She misses you."

"She's surviving Vivian without you?"

"So far."

153

And she would keep surviving Vivian if Allie kept her mouth shut. Jules had felt obligated to tell Vivian that Simon knew about their relationship. She wasn't about to squeal on Allie. Vivian might turn on Allie in full wrath, which would be like fire-hosing a saltine.

Besides, Jules didn't think Allie would tell. She couldn't imagine it. In fact, it was almost a comfort that someone knew about them and didn't disapprove. Well, two someones, if you counted Ellen. Although Jules had no idea if Ellen, too, had put together the pieces or if she just knew that Jules was an extra dinner guest sometimes. Jules didn't want to work all that out either.

Simon returned to his office, leaving Jules to open her laptop again. Enough futile brainstorming. She must have a million emails waiting right now, and she was on company time. Besides, she hadn't gotten that sign she desperately needed, so writing would have to wait.

Just then, her text tone sounded. Jules glanced at the display. Whoa, what a weird coincidence. It was Allie.

Hi Jules!! This is so random, but I remembered you said you didn't have time to find things to write abt & I thought I'd tell you that one of my fashion profs emailed everybody abt an essay collection she wants submissions for

A moment later:

I can get you her info if you want

A moment after that:

IDK what the essays are supposed to be abt tho

And then:

Fashion I guess

Jules stared at her display in dumb astonishment. As she did, more gray text bubbles appeared on the screen until Allie's final one.

So weird I just got that email this morning right?? Maybe it's a sign!!!!!

It took Jules a full minute to type back:

Must be! I'd love her info. TYSM!

Moments later, Allie sent a text with her professor's email address and a link to the call for essays.

Jules gave the page a careful look. To her surprise—and relief—it wasn't an academic collection. Instead, the book was forthcoming from a Big Five publisher intended for a general audience about queerness in fashion.

She'd already written about that—an article in *Salon* about the lack of genuine queer representation in the industry. There was certainly more to say, enough that Jules already had material but wouldn't be repeating herself.

All submissions were anonymous. The hook of the collection was that it didn't feature the usual big-name authors. The opposite—ordinary people would have the opportunity to submit their ideas. The book would be marketed as "original ideas from authentic voices."

The reviewers wouldn't know that Jules Moretti, Vivian Carlisle's protégée, was the author. Nobody would unless she got accepted and published, thanks only to her writing.

Don't get your hopes up, Jules ordered herself. *They're only taking twenty essays, and there will be tons of submissions.*

But she could be in with a shot. She'd worked at a magazine long enough to know that most of the submissions would be lousy. Jules would bring an insider's perspective, and she could expand on some ideas that had been intriguing her for a while.

Well, she'd wanted a sign, all right. Jules leaned on her elbows and exhaled heavily. She didn't really believe in that stuff, but if this was what coincidence looked like, she'd take it.

Vivian wouldn't believe it either. Not that Jules would tell her right away. She didn't even have an idea yet.

But for the first time in a while, she had motivation, and that was worth more than all the world's ideas put together.

155

For the next two days, she and Vivian had to content themselves with texts, but for once, Jules wasn't moping. She was working. It reminded her of months ago when Simon had put her in touch with *Salon* and she'd had to throw an article together in just a few days. She'd given up sleep and looked so tired that Vivian had actually called her out on it.

It wasn't quite that bad this time. The deadline for the essay collection wasn't for another month. Jules wanted to get it finished and in early, though. The closer they got to Vivian's due date, the less flexibility she'd have.

Another plus of writing the article: it let her worry less about how she'd feature in Vivian's busy life once the baby came.

Around ten o'clock, Jules blearily finished another cup of coffee and typed more notes:

Gucci website currently featuring models assigned male at birth wearing skirts & carrying purses. Bolder than most "gender neutral" fashion marketing but super expensive. Queer community has less money overall than straight people (exception: cis gay white men). Mere voyeurism for a wealthy audience?

She blew air through her lips loudly enough to make it a raspberry. Vivian would have raised an eyebrow at that and then told her how to make her idea better.

Jules hadn't told Vivian about the article yet. It just didn't seem like the right moment. Besides, she couldn't ask for her help. This was something Jules was going to do on her own, independently of Vivian, Simon, or any other connections she had.

Just then, her phone rang. It was Vivian, as if Jules had mentally summoned her.

"Hello," Vivian said.

From the exhaustion in Vivian's voice, Jules could tell it wouldn't be a long conversation tonight. She drooped. She was tired too, but she'd looked forward to catching up. It had been three days since they'd spoken.

It also wasn't the time to tear into Vivian about it, not when they were both dragging and prone to being unreasonable.

So she just said, "Hi. How are things?"

"Oh, fine," Vivian said. "I can't speak long. I'm about to fall asleep where I sit. You're okay?"

"Okay enough," Jules said, disappointed even though she'd expected it. "So, what's got you so tired tonight?"

"What doesn't?" And then Vivian was off and running, telling Jules about getting *Du Jour* ready to transition to Beatrice LaSalla's leadership and pushing Human Resources to the breaking point because both Mr. Barnhardt and Mr. Oppenheimer wanted to clean house.

"And not that I object to hiring the most competent people, of course, but, I mean, really," Vivian said, exasperated. "Couldn't they have waited to cull the section heads until we could hire people who actually know their way around a publishing business?"

"Yeah," Jules said, trying not to yawn. She was more tired than she'd thought. Which was funny because now Vivian sounded a lot more energetic.

Maybe Vivian was some kind of energy-sucking vampire who operated over the phone. Jules wouldn't put anything past her even now. Especially now.

"But you're looking after yourself, right?" Jules asked. "You know. Eating and stuff. You said you would."

"Yes, yes," Vivian said vaguely, which meant she'd probably skipped a meal or two. "I've been counting calories, Julia, believe me. Anyway, I'd better go."

"Okay." Jules worried her bottom lip. "Can I call you tomorrow?"

"Don't bother." Vivian sighed. "I've got dinner with Stan again. I don't know what you were so worried about, Julia. He's incredibly dull one-on-one."

"And incredibly handsome," Jules said darkly. Then she added, "But his ears don't match up."

"They—you know, they don't, do they?" Vivian said. "I've never thought about that before. Now it's going to be all I see whenever I look at him."

"Happy to help." Jules smiled in triumph. "Believe me. Have a good time with Mr. Ears tomorrow."

"What are you, five?"

"You know what I bet you'll do? I bet you'll look at him and say something like, 'I'll have the ears. I mean the chicken.'"

"You're a horrible person," Vivian said.

"Hold that thought," Jules said. "I'll see you on Sunday. I love you."

Tonight Vivian didn't forget to return the words. "I love you," she said, warming Jules up more than her cup of coffee ever could.

Sunday, Jules thought. *We'll talk about this then. We'll make it work. It'll be fine.*

All this could be fixed, and everything could be fine.

Jules looked back at her notes. In spite of the coffee, she was so tired that they seemed to blur in front of her. Time for bed, where she'd probably dream of androgynous Gucci models in skirts. Or if she was lucky, Vivian.

At least then they could hang out in her dreams, if nowhere else.

CHAPTER 19

JULES WENT TO A PARTY on Saturday night at a fashionable designer's fashionable loft studio, where she met many fashionable people and sipped fashionable new drinks that more often than not tasted terrible. She didn't have the time of her life or anything, but some of the people there were funny and cool, and they even seemed to think she was funny and cool too.

She'd missed that. She hadn't had fun at a party since college, where she'd had tons of friends and nobody spent all their time checking the labels on people's shirts.

Tonight had a laid-back atmosphere, and after a couple of drinks, even the snobs were mellow enough to hang out with. There were even a few people from *Du Jour* who came over to say hello and caught her up on all the insanity Vivian hadn't seen fit to mention.

Jules tried to change the subject pretty quickly, though. It was nice to spend an evening talking about things not related to the chaos of her old job.

Still, even though the party was fun, Jules was much more excited the following evening as she took the subway to Vivian's neighborhood. If it had been a long time since they'd talked on the phone, it had been a lot longer since they'd seen each other and kissed and—

Two weeks, Jules realized with shock. She hadn't even laid eyes on Vivian in two whole weeks. It had felt like a long time, but she hadn't realized it had been *that* long. Her heart pounded. She couldn't wait.

But she was destined for disappointment. When she emerged from the steps of the 72nd Street station at 6:55 p.m. sharp, she saw that she'd received a text from Vivian.

I'm running late, but Ellen will let you in.

Jules stared at it. Was she for real? On a Sunday, *their* Sunday, after two whole weeks?

She stepped out of the foot traffic and texted:

Where are you & when will you be back?

My office. Give me until 8. Dinner should be ready. Don't wait on me if you're hungry.

Don't—? Jules's hand clenched on her phone.

Then Vivian added:

I'm sorry. I thought I'd be finished by now. I'll be there as soon as I can.

An apology was more than warranted. Vivian also didn't give many of them. As mad as she was, Jules could still recognize a momentous event when she saw it.

I'll bet she apologized to her ex-husbands too.

The thought sent a chill through Jules's body. She banished it immediately. It wouldn't do to let anger spiral.

She replied to Vivian:

Ok, see you soon

That had better be true.

Vivian didn't get home until a quarter to nine—forty-five minutes past her own deadline. She'd texted Jules an update along with a photo of her office, freshly painted and with one wall papered with an abstract pattern. Weirdly, that one reminded Jules of the accent wall she'd painted in her own apartment in a series of geometric shapes.

Jules texted:

Looks like my wall

That's the idea.

"Aw-w," Jules said aloud before she could help herself.

That could be why she felt more magnanimous when Vivian got back, even though she was starving. Eat dinner without Vivian? No way.

The front door opened and closed. Jules heard it from the den. She got up from the couch and quickly headed to the foyer, where Vivian was hanging up her coat, shoulders bowed and face lined with weariness.

When she saw Jules, she gave her a genuine—if apprehensive—smile. "Good evening," she said.

Two weeks. Jules couldn't believe it. No matter what, Vivian was a sight for sore eyes tonight.

"Hey," she said quietly, coming forward for a kiss.

Vivian returned it readily, taking hold of Jules's shoulders and sighing against her mouth when their lips parted.

"Sorry I'm late," she said. "I—"

Jules cut her off. Vivian looked like she was about to keel over. "Come on," she said and took Vivian's hand, tugging her toward the kitchen. "You haven't eaten yet, have you?"

For once, Vivian allowed herself to be led. She sat at the table while Jules warmed their plates in the microwave. The food, a savory chicken dish, wouldn't be quite as good as it was when it was freshly cooked, but it still smelled great.

Vivian picked up her fork, glanced at Jules, and said in a low voice, "So, how have you been?"

Jules took her cue and started talking so that Vivian could eat her meal without having to respond. Her eyelids fluttered in pleasure at the first bite, and Jules wondered if she'd even remembered to eat lunch. Anger gathered in the pit of her stomach, but she mastered it and barreled on, shoving mouthfuls of chicken into her mouth between anecdotes about her week. By the time she was done, Vivian had nearly finished her food.

"You want some salad?" Jules asked. "There's spinach and stuff in the fridge. It'll be good for you."

Vivian didn't look at Jules as she took one final bite. "Is all this pampering meant to return me to full strength before you let me have it?"

Jules pursed her lips, but Vivian didn't look up. "I don't know," she said.

Vivian tensed.

"I don't want to fight with you." Not when it had been so long since they'd even seen each other. "I just need to hear that this is only one time, and we'll see each other more often, and this won't be forever."

"It won't be," Vivian said immediately. She pushed her plate away. "It's only temporary. But there are certain things I have to do, Julia— responsibilities I have whether we like it or not."

"I know that," Jules said, trying not to sound offended. Hadn't she been telling herself that for weeks now? She could be what Vivian needed her to be. "I said that."

"Good." Vivian glanced at the clock. Nearly nine thirty. "It's late. I… know better than to ask if you can stay."

"Um, is that you telling me I can't?"

Vivian's glare was swift. "Of course not."

"Then I can stay. I just have to leave really early so I can go home and change. This is our time, Vivian. I want it."

"So do I." The words could have sounded defensive. Instead, Vivian's soft tone made them warm, wistful. "I like it when you stay. In fact, you could bring a few more things over, if you want."

Jules imagined her toothbrush in the guest bedroom's bathroom next to a sampling of her cosmetics and hair supplies. She pictured getting ready in the morning while Vivian did the same thing down the hall, mercifully distanced so they didn't elbow each other and mix up their cosmetics. Somewhere, she'd heard that separate bathrooms were the secret to a successful relationship. It made sense to her.

She cleared her throat. "Sure, that could work. If it's okay with you."

Vivian smiled and then raised her water glass to her lips as if to hide it. "Yes, Julia. It's okay with me. Do you know what else would be okay with me?"

That wicked gleam in her eyes was all too familiar by now. Jules's stomach did a hopeful flop. "Aren't you tired?"

"Yes. That's why it'd also be okay with me if you did most of the work."

"So what else is new?" Jules grumbled, a protest without teeth. She hadn't expected this, but after two weeks, no way was she turning down an opportunity. She rose to her feet. "Dishes can wait. Let's get a move on."

"Oh, the romance," Vivian said but gamely led the way to the stairs.

The combination of good food, sex, and rest relaxed Vivian. In fact, it relaxed her enough that she lay naked next to Jules, playing with a long lock of her hair. By now, it was half past ten, but Vivian looked more energetic than she had before.

Jules pointed this out, and Vivian chuckled.

"I've always been a night owl," she said softly, "ever since I was a child."

She never talked about her past. Tonight there was a new note in her voice: pensive and vulnerable. A gift, maybe, waiting to be opened.

Even though she was exhausted, Jules wasn't going to wait to open it. "Yeah? What else were you like as a child?"

"Well..." Vivian's hand drifted to rest on her rounded abdomen as if she were telling a story to her daughter as much as to her lover. "I was restless. I couldn't stay still. I was the youngest of three children, and by the time I was born, my parents didn't have the same energy to devote to me."

"So you got away with murder," Jules said dryly.

Vivian chuckled. "My siblings certainly thought so. Not that there was much to get away with around there. You know where I grew up."

"Toledo, Ohio," Jules said. "You said you wanted to get out."

"'Wanted' is an understatement. Our house had torn window screens that my dad never fixed, and mosquitoes invaded during the summer. I wore my sister's hand-me-downs, even though we were different sizes, and that's why I learned to sew. I grew up pricking my fingers on needles and scratching at bites until I was old enough to replace the damn screens myself. Hell yes, I wanted to get out of there."

It seemed impossible. Were there pictures somewhere of this younger Vivian in ill-fitting clothes? Yearbooks or photo albums? Jules doubted it—not in this house. Maybe they existed somewhere else.

"Is your family still there?" she asked. "Do you ever visit the Carlisles of Toledo?"

Jules had kept her voice light and teasing in case this was a sensitive subject. Even so, she was surprised by how long Vivian took to answer.

"There are no Carlisles in Toledo," she said. "At least none that I'm related to."

Just as Jules was about to press for more information about that, she remembered Simon saying to her: *Vivian Carlisle isn't even her real name.*

"There are, however, a few Fluhartys," Vivian concluded. "And occasionally—very, very occasionally—I visit them."

It took Jules a second to catch up. Maybe it was post-orgasm brain fog. That might also have been why she blurted out "Fluharty?" as if it was the craziest thing she'd ever heard.

Vivian sighed and scooted back just enough that Jules could see her face better. Her blonde hair was plastered to her forehead with sweat, and a wry smile hovered around her lips. "Correct."

"Vivian Fluharty," Jules marveled. "For real?"

"Um…" Vivian said.

After a pause, Jules said, "Not even Vivian?"

"Not even that."

"So what's your first name? Out with it. You know I'm sworn to silence."

"Maybe you should sign an NDA first."

Was Vivian kidding? It seemed impossible to tell.

"Jennifer," Vivian sighed. "Jenny for short."

Jules tried to put the two words together in her head. Aloud, she said, "Jenny Fluharty."

"Laugh and I'll make you regret it."

"I won't," Jules said, pinching her thigh so she could keep her promise. "*Ow*. I mean, of course it's not funny. It's just hard to wrap my head around you as someone really named Jenny Fluharty."

"That's because I'm really named Vivian Carlisle." Now Vivian's voice had the razor edge that Jules—and the rest of the world—was used to. "I changed my name as soon as I turned eighteen. That caused a hell of a family scene, I don't mind telling you. I didn't care. I chose my name, and it means everything to me. It's who I am."

"I get it," Jules said quickly. She rubbed her hand over Vivian's bare arm to soothe her. "Anyone should be able to choose their name if they want to. I love your name. It's beautiful."

If she added "just like you," Vivian would scoff, but it was implied.

Vivian's fingertips glided over Jules's forearm, stirring the fine hair there. "Yes. As is yours, Julia."

"Thanks. But..." It was finally time to ask Vivian about something she'd wondered before. "Everyone else calls me Jules. Why don't you?"

Vivian hummed. "I wondered if you'd ever ask me that."

"So what's the answer?"

"*Julia* is elegant. Musical, even. I like how it sounds, and I don't want to use a nickname." Vivian nestled in closer to Jules. "That's how it started, anyway."

Damn. Sex was making her voluble tonight. Jules wasn't going to waste a moment of this. "And now?"

"As you said yourself, everyone else calls you Jules." Vivian gave her a long look. "I'm not everyone else."

"No kidding," Jules said fervently. She tilted her head for a swift kiss.

Vivian returned it and then yawned hugely. "I think I'm losing my second wind. *Ah.*" She shifted with a grimace, touching her belly again.

Jules put her hand over Vivian's. Beneath their entwined fingers, the baby kicked.

"Wow," Jules said softly. "It's amazing every time."

"I'm sure it is from the outside. Just be thankful it didn't happen, say, twenty minutes ago."

Vivian glowered at her belly, but Jules wasn't fooled, not when the glower turned to a soft look of fondness.

"Dishes are on me," Jules said.

Vivian looked even more grateful than she had after arriving.

The night wasn't as restful as it could have been. Now entering her final trimester, Vivian was having trouble sleeping. She used a maternity pillow that bumped into Jules every time she moved. She got up every four seconds to pee and couldn't seem to get comfortable.

Jules still didn't want to be anywhere else. On a night she'd otherwise have spent working on her article, she'd vastly rather be here, jostled awake again and again.

Vivian finally settled down for good around three a.m. Jules spooned up behind her and rested her arm over Vivian's rounded belly.

"We can have both," she whispered, softly enough not to wake Vivian. "Our jobs and this. Don't you see? Can't we try?"

Vivian, sound asleep at last, did not reply.

CHAPTER 20

THAT THURSDAY, SIMON HAD LUNCH with Jules in his office to go over his monthly expenses. When they were finished with business and had twenty minutes left on their schedule, he sipped his flavored water and said, "So, when may we expect your tedious moping to be over? It's been a month since you started walking around looking like somebody killed your dog."

Tedious? Nice. But of course Simon had noticed.

"I'm not moping," she said. How to fob him off? "It's just—right now it's that time of the month, and I usually get a little depr—"

"Thank you for sharing," Simon said, though the look on his face told Jules he only half believed her.

"You asked," Jules pointed out and smiled in spite of herself at the uncomfortable look on his face.

"So I did," Simon sighed. "Okay, my evasive friend. Oh, changing the subject entirely, of course, how's Vivian these days? Busy decorating her new throne room?"

Okay, maybe he believed her less than half. "Yeah, she's busy," Jules said, poking at the remains of her salad. "You know, like you'd expect."

"Yes, well," Simon said. "I notice you've been making some friends around the office. That's good. I hope you're still planning to come to Maxwell's concert on Friday."

Oh jeez. "Yeah," Jules said, rolling her eyes. "I am. It's almost like I'm getting a life."

Simon raised his water bottle in a smirking salute.

"You're one to talk," Jules added. "I'm not the only one looking forward to this concert. Gee, I wonder if anything might come of it?"

"Don't worry. You'll be the last to know."

"I will not," Jules said with a grin. "I'll be the one arranging your lunches and ordering flowers for him."

"Don't get me hyped up. DMs aren't a big deal. He probably DMs tons of guys."

"Ooh. He's messaging you? This is news to me."

Simon wadded up his sandwich wrapper and tossed it toward the trash can in the corner of his office. It bounced off the edge and fell to the floor, where its edges slowly unfolded, revealing traces of lettuce and sriracha mayo. "Did you know that a few people out there practice something called 'work-life balance'? And have these weird things called 'boundaries'?"

"Sounds fake." Jules put the plastic lid over her salad, pressing the edges together with a satisfying click. "Look, life is short, okay? If it makes you happy, go for it with him. All's fair in love and war."

He chuckled and then grew serious again. "All is fair, Jules. Do what you have to in order to get by. Look out for number one. Do you understand what I'm getting at here?"

Jules frowned at him. "Yes, but I don't agree. Relationships don't have to be like work. It's not about always watching your back."

"It's such a treat watching you grow up inch by agonizing inch," Simon said, "but sometimes you stall."

Jules glared at him, fed up to the teeth with the patronizing attitude, but before she could snap, he said in a conciliatory tone, "Look. Just take care of yourself. I've been watching you wilt for a month now, and it's bothering me. Don't spread yourself too thin." He paused. "Don't kill yourself for somebody who won't return the favor."

"What makes you think she wouldn't?" Jules snapped.

"Oh boy. Now I remember why some boundaries are bigger than others."

There was more he wasn't saying. The last time Simon and Jules had talked about this, he'd raised worries about how Vivian's relationship with Jules could impact Adrian & Jo. His concern here wasn't entirely that of a friend. Jules had to remember that.

"We're being circumspect," she said. "You haven't heard anything, have you?"

Simon shook his head. "No. You're handling that part of it well, I admit. Until—unless—something goes wrong in that quarter, I'm thinking more about how you're handling the other parts."

"It's not like I don't have my own stuff going on," Jules said, defending herself from accusations he hadn't exactly leveled. "Besides, it's a hard time for her. I'm not going to be like her husbands. I can be there for her."

"Good," Simon said slowly. "So long as you're not just there for her to wipe her feet on when she comes home."

"What are you—oh. Doormat. I get it." Jules scowled. "Cute. But I'm not."

"If you say so," Simon said, "but she brings that out in people. You know she does. Just keep it in mind. Do what you have to do," he repeated. "I did. And it saved my sanity."

"You sure about that?"

"Now look who's the cute one."

"It's always been me. I've always been ten times cuter than you. We could take a poll. I'll win by a landslide."

Instead of replying, Simon wadded up his paper napkin and chucked it at her nose. This time he hit his target.

The next night proved Simon to be a prophet. Afterward, Jules still couldn't believe it had happened.

"Sunday's up in the air," Vivian said over the phone. "I've been invited to a weekend business retreat in the Hamptons, and I don't think I can get back in time."

Jules's hand clenched hard on her water glass. "Wait. We can't see each other on Sunday at *all*?"

"I don't think so," Vivian said apologetically. "But are you free tomorrow night? My previous engagement just canceled."

Jules set her glass down on the coffee table so hard it almost cracked.

Vivian's *previous engagement* had just canceled. Vivian didn't cancel it so she could have time to be with Jules when they couldn't meet on their usual day.

In spite of this, Jules almost said yes. The word sat on the tip of her tongue. It was still time they could spend together, right? Wasn't that more important than Jules's pride, her…

Her self-respect?

Doormat, Simon's voice said in her head.

"I can't," Jules heard herself say. "I'm going to a concert. I told Simon I'd be there. Lots of other important people will be there too."

"Oh," Vivian said after a moment of silence.

"But"—Jules licked her lips and hoped what she said next got through—"I *could* cancel. Some things matter more."

"Don't feel obligated," Vivian said calmly. "Sounds like it'll be a good opportunity for you. Meet people. Make contacts."

"Well, yes. But—there will be other opportunities, you know? There are always parties and concerts and meetings. Isn't it about having the right priorities?"

"Go to the party, Julia," Vivian said.

Jules set her jaw. "I'm saying you're more important." She took a deep breath. "*We're* more important. Do you understand what I mean?"

"Go to the party," Vivian repeated. Her voice was very, very firm. "My invitation is rescinded. Don't show up here. Network instead. That's what's important."

Jules actually felt like she'd been punched in the gut. "No. You can't say that. You can't tell me what's most important to me."

Didn't Vivian get it? There *would* be other events, and they'd be full of the same people, and they'd serve the same drinks, and they'd all blend into each other, and in ten days, never mind ten years, Jules wouldn't remember anything about them.

But this, her relationship with Vivian, was one of a kind. She didn't want to wake up one morning and realize she'd ignored the most important thing ever.

"No, I can't," Vivian said dryly, "but I can tell you that I'll find some way to keep myself busy on Friday night as well. And on other nights. It's fine to have a thriving career, Julia. Better than fine. Do whatever you can to develop yours."

"Okay, I really don't know how else I can put this," Jules said. "I know it's fine. I love my job. I love you more. I don't want to miss you."

Vivian said in exasperation, "You're not missing me. I'm not going anywhere. I know it's been hard. It won't be for too much longer."

"It won't be, huh?" Jules said. Then she heard the words coming out of her mouth. "How often have you said that before?"

Oh...shit.

There was a long silence, during which Jules bit her lip and wondered if she even should have picked up the phone.

Then Vivian said, "Excuse me?"

Crap, crap, crap. "I just meant—"

"How often have I *what?*"

Jules could picture Vivian's face now. It would be turning red, and not in the sexy way but in the twisted, angry way that meant she knew what was coming.

Yes, Jules realized with a flash of clarity. Vivian knew what was coming. She'd done this before, and she had always hoped it would end differently. But how could it?

There was no use in turning back now. "How many times did you and your ex-husbands talk about this? I mean it. It's not a rhetorical question. How many times have you had this discussion?"

"What discussion?" Vivian snapped. "What discussion am I about to be blindsided with? Please be explicit."

"I'm not blindsiding you," Jules said, trying to stay cool. "I'm just asking. How many times have you told somebody, 'I'll just be busy for a little while. Things'll calm down after this photo shoot' or something?"

"I don't believe this."

"Just answer the question," Jules said. "Can you do that?"

"We talked about this from the very beginning," Vivian spat. "You knew all along how I felt. How my partners never understood."

"I know they didn't, but there's got to be room for—"

"I thought that you understood. That you would be different."

"—for compromise. I *do* understand. I *am* different."

"How?" Vivian asked.

There was a note in her voice that Jules had never heard before. It made her feel sick, even though she couldn't say why exactly.

Vivian continued. "If I've had this conversation a million times before, how can you possibly say you're different?"

"Because I am! I'm not Robert!" When was Vivian going to understand that?

"Then where is this coming from?" Vivian demanded. "What are you saying?"

"I'm just saying that maybe we could compromise!" Jules said, curling her free hand into a fist. "I know nothing's going to be perfect. But we used to talk on the phone a lot more. We'd see each other once a week. I don't think that's too much to ask. Do you?"

"Of course not, but you don't get it," Vivian said.

Jules went rigid. Of all the patronizing—

"Haven't you been listening to me?" Vivian asked. "If I could see you more often, I would—I'd see you every day—do you think I don't want to? Everything's chaos, Julia, and at the moment I don't have a choice."

Jules sat bolt upright on the sofa. "What?" she said. "What did you say?"

"I said, at the moment I—"

"You don't have a choice. No, you do have one," Jules said. "You always have a choice. You always own your decisions, Vivian."

"I am owning my decisions," Vivian snarled. "I'm telling you that this is the decision I've made, and if I want to see it through, then this is what I've got to do. Can you really not see that?"

"I know you're going to see it through," Jules said in pure frustration. "That's what you do. But things have to change."

"Things have to change," Vivian repeated, a sudden hitch in her voice.

"Don't you think so? Vivian, we're in a committed relationship, and I'm lucky if I get to see you once a week. You know that if you want to, you can stay as busy as you are right now forever."

"If I *want* to?" Vivian asked thickly.

"Or you could take a night off once in a while to be with me. I'll do the same. You're part of my life now, and I'm part of yours, aren't I?"

"You are," Vivian said. "You are." And that was when Jules realized Vivian was crying.

Her insides went hollow and cold. She felt like the lowest creature on earth. Lower than slime. She was hitting Vivian at her weakest point, and they both knew it. They'd needed to have this conversation, but Jules hadn't wanted it to happen like this, so full of anger and recrimination.

Just a few nights ago, they'd been cuddling in bed while Vivian told Jules things she'd never told anyone. Why couldn't they talk about this that way? Reasonably, tenderly?

"Vivian," she said, her own voice shaking, "maybe I should come over. We can talk this out in person."

"Will it make a difference?" Vivian said. She sounded like she was choking. "It never does. Oh, my God."

"Vivian, please calm down," Jules begged. To her horror, she realized she was tearing up as well. How had they gotten themselves into this, and so quickly? "I'm not calling anything off. Nothing's ending. I'm just saying that once a week—"

"No, you're not," Vivian said. "You're not saying that at all. For now, it's once a week. Then you'll wonder why we can't be together more. Then you'll—" She stopped.

"Vivian, no." Jules used her free hand to wipe her eyes and then cover them. "I'm not trying to say any of that. I'm saying we can compromise. Why can't I get a place on your schedule? Don't you want things to be different this time?"

"I thought they would be," Vivian said, her voice dull.

"They will be," Jules insisted. "Come on, we're not giving up. We're good together, aren't we? When we *are* together."

Vivian was silent.

"What are you thinking?" Jules asked desperately. "Just talk to me."

"I'm thinking, all right?" Vivian didn't sound like she was crying anymore, thank God. "And I'm seeing a pattern."

"Yeah, well, so am I," Jules said. "We have to break it. Won't it be good for you, anyway? Not just being with me, but taking a few nights off? Taking care of yourself?"

"Oh, now this is about me," Vivian said. "Maybe you should have started that way. It would have made the sucker punch a lot more effective."

Jules's jaw dropped. "No! I have to work at it too. I know I'm not perfect."

"Oh good," Vivian said. "I've been wondering when you'd figure that out."

Jules's mouth snapped shut. Then she said, "What?"

"Ms. Relationship Expert," Vivian said. "Everything's so easy, isn't it? Everything's so black-and-white. You know exactly what we need. You know exactly how to heal me because God knows I must be broken somewhere."

"I've literally never said that. I've never even thought it!" Jules dragged her hand through her hair so hard that her scalp hurt. "I'm not telling you to quit your job. You're not listening to me. You're hearing things I'm not even saying!"

"No, I hear what you're saying," Vivian said. "You don't. You don't know how many times I've heard—"

"Vivian, *I'm not your fucking asshole husbands!*" Jules's throat felt sore. "Can you just listen for five goddamn seconds?"

Silence.

"Hello?" Jules prodded. "Hello?"

She looked at the screen. It was her home screen. Vivian had disconnected.

"Oh no," Jules said, staring at the phone. "No, you did not just do that."

She redialed with a shaking finger. She wasn't surprised when she got sent straight to voicemail, but she was still incensed. "Hanging up in the middle of a conversation. *Real* mature. Maybe you're the one who just turned twenty-six!"

Then she ended the call and flopped back down on the couch, seething. She stared up at the ceiling, her vision swimming. Then she hopped up and prowled around the room while her mind whirled with a dozen things she wanted to say to Vivian and absolutely *would* the moment she got the chance. This was way too much to convey in a text. In fact...in fact—

Jules dialed again and got sent to voicemail again. "Okay," she said. "I am calm. I am reasonable. No. No, I am not. I have not been calm and reasonable since the day I met you, and I can't believe you hung up on me when I was trying to tell you something important, and I can't *believe* you called me Ms. Relationshi—oh, shit."

She ended the call again. So much for reasonable.

Jules sat back down on the couch, dropped her head down between her knees, and breathed deeply. After a few moments, she raised her head again and dialed Vivian's number.

"I'm calling you tomorrow," she said, enunciating very clearly so that Vivian's voicemail wouldn't miss a single word. "Stop freaking out and get some rest. I hope you sleep well. We are not breaking up. Good night."

That had to be the dumbest message she'd ever left on anybody's phone, including the drunk dial she'd made to her least favorite professor's office at three in the morning.

But she'd said what she wanted to say. So that was that.

Besides, Jules couldn't believe what had just happened. Maybe Simon was right and she'd been a doormat. Someone who'd said it was good enough to see her girlfriend once a week or less. She'd asked for crumbs. And Vivian hadn't even wanted to give that much.

No, Vivian did. She'd said she wanted to see Jules more often. She'd said she wanted to see Jules *every day*. That was exactly how Jules felt. So what was her problem?

In spite of her own injunction to Vivian, Jules couldn't stop freaking out. She definitely didn't get any sleep. She paced, muttered, tried to watch television, then paced some more. At two a.m., she left her apartment to pace the sidewalk outside for a change of scenery. Too bad the bagel place was closed.

At seven thirty a.m., after getting not a single minute of sleep, Jules showered, did her makeup, and headed for the subway to go to work. She was going to be absolutely useless today. The concert tonight would be torture. And while part of her hoped that Vivian felt like shit too, the greater part hoped that she'd calmed down and felt better because she didn't need to get so worked up right now with the baby and all.

God, Jules thought, slamming a sheaf of paper into the three-hole punch and pushing down viciously. *It must be love.*

Then five p.m. arrived. After hours of work, Jules was now staring at a sleeping laptop screen because she couldn't think of a single thing to do, say, or write that would be of use to anybody on the planet. Even her article refused to budge.

This was no good. Any of it. They had to do better than this. They had to be better than this. Because Vivian had been right when she'd made her offer to Jules in London: they suited each other. And Jules had been right last night: they were good together. When they were together.

The office was quiet. Jules picked up her phone with a shaking hand, though she didn't know if it was shaking from nerves or fatigue. She dialed Vivian's number.

And Vivian picked up.

"Hello?" she said. Her voice sounded thick and raspy.

Jules wondered if she'd been crying again and got a lump in her throat at the thought. "Are you okay?"

"What?"

"You sound sick. Are you okay?"

"No," Vivian said flatly. "You woke me up."

Jules looked at the clock to confirm that it was, in fact, five in the afternoon. "Why were you sleeping?"

"Because I didn't sleep well last night, and somebody told me to get some rest," Vivian said. "I took the afternoon off. How do you like that?"

Jules blinked, stunned. "I'm glad. I like that. But you're all right?"

"I'm sleepy," Vivian growled, "and I'm not in the mood for round two."

"Neither am I," Jules said. "I hate fighting with you."

"You certainly gave the opposite impression." Vivian made a grunting noise. Jules imagined her sitting up in bed. "Anyone who thinks *I* like laying down the law should meet you. It's an education."

Jules opened her mouth to deny it but said instead, "I had to say my thing. Now you know how I feel." She paused. "Don't you?"

"Yes," Vivian said. "I guess I do."

"Tell me, then," Jules said, suddenly very uneasy because she wasn't sure Vivian had heard the right message. "Tell me what I meant because maybe I didn't make it clear. You know. How I love you and want to see you more."

It sounded a lot simpler this afternoon than it had last night.

"Sounds like I don't need to tell you," Vivian said. "And you know how I feel."

"Yeah," Jules said. "You said you wish you could see me more. You said if you could see me every day, you would."

"Yes." Vivian sounded exhausted and sad. "I would. But, Julia—"

Jules opened her mouth and the words "What if we tried living together?" fell out of it.

Then Jules didn't say anything else.

Vivian didn't say anything either.

Jules kept not speaking, and so did Vivian, and they remained on the phone in silence for ten million years or something that felt like it.

Then Vivian said, "How's that, dear?"

CHAPTER 21

JULES COULD POSSIBLY HAVE APPROACHED this better.

She could have prepared. Taken notes. Maybe thrown together a spreadsheet, added market research, and presented Vivian with a portfolio to make her case.

The trouble was that the idea had been living in her subconscious this whole time. The minute it had popped into her conscious mind, she'd blurted it out. Now it was too late to take it back.

She bit her lip. "I guess that sounds unreasonable."

"That's an understatement," Vivian said tightly. But she didn't say *no*.

That might be worth holding on to while Jules processed this out loud. "I can't believe I'm saying this. I really can't. But I think we should try it." She took a deep breath. "I want to live with you. I want to see you every day, and there's no other way we can pull that off with things the way they are now."

"You have lost your mind."

"Probably," Jules said helplessly. "Do you have a better plan?"

"Yesterday you were saying we could see each other once a week, and now you want to live together?"

"I—"

"Do you know what the press would say?"

Again, not "no." Not "I don't want to."

"Maybe nothing," Jules said. "Why would they automatically assume I'm your girlfriend? This is a difficult time for you. I'm your friend, and you need somebody to help you out."

"You've got to be kidding," Vivian said.

"We could deny everything. I'm totally okay with lying about it for a little while. Anything that means we can just get on with it."

"Get *on* with it?"

"I like having dinner with you. I like being there. We pulled it off over Christmas, didn't we? And even during fashion week. Don't you think we can?"

"You want to live with me."

"Yeah. With you. And the baby, when she shows up. God, the baby. Vivian, of course I want to be there for that! You'll need me for that."

"Are you aware that we've been together for three months, Julia?"

"Well, it feels like a lot longer," Jules said, then closed her eyes in despair. "I mean—"

"I see."

Jules could just picture Vivian's left eyebrow climbing ever higher.

Vivian continued, "You think this will solve everything. Did you forget that I lived with my husbands as well? Don't blame me for comparing you to them," she added sharply. "What else am I supposed to do?"

"They wanted you to be a good little wife," Jules snapped. Well, she guessed that's what they'd wanted. "I don't. I don't want to be one either. But I'd see you in the morning, and I'd see you at night, and we'd at least try to come home for dinner, wouldn't we?"

"You want to live with me," Vivian said faintly. "You're serious."

All Jules could think to say to that was yes.

The more she thought about it, the less rational it sounded. And so far, doing the irrational thing had worked out pretty well for the two of them.

"You leave messes in the bathroom," Vivian said.

"I won't," Jules promised. "Not ever again."

"We'd be some kind of horrible lesbian cliché. And we're not even lesbians. Do you know what it's called? U-Haul syndrome."

"Not if we get professional movers," Jules said, then shut her eyes again. *Oh God.*

"Lovely. I can tell you're taking this seriously. You really think this is a good idea?"

"You're the one who convinced me we should be together in the first place," Jules reminded her. "Now it's my turn."

"Living together is different."

"I know. I lived with my ex-boyfriend. And my place is a lot smaller than yours."

"Oh, you lived with your ex? And you still broke up. Imagine that."

"Do you have a better idea?" Jules asked, about ready to tear her hair out from sheer frustration. "I'm open to one. Listen, I really can see why you wouldn't want me to live with you. It makes sense you wouldn't want me in your hair all the time."

Vivian valued her space and privacy. Really, it was a miracle she hadn't shut Jules down completely and declared the subject closed.

"No, that's not..." Vivian began. "That isn't a..."

Jules waited. When Vivian didn't continue, she asked, "That isn't a what?"

After a period of silence, one that felt far too long, Vivian said, "I guess we can give it a shot."

Her tone suggested another kind of shot. The sort a firing squad gave you.

"Give it a shot?" Jules repeated, hoping she'd misinterpreted.

"Yes, Julia, that's what I said. If this...invasion is what you need to feel secure in—"

"*Invasion?*" The world was starting to haze red. Okay, so Vivian didn't have to be thrilled about the idea, much less say yes, but she didn't have to think of Jules as a hostile occupying force either.

Jules didn't need the moon and stars—although they would have been nice—but she didn't want to move in with an unwilling Vivian. Who'd ever want to live with a partner under those conditions?

"If that's how you feel about it, never mind," she growled. "'Invasion'? Jesus, Vivian, come on. I won't force you into something you don't want."

"Force me? Wait. Are you walking it back?"

Just then Simon stepped out of his office. "Ready to go?"

Jules glanced at the time on her computer monitor. Shit! They had to head out. There would be an hour or so of schmoozing before the concert, and Simon wanted to be there for that.

"Sure thing!" Jules chirped at him. "Just let me grab my bag."

"*Julia,*" Vivian said in her ear.

Simon waited expectantly.

"Gotta go," Jules said, trying to sound casual. "We'll talk later, okay? Bye."

She had to forego the *I love you,* but Vivian would have heard Simon's voice in the background. Surely she'd understand.

Given the way Jules's phone rang immediately, Vivian might possibly not have understood.

Well…tough luck. Disappointment sat like a stone in Jules's stomach. Her solution might not have been the most logical one in the world, but at least she'd thought of something. Vivian didn't seem inclined to do that, and she was the best problem-solver Jules knew.

Just not when it came to this.

"What's going on?" Simon asked as they headed to the elevator. "Everything okay with the new warehouse coordinator?"

"Oh yeah," Jules said quickly, silencing her phone. "No worries. Everything is super great."

Maxwell Walker might not be much of a musician, but he was handsome, rich, and clearly into Simon. He'd also dressed for the occasion. Jules had never seen a billionaire in a ripped Manic Street Preachers T-shirt before, but there was a first time for everything.

She might be the wingman, but she hardly had to do any talking. Simon introduced her as his assistant; Maxwell shook her hand and then turned his attention back to Simon like a heat lamp.

"We've got a definite sound," he said, raising his voice enough to be heard over the clatter of roadies setting up the stage and guests arriving for the show. "Think Babybird, Strangelove, Ultrasound. That kind of thing." He scratched the back of his neck and looked a little sheepish. "Hard not to follow in the steps of the giants you listened to in high school."

Jules made a note of the band names. Judging by the blank expression on Simon's face while he nodded, they'd be looking them up the moment Maxwell left.

A man in his midfifties walked up to them, dressed fake casual in an unbuttoned plaid shirt and jeans that were clearly brand-new. "Max, buddy! Setup looks great! Listen, sorry to interrupt, but I was wondering if we could talk about—"

"Not now," Maxwell said, never taking his eyes off Simon.

The man looked surprised. "What if I said the words 'ten million dollars'?"

"I'd say come back when you've got ten times that, and we can talk after the show. Simon, I saw you at London back in February. I never got a chance to say hi, but…"

Simon looked like he might actually swoon.

Jules clearly wasn't needed here. She wanted to take out her phone and see if Vivian had texted her, but that would be rude, so she looked around instead.

The Cutting Room was half concert venue, half restaurant, filled with tables and chairs both on the ground floor and a balcony surrounding the main room. Side rooms filled with comfy-looking couches and chairs branched off. A curved bar, already well populated, swiped around the side of the room. A gigantic chandelier decorated with real guitars cast an orange glow over everything.

No room for a mosh pit. That was probably for the best.

Jules liked it a lot. She'd better enjoy it now because there was going to be a lot less time for this kind of thing after the baby came. This wasn't really Vivian's kind of place anyway.

Dammit. She'd meant to stop thinking about that for a little while.

"Who the hell is Babybird?"

Jules nearly jumped. She looked back to see Maxwell heading toward the stage, surrounded by hangers-on, while Simon leaned toward her anxiously. "Um—"

"Come on. I want a table at the front. Or would that be too obvious? I don't want him to think I'm desperate or anything."

In the end, they sat in the first row but not right in front of the stage. They also bent over Simon's phone, looking up the bands Maxwell had mentioned. Meanwhile, Jules's phone had to be burning a hole in her purse from how hard she was ignoring it.

"They were 1990s British indie," Simon groaned. "And he's not even British. I knew he couldn't be perfect."

"From what I've heard, there are twenty billion better things about him."

"And a great ass," Simon said dreamily. "Did you see how many people tried to come up to him while he was talking to me?"

Jules hadn't been paying nearly enough attention for that. She smiled and nodded anyway.

"He's into me. Maybe. I'm pretty sure? Oh boy, here we go."

The main lights went down, the stage lights came on, and Maxwell bounded onto the stage with more applause than new guitarists normally merited. After some quick introductions, the band crashed into its first song. It did indeed sound like a mishmash of 1990s British indie bands.

It wasn't Jules's favorite genre by a long shot, but she guessed it sounded okay for what it was. In the meantime, she looked at her phone.

Vivian had left her four voicemails. Four. Who did that? Evidently Vivian, too, felt that some things couldn't be expressed via text.

That might not be a good thing at all. Jules's stomach knotted. To hell with this concert anyway.

She touched Simon's shoulder and yelled in his ear, "I've got to step out for a second and call Keisha."

Simon nodded, never looking away from the stage.

Jules walked until she found one of the side rooms. People sat talking on the couches, but if she stood in the corner with the phone pressed to her ear, she could hear.

The first voicemail went:

"Pick up the phone, Julia. What the hell are you thinking, leaving the conversation like that? I said yes, didn't I? Isn't that what you wanted? Call me back immediately."

Jules scoffed loudly enough for a couple of the people on the couch to look at her.

Vivian thought that her reluctant yes was supposed to thrill Jules, was actually what Jules *wanted*. Meanwhile, Jules couldn't think of anything she wanted less.

The second voicemail had been left about ten minutes later.

"All right. I guess you're out at that...whatever with Simon. At least, that better be why you're not answering. Look, I understand that my agreement

might not have sounded wildly enthusiastic. It's just that this is very soon. It's quick. It's not that I'm—it's not that I don't want—" A heavy sigh. *"Just call me."*

Jules's heart sank. Talk about not being "wildly enthusiastic." Was Vivian saying no? She almost didn't want to play the next voicemail.

She did, though. It had been left fifteen minutes later and was almost a whole minute long.

"I'd already been thinking about it, you know. It's not like the idea never crossed my mind, although I'm sure you thought you were being incredibly original. But unlike you, I was giving it due consideration. I was—all right, that sounded a little harsh."

A little? Jules snorted.

"I didn't want to put too much pressure on you. As I said, this is very fast, and I know our situation is...complicated. But if it makes you feel better, then...then yes, I've missed you. More than you know. Of course I want to see you more often; of course I know it's only going to get harder. I know—"

A pause ensued, so long that Jules checked the phone to make sure it hadn't died in the middle of the message. Then the message continued.

"I just want to make sure you've thought this through because I have. I'm not trying to be condescending. I just—don't want you to regret it. I couldn't stand that. I said I'd make you happy, and I refuse to start by hustling you into a situation you're not ready for."

A situation Jules wasn't ready for? Like, say, getting into a romantic relationship with her pregnant boss, going from zero to sixty in two seconds? That seemed like a bigger deal than sharing a roof with someone. Was Vivian for real?

Maybe Vivian had realized how that sounded because, after another pause, her tone became wry.

"I mean, another situation. I want this to come from you, and I need you to mean it. Do you understand? Not something you just suggest off the top of your head because you're out of other ideas and you end up shocking the hell out of me. It should be something you've thought about, something you've chosen because you can't…because you can't imagine not choosing it, or…"

Fabric crinkled beneath Jules's fingers. That was probably because she'd grabbed her blouse over her heart and was clutching it for dear life.

Vivian cleared her throat.

"Anyway. That's what I'm asking for. Give it some thought, real thought, and if you change your mind, there's no need to bring it up again. But if you don't—if it is truly and honestly what you want—"

Jules's chest ached from holding her breath.

"Then yes. Yes, Julia. Come and live with me."

The voicemail ended. Jules looked at her screen. It was blurry. Oh shit. Did she have actual tears in her eyes? Was that why her face was hot and she was dizzy?

She blinked. Something wet streaked down her cheek. Yeah, those were tears.

There was a final voicemail. Jules pressed Play with a trembling finger.

"One more thing. If you do say yes, you're not bringing that god-awful sofa. My house isn't an IKEA."

Jules laughed so loudly and suddenly that everyone on the sofa turned to stare at her again. Their curiosity only made her laugh harder, and she waved wordlessly at them as she called Vivian back.

Vivian picked up on the first ring. She said only, "Well?"

"My sofa isn't IKEA," Jules said, "but I can live without it. Just as long as I don't have to live without you."

CHAPTER 22

"How can you have such a huge house with no extra room?"

"You make it sound cluttered, Julia. It's simply well put together."

"I'll say."

Jules had her hands on her hips as she looked around Vivian's bedroom and contemplated the next step.

As usual, Vivian was wasting no time. They'd agreed the day before to move in together. Now she and Jules had just spent the past forty-five minutes doing a walk-through of Vivian's carriage house. The end result was that Jules might be able to squeeze in her favorite puffy ottoman somewhere. *Maybe*.

"I'd like to find somewhere for my living room curtains," she said. "I made them myself."

"I, er, remember," Vivian said politely. "There's a bedroom on the top floor that doesn't see much use. I think they'd go with the color scheme in there."

Jules glared at her.

Vivian shrugged. "I'm giving you Robert's closet. Tell me you're not coming out ahead."

Jules bounced on her toes before she could help it.

Vivian saw and didn't bother to repress a smirk.

Robert's closet—no, *Jules's* closet—was a glorious cedar creation. A hallway ran through its middle, and a padded full-length bench rested at the end before a floor-to-ceiling mirror. There were seven shoe shelves alone. Ceiling speakers could pipe in music. Not that Jules needed it—she'd heard angels singing the moment she first stepped inside.

At the thought, she glanced at a place she had yet to enter: the double doors leading to Vivian's own closet.

"I'm not sure you're ready for that," Vivian said mildly.

"What, it's like looking into the Ark of the Covenant?"

"Something like that. But be my guest." Vivian strode to the doors, opened them with a flourish, and stood aside for Jules to enter.

Jules walked past her, holding her breath. Then it rushed out of her in a *whoosh*.

Vivian's closet, wallpapered in soothing shades of gray and white, didn't just have a hallway. It branched off into two side corridors at the end. Both sides of the hallway were lined with glass-fronted shelves, behind which sat an endless array of shoes and handbags. At the end of the hallway sat an island with a white marble counter and a silver mirror. The whole place was illuminated by lights placed as strategically as if they were highlighting museum exhibits.

Racks upon racks of designer clothing. Dozens of hooks for silk scarves. A whole station for jewelry and watches that could be rotated.

Jules turned down the left hallway, Vivian's tread soft on the Berber rug behind her. This seemed to be the intimates section: a rack with delicate robes and chemises and carved cabinets that held panties and bras. Rollout shelves held multiple sets of pajamas and slippers.

In the middle, incongruously, sat a high-backed chair of ornately dark carved wood. It was richly upholstered in red and gold and didn't match anything else in the space.

"The closet doesn't hold everything, of course," Vivian said casually.

"I know. I coordinated the rotations." Jules had been responsible for arranging the transport of Vivian's seasonal wardrobes from her home to an upscale storage unit. Yet even with that, the closet was a revelation.

Suddenly, music began to play: "Morning Mood" from Grieg's *Peer Gynt*.

Jules turned to see Vivian holding a remote in her hand.

"So what do you think?" she asked.

Jules wanted to say something smart-assed or pretend to be unimpressed. There was no point; her face had already given everything away. "I want to set up a church in here. Our Lady of Unbelievable Awesomeness. It's way bigger than your bedroom. I could get lost."

"You should have left a trail of breadcrumbs."

"I don't think we want the ants." Jules reached out to touch a silk chemise in a delicate shade of peach, trimmed in ivory lace. "Wow. I bet this looks amazing on you."

"Give me six more months and we'll see." Vivian's voice contained a speculative note in it.

Jules glanced at her curiously, only to see Vivian looking back at her with a gleam in her eyes. Jules had come to recognize that gleam well.

"What are you thinking?" Jules asked softly, still stroking her fingertips over the silk.

"That pretty piece won't fit me for a while, but I'd be curious to see it on you."

"Um…" Pre-pregnancy, Vivian had been thinner and less curvy than Jules. "I'm not sure it'd fit."

"There's only one way to find out."

Even though it was growing late—another night after they'd both been on the run all day—Jules found herself returning Vivian's interest with… well, interest. So while Vivian watched, she stripped down to her panties and shimmied the silk over her head, knowing Vivian could see the bounce of her breasts as she did so.

Those breasts strained against the front of the chemise, which had definitely been designed for someone more angular than Jules. The silk hugged the curves of Jules's hips as well and stretched tightly over her ass.

Vivian looked Jules up and down from the crown of her head to her toes. She didn't say anything. She didn't have to.

Jules's nipples hardened into peaks before her gaze, and a familiar ache began to pulse between her thighs.

"Like what you see?" Jules asked hoarsely.

"I see what you meant about church," Vivian murmured. She set the remote on a shelf, stepped forward, and stroked her fingers through Jules's hair. Then her hand drifted downward, her fingertips brushing Jules's cheek on the way to her bare throat. "I'm feeling reverent too."

Jules caught her hand. Then she kissed Vivian's palm, tasting the skin before taking one of Vivian's fingers in her mouth and sucking.

"Oh!" Vivian gasped.

"You're supposed to keep your hands to yourself in church," Jules said around her fingertip. She nipped gently, her eyes closed. Easier to savor that way. "So hands off."

Vivian's other hand brushed over Jules's hip, smoothing the silk there. "Uh-uh."

Jules opened her eyes to see Vivian's hot electric-blue eyes fixed unswervingly on her.

L'heure bleue, Jules thought. That mysterious time just between day and night when the sky begins to darken. When anything seems possible and nothing seems quite real. *My favorite hour.*

She took her mouth from Vivian's fingertip, pushed Vivian's other hand away, and stepped back.

Then she sat down on the carved chair while Vivian watched her, eyes still burning.

"I thought this chair didn't fit in here at first," she said, "but of course you'd have a throne lying around somewhere."

"It fits," Vivian said evenly. "You just have to have the right vision."

Jules arched forward slightly, pressing her chest out. The silk strained at her sides. "How's this vision working for you?"

"It's working very well. Let me tell you what I see. I see a beautiful woman playing at being queen, but the whole time I've got her right where I want her."

Jules stopped breathing.

Vivian stepped forward. The fire in her eyes spread outward until Jules saw her as a creature of heat alone. The air seemed to ripple around her.

"Open your legs," she told Jules.

As if of their own accord, Jules's thighs parted, showing Vivian her panties.

"Already a wet spot," Vivian observed.

"God," Jules gasped.

"I'm not allowed to touch?" Vivian asked. "Fine. You'll do it for me. Start with your breasts."

Jules's fingers were there before Vivian finished talking. She circled her nipples, hard through the silk, before stroking them. Her own touch sent a jolt through her, and she couldn't stop a little cry.

Vivian nodded. "Good. Very good."

"Now what?" Jules groaned.

"Now," Vivian said, "you take initiative."

Fuck, yes. Already Jules didn't want to wait. She slid her hands down her hips.

"So impatient." Vivian's voice was a lioness's purr. "That wet spot's growing by the second."

"Get a good look," Jules panted, "'cause you're not touching this tonight."

She slid her left hand beneath her panties' waistband. Vivian had done this to her too when she'd had Jules on the kitchen counter. The pressure had driven Jules wild, the way the fabric had forced Vivian's hand harder against her. Now she took advantage of it as she pushed a finger inside herself. Vivian had been right: she was already slick.

Vivian inhaled sharply through her nose.

"Oh, honey," Jules breathed. She slid another finger in and began to rock down on her own hand. Back and forth. Then faster. Then harder…

Vivian never looked away. She had Jules right where she wanted her, she'd said.

Vivian wants me here, Jules thought. *I'm going to live with her because she wants me here, because she loves me.*

That did it. Jules clenched, gasped, and cried out before Vivian's devouring stare.

As she relaxed in the chair—Vivian's throne—she sighed. Then she raised her fingers to her mouth.

Vivian moved more swiftly than should be possible for a woman in her condition. This time it was her turn to suck Jules's fingers, licking them clean.

"Wow," Jules whispered, "this living arrangement is off to a good start."

"Like they say"—Vivian bestowed a final kiss to Jules's fingertips—"begin as you mean to go on."

CHAPTER 23

EVERYTHING WAS SETTLED. WELL, ALMOST everything.

The movers were settled; luxury moving companies could move swiftly to accommodate the super-rich. The date was settled; Jules had asked for a day off and Simon hadn't asked questions. What wasn't settled was telling her current landlords about her plans.

That sort of thing was complicated when your landlords were also your parents.

Especially when those parents hated Vivian Carlisle, whom they'd once suspected of sexual harassment or worse.

Jules sat on her not-IKEA sofa, surrounded by boxes. She'd been packing all week, late into the night. It was mostly her clothes, books, and personal items. Habitat for Humanity was coming to get her furniture and kitchen stuff. After that, there would be some odds and ends to take care of but nothing huge.

She was taking a huge risk with this move. If it didn't work out, she'd be left with very little in terms of starting over. She'd have to move to an outer borough, find roommates, all while crying herself to sleep.

No, she told herself. *It won't be like that. This is going to work out.*

Jules looked at her tablet. She'd taken notes on what to say to her parents. Words could fail in a time like this. The last thing she wanted was to come up empty-handed when she tried to explain the inexplicable.

Her relationship with Vivian was something to be proud of. Still, the thought of telling her mom and dad about it made Jules want to crawl under her desk and hide. It would be even harder now that things between them were so serious.

What would her parents say? Would they argue, plead, or just yell? Come after Vivian with a sledgehammer? They probably wouldn't throw a housewarming party.

Jules supposed she was to blame. She'd sure laid it on thick, those first few months at *Du Jour*, about how unreasonably demanding Vivian was. Her stories had gotten even more hair-raising once she'd moved to being Vivian's assistant. Her parents had often disapproved, saying there was no need for anyone to be so tyrannical.

And then Vivian had gone and snatched Jules from her family's bosom during Christmas.

Her parents had thought Vivian was trying to seduce her. *Oh God.* Jules wanted to laugh hysterically. She imagined it wouldn't go over well if she told them she'd had to drag Vivian into bed inch by inch.

She and Vivian had discussed the matter a little over the past week. They'd gone through various strategies, including telling Jules's parents what they'd discussed telling the press: Jules was moving in just to help Vivian out. That idea hadn't lasted long, since Jules didn't want to lie and her parents weren't idiots.

In the end, Jules decided there was nothing for it but to tell the truth. Rip off the Band-Aid. Vivian had agreed wholeheartedly.

Jules suspected it was what Vivian had thought all along but that she'd wanted Jules to come to the same conclusion on her own.

No sense in putting it off. Jules reached for her phone with a sigh.

"You're moving?"

Jules couldn't blame her dad for sounding so surprised. There was no obvious reason for her to give up an apartment that she could never have afforded on her own.

"Yeah," she said. "I'm sorry for the last-minute notice. I know it's sudden. But I just want to say I'll—"

"Wait a minute, sweetheart."

Jules didn't wait a minute. "I'll clean the whole place top to bottom after I move out. And I'll reach out to your property manager about listing it right away. You won't have to worry about—"

"Jules, hold it. Why are you moving? Hey, Laura, come here—Jules is on the phone."

Jules suppressed a groan.

"Hello? Jules?" Her mom sounded alarmed. "Did your father just say you're moving? What's the matter? Is something wrong with the apartment?"

"No, everything's fine with it. It's great. I want to thank you for letting me stay there for so long, in fact. I know you missed out on a lot of money from renting it, which is why I want to take care of everything before I—"

"Why are you moving?" her mom asked. "Where are you going?"

Jules put her phone on speaker and placed it on the coffee table. That made it easier to push both her hands through her hair. "West Seventy-Third."

A brief silence. Then her dad said, "The Upper West Side?"

"Yep."

"Jules, what are you doing moving to the Upper West Side? How can you afford it?"

"You're moving in with someone," her mom said flatly.

Jules's stomach twisted.

"Why would she move in with someone?" her dad asked. "She's practically living for free in our place. Someone should move in with *her*, like Aaron did. Right?"

"Well, I don't know, Eric. I'd say Jules could explain it to us."

Sweat was gathering in Jules's palms and at the small of her back. "Um...well, yeah. I am moving in with somebody."

Her mom sighed heavily.

"Who's somebody?" her dad asked. "Is it someone you're, uh, romantically involved with? You haven't mentioned seeing anyone."

Jules's lips felt desiccated from nerves. She licked them. "No, I haven't. I'm sorry about that. I-I wish I'd mentioned it before now."

She really did. It had seemed impossible to tell her parents about her relationship with Vivian. Sometimes she'd longed to so that she could ask their advice about being a partner, a professional, and possibly a parent all at the same time. Most of the time, though, she'd been desperate to avoid their questions and judgments.

Those questions and judgments would have been easier if the bomb Jules was about to drop had been smaller.

"So it is romantic?" her dad pressed.

"Obviously," her mom said. "Jules, how long has this been going on? How long have you been with...whoever he is?"

"She," Jules said.

Another pause. Jules's heart was hammering so hard, she could feel it in her throat. *Just say it. Say it's Vivian. Just get it over with.*

"Is that why you didn't say anything?" Her father's voice was gentler now. "Sweetheart, you know we're not—you know we'd be supportive."

"Of course," her mother added. "We were fine when you dated the other girl, weren't we?"

If by "fine" you mean "well-intentioned and awkward," then yes, Jules supposed they'd been fine. "Yeah, you were okay. That's not the only reason I didn't tell you."

"Then what is it? You were afraid we'd disapprove of something else?"

Jules fixed her eyes on the candle she'd placed on the coffee table. She'd lit it so that a warm, comforting lavender aroma would float through the air. Now she kept her eyes on the dancing flame.

"It's complicated," she said. "I wanted to keep it private at first. I wanted to tell you too, but I didn't know how things were going to turn out. It just seemed better to sit on it until I knew where things stood." She licked her lips again. "Now I do."

"It sounds like it, if you're moving in together," her dad said.

"Tell us about her!" her mom chirped, clearly overcompensating for her earlier lack of enthusiasm.

"Well, she's...she's..." *She's an icon. She's a tyrant. She's a genius. She's probably the love of my life.*

"She's Vivian," Jules said.

Silence, sudden and absolute. Jules put her sweating palms on her thighs to ground herself.

Then her mom said, "Vivian who?"

Jules's breath rushed out of her all at once. She wheezed, "*What?*"

"You—you don't mean Vivian Carlisle, of course," her mother said with a wobbly laugh. "Your old boss. Isn't that silly? For a moment, I thought... It's just that you've never mentioned knowing anybody else named Vivian. But really—"

"Jules," her dad said, and nothing else.

The candle flame disappeared when Jules closed her eyes. "No, Mom. It's Vivian Carlisle. I've kept in touch with her since I got fired." *All kinds of touch.*

"What does that mean?" her mother whispered. "Jules, what does—it's not really romantic, then. Maybe I misunderstood. You became friends while you were working for her. So you're...moving in to help?"

"We did become friends." If only she knew the words, any words that would make this less horrible. No prepared script would do it. "Friends and—" She paused, swallowed, and started again. "Friends and more."

"No," her dad said. "No. Oh no."

"Dad—"

"I knew it," he said.

His voice had started to get the rough edge to it that Jules had only ever heard a few times during her childhood and youth. It had scared her far more than anything Vivian had ever managed. Because when her dad spoke like that, it wasn't like you'd just screwed up the coffee order. It was nuclear winter on the way.

"At Christmas," he continued. "I knew she was up to something like this."

"No," Jules said at once. "Nothing happened at Christmas, Dad. I'm serious. I told you it didn't."

"Then when?" her dad roared.

Jules rocked back against the sofa in shock at his raised voice.

"When did she go after you? It was while you still worked for her, wasn't it?"

"She didn't go after me," Jules said, her own voice climbing. "She didn't make me do anything. She's never done that."

"Jules," her mother moaned, "was this why you were fired?"

"No! That was Mark Tavio, not her."

"Was it because of her? Did he know about her and you? Does everybody know—" Her mother's voice cracked. "Does everybody know but us?"

"Nobody knows," Jules said, covering her eyes. "It has nothing to do with why I got fired. It has nothing to do with any of that. Mom, Dad, nobody knows, just..." *Don't say Simon.* "Just us."

"So when do people find out?" her dad demanded. "When you end up all over the tabloids and social media and your life is over? That's if taking care of her kid while she's off living the high life doesn't do it first."

"What? It's not like that," Jules snapped. "I'm not her babysitter. We hired a nanny, for Christ's sake."

"*We?*" her mom said.

"Yes. I was there. I was part of the hiring decision. We've had a lot of talks, and I'm part of the decisions. She's not my boss anymore."

"But you only got fired a couple of months ago," her dad said. "This predates that, doesn't it?"

This was why he had a successful law practice. He was a ruthless cross-examiner.

Jules took a deep breath. "Yes. We got together before I was fired."

"Jesus Christ, Jules."

"Can she get fired for that too, Eric?" her mom asked. "Not Jules, I mean...*her.*"

"She certainly should," her dad said grimly. "I'm guessing she thinks she's above the employee handbook. And she's probably right."

"*She's* got a name," Jules said between her teeth. "It's Viv—"

"Vivian Carlisle. Yes. I know it well. So do a lot of other people. Jules, I never cared about this kind of stuff until you worked in fashion, but I've read into it a few times now, and...she's famous, sweetie."

Jules waited for more. When it didn't come, she said incredulously, "I know that. Well, she's famous in fashion, anyway. She's not a movie star. The paparazzi don't mob her unless..." She trailed off.

Her mom picked up right away on what she'd been about to say. "Unless something happens. Like when she got pregnant. Or, say, when people learn she took up with her assistant who's young enough to be her daughter."

"Ew, Mom! I am not!" They were sixteen years apart. Yes, it was possible, but Vivian would have had to start pretty early.

"I looked her up on Wikipedia. She's forty-two. That's the same age as your aunt Mary."

Vivian didn't belong in the same category as Laura Moretti's youngest sister, who lived on the West Coast, raised Pomeranians, and smoked a pack a day.

"She's the same age as a lot of people, Mom," Jules said. "So am I."

"And her birthday's in October. Then she'll be forty-*three*."

"That's how it works," Jules agreed. "Listen, I get that you guys don't approve. Like I said, it's complicated."

"In some ways, it's very simple," her dad said. "And by that I mean it's a bad idea. Plain and simple."

"Dad…"

"I've got to be blunt. You have no idea what you're doing," he said. "No idea at all. She is using you, and you can't even see it, and we did not raise you to be *this stupid*."

"I'm not being stupid." Jules looked at her candle flame again. Best case scenario: it suddenly raged out of control and set the apartment on fire, giving her an excuse to escape this conversation. "She's not using me, and I know what I'm doing. It was my idea to move in with her. I've had to talk her into a lot of things."

"Oh yes," her mother said. "I just bet you did, Julia. Is that what she's got you thinking now? That it's all your idea?"

"No, it wasn't all my idea," Jules pleaded, "but part of it was. Mom, Dad, I'm not a puppet. Nobody's pulling my strings. We've worked this out together. We know it's going to be hard."

"No, you don't!" her mother cried. "Honey, you don't—"

"It's my fault you think she's awful. I've said some bad things about her, but she isn't—"

"You don't have any idea how hard it'll be. You're so young. Oh, my God."

"She's wonderful, Mom. Yeah, she can be difficult too, but it's really good. I'm happy with her, and I just want to make you understand!"

"Oh, I understand," her mother said. "I understand all right, and so does your father. I think we understand perfectly."

"No, you don't." Jules balled her free hand into a fist on her thigh. "She's the best thing that ever happened to me. I know it's crazy, but that doesn't mean it's wrong." She took a deep breath, trying to regain her calm. "I love her, and she loves me."

"So what does love look like?" her mother asked. "You show up everywhere on her arm? Everyone calling you a—*you* know what they'll call you."

"Laura," her dad said.

"I'm sorry, Eric, but Jules needs to admit this to herself. People are going to say awful things about her. Nobody will take her seriously as a writer or anything else. Is she ready for that? Or is she just going to be a dirty little secret?"

"You could ask me instead of him," Jules growled. "And yeah, people are going to say shi—crappy things. I'll deal with it. I don't have much choice if I want this. And I do want this. More than anything."

"Well, I can tell you've really thought this through."

"Okay." Jules's eyes stung. "I think this conversation has gone about as far as it can."

"Don't be childish, Jules."

"I'm not." But Jules felt very childish indeed when she dashed the back of her hand over her eyes and it came away wet. "But we're all getting upset, and when your parents talk about you as a gold digger, it's time to hang up."

"Don't twist my words," her mom snapped.

"Your mother did not call you that," her dad added. "That's unfair. We just don't want you to stick your head in the sand about what's happening."

Jules's phone pinged with a text. She leaned forward to see the screen. The flame of the candle flickered in the reflection.

Vivian had texted:

I hope it's going well.

"I wish," Jules muttered.

"What?" her mom said.

"Nothing." Jules sniffled. Hopefully, they couldn't hear it. "I've got to go. We'll talk later after we cool off."

"Jules, I am perfectly capable of cooling down and talking right now."

"Well, I'm not. Good night."

Jules stabbed the screen to end the call. The phone flashed back to the home screen where Vivian's text waited patiently for her.

A tear, singular and pitiful, rolled down Jules's cheek. Her chest ached. She replied:

Just got done. It wasn't great

She hadn't expected an instant response, but within moments, Vivian replied:

Are you all right?

I'll be ok. It was just hard. They didn't listen to me

This wasn't the kind of conversation Vivian liked to have over text. She'd call soon. Jules lacked the energy to do so herself.

Then Vivian texted:

I'd like to come over, if you're up for it.

Jules's eyebrows tried to climb all the way up to her hairline. She replied:

Isn't it too far?

How many times have you made the trip to my place? I'm at the office anyway. It's closer than my house.

Of course Vivian was at the office. Jules snorted.

Then yeah, I'd like to see you. When will you get here?

On my way.

It took roughly thirty minutes to get from the Koening Building to Jules's place. There was enough time to do a quick clean before Vivian got here.

Jules looked around at all the boxes, felt the sad weight of her bones, and thought, *Nope.* Instead, she flopped back onto the sofa Vivian hated and closed her eyes for a second.

At the end of that second, a sharp knock made her open her eyes again. She felt unusually fuzzy. She looked at her phone and saw that half an hour had passed.

There was another knock, followed by Vivian saying, "Julia."

"I'm here," Jules called. She rose and shuffled to the door, feeling weirdly out of it. The exhaustion of the last few months seemed to be catching up with her.

Or maybe it was just that she'd never had a conversation like that with her parents before, and she hadn't realized how it would knock her on her ass.

When she opened the door and Vivian's eyes widened, Jules realized she must look even shittier than she felt.

"Let me in," Vivian ordered before Jules could greet her. "Sit down, and I'll get you some water."

"Can I have something else?"

"I don't think alcohol is a good—"

Jules leaned in and got the closest hug she could manage with Vivian's belly in the way.

After a startled pause, Vivian's arms went around her too. She held Jules for a moment, and Jules ordered her tears to retreat.

"Thanks," she said thickly. "I needed that."

"And now you need to sit." Vivian's voice was gentle. "That awful couch is calling your name. Just give me a minute."

Jules waited obediently on the couch while Vivian moved around in the kitchen, opening and closing cabinets.

"You've packed up all your glassware," she called.

"I'm getting rid of it. I don't think you'll need my glassware, or pretty much anything else I have."

"Hmm. Let's see. Thank God you have some plastic cups."

The sound of running water. Now that Vivian was here and fussing over her, she felt better, like a warm hand had caressed her arms and soothed the goose bumps away.

Vivian gave Jules the water and sat on the couch with a groan. "Tell me everything."

Jules wasn't about to tell her everything, but she landed on the most salient points. She ended by saying, "And I was so upset that I had to hang up. I couldn't talk to them anymore."

"I'm sorry," Vivian said.

"Why? It's not your fault. It's mine."

"No, Julia, it's not mine, and it's not yours." Vivian sounded very firm on that. "Why does it have to be somebody's fault?"

Jules winced. "Well, when I started working for you, of course they wanted to hear all about you, and—"

"Ah." Vivian's lips quirked but she got them under control. "Say no more."

"Then there was Christmas. They thought you were—" Jules cut herself off, horrified at what she'd nearly confessed.

Vivian frowned. "Thought I was what? Selfishly stealing you away?" She gave a rueful chuckle. "Well, they were right."

It would be the worst idea ever to tell Vivian what Jules's parents had really feared. "They don't understand. They think I don't know how to make my own decisions."

"They think that?" Vivian rolled her eyes. "Have they met you?"

"Huh?"

"'Vivian, let's have sex. Tell me you love me. We need to live together. Don't forget to eat your breakfast—'"

Jules managed to smile. "Maybe I should have let you talk to them for me."

"No, thank you," Vivian said. "Julia, if your parents ever want to speak to me civilly, we can do that. But I've had more than my share of run-ins with evil in-laws."

Then she pinked.

Jules grinned—not so much at the term as at how Vivian was starting to look uncomfortable. "*In-laws*, huh?"

"It's just a phrase," Vivian said in exasperation.

"Slow down. I think we're moving a little fast here," Jules said, grinning harder and feeling much better.

"The parents of my *significant other*." Vivian rolled her eyes again. "There."

"Got it." Jules took a deep drink of water. "Thanks for making me laugh, anyway."

Vivian harrumphed.

Jules leaned in and rested her head on Vivian's shoulder. "You feel nice. I like the cashmere."

"My pregnancy's doing you a favor. Before I gained weight, my shoulders were like knives, I'm told."

"I'm sure they will be again," Jules said comfortingly.

"I can't stay the night. I managed to sleep on your mattress before, but it's not happening now."

Jules put her hand on Vivian's belly, stroking it up and down, mesmerized, as usual. There was a kid in there, one who would develop a personality, talents, and interests they couldn't imagine yet.

There was more to the world—more to Jules's life—than an argument with her parents. A lot more.

"Would you like to come back with me?" Vivian asked.

"I would." Jules had left enough things at the carriage house by now that she didn't have to trek back to her apartment before work. "I want to come back with you and stuff my face with that chocolate ice cream you keep pretending you don't have."

"I thought we had an unspoken agreement," Vivian said. "You pretend you don't see the ice cream, and I pretend not to notice that there's less of it every time you visit."

"I won't be visiting soon. I'll be living there. You'll be stuck with me."

She'd meant to sound light, carefree. Funny, even. Her voice wobbled on the final word.

Dammit.

Vivian looked around at all the boxes. Then she put an arm firmly around Jules's shoulders.

"That green velvet ottoman," she said, pointing with her free hand toward the furniture in question. "Isn't that your favorite piece?"

"Yeah, it was my grandma's." Jules was sad to see it go, but it wouldn't match Vivian's décor at all. Hopefully, it'd find a good home. "What about it?"

"The rug in the den has some green in it. It'll match well. We'll just swap it out with the white footstool."

Vivian's tone was businesslike, nearly brisk. She might have been telling a photographer what props to include in a photoshoot.

Even so, the tears Jules rubbed dry on Vivian's cashmere were happy ones.

CHAPTER 24

VERY EARLY ON SATURDAY, TWO burly men from Black Tie, White Glove Movers carried Jules's things into a truck, appearing amused that Jules had already packed all of it up. "We do stuff like that too, y'know," one of them said. "It's part of the job."

Her possessions huddled in one pitiful little corner of a vast truck; it was mainly clothes, books, knickknacks, and the ottoman. That was good. This wouldn't take long. Discretion meant that they had to be in and out as quickly as possible.

Thank goodness for what Vivian had said once about the neighbors being uninterested in her comings and goings. Besides, by the time the movers drove away, it was just creeping up on ten in the morning, and Jules doubted very much that enough people had been up and about to notice them.

Dear God. Jules Moretti, moving to West 73rd Street, just off Central Park. Who'd have thought it?

Had Vivian felt the same way when she'd arrived?

In spite of her excitement, Jules knew she'd miss her apartment. She'd lived there for years. It had been familiar when everything else in her life was up in the air. Now she was in for another big adjustment. She was over the moon about it, but that didn't mean it was easy.

She felt a little better when she began hanging up her clothes in her massive new closet. She felt better still when she unpacked her shoe collection.

Best of all was the feeling when she saw that Vivian had cleared out all three bookcases in Robert's old room. She could fill them with her own library. Her collection was modest in comparison to Vivian's, but there was something about having books that made the space feel more like her own.

She was nearly done by two o'clock and helped herself to a late lunch from Vivian's—*their*—fridge, still trying not to feel like an intruder. This was going to take getting used to. She might as well start working on that, and when she finished eating, she set off to explore the house.

Jules had seen more of the Carlisle home than most people had, but she'd never had the grand tour. It had felt rude just to walk around on her own. No longer.

The house seemed much bigger indoors than it did from outside. On the outside, it was a ritzy house that looked shorter than its neighbors, but once you got inside, it was like you'd walked into some alternate dimension where the rules of space did not apply. The place felt freaking huge.

There were three floors, plus a cellar. Jules had seen all of the ground floor at least: the foyer with its Lichtenstein painting, the kitchen where she and Vivian had shared so many meals, and, of course, her beloved den. The first floor had Jules and Vivian's bedroom, Robert's ex-bedroom, and a third bedroom that had been cleared out to serve as the nursery—which they really needed to get started on, all things considered.

Vivian's office held court on the second floor, along with another bedroom, two fabulous bathrooms with whirlpool tubs, and a media room with an enormous screen and stadium seating. The third floor seemed an afterthought with two more bedrooms, some storage space, plus a locked door that led up to the roof.

Jules was especially intrigued by the dumbwaiter. Nobody used it, but it was almost a hundred years old. Vivian hadn't bought a sleek new condo—she'd wanted a place with history.

The third floor was as immaculate as everything else in the house, but it was obvious that nobody had stayed in the bedrooms in a long time. In fact, the whole floor had an abandoned feeling about it, as if Vivian had never quite figured out what to do with it and had given up trying after she'd decorated it.

The ground floor, a more public space, featured photos of Vivian with various luminaries. There was also a prominent picture of her hard at work at her desk on her first day as editor in chief of *Du Jour*.

However, there were no family photographs anywhere. After what Vivian had told Jules about her birth family, that wasn't so surprising. Any photos of Robert were no doubt long gone. That absence spoke volumes. Vivian looked like a woman alone with a thriving career and nothing else.

Not anymore, Jules thought. *We're going to fix that.*

They might not hire a photographer to stage photos of the two of them, but she and Vivian were going to get some selfies and candids in here. To say nothing of when the baby arrived. Jules was going to go nuts taking pictures of her.

One way or another, this place was going to be hers too.

She already had an idea of where to start.

"I should have seen this coming," Vivian said.

"You sure should have." Jules carefully straightened her handmade rust-colored curtains. What had Vivian been so worried about? They looked just fine in the master bedroom.

"The original curtains were custom-made for this room in Italy."

"My family's Italian. And if you're worried about exclusivity, I promise nobody else in the world has a Jules Moretti creation in their house."

"I thought we were making life-altering decisions as a unit."

"Ha-ha." Jules sat down on the edge of the bed in relief. It might seem like a small, even petty, thing to someone else, but it would mean so much to open her eyes in this bedroom every day and see a piece of herself in it.

She said, "Well, all my stuff's here. I have to take care of cleaning and listing my old place, but other than that…it's done."

Even she could admit that sounded a little dramatic. Judging by Vivian's snort, she agreed. "Actually, it's just beginning."

"True. Hey, hold that thought." Jules stood up and whipped out her phone. "I want to commemorate the day I moved in."

"A selfie? Really?"

"Who else is going to take it? Say 'cheese.' One…two…"

"No," Vivian said.

"Oh, come on, I just want—where are you going?"

"Follow me. You might learn something."

A few minutes later, as they sat on the loveseat, Jules had to admit that Vivian was right to take the picture in the den. The light was better. And for a woman who never took selfies, she was excellent at it. Way better than Jules.

"Look at the camera," Vivian said in exasperation on the third attempt. "You keep looking at me, so your eyes are going the wrong way."

"Sorry," said Jules. She couldn't help it. Vivian was as mesmerizing on a selfie display as she was everywhere else. How could Jules not look at her?

She got it together and looked at the camera lens instead. It wouldn't do to look too goofy.

"*Thank* you," Vivian said and took another picture. Then she examined it and said, "Adequate."

It seemed more than adequate to Jules. The angle was perfect, and by the time Vivian had finished adjusting the colors and contrast, Jules could have sworn it was a professional job.

"You don't run fashion magazines for two decades without knowing how to take good photos." Vivian dropped the phone back into Jules's waiting palm. "We can do better, of course. Favour Adamu is a new photographer I've got my eye on. She's got a gift for portraiture and could use a boost to her portfolio. We could schedule something."

The look she turned on Jules then was serenely curious as she waited for a response.

Is Vivian ready for that? Jules's mother had asked only days ago, referring to Jules's coming out as Vivian's lover. *Or am I just going to be a dirty little secret?*

"Her portfolio," Jules said carefully, "which I'm assuming is public."

"You assume correctly. Julia, I know these are big changes for you, and they're about to get bigger." Vivian rested a hand on her belly. "I don't want to rush you. I'm willing to push the story that you're just here to help me. But I can't promise how long people will believe it, and it's better to control your narrative instead of letting others do it for you."

"Yeah, I know." Jules propped her elbows on her knees and looked moodily at the Berber rug. Vivian had been right: the green accents did match the ottoman. "I want to come out, Vivian. I'm not ashamed of us. It's just a lot."

"It is," Vivian agreed. "Cruel things will be said. I'm used to them."

Are you? Jules wondered.

"But you're not," Vivian continued. "You've got to build up walls against them. The only thing that'll do it is time."

Walls. Vivian had so many walls that no siege could be long enough to knock them down. That was what it took to protect herself from public opinion?

You didn't go to those lengths when you were inured to something and didn't care anymore. Vivian's self-confidence was magnificent to behold, but even she couldn't be totally immune to that kind of cruelty. It must be impossible to get used to it.

Jules gave Vivian a sidelong glance. It was time to tell her about something. She'd waited too long already.

"My mom said nobody would take me seriously as a writer once we came out," she said, "because everyone would assume I only got published because of you."

Vivian's expression closed. "You've said the same thing yourself. That's something else we can't do anything about. You'll just have to prepare yourself for it and get on with your career anyway."

"I've already started." Jules shifted on the couch. "I'm working on an essay for a collection about queerness in fashion. All the submissions are anonymous, so nobody will know it's me."

Vivian looked surprised. "Really? I know the collection you're talking about. Why didn't you mention it to me?"

Jules stared at her. "Why didn't *you* mention it to *me* if you knew about it?"

"Because you didn't want me interfering in your writing career again. That's why."

Fair enough. "Well, Allie told me about it. I want to submit the essay this week. I meant to be done by now, but, well"—she gestured at her surroundings—"life and everything. I know it's a long shot that it'll be accepted, but if it is, that's definitely something that's all mine."

"It's not the worst idea," Vivian agreed. "All right. Let me know if you want help with the writing. I'll stay out of it otherwise."

"Thanks," Jules said in relief. Vivian wasn't offended, obviously. It was unlikely that she'd have time to help with the writing, though, if Jules wanted to submit it in the next few days.

"As to the other thing," Vivian continued, "us going public, that is, are you busy on Memorial Day?"

"Um, no. But aren't you going to Rhode Island for that fancy boat race?"

"The Annual Regatta, yes. From the New York Yacht Club. It's three days long, but I refuse to put myself through that. Still, Stan Oppenheimer and Geoffrey Barnhardt are co-captaining a boat, and if they don't win, they'll be completely insufferable."

"I hope they win, then. But what does that have to do with me?"

Vivian just gave her a long look.

Jules's fingertips began to tingle. Her head buzzed. Was that a sign of stroke?

"You're inviting me?" she asked numbly.

"It's just a thought." Vivian's look never swerved from Jules's face. "A way for us to dip our toes in the water, no pun intended. You'd fly up with me on Monday afternoon, we'd stay for the celebratory dinner, then fly back."

Jules had taken short flights with Vivian on private planes before. Never as a guest, though. Never as a…date.

Vivian continued, "There are no paparazzi at this event. It's about the establishment, not celebrities, so there's little public interest. Somebody might film us on their phone, of course."

"Of course. Right." Jules's head spun. Was this really happening? Were they actually talking about coming out?

This was a million miles ahead of coming out to the nanny. Vivian wanted Jules on her arm in front of the establishment—in front of the whole world.

"What do you think?" Vivian asked. "I won't pretend it's without pressure, but it's no fashion week or a movie premiere. But I'm not—" She cleared her throat. "I'm not making all the decisions. I won't push you to do anything you're not ready for. We can wait. Or maybe you have a different idea."

Jules had never been to a regatta. What did you wear? How did you talk to people? She didn't know anything about yachts.

"You don't have to answer me now," Vivian added. "Google the event. See what you think about it."

"Do I have to get on a boat?" Jules asked. "Because I get seasick. That's my only objection."

Vivian's breath caught. Her hands clenched on her lap. She sent Jules a look that said, *Be very certain.*

Jules sent one right back that said *I am.*

She was—more than she would have believed even an hour ago. Perhaps because the matter wasn't speculative anymore.

Vivian wasn't talking about coming out as a regrettable inevitability. She had a plan. It involved introducing Jules to some of the most powerful people in her own social circle as her equal. More than that: as someone she loved.

Besides, even if Page Six somehow found out and tore Jules apart, it couldn't be worse than her own parents saying the same thing.

"I know we're in for some hard stuff," Jules said. "Maybe I'd just like to see you kick ass at this too."

Surprise flashed across Vivian's face. Moments later, undeniable pleasure followed. Her mouth widened into a smile that made Jules think of sharks circling a ship.

"You know me, Julia," she said. "I never disappoint."

CHAPTER 25

As an assistant, Jules had attended a lot of fancy events with Vivian. At first, of course, it had been in a purely official capacity. Then there had been a couple of strange hybrids of professional and personal: Christmas Day at the Ritz, the New Year's Eve ball, and, of course, the destruction of Mark Tavio.

This was the first time she'd ever been somewhere with Vivian purely as her guest. It was just the two of them too. Vivian had declined to bring Evan, her new assistant, the one she'd hired to replace Allie and whom she described as "not a huge disappointment." Instead, Jules alone hovered at her side and tried to look like she belonged.

It should have been easier; she was used to being at Vivian's side. It *looked* the same. But it wasn't.

The Annual Regatta was the highlight of the year for the New York Yacht Club. Every summer, the city's elite arrived in Newport for three days of boat races. From what Jules could tell, the racing wasn't really the point unless you were actually *in* the race, in which case it was your reason for living. For most people, the point was—as always—the schmoozing.

Jules had developed decent schmoozing skills as an assistant. That was different. That was professional; people expected and respected the hustle. In an environment like this, you had to pretend you weren't doing it, all while wearing a dainty dress and cutesy hat.

Jules adjusted her cutesy hat for what felt like the millionth time. She had to; it was windy.

She and Vivian stood beneath a large white tent on the grounds outside the Harbour Court clubhouse that overlooked Brenton Cove. Guests milled around them, the women in cocktail dresses and the men in sports coats, going to and from the bar and dining on hors d'oeuvres.

The clubhouse had begun life as a mansion in the Gilded Age, when America's newly wealthy families built houses like those of the European dynasties from whom they claimed descent. Now it served as the home base of the yacht club as well as the venue for tonight's gala dinner.

And a place where I feel like an alien, Jules thought. She took a long sip of her champagne.

"George," Vivian said, reaching out to shake some guy's hand. He was portly and balding.

Once Jules had known the highflyers Vivian interacted with. They'd been fashion people. Not here. In her new position, Vivian had to broaden her audience. Today that audience included bankers who owned yachts and who'd rather talk about the stock market than Shiseido.

So Jules looked on, mystified, as Vivian greeted George like an old friend and he shook her hand heartily in return.

"Vivian! Great to see you in person!" he said. "After a dozen conference calls, it feels like I know you."

Vivian kept smiling, although George's presumptuousness surely curdled her stomach. "It's nice to see you too. And this is…?"

George turned to the willowy blonde on his arm. She seemed to be in her early thirties to his late sixties and had a painfully wide smile. Her teeth were so white that Jules adjusted her sunglasses.

"This is my wife, Kyra," George said. "She's been dying to meet you."

"I'm the biggest fan of *Du Jour*," Kyra said eagerly, holding her Louis Vuitton clutch to her chest. "I've read that magazine since I was a kid. When George said you'd be here, I said I'd kill him if he didn't introduce us." She stepped back and struck a pose. "Recognize the dress?"

"Of course," Vivian said. "Monique Lhuillier, the March issue. Lovely."

"Oh, my God! I'm so glad you like it." Kyra clapped her hands and bounced on her toes, which was risky, considering her four-inch heels. "That means, like, the world. Seriously! I can't wait to post on Insta that Vivian Carlisle liked my look."

"Be my guest," Vivian said with a layer of sugar over the scorn.

"Well, best to get going, sweetie," George said, looking at his empty beer bottle. "We don't want to bother Vivian."

Kyra looked crestfallen but said, "It was *so* nice to meet you. We'll totally have you over to the house sometime. I've just redecorated."

"I hope you enjoyed the races," George said, glancing away and smiling at another couple.

"We didn't go to the races," Vivian said slowly. She looked at George and Kyra, then at Jules, then back at George and Kyra. Her brow wrinkled. "I couldn't fit them into my schedule, unfortunately."

"Oh, that's too bad. I hear your guys won. Enjoy the dinner, anyhow—it should start any minute."

"Before you go," Vivian said, "let *me* introduce Julia."

Jules's heart stopped. The first introduction of the night. The first introduction *ever*.

Both George and Kyra looked a little stymied. Then George said, "Oh, okay. Your assistant, right?"

Vivian glanced at Jules, giving her an unmistakable way out. A last chance for Jules to change her mind.

Jules held her breath and nodded her permission.

Vivian turned back to George and Kyra. "No," she said. "My girlfriend." The words were out.

Maybe Jules's heart would never start again. She couldn't bear the suspense. What would happen now? A raised eyebrow? A sneer? Gossip spreading like wildfire throughout the tent?

"Oh, okay!" Kyra said, flashing a smile at Jules.

George shook Jules's hand. "Nice to meet you too. Sorry. We thought you were just a... Well, anyway, it's nice to meet you, Julia."

Nearly too stunned to speak, Jules said, "Thanks. You too."

Was that all there was to it? It couldn't be. Was it really?

"These things are always so boring when you're alone," Kyra said confidingly to Vivian. "Before I met George, I went everywhere with my girlfriends too. Bye-ee!"

Jules opened her mouth, but they'd already turned to go and were disappearing into the crowd.

Vivian turned to Jules. For the first time since Jules had known her, she had a completely flabbergasted look on her face.

Before she could stop herself, Jules laughed. Talk about an anticlimax. "Oh boy."

"Was that unclear?" For once, Vivian didn't sound sarcastic or impatient. She seemed genuinely confused.

"Apparently."

"I don't understand. Who talks about their friends as their *girlfriends?*"

"Women do it all the time," Jules said in surprise.

Vivian glared at Jules. "Not the women I know."

"That's because nobody in the fashion industry wears straight goggles. You're mingling with civilians now."

"But it's so...infantile." Vivian looked around with a blistering stare as if the New York Yacht Club was wholly to blame for heterosexuality. "Now what am I supposed to call you? My partner?" Her lip curled as if the notion was too prosaic for words.

"How about your piece of ass?" Jules suggested.

"Julia," Vivian said reprovingly, but her lips twitched.

"Your number-one babe."

"No." Vivian turned and headed for the bar.

Jules accompanied her. "Your hottie."

"Not that either."

They reached the bar. The bartender smiled at Vivian. "Good evening, ma'am. What can I get for you?"

"Perrier."

"Sure thing. Anything for your friend?"

"Oh, she's not my friend," Vivian said. "She's my pain in the neck."

"The old ball and chain," Jules said with a straight face.

He shrugged and smiled. "Okay. Anything for you?"

Before Jules could ask for a vodka on the rocks, hold the rocks, a bell rang. The summons to dinner.

"Hmm," Vivian said. "What if we—"

She placed a hand on Jules's back and gave her an inquisitive look.

Even here like this, Vivian's touch sent a ripple of heat through Jules. Jules couldn't repress a shiver. She managed, "Sure. Yeah. That might work."

But as they proceeded into the dining hall amidst the throng, nobody seemed to notice. They simply parted before Vivian like an upper-crust Red Sea, giving her obsequious smiles.

"I think it looks like you're just guiding me," Jules said as they approached their table. "Maybe if we'd held hands?"

"Or linked arms. Too late now." Vivian nodded toward the people sitting at their table. "Well, we can at least make it unambiguous with *them*."

"They" were Geoffrey and Tilda Barnhardt, plus Stan Oppenheimer and a beautiful woman who looked about ten years his junior.

Everyone rose when Vivian and Jules approached. Looking at them, Jules felt a sense of déjà vu: it was way too much like the night Vivian had unseated Mark Tavio. Still, better than sitting with complete strangers for an occasion like this. Or with George and Kyra.

"Vivian!" Geoffrey said as they reached their seats. "You look fantastic."

Vivian did. In deference to the written dress code, she was wearing a cocktail dress. In defiance of the unwritten dress code, it was neither summery nor romantic. When surrounded by a sea of florals and ruffles, she wore a glittering black Chanel sheath that clung to her rounded stomach, topped off by an emerald-green bolero jacket. A black Merve Bayindir fascinator perched at her temple, contrasting elegantly with her short blonde hair.

Meanwhile, Jules was in a ruffled floral Vince Camuto dress and floppy hat, but at least she felt really cute in them.

"Thank you, Geoffrey." Vivian allowed him to pull out her chair for her and sat down with a tiny groan she couldn't hide. "I hear congratulations are in order."

"We won the around-the-island race!" Stan proclaimed, lifting his water glass. "Broke the record! Well, almost."

"How are you feeling, Vivian?" Tilda asked.

Geoffrey returned to his seat, leaving Jules to pull out her own chair. Yet again, nobody had looked at her or acknowledged her. She sat down, repressing a growl of exasperation.

"Never better, actually." Vivian glanced at Jules. "I—"

Before she could continue, Stan Oppenheimer placed his hand on his companion's back. "Vivian, I don't believe you know my date, Aliyah. She's just moved to New York from Boston."

Aliyah was a slim Black woman with a cloud of natural hair. If anybody felt more out of place in this crowd than Jules, it had to be her. Nevertheless, her smile seemed unforced and gracious. "It's nice to meet you, Vivian. I've heard so much about you."

"A pleasure," Vivian said politely. "And what do you do?"

"I was just hired as a senior analyst at MetLife. Stan and I met over talks about restructuring Koening's insurance plans."

"Wonderful. This is Julia," Vivian said, turning to Jules and placing a hand on her shoulder. "She's *my* date."

Jules held her breath.

"Just like at that wonderful dinner, I see," Tilda said, smiling at Jules. "She must be a big help to you if you brought her back for round two."

Vivian's expression was a study in disbelief.

It wouldn't do to laugh. It wouldn't do at all. Keeping herself under control, Jules said, "I'm actually—"

"Geoffrey!" Stan said. "Tell Vivian about that final leg of the race! You were an absolute monster at the helm."

"Oh. Well." Geoffrey shrugged modestly. "The wind was at our back, so—"

"Julia is my significant other," Vivian said. "In fact, she just moved in with me. She is not my assistant, and we are not platonic friends."

Silence fell. Tilda Barnhardt's water glass stopped about halfway to her mouth.

"I just wanted to clear that up," Vivian added. She put her hand over Jules's on the table. "Since you interrupted Julia before she could explain. Now, Geoffrey, what were you saying about the wind?"

"I, er..." Geoffrey looked back and forth between Jules and Vivian. "Well, it was—"

The server stopped at their table. "Good evening, ladies and gentlemen. May I describe our wine offerings?"

Everyone mumbled agreements that sounded far too relieved.

Jules was very grateful for Vivian's hand over hers. It kept it from trembling. She couldn't do anything about the hand she kept fisted in her lap under the table.

When the server departed, Stan leaned in. The pause had apparently been enough for the awkwardness to dissipate.

"Just checking," he said, "but, Vivian, are you joking?"

Jules's hand clenched harder in her lap.

"I'm not," Vivian said coldly. "What kind of question is that?"

"No, no. It's just that you never mentioned…" Stan looked at Jules and then at Vivian's belly, as if he couldn't decide whether to bring up the gender thing, the former assistant thing, or the pregnancy thing first.

"Of course I didn't. It puts us both in a vulnerable position, especially Julia. We wanted to wait until we were more secure."

"Hmm. I can understand that." Tilda looked far less rattled than either man at the table. Coolest of all was Aliyah, who had no skin in the game and merely watched the proceedings with obvious interest.

"So you're coming out?" Tilda added. "Officially?"

"Trying to," Jules said. She'd get herself into this conversation come hell or high water. "It's been weirdly difficult."

"How so?" asked Geoffrey, clearly getting his bearings.

"Well, we were just talking to this couple, George and Kyra…"

Jules drew on her skills as a writer in telling the story: emphasizing the humor without mocking anyone, hitting the beats as if she were leading up to a punchline. By the time she finished, everyone was chuckling and the tension had ramped down.

Vivian gave her a small proud smile when she was done.

"Our son's double-majoring in gender studies along with business," Tilda said casually as two servers set down their wine. "It's really helped him as he's transitioned. Hasn't he mentioned something like this, Geoffrey? What Jules just described?"

Geoffrey looked thoughtful. "Oh yeah. Before, um, *he* transitioned, he was dating a girl who also looked, you know, feminine and everything. Said everybody seemed deliberately to ignore them as a couple."

"There's a term for it," Tilda said. "He sent me an article, but I can't remember. It started with 'hetero.'"

"Heteronormativity?" Aliyah suggested.

Stan looked at her in obvious surprise.

Tilda snapped her fingers. "That's what he called it! The idea that being straight is the default."

"But it is, isn't it?" Stan asked. "I mean in terms of numbers."

Jules and Vivian gave each other a wide-eyed look.

"It's more than that," Aliyah said. "Just look at what's happening to Vivian and Jules. That's twice they've tried to come out, and nobody's even listening."

"Ridiculous," Geoffrey agreed.

"I'm open to ideas," Vivian said dryly.

Four faces looked apologetically back at her and Jules.

"What are we supposed to do?" Vivian continued. "Make an announcement in front of everyone, or just make out at the table?"

Jules's face flamed.

"Well—I hate to ruin the surprise—but you *are* going to be asked to present the cup to me and Geoffrey," Stan said. "Maybe then? Kidding, kidding."

"I sure hope so," Vivian replied.

This conversation was making Jules's head spin. She'd expected judgment or questions about their relationship, or at least awkward silence and changing the subject. Not whatever this was. Strategy?

Then she realized that was exactly right. These were Koening's new top executives, and they were pulling together to shape the narrative for the company.

Tilda confirmed Jules's suspicions when she tapped the table and said, "We need something unambiguous but tasteful."

"And official," Aliyah suggested, "since people aren't picking up on cues they normally would."

"Official. Hmm." Vivian glanced at Jules, and a lightbulb seemed to go on over her head. She leaned into Jules's side and murmured, "What would you think about giving an interview?"

"An interview?" Jules squeaked. Unfortunately, she did it loudly enough for the rest of the table to hear.

"Oh, that's a good idea," Geoffrey said. "God knows we've got the outlets for it."

"Easy to make sure they ask just the right questions," Tilda added. "There could be—"

"What do *you* think?" Vivian repeated, never looking away from Jules.

"I-I don't know." Jules twisted her linen napkin in her lap and tried not to sound horribly young and lost. "It seems a little artificial."

"Well, the natural approach isn't exactly working," Stan pointed out.

That was true. The Barnhardts were also correct about Koening publications asking the right questions. Controlling the story from the word go.

"It'd be one of Vivian's own magazines?" she asked.

"What else?" Geoffrey said. "It'd let us get out ahead of this before it becomes a PR disaster."

Vivian bristled.

"Sorry," he said, "but it's the truth. We all know it."

Suddenly, Simon's warning rang in Jules's ears. The one about how this could tank Adrian & Jo if word got out because people would call Vivian a predator and Simon would be tainted by association. The same would be true of the whole Koening group.

Vivian and Jules should have thought of that. Well, Jules should have. Vivian had focused only on the impact to her and Jules as individuals because she'd spent so long stepping on anyone who got in her way professionally. It had clearly never occurred to her to care about company image, since her own image had been victim to the media for so long. What was one more attack if it got her what she wanted?

"Geoffrey—" Vivian began.

"He's right," Jules said quietly.

Vivian frowned at her.

"This could look bad," Jules said, "beyond what you and I were talking about earlier. Maybe we should be a little more, uh, deliberate about how we frame things."

"Think of the clicks too," Stan said. "Traffic would go through the roof. Er, not that that would be the primary consideration."

"Not that it would," Vivian said dryly. "I don't know that any of our imprints are a natural fit for this, though. It'd seem forced, as if we're only doing it for a circulation bump. That might be worse than not doing it at all."

Aliyah leaned forward, propping herself on her elbows. Once this was over, Jules was definitely asking her where she'd gotten that blue kimono-sleeve dress.

"I don't know if you want to make this the focus," she said, "but what about a queer masthead like *The Advocate*?"

"That's not the focus," Vivian said firmly. "Not for me, anyway. I'm not out to make a political or social statement. Besides, Julia's the only woman I've ever been interested in."

"People might like that, you know," Stan offered. "It sounds romantic."

"That's…because it is?" Jules glanced at Vivian. "But we're two women having a relationship, which *is* queer."

"Yes," Vivian replied. "So what? I still don't want to slap a sticker on my forehead announcing my sexuality. It's nobody's business, and I've got no interest in summing up our relationship with one adjective."

Jules stared at her. Well, that was…direct.

Vivian looked back and shrugged. "What? I don't use labels. I wear them. I'd never speak for you, but—Tilda, what are you doing?"

"Taking notes." Tilda's fingers flew over her phone screen. "'Don't use… labels…wear them.' That's a good sound bite. We should remember it."

"You have *absolutely* been waiting to say that," Jules told Vivian.

Vivian replied only with a modest smile.

CHAPTER 26

"This is ridiculous." Vivian slapped Jules's phone back in her palm with unnecessary force.

"Agreed." Jules looked back down at the Instagram post. A quick search had found an account for Kyra Jenkins, the socialite she and Vivian had met the night before. Kyra had taken a picture of herself in the ladies' room of the Harbour Court Club and captioned it:

OMG. You'd never believed who loved this dress... #VivianCarlisle herself. TOTAL ICON. I only wish I'd gotten a selfie w/ her!! You'll just have to take my word for it!!!! She looked amazing & was there w/ a girlfriend as her "date"... I love when women prove they don't need a man to have a good time, stay strong Vivian!!! #OOTD #DuJour #Feminism

"The comments aren't much better." Jules laid her phone on the nightstand and tried not to laugh at Vivian's disgusted expression. "At least she's right that we don't need a man to have fun."

"The first time I *breathed* near Robert in public, everyone speculated on when we'd get married." Vivian walked—no, stomped—over to the bed and lay down, propping her back up against a stack of pillows with a groan.

"It's infuriating, but I still think we should stick to the plan." Jules turned off the overhead lights, leaving Vivian illuminated by one lamp that cast its glow over the bedroom.

"I know," Vivian growled. "And we will."

The plan had been concocted in painstaking detail during and after the Annual Regatta dinner. Jules, always a big fan of having a schedule, approved wholeheartedly.

For starters, she and Vivian had agreed—weirdly enough—*not* to come out right away. By the end of the night, Vivian had been swaying in exhaustion, and Jules had gotten her to admit that she could do without another media storm for a while.

In lieu of that, they'd agreed to do an interview a few months after the baby was born. Life would hardly be peaceful and quiet, but at least by then they'd have adjusted to the new routine and have time to enjoy being together before public opinion blew up in their faces.

In the meantime, Jules would lay relatively low, and further public appearances would be kept to a minimum. As Tilda had put it, "It doesn't mean you can't go out to dinner once in a while, but hold off on the red carpet."

"Well, of course," Vivian had said sourly. "Who'd look twice at two girlfriends having dinner together?"

There were contingency plans in case the truth got out before they were ready to go public: PR spin doctors to call, scripts to trot out, lies to tell ("Vivian never *once* expressed interest in me while we worked together"). But for now, rather than a grand gesture, rest seemed called for.

Looking at the gray tinge beneath Vivian's cheeks, Jules could only think it was the right decision. Good thing their original plan had gone awry. What would tonight be like if the press was camped out on their doorstep instead of leaving them in peace?

She stood over the bed and looked down at Vivian. "Want some water?"

"Not enough to get up six times tonight instead of five. Ugh. Tell me something good."

"Er, are you quoting Chaka Khan, or is that a request?"

Vivian covered her eyes with a hand and sighed. "Stevie Wonder wrote that song, and yes, it's a request. I feel like a lead balloon, my feet are killing me, and people are idiots. Please tell me something to make me less homicidal."

"My article in *Modernity* comes out on Wednesday," Jules offered.

It had the hoped-for result. Vivian looked back at Jules and smiled in pleasure. "That's right. We'll have to celebrate."

"Yeah." Jules didn't ask *how* or suggest going out to dinner since that would just remind Vivian of heteronormativity all over again. Instead, she sat down on her side of the bed. "I get why you have a king-sized mattress, but I feel totally lost at sea. It's like the Boston Marathon just to get next to you."

"At least one of us is getting a workout. But if you really want to get close, I have a suggestion."

That couldn't have been innuendo, not with how exhausted Vivian looked tonight. "Yeah? What?"

"Look in the drawer of your nightstand."

Jules did and laughed when she saw a bottle of massage oil with a French label. "I can take a hint. This looks like good stuff."

"You wouldn't believe," Vivian said dreamily. "You gave me a foot rub once. I need an encore."

Jules wondered if she'd tried to rub it on herself before she remembered that Vivian couldn't even see her feet now, much less touch them. She felt a surprising pang of jealousy: who exactly had helped Vivian discover this unbelievable oil?

"My pedicurist recommended it," Vivian added, and Jules instantly felt ridiculous. "She's incredible. Well?"

"Let me get a towel." Jules hurried to the bathroom. She didn't want to get oil all over her own pajamas or on Vivian's sheets, which probably had a ten thousand thread count or something.

She returned with a towel, laid it over her lap, rubbed the oil between her palms, and set to work on Vivian's left foot.

"Mm," Vivian groaned. "Maybe you're incredible too."

"No maybe about it," Jules said and squeezed. "This is good for you."

"Good for *me*? You're smarter than that. Five more minutes of this, and you know I'll give you anything you want."

Really? Huh. So five minutes later, Jules said, "You know what I want? Let me split the utilities."

Vivian, who had shut her eyes in ecstasy, cracked one open. "What? Why?"

Jules rolled her eyes. "Why not? I'm not asking to pay rent or anything"—few things would have insulted Vivian more—"but I should contribute something to the house."

221

"Oh, don't be ridiculous," Vivian said.

"I want to. I mean it."

Vivian closed her eyes again. "Whatever helps you sleep at night. I can't help noticing that your hands have slowed."

Chuckling, Jules resumed the massage. About ten minutes later, she'd worked Vivian's legs from calf to toes, and her hands were starting to cramp. "Okay. Fifteen minutes. I'm done."

"No," Vivian protested. Whined, almost.

"Yes," Jules said firmly, wiping her hands on the towel. "My hands hurt. And I'm pretty sure all the muscles in your legs are like boiled pasta by now."

"True," Vivian admitted. She flexed her toes and looked every bit as happy as she did after sex.

Jules swallowed hard.

Then Vivian looked at Jules, and Jules started to sweat.

"Come here," Vivian said.

"But you're not feeling—"

"Come here," Vivian repeated, stretching out one arm, and Jules was pretty sure she'd never be able to resist an invitation like that.

She scrambled to sit next to Vivian, who murmured, "I'm sure kissing is good for me too. You're not done spoiling me, Julia."

"Never." Jules cupped her jaw and leaned in.

Vivian's mouth still astonished her. So warm, so luscious, so… She took her time kissing and nibbling, just as she always had.

Vivian teased her right back, appearing completely content to linger, to kiss as an end in itself instead of as a prelude to sex. And wasn't that a surprise? Well, maybe she was just taking what she could get.

Jules was too. It had been too long since they'd had this, even this, just lots of kisses. She could hardly believe it.

Eventually the nibbles turned into more until they were kissing deeply and Jules's breaths had turned into groans.

Vivian was panting a little too.

Aching, Jules pulled away. "Okay," she managed. "I think that's, um, enough for me." It was one of the biggest fibs she'd ever told.

"Is it?" Vivian said.

"Well—"

"Is it?" Vivian repeated, her voice a husky whisper. She slid her hand beneath the elastic waistband of Jules's pajama pants.

Jules gasped and thrust her hips forward.

"I don't think it is," Vivian murmured. "I don't think it's enough for you at all."

"Please," Jules said before she could stop herself. "Please."

Vivian pulled her hand out just long enough for Jules to tear off her own pants and underwear and then her fingers were inside Jules, twisting and rubbing, the thumb pressing against Jules's clit.

Jules grabbed Vivian's face and kissed her fiercely, then bent and began mouthing at her throat and as much of her chest as she could get to without tearing Vivian's shirt off.

"Oh you. Oh, you tease," Vivian gasped, thrust her fingers in harder, and made Jules come in a single heartbeat. It felt fantastic. More than. It felt... There probably weren't even words for...

When Jules sagged down against her, panting and useless, Vivian pulled her fingers out and added, "I was trying to be nice to you, and you had to get me worked up when I feel like a beached whale."

"Whatever," Jules mumbled against her shoulder, still quivering with satisfaction and enjoying Vivian's smell. "I spent almost two months after Christmas being completely sexually frustrated. Now it's your turn."

"It's your giving nature that enthralls me," Vivian said.

Her sarcasm couldn't conceal the truth. Vivian did love Jules's giving nature because she got off on being teased just like this. She might not feel like actually having sex, but she sure liked the promise of it.

"Well, whenever you've ready, I'll be waiting," Jules said. She smoothed a hand over Vivian's silk-covered belly and grinned at the way Vivian's nipples were standing at very obvious attention. "Here I am, waiting. Respectfully."

"I hate you," Vivian said, her calm voice belied by her rapid breathing.

"I'm pretty terrible," Jules agreed. She glanced at the clock. It was after eleven. "You sleepy yet?"

"I'm getting there," Vivian admitted. She sighed. "The days seem so long, and yet they go by so quickly. I've always wondered how that works."

"Me too," Jules said. "I think about what I do every day, and there's so much stuff, but then I look back and the whole week disappeared when I wasn't paying attention."

"Yes," Vivian said. "Tomorrow I've got to write my final editor's letter for *Du Jour*. I'm honestly stuck. How do I wrap up ten years?"

"Jokes are good. People love jokes. And riddles."

"Oh good. You can write it for me."

"Sure. I'm submitting my essay to that collection tomorrow, so obviously I'll have a ton of free time." Jules hopped off the mattress—Vivian glared because, Jules knew, she wasn't about to hop anywhere—and tugged down the duvet and sheets.

Vivian helpfully lifted her rear and then her legs. Then she reached for the U-shaped maternity pillow next to the bed that helped her sleep comfortably on her side, and Jules drew the bedclothes back over her.

"Night," she said, turning off the lamp.

"Good night." Vivian hooked a knee over one of the pillow's legs. "Sleep well, my nonromantic girlfriend."

Jules scooted in until she could spoon Vivian from behind. "You too, bestie. Y'know, it is kind of funny, since we started off our relationship being platonic."

"I think our definitions of humor differ."

Jules still felt warm and satisfied between her thighs. It made her generous enough to reach over and rub soothing circles over Vivian's belly.

"Mm," Vivian said, and added, "now *that* you can do until I fall asleep."

Just then, the baby kicked.

"Oh no," Vivian groaned.

Jules didn't think it was "oh no" at all. "Well, hello there," she said as she felt another movement beneath her palm.

"So much for sleep," Vivian growled. "I hope she settles down soon."

Jules kissed the back of her neck. "I know life's been hectic, but we really should start getting the place ready for her. Do you want your regular designer to do the nursery?"

"Yes, but I was planning to have Evan coordinate all of that."

Vivian's new personal assistant? What the hell?

"Are you serious?" Jules asked.

"What? You've been busy, and it's not going to let up. That's what personal assistants are for, if you remember."

"If it was your office or the living room, sure," Jules said, stung, "but I want to be involved in the nursery. Once I've submitted my essay—"

"Fine," Vivian sighed. "Just tell my designer to run everything by us before he orders anything. Also no cutesy honeybee motifs. I hate bees." She shifted restlessly in the bed. "And being this pregnant. I hate that too. I'm ready to see my feet and be able to sit at a reasonable distance from my desk."

"Not long now," Jules said.

"No," Vivian said quietly. She put her hand over Jules's, and they lay there together holding her belly. "Not long now."

CHAPTER 27

NOT LONG NOW.

Over the next few days, as Jules used every lunch break to coordinate the nursery process, she thought of that often.

Vivian was due on July 16. The time until then would fly by, and at the end of it—if all went well—she and Jules would find themselves with an infant on their hands.

None of this was a surprise. But when Darius, Vivian's interior designer, sent over sketches and links to various nursery necessaries, it all seemed a lot more real. Real in a way that it hadn't since Jules had first seen an ultrasound printout.

Jules sent Darius an email signing off on the custom crib and thought: *What am I going to be to this child?*

She got a brief break from her thoughts when she emailed her article to the collection and held her breath until she got the we'll-get-back-to-you-soon email the following day. And then they started up again.

Jules should have been thinking about this all along. So many other things had grabbed her time and attention recently, but now she and Vivian were living together, settling into their life and preparing for the baby.

More than anything, she wanted to ask her parents' advice. The thought was too painful. They hadn't spoken since their blowup, and that was over ten days ago now. She and her parents had gone longer without talking, but not much, and never because they were angry. It sucked.

Her parents weren't her only family, though.

She and her sister Robin had always gotten along well, but Jules wouldn't have called them super close. They didn't talk often. She hadn't turned to Robin for advice when she'd been wrestling with her feelings about Vivian. Since the fight with her parents, Robin hadn't reached out. To be fair, neither had Jules, but, really, there was only so much she could be expected to take on at this point.

But at the end of a long day, and when Vivian was still at the office, Jules found herself in the media room. She fired off one last email and looked at the giant, silent projector screen. She had no urge to turn it on, read, scroll social media, or do anything except talk to someone in her goddamn family about what was going on with her. Sometimes you just needed perspective from people who'd known you literally since birth.

She texted Robin:

Hey, how's it going?

After a moment of consideration, she gathered her courage and followed up with:

I miss you.

Then she sat back in the recliner. It was genuine leather and had cupholders plus heating and massaging functions.

The media room was set up like a movie theater, but she and Vivian had never used it. It was a lot nicer to watch movies on a normal television while snuggling on the couch. The room had probably been Robert's idea.

But when you were alone, there was nothing like getting massaged by your chair. Jules pressed a button on the arm and sighed in bliss when the rollers beneath the leather began to work against her back.

She should have brought a glass of wine. That'd be a good way to wind down and wait for Vivian to—

Her phone rang, disrupting her thoughts. It was Robin.

Jules hadn't expected an actual call. She answered right away. "Well, hi there."

"I've missed you too," Robin said.

At her sister's voice, Jules's heart went wobbly and warm. Tears pricked at her eyes like someone had pushed a button on her. She hadn't realized how it would feel to hear from her family after everything that had happened.

"Y-yeah." *Whoops.* She hadn't meant to sound so choked up. Jules cleared her throat. "How are you?"

"I'm good. Mark's good. Everything's…" Robin trailed off.

Then silence. It went on long enough that Jules said, "So are the wedding plans—"

"What are you doing?" Robin asked.

She should have known it was too good to be true. Jules mashed the Off button on the armchair. The rollers against her back no longer felt soothing.

"I can't do this with you too," she said.

"No, I didn't call to yell at you. I'm sorry I didn't get in touch before. I just didn't know what to say, and I was hoping you'd tell me what the hell's going on."

"What did Mom and Dad tell you?"

"Uh…" Robin's voice went evasive. "That you've moved in with your old boss and that you're, like, having an affair with her. Not a *lot* of details."

"That's because they don't know details. They don't know them because they freaked out on me and couldn't have a rational conversation."

"I figured," Robin said to Jules's surprise. "Dad can be a brick wall. And Mom's always been dramatic."

Jules couldn't stop a smile. She and Robin had complained about that many times together when they were teenagers.

"Jules, I don't want to get on your back. You know I love you; you know you've got my support."

"Thanks," Jules whispered.

"But I've got to ask you. Are you sure this is a good idea? I mean, after all you said about this woman when she was your boss—"

"*Vivian,*" Jules growled.

"Yeah, okay. Sorry. After all you said about Vivian *when she was your boss*, we're suddenly supposed to believe this is some healthy thing?"

"I can't make you believe anything." Jules closed her eyes.

"I'm not asking you to," Robin said in exasperation. "But this is weird, and I'm not going to pretend it's not. Mom and Dad didn't approach it right, but all they want is for you to be happy."

Jules looked at the blank projector screen. She should have put on a movie instead of texting her sister. A dumb action blockbuster—or *Carol.*

"Then they shouldn't try as hard as they can to make me unhappy," Jules said. "They're doing that, not Vivian. Vivian's making me super happy, in fact."

"Well, that's...good. Can you tell me more about that? Like, she's having a kid, right?"

Jules knew where this was going. "Yep."

"So how do you fit into that? You're living with her, so are you going to coparent?"

Coparent. The word created a tug of longing inside Jules that she couldn't deny but that she knew better than to trust. Setting up a nursery and taking baby pictures was one thing. Raising a kid was something else. She'd babysat enough to get a glimpse of that, and everyone said nothing could prepare you for being an actual parent.

"Vivian said she wouldn't ask me to," she replied. "She said I could be as involved as I want to be. But I want to be involved, Robin. I've been in on this from the beginning, and when I think about the baby, I just feel..." She was clutching her T-shirt over her heart. She hadn't meant to do that. "I can't explain it."

"What about your job?"

"Oh, it's awesome. I really like it. Simon's great."

"I didn't mean that," Robin said in exasperation. "I meant how are you going to do your job and also take care of baby stuff *and* your writing? Are you going to quit?"

"Quit?" Astonishment prickled over the back of Jules's neck. "What are you talking about?"

Robin sounded quite reasonable when she said, "Vivian's loaded, right? I just wondered if you're going to quit your job and write full time. That'd give you more flexibility in terms of the kid too."

It took Jules a moment to recover her voice. Robin had just blown her mind. Such a thought had never occurred to her, and Vivian had certainly never suggested it.

"I'm not quitting," she said. "Vivian's not going to *keep* me. I wouldn't like that."

"Would she?"

Good question, actually. Vivian had often expressed the desire to do nice things for Jules, to take care of her and make life easier. Hell, she'd probably be thrilled to finance Jules's writing career until—or if—Jules found success. It would be a way for her to help Jules's dreams come true.

But she'd never offered because she understood how it would make Jules feel.

"We're on the same page," Jules replied. "She doesn't want me to feel like a dependent. As to the rest, we're hiring a full-time nanny. I won't be changing diapers all day. Neither will Vivian."

"I'd like to see her change a diaper," Robin said dryly. "Well, I'm glad you care about your independence. That'll make Mom and Dad feel better, you know."

A vibration hit the back of Jules's throat, a growl she hadn't known was coming. It felt strangely good.

"Then they could call me," she said, "or text. Or send a fucking telegram, if they wanted."

That'd be something, wouldn't it? *HI JULES STOP WE FULLY SUPPORT YOU STOP SORRY WE ACTED LIKE DICKS STOP.*

"Or *you* could do those things instead," Robin said.

"No, I couldn't. Not after they said Vivian's a predator and called me stupid. That was awful, and I'm not going to act like they never did that and everything's fine."

"I think they want to reach out. They just don't know how. Neither did I."

"It's not all that complicated. You just say, 'Hey, I hope you're okay. Want to talk?'"

After a pause, Robin said again, "I'm sorry. I should have."

"Yeah. Well, we're talking now." Jules took in a big breath. "And I'm sick of talking about me, so how are you? How's the wedding planning going?"

"Ha! Mark and I looked into the average wedding cost, and now we're eloping. You're sworn to silence."

For the first time all night, Jules laughed. She pulled her knees up to her chest, wrapped her free arm around them, and settled back into the cushy recliner.

"My lips are sealed," she said. "Tell me all about it."

You couldn't choose your family, but sometimes it wasn't all bad.

CHAPTER 28

THAT SATURDAY, SIMON TOOK OFF his glasses and rubbed his eyes. "Gosh," he said, "it's such a beautiful day outside."

"At least our air conditioning's working." Jules glanced out of Simon's office window to where the heat shimmered in the evening air.

Early June in New York was usually pretty temperate. Not this year. Getting to work from the subway station had been a slog.

The city was miserable in hot weather. Bicyclists seemed actively murderous, sweating through their jerseys as pedestrians jumped out of their way. Drivers honked with even less provocation than usual. Humidity made the air itself hostile, ready to throw its weight around and knock everybody flat.

Jules and Simon had been throwing back ice water all afternoon and running the A/C at full blast. She didn't like to think what the power bill would be.

"Vivian's up to her elbows in work at home anyway," Jules added. "All the last-minute details before she goes on leave. We're going out to lunch tomorrow, though. Since my *Modernity* article came out and all."

Home. She was almost used to saying that. Simon almost seemed to be used to hearing it, judging by how his eyebrows had stopped jumping every time she said it.

"That's right! Congrats. And I won't call you in tomorrow," Simon promised. He straightened the papers on his desk. "But it just wouldn't be a proper Saturday if we didn't have to come in once in a while and work our little heinies off."

He rubbed his hands over his forehead and yawned before adding, "Changing the subject from your domestic bliss to mine, did I tell you I'm buying my townhouse?"

"Yeah?" Jules asked, impressed. Simon lived in the West Village. A townhouse there was no small change.

"Yes. The landlord's selling, and I don't want to leave. I'll have a housewarming party. Get me something expensive."

Jules grinned. "I'll get you a buff guy to decorate the place. How about that?"

Simon arched an eyebrow. "I don't need one, thanks very much."

"Oh?" Jules leaned forward eagerly. "You and Maxwell going out again?"

"Tomorrow night to Masa." Simon's eyes filled with stars at the thought of the most expensive restaurant in the city. "I think he wants to whisk me to Lake Como too. At least I assume that's what he meant when he said, 'I'm going to whisk you to Lake Como.'"

"Bad timing on your place going on the market, then," Jules said sympathetically. "Buying's going to give you less, uh, flexibility in the future."

"You mean it'll make it harder for me to sidle into his Upper East Side penthouse."

"Not exactly," said Jules, who'd meant exactly that. "Just that, you know, you're a little more…tied down."

"I want my own place. I like my independence. Not every queer couple moves in together within two seconds."

Jules looked down at her tablet. "Low blow."

A moment later, a Post-It Note appeared beneath her nose as Simon reached across the desk. It read:

Sorry about that.

Jules looked up just in time for him to stick it on her nose. He wore a rueful smile.

"I didn't mean to be shitty," he said. "Look, I should have said this a while ago: I'm sorry I hit the panic button when we talked about Vivian and you. All that stuff about the sky falling down on top of Adrian & Jo."

She raised an eyebrow. "You're not worried about that anymore?"

"No. Well—not *as* much. It seems a little less dire, now that you've got an actual plan. I mean, it's so great you have a plan. Always smart to have a plan."

Jules raised her other eyebrow.

"Plus my boyfriend thinks I'm being an ass about it. You know, gotta keep him happy and all."

Jules waited.

"Look, if you're waiting for me to say that I love you and I'm glad you're happy, you'll be waiting a long time," Simon growled. "Can we accept that I've evolved and move on?"

Jules took the Post-It off her nose and wrote on it, *I'm happy for you too.* She showed it to Simon and then stuck it on his forehead.

"Aw-w," Simon said, the sarcasm belied by the pink in his cheeks. "But enough sentimental stuff. Back to the projected July revenues. I think—"

Jules's phone rang.

She glanced at it to see who was calling. Vivian. That was strange. Vivian knew perfectly well that she was working, and she was plenty busy herself. Jules gestured to Simon's office door. "Uh, can I take this? I'll just step outside to my desk."

Simon peeled off the Post-It and waved Jules away benignly. "At some point, I'll ask you to tell her I said hi. Today isn't that day."

"Hello?" Jules said as she reached her desk. "Everything okay?"

"Are you free to leave work?" Vivian asked without preamble.

Jules frowned. "Not really. We're in the middle of the reports for—"

"I hope you're not working too hard," Vivian said, and for some reason the tone of her voice made the hairs on Jules's arms stand up. "Because you need to come home. We have some unexpected guests."

"Some what?" Jules glanced back at Simon, who was watching her curiously from his desk. "Guests?"

"Your parents are here," Vivian said blandly.

Jules's heart stopped, and her whole body suddenly got cold. She must have done something with her face too, because now Simon looked alarmed.

"My what?" she croaked.

"Standing right in front of me as we speak, in fact," Vivian continued, using the syrupy voice she always used for people she hated but had to be nice to until a better alternative presented itself. "What an amazing surprise."

"My—"

"I've already got Ellen making an appetizer, but you definitely don't want to miss dinner. I'm sure we'll be able to fill two extra plates for them."

"When you say my parents are there…" Jules began, leaning back against her desk for support.

Simon's jaw dropped.

"Yes, that's absolutely what I'm saying."

"You're kidding me. They're right in front of you? They're…they're… they're—"

"Hurry home, *dear*," Vivian said and disconnected.

Jules stared blankly at the wall and prayed that she'd just hallucinated the last fifteen seconds, even as she knew she hadn't. Then, dizzy, she turned back to Simon, whose eyes were as wide as her own had to be.

"So can I come and watch?" he asked.

"I have to go home now," Jules managed.

"I know, darling," he said, reaching for his own phone. "I'll call your Uber while you take deep breaths. Want a shot from my liquor cabinet?"

"Yes," Jules said. Then she added, "No."

"Deep breaths," Simon reminded her as his fingers tapped on the display.

Jules sat at her desk and cradled her head in her hands.

"How do they even know where she lives?" Simon asked.

"I texted Robin the address after we talked," Jules groaned. "I figured somebody in my family should have it."

"Rookie mistake. You should have just pretended you died."

Not a bad idea. In fact, before tonight was over, Jules might not even have to pretend at all.

The situation was about as bad as she'd expected.

In the den, Vivian sat in one armchair, gracefully poised in spite of her swollen belly. She was smiling like a crocodile at Jules's parents, who sat on the loveseat and were glaring right back at her. The coffee table sat marooned in the middle of it all, offering a charcuterie board that nobody had touched.

The heat outside had seemed oppressive, but it was nothing compared to the icy atmosphere in the house. Frost was sure to start creeping up the walls any second now.

Vivian and her parents turned to face Jules as she stood at the door.

Stay calm. Jules had rehearsed her approach during the Uber ride. She wasn't going to charge at her parents with questions and accusations, as much as she wanted to. She wasn't going to act like this was normal and fine either. There had to be a balance, and she'd strike it.

She had to. Looking around the room, Jules saw that her parents were rigid with tension. Vivian's smile belied her fury. It would be up to Jules to somehow keep the peace if this…encounter…was going to be productive at all.

It was weird to be the youngest person here but also the adult in the room.

Her father rose to his feet, giving her a tight smile even as he came forward for a hug. He squeezed her very tightly, almost to the point of pain, while she patted him awkwardly on the back.

"Hi," she said as he pulled away. Jules looked back and forth between him and her mother, who continued to sit on the loveseat with an unusually blank expression on her face. "I had no idea you guys were coming."

"Neither did we," her dad said, trying to sound hearty as he sat back down next to her mom. "It was pretty impulsive. We bought the train tickets last night and came up this afternoon. Stowed our luggage in a hotel. We, ah, wanted to have a look at the apartment and see if it's ready to rent again. And Robin said you'd given her your new address, so we thought while we're here, why not?"

Yeah, right. Also, Robin was dead meat. Jules folded her arms and said, "Really. So how's the apartment? I had the cleaners in a couple of days ago. Does it look okay?"

For a second, her dad looked befuddled. Then he shook his head and said, "Oh. Well, it's—"

"We haven't gone there yet," Jules's mom said. "We decided to come here first."

Jules's dad gave her mom the quick frown of someone who didn't want to go off script.

"Ah," Jules said.

"Yes," her mother said, glancing at Vivian. "We haven't seen you for a while, after all. It's been a long time since Christmas, hasn't it?"

Oh shit.

But Vivian replied with perfect equanimity. "Time flies, Ms. Moretti. Christmas seems like years ago."

"It really does," Jules's mom said.

The second armchair sat empty. Jules ignored it in favor of standing next to Vivian's chair and resting her arm on the back of it. She wished she hadn't sweated so much today. Her hair probably looked like shit too.

"How long are you staying?" she asked. "You said you got a hotel. Gonna make a trip of it? See a show?"

"*Waiting for Godot* is playing at the Jacobs," Vivian said. "The reviews are excellent, if you like the absurd."

Laura Moretti's glare became downright blistering, a laser of heat through the ice of the room, aimed right at Vivian.

Jules's father cleared his throat. "Just one night. We've got tickets out for tomorrow afternoon. We wanted to leave some extra time for, ah…"

When he didn't finish, Jules said in some confusion, "For inspecting the apartment?"

"We thought you could use the time to pack," her mom said.

Vivian sat up extremely straight.

Jules *must* have misheard. "Sorry. The time to…what?"

"We'd like you to come home with us, Jules," her mom said, now resolutely looking at her as if Vivian didn't exist. "Just for a little while."

"You've got to be kidding," Jules said. "I mean, you have to be."

"No," her dad said, "we're not. Not at all."

Jules looked down at Vivian, expecting that Vivian would look right back at her to share her incredulity.

Instead, Vivian kept her gaze trained on Jules's parents. Her hands sat placidly on the arms of her chair, but Jules could see a twitch at her right temple.

So much for the diplomatic approach she'd been planning.

"What are you doing?" Jules asked. "How can you come here without calling and tell me you want me to come back to Philadelphia with you? Are you nuts?"

They had to be. Jules would never have imagined her steady, level-headed parents pulling a stunt like this in her wildest dreams.

"Maybe so," her dad admitted, unclenching one of his hands and rubbing it over his forehead. "But we had to see you in person, Jules. This can't happen over the phone."

Then he added, "We tried, didn't we? You wouldn't listen to us. We wouldn't listen to you. It's got to be face-to-face." He looked back at Vivian. "And I'm not going to lie. We had to get a look at you too."

Vivian did not deign to reply. She just kept watching Jules's parents with that same cold unwavering stare, as if challenging them to tell her what they saw.

Jules slid her hand down from the back of the armchair to rest on Vivian's shoulder and gave her a tiny squeeze.

"I just want to know," Jules's mother said, her voice trembling with anger, "I just want to know, *Ms. Carlisle*, what it is you want out of a young woman who was working for you? Who looked up to you, who admired you, who'd do anything for you?" She swallowed hard. "You're about to be a mother. Think about your own child and then look me in the eye and tell me, if you can answer that question."

"I can," Vivian said, "but I won't. You can't possibly think I'm interested in justifying myself to you."

Jules's dad's control finally broke. He leaned forward in his chair, his mouth pulling back into a snarl.

"I don't give a damn what you think about us," he said in a low voice. "And I don't care who you are or how much clout you have. This is about my daughter, and I want to know what your intentions are."

"If this is really about me, maybe you should talk to me too," Jules snapped.

"They're not here to talk to you, Julia," Vivian said. "They're here to judge me and then rescue you. Isn't that right, Mr. Moretti?"

Her dad's face flushed. "I've had enough of this." He stabbed his finger at her. "You're exploiting my child, and you're telling her it's love."

"Stop it, Dad," Jules said instantly, but he ignored her.

"Maybe you do this all the time," he continued. "I wouldn't know, but she's been killing herself for you, and if you can't see that—"

"Dad!"

"She's done everything for you," her mother rasped. "How can you ask for even more and still sleep at night?"

"I actually sleep very well," Vivian said, "especially when Julia's here."

Jules yanked her hand off Vivian's shoulder and forestalled her parents' enraged response by barking, "Not helping!"

Vivian turned to glower at her, but Jules glowered right back. "Stop baiting them! They came here to talk." She glared at her parents too, like she never had before. "So talk to me. Tell me what you think you're accomplishing by coming here like this and insulting us both."

"I don't know," her dad said to Jules's surprise. "I told you it was an impulsive thing. We don't have a plan."

"Except taking her back to Philadelphia," Vivian pointed out.

"Will you stop it please?" Jules said. Even Vivian ought to know that this was not the time to stir the pot. "I'm not going, okay? I'm staying here."

"Fine. Then stay here. I mean in New York," her dad said, holding up his hands. "We're not going to kidnap you, for God's sake." He glared at Vivian. "Like I said, we had to see for ourselves."

"So," Jules said, "what do you see?"

"I see what's here," her mother said through gritted teeth. She looked at Vivian. "I see a forty-something woman who is pregnant and who—"

"Forty-two," Vivian said, "for the sake of accuracy."

"Vivian," Jules growled.

"*I see,*" her mother continued, looking like she was two seconds away from hurling the charcuterie knife across the room, "somebody who uses people for a living and treats them like chess pieces and who thinks she can treat my daughter like one. Well, let me tell you something about me."

"Dinner is ready, Ms. Carlisle," Ellen called from downstairs, sounding both hesitant and proper.

Her voice snapped all four of them back into reality.

Jules realized she was trembling: anger, nerves, sheer adrenaline. Plus words she couldn't assemble in any coherent, useful order.

Vivian wasn't trembling. She said calmly, "Julia?"

"Yes?"

"Why don't you go down to dinner—"

"*What?*"

"—with your father," Vivian finished, giving Jules's mom a level stare. Jules's mom narrowed her eyes, which still glittered with fury.

"I'm not sure that's a good idea," her dad said, giving Jules's mom a quick look.

"Me either," Jules agreed.

"Go, Eric," her mom said. "You go on downstairs. You too, Jules. I want to talk to this...this—"

"Yes, yes," Vivian said softly. "We'll talk, Ms. Moretti. We'll get everything straightened out just fine."

Jules looked at her dad. He appeared as apprehensive as she felt.

Gentle pressure on Jules's hand. Jules looked down to see that Vivian had placed her hand atop Jules's own.

"It'll be all right, my love," Vivian said softly.

Next thing Jules knew, she was standing in the kitchen on wobbly knees. Her cheeks burned. In place of coherent thought, her brain ran the fuzzy buzz of radio static.

You're a goner, she thought, as she came back to herself. *She calls you "my love" and you have an out-of-body experience right in front of your parents.*

Something clattered. Jules realized she'd been staring blankly at the kitchen island. On the other side, Ellen was setting the table with four plates. The usual centerpiece was gone, replaced with serving dishes of shrimp, orzo, and roast vegetables.

Vivian's house had a formal dining room, but it clearly wouldn't be called into service for this occasion. Good thing too. The last thing they needed was for Jules's parents to freak out over the silver service, fine china, and crystalware. At least this way everyone could pretend that things were sort of normal.

"I didn't know whether to prepare a dessert, but I can call Barachou for an order of cream puffs," Ellen said, wiping her hands on a dish towel. She smiled at Jules's dad. "You've got to taste them to believe them."

If anything could make this evening more awkward, it would be a DoorDash interruption. Besides, Jules couldn't guarantee they'd even make it through dinner if her mom stormed out of the den and dragged her dad away.

Luckily, her father cleared his throat, patted his middle, and said, "Oh, thanks, but no thanks. Laura and I are trying to cut back on the sweets."

"Nothing for me or Vivian either," Jules said. "Thanks so much, Ellen."

"Of course. Good night, Jules. Sir."

"No *sir* necessary," her dad said quickly.

Ellen gave them both a polite smile and departed without another word.

Jules and her dad seated themselves, silently ladled food onto their plates, and started picking at their meal, not looking at each other.

"Think they'll kill each other?" Jules asked.

"No way to tell," her dad replied.

They picked a little more. The shrimp dish was one of Jules's favorites. She couldn't taste it much right now.

"I just think you're too young for all this, honey," her dad said, finally meeting her eyes. He didn't look angry now, just serious and frustrated. "I mean, what role are you playing here? Stepmother or what?" He shook his head before she could answer. "I thought you wanted to concentrate on your career. I thought that's why you and Aaron fought so much."

Jules knew she had to tread very carefully now as she put into words what she'd been thinking for months. "I did. I do. But it was all...out of balance then. I worked all the time, and I didn't care enough about him to make room for him. I can't blame him for leaving."

Her dad shrugged. "Neither can I. That's not a knock on you, sweetie—people your age are figuring out their priorities. But Jules, when did this start? With you and her...I mean Vivian."

Jules thought briefly before deciding that there was no sense in lying about it.

"The second time we were in London," she said. "At the end of fashion week."

"That was in February, right?"

Jules nodded.

"I remember thinking you sounded pretty bad before then," her dad said cautiously. "It wasn't anything you said exactly. You just sounded off."

"But I sure perked up in March, didn't I?" Jules asked and dared a tiny smile.

Her dad didn't take the bait. "Whose idea was it? Hers or yours?"

"Hers," Jules admitted.

Her father's eyes darkened.

"But it wasn't like that, Dad—really," she added quickly. "It wasn't sketchy or sleazy or... You know what it was?" She blinked as she realized it. "Proper."

"Proper?" Her dad stared at her. "Jules. Nothing about this is proper."

"No," Jules said and suddenly laughed as she remembered the February morning when Vivian had solemnly declared her intention to have a celibate romantic relationship with Jules. "It was. Oh wow. I just thought about it. It was downright old-fashioned almost."

She saw the aghast look on her father's face and quickly sobered up. "Sorry. But it was. It was fine. Dad, I agreed to this. She didn't make me do anything. Nobody could make me do anything like that."

"Well, you weren't afraid to stand up to her," her dad said, looking like it pained him to admit it. "I was glad to see that at least. Not that she listened," he added darkly.

"Not this time," Jules admitted. "But, yeah, I'm not a doormat." Best not to add "anymore." "I don't work for her. She's not my boss in here. She never has been, not like that. It was my idea to move in. I had to talk her into it."

Her dad looked appalled again, and Jules said defensively, "Well, we have new jobs, and we started working all the time and never seeing each other. At least this way we can."

Her dad rubbed his hand wearily over his forehead.

"Oh, Dad, come on. I know you don't approve. I get it."

"Do you?" he asked, lowering his hand and looking at her.

"Yeah," Jules said, "I do. But that's not going to stop me." She took a deep breath. "I'm playing for keeps on this one, Dad. I'm not letting her get away. This is it."

"Playing for keeps?" Her dad lifted his eyebrows.

"Yeah," Jules repeated, realizing as she said it how extraordinary *it* was. Her thing with Vivian, playing for keeps. They'd been doing that from the very beginning, hadn't they? There had never been any talk between them of testing the waters or keeping it casual or getting to know each other better or doing any of the stuff you'd normally do. They'd both known from that first conversation in the kitchen that it was going to be serious, that they were going to risk everything without knowing what came next.

Why hadn't Jules ever thought of it like that before?

"Jules?" her dad asked, sounding worried.

"It's working, Dad," Jules heard herself say as if from a great distance. "It's good. You don't know how good." Even when it was hard.

When it was hard with Aaron, it hadn't been good. It had been over.

"I know you're worried about me not having time to work," she added, "but it won't be like that. There's going to be a nanny and, uh, stuff."

"Stuff? You mean staff. Servants and nannies and drivers and…" Her dad exhaled heavily. "I don't want you to be some rich person's little plaything."

Jules opened her mouth.

Her dad held up his hand. "I know. I know. You love her."

"Yes," Jules snapped. "I do. And she loves me."

Her dad sat back in his chair. "I want you to be with someone you love, Jules, but I also want you to respect yourself. I want you to be able to look at yourself in the mirror and admire the person you see there." He gave her a direct look. "Can you do that? Honestly?"

"Yes," Jules said, looking right back. "Honestly, yes, I can." She could. More than ever, now that she'd stood up for herself to Vivian, her parents, and everybody else. "I don't know how else to put this, Dad. I'm okay here. I'm happy here."

"You seem happy," her dad allowed. "That's all we want for you, whether you believe it or not. Your mother and I just—"

A door down the hall opened and shut. The den. After a few moments, they heard footsteps.

Jules held her breath as her mother and Vivian arrived in the kitchen. She suspected her father did too.

Neither of them had a black eye, and nobody appeared to be missing any teeth. Her mother wasn't even flushed with anger anymore. In fact, she was kind of pale. Pale and thoughtful looking.

Vivian's face was as blank as ever. "Are you sure you won't have some dinner, Laura?" she inquired.

"No, thanks," Jules's mom said, turning a hooded gaze onto Jules. "I think we'd better be going. Come on, Eric. I'd like to go back to the hotel."

What the hell did that look mean? Usually her mom was more of an open book than this. Jules forced herself not to look to Vivian for help; they could talk after her parents left—which seemed to be imminent.

Jules's father rose to his feet, frowning in concern. "Well, wait a minute. Can't we—"

"Eric, please," her mother said. "I'm very tired, and Vivian is too."

Vivian is too? Jules and her father exchanged an astonished look.

"Jules, we'll call you tomorrow," her mother said. "If you can, we'll meet for lunch and talk some more then."

Vivian and Jules were supposed to go out to lunch to celebrate Jules's *Modernity* article—a rare public outing for them. It seemed like a trade down, to say the least, to spend it with her hostile parents.

"That'd be a good idea," Vivian murmured, looking at Jules, clearly thinking the same thing.

Her dad opened his mouth again, and her mother said, "Eric, please."

"Right," her dad said. He'd been calm and resigned with Jules a few seconds ago, but now he was glaring again at Vivian.

Vivian looked back serenely. "Good night, Eric."

"Good night," Jules's dad said tightly. He glanced quickly at his wife and then at Jules before leaning in to give his daughter a brief kiss on the cheek. "Hope we'll see you tomorrow, Jules."

"Er, yeah. Me too."

"Let me call my driver," Vivian said. "There's no reason for you to take an Uber."

"No," Jules's dad growled. Then he glanced at Jules, perhaps saw her bristling, and added, "No, thank you. It's a nice night. I think we'll walk for a little while."

"Of course," Vivian murmured.

Jules's mother gave Vivian a long look, then turned to look at Jules before leaning in and kissing her cheek. "Good night, honey," she said. "We'll see you later."

We'll see. "Night."

Her parents left. As soon as the front door closed, Jules's knees got wobbly again, and she sat down hard on her kitchen chair as if all the adrenaline had left her body at once and never planned to return.

Vivian sat down too in front of one of the empty plates and began to help herself to shrimp and orzo. She looked unenthusiastic about it, but she needed the calories.

"Let me warm that up," Jules said blankly.

"Don't worry about it." Then Vivian ate silently while Jules tried not to stare at her.

Finally, though, Jules couldn't stand it any longer. It was still difficult to speak during the silences when things were tense and Jules knew Vivian would prefer her to keep her mouth shut. But now she said, "I'm sorry. I didn't know. I never would have imagined they'd—"

"Looks like it runs in the family," Vivian said coolly. "Inviting yourself into my house, I mean."

"Hey," Jules said, stung. Vivian might have felt ambushed, but so had Jules, and she didn't need her girlfriend to snipe at her. "I said I didn't know they'd do this."

"There are some other things you didn't say," Vivian replied, slicing through Jules with her cold eyes.

"What are you—"

"For example, you never said your parents thought I was molesting you over Christmas." Vivian dropped her fork on the plate and leaned back in her chair, her eyes glittering with anger. "Or words to that effect."

"Oh, my God," Jules groaned, hiding her face in her hands.

"It was wonderful to hear it from your mother instead. I can't tell you how much I enjoyed that."

Jules stared at Vivian through the cracks in her fingers. "Why the hell would I ever have told you about that? I can't believe she said that to you."

"Why not?" Vivian snapped.

"Because they grilled me about it, and I told them they were wrong!" Jules threw her hands in the air. "Jesus Christ. I'm going to call her right now, I'm going to—"

"That won't help anything," Vivian said, and picked up her fork again. "So settle down. Your mother and I spoke…politely…once we'd gotten past that charming moment."

Jules didn't exactly feel like settling down. What had her mom been thinking? "What did you say?"

"I said what I had to say." Vivian's glare was lethal now. "Don't you know me by now, Julia? I knew everything about your parents from the moment they set foot in our house. And I knew to tackle your mother first. If it works, she'll bring your father around, and I'll never have to deal with this ridiculous drama again."

"But what did you say?" Jules persisted, leaning forward. "I mean, she didn't look happy, but she didn't look mad anymore. Not exactly."

Vivian's lips pinched. "I did what I said I wouldn't do," she said. "I justified myself to her. I explained myself and my situation and my feelings—things that she had absolutely no right to know, whether she's your mother or not—"

"But...but why did you—"

"Because it worked," Vivian said flatly. "I knew it would. That's what it took. So I did it." Her mouth quivered with anger; her eyes were practically throwing off sparks. "I always do what it takes. Haven't you noticed?"

Jules felt breathless. "Do what it takes to—"

"To keep you." Vivian looked her right in the eyes. "To keep you with me, and to keep them off our backs. I don't want a rift between you and your parents. It'd come between us too."

"No!" Jules said at once. "I would never have gone back with them. You don't really think that, do you?"

"No," Vivian said, "I don't. Not for an instant."

Jules opened her mouth, then stopped and looked at Vivian's face. Vivian was serious. Vivian meant it.

Vivian knew that Jules would not leave her, knew she hadn't thought about it for an instant.

Vivian—Vivian Carlisle—had absolute faith, absolute trust in Jules's love for her. Vivian, who trusted no one.

Jules gulped as the room spun around her.

Vivian continued. "But I hope you understand that everything'll be a lot easier if you're not estranged from your parents. And at this stage of the game, anything that makes life easier or more pleasant..." She shifted in her chair and winced. "Well, you can imagine how I feel about that." Then she frowned at Jules. "What's wrong?"

"Nothing," Jules said faintly. At least the room had slowed down. Faith and trust and love. "I'm glad you... I mean, I'm sorry you had to—"

"I want you to be happy," Vivian said, "here with me. I don't want you to have regrets." Her jaw hardened. "If that means I have to...*explain myself* to your parents, then I'll deal with it."

"Thank you," Jules whispered.

"Don't thank me," Vivian said. "I'm pretending your mother is this shrimp." She stabbed said shrimp with her fork and shoved it in her mouth, chewing ferociously.

"Oh. Right."

Vivian swallowed. "I'll say."

"You do make me happy." Jules gulped. "I thought about that when I was talking to my dad. I couldn't explain it, but we work. You and me."

"I'm pretty sure I've made that argument myself. To you, in fact." Vivian took a bite of cold orzo. She wrinkled her nose.

"Are you sure you don't want me to warm that up?"

"You might as well," Vivian growled and pushed her plate away. "I skipped lun—" She stopped herself, but she was too late to keep Jules from scowling at her. "No. I don't want to hear it tonight."

Jules grabbed her plate and stomped over to the microwave. "Oh, my God." She stuck the plate inside, pressed buttons, and listened to the low-level whir. Then she turned back around to see Vivian watching her from the table, her face inscrutable.

Jules snorted with laughter before she could stop herself. "I can't leave you alone for a minute, can I?"

"You're the giggliest woman I ever met. Really."

"Yeah." Jules stuck her hands in her pants pockets and sauntered over to Vivian's chair, grinning down at her. "I owe you the foot rub of a lifetime too."

Vivian's stoic face finally cracked as she bared her teeth at Jules in a savage smile. "You have no idea."

"I have some idea." The microwave beeped, and Jules set the warmed-up plate back in front of Vivian before seating herself.

As Vivian ate, Jules looked at the rise of her belly, just visible over the table's edge. "I dunno," she said slowly, propping her elbows on the table as though thinking through what she was about to say. "They were out of line, but I kind of wonder if I'd act any differently, don't you?"

Vivian took a sip of water and waited.

"What we're doing looks bad from the outside. Bad enough that we need a PR strategy to handle it. And if *she* did what I'm doing"—Jules looked again at Vivian's belly—"I think I'd freak out too."

Vivian's gaze softened. She sounded reluctant, but she admitted, "I thought the same thing, although I hope I wouldn't white knight myself into somebody's house."

"Of course you wouldn't. You'd summon them to our house and make them explain themselves."

That was enough to make Vivian laugh out loud, something rare enough that it still shocked Jules like a fuzzy sweater on a dry, cold day.

"Hey." Jules leaned forward and propped her chin on her hands. That soft look in Vivian's eyes, the warm note of her laugh, indicated that it was time to ask a big question. "I know you're not the *most* into talking about feelings, but how are you feeling about this? About her?"

For a moment, Vivian's face closed into an expression Jules knew all too well from her time as an assistant. It was the expression that said *None of your business* with a side of *How dare you?*

Then Vivian appeared to remember she wasn't dealing with an assistant, colleague, reporter, or even an ex-husband. To Jules's great relief, she took a deep breath and visibly relaxed her expression.

God, Jules thought, *she must have walls behind walls.* It was pretty remarkable, in fact, that after so long, Vivian could recognize a wall and consciously take it down.

"Eager," Vivian said.

Jules hadn't been expecting that. She'd expected Vivian to say she was unafraid. Vivian could also have said again that she was just ready for the pregnancy to be over. But Jules hadn't thought she'd say she was eager, much less have a slight sparkle to her eye.

It brought a wide smile to Jules's own face. "Yeah?"

"Yes. I don't want to sound too sentimental, but this is going to be a little person. I think she's got a good chance of being a remarkable person."

"Better than good," Jules offered.

"Yes." Vivian patted her belly and gave it a half smile. "And she's starting off with every advantage in the world. But I don't want to spoil her. I had to claw my way to where I am, and it's why I can do what I do. I'm not saying she won't have every opportunity, but she's the one who'll have to take advantage of it. She'll have to prove herself to the world."

Jules grinned. "And when she's gotten to where you are, it's the other way around, and the world's got to prove itself to her."

"If she pulls it off. I can't wait to meet her, but I've seen too many society kids who think they're owed everything and whose parents barely know them. They'll hire a lawyer to get rid of their DUIs and then never talk to them about it. I won't be one of those parents. I refuse."

"Yeah." Jules took a deep breath. *Say it.* "So do I."

"I certainly hope—" Vivian finally appeared to hear what Jules was saying. She cocked her head and said, "You *also* won't be one of those parents?"

"Nope." Jules reached out and took one of Vivian's hands in her own. "But I'll be *a* parent. Not just someone living in your house who helps decorate the nursery. Everyone keeps asking me what role I'm going to play, but I've been there since the night you found out. I'm all in—if you'll let me be."

After all, Vivian didn't have to allow Jules to coparent. Technically, legally, Jules had zero rights to this child at all. Whatever Vivian said went, and it could change at any time.

Vivian let Jules hold her hand, but she didn't return the squeeze, and she kept looking Jules in the eye. As always, her gaze probed right to the bottom of things.

Once upon a time—what seemed long ago—Jules had tried not to let Vivian see her heart. Now she returned Vivian's gaze fearlessly. She had nothing to hide.

"It'll mean sacrifices," Vivian said. "Nanny or not, she'll take up more time than we realize. Everyone tells me that. And it's easy to be confident at your age that you can handle anything. I'm not patronizing you," she added, lifting her voice before Jules could protest. "It's just the truth. I remember it myself."

"You two are a package deal," Jules said. "I'm in your house, and I'm your partner. No, I didn't plan on any of this, but neither did you."

For a moment, a hopeful look crossed Vivian's face. Desperately hopeful. Then it was gone.

"I'm not refusing you," she said, "but we've just had an emotional evening, and this isn't the kind of offer I'll accept off-the-cuff, no more than I accepted your suggestion to move in. We can talk more later. We *will* talk more," she amended.

Later, Jules thought, *after the baby's born, in case I change my mind.* That was obviously what Vivian meant.

Jules wouldn't change her mind. The thought of a baby was scary as shit; even now, her stomach tumbled at the thought of the responsibility. That didn't change facts. The fact was, Jules was where she was meant to be.

If Vivian needed time to see that for herself and accept it, so be it. Jules wasn't going anywhere.

"Yes," Jules said. "We can and we will talk more."

CHAPTER 29

In lieu of a celebratory lunch with Vivian, Jules met her parents at Tom's Restaurant. They'd always been big *Seinfeld* fans, and Jules had seen every episode and deleted scene on DVD while growing up. Even in the midst of family conflict, her parents seemed to enjoy sitting in the same diner where Jerry and his friends had talked about nothing all day.

She'd fully planned to tell them off, just as she'd told Vivian she would the night before. But something about the way they looked at her today told her it wasn't necessary and stopped her in her tracks. They seemed resigned, if not reconciled. Tired, almost.

Instead of jumping into the animosity of last night, her dad said, "The apartment looked good this morning. Thanks for taking care of all that."

Okay, that was a civilized note to start on. "Least I could do. I'm glad everything's all right."

"We should be able to get it rented pretty quick."

"Great."

Normally, Jules's dad could exhaust the topic of the rental market. This afternoon, though, he seemed out of ideas.

The Morettis sucked on their soda straws in awkward silence.

Rip the Band-Aid off, Jules thought. "So, Mom, what did you and Vivian say to each other?"

Her mother frowned at her. "She didn't tell you?"

"Sort of," Jules said evasively. "She said that she talked about, uh, how she felt. About the situation and me."

Vivian would rather give up a couple of ribs before she recounted that embarrassing conversation in detail. Jules hoped her mom would be more open to giving a blow-by-blow. What they'd said to each other in private wasn't Jules's business, but she couldn't help wanting to know.

"She did." Her mother and father exchanged glances, which meant that they'd talked about everything and weren't going to tell Jules much of it. "I'm not going to pretend I'm happy. She's a hard woman to like, and I don't think this relationship is good for you."

Jules stiffened.

"But…" Now her mother sounded almost pained. "I'm willing to believe that she's sincere in how she feels about you. Which is better than what I was thinking."

"I'll have to take your mother's word for it," her dad said. "She's a pretty smart lady."

Jules's mom rolled her eyes and elbowed him, and for the first time since last night, something like a real smile lingered around her mouth.

It disappeared quickly, though, when she looked back into Jules's eyes. "You're an adult, honey. But you'll always be our baby too. I know in my head that this isn't our business"—she tapped her chest and her eyes filled with tears—"but I don't know it here."

"Oh no, Mom," Jules gasped. She reached over and grabbed a wad of napkins from the dispenser on the table. "Don't cry. Don't do that."

If her mother cried, then Jules would cry, and her dad would try to pretend he wasn't there, and that'd be it for conversation.

"I'm okay," her mom said thickly and blew her nose.

Just then, the server arrived with their plates, and they all gratefully diverted their attention to the greasy food.

"Think this is what Jerry and Elaine ate?" Jules's dad asked around his tuna salad sandwich. "I used to know, but it's been a while."

"No idea," Jules said, relishing the bite of her burger. "Don't care. Yum."

"At least you're eating a burger," her mother said, sniffling as she ate a french fry. "I was afraid you'd live on salad like all the other girls I see around here."

Jules couldn't remember the last time she'd eaten a burger, actually, but it didn't seem wise to mention that. Instead, she took another enormous bite. "No salad on this plate."

Her mother seemed placated, at least enough so that the Morettis all finished their food in more or less peaceful silence.

Jules wistfully remembered roast beef sandwiches for lunch on Christmas Eve, the last meal they'd shared. What would the next family meal be? And when?

Such sad reflections occupied her mind until her dad wiped his mouth and looked at his watch. "We should get back to the hotel and pack up. Our flight's at four. We'll be cutting it close." It was nearly one. "Thanks for meeting us, honey."

"Yeah," Jules said. "No problem." She looked at them across the table and they looked back. "Um. You sure you don't want Ben to take you to the station? That's Vivian's driver. He could tell you about all the dumb stuff I've said and done in the car."

"No," her dad said. "No, thanks."

But her mother looked thoughtful. "Actually—"

"No, Laura." Her dad sounded very firm. "We did what we came to do. We're not using the driver as an informant."

Her mother sniffed but didn't deny the charge.

"Based on what I've seen of Vivian, I'm betting she doesn't open up too much in front of the help, anyway," her dad added.

"Not too much," Jules said. No reason to mention that Ben had probably seen—or figured out—plenty over the years. Nor that he kept Vivian's secrets on pain of death, including her relationship with Jules. "You sure?"

"We only brought overnight bags, so there's not much to carry," her mother said. "We might even take the subway. But your father's right; we need to go."

They all rose to their feet and headed for the door. They would part ways in a moment: Jules was returning home while her parents were off to Penn Station. They walked one block together before arriving. There were hugs, and her mother looked like she was about to cry again, but thankfully she held it together—at least until she and Jules's father were out of sight.

Jules watched them until they were underground, waving as they turned around right before they disappeared.

Then she looked up the sky, inhaled deeply, and let her breath out again. It was over. It was over, and it was a nice day, a Sunday afternoon when Vivian didn't expect her back at any particular time.

Jules decided to detour a little. She'd head south through Riverside Park, look at the joggers and the people playing Frisbee with their dogs and everybody else, and just keep walking until she was finally home.

Over the next couple of weeks, life returned to normal, or as normal as it ever got. Simon had seemed a little disappointed that Jules's parents' visit hadn't resulted in nuclear war. Still, he was glad they were talking to her again.

In a historic moment, Jules's mother had even mumbled over the phone that she hoped Vivian was getting enough rest because God knew it would be in short supply in a month. Granted, she'd immediately segued into Jules's and Robin's infancies, but Jules had still been shocked breathless.

As for Vivian, Jules didn't know if she was getting *enough* rest, although she was making an effort. With less than a month to go, she looked more exhausted than she had since her first few weeks. These days, she came home, ate dinner, and promptly collapsed into bed, reading and making notes. Her laptop was always at hand so she could work from home as much as possible.

For her part, Jules was trying to walk the fine line between being home and being at work, doing her utmost at both places and, on top of it all, trying to build up some more goodwill with Simon, at least enough that she wouldn't get smacked down for her greed. But there was something that she really needed.

"Vacation time?" Simon said on June 27. "For the week after July 12. Let me think. What else is due to happen right around then?"

"Just a few days, Simon," Jules argued. "I'm not asking for my two weeks in one gulp."

She wished she could, but leaving some in reserve, just in case, seemed a good idea. Actual family leave was out of the question, since she and Vivian didn't have any kind of legal arrangement or relationship.

Simon sat back in his chair, looking resigned. "I've worked with people who have newborns in the house. Do you know what I have to look forward to when you get back?"

Jules shook her head.

"Watching you shuttle between work and home for five days on no sleep. You'll start showing up unshowered. You'll forget the name of our business. And my name. And your own. And my personal favorite: you will be completely unable to talk about anything but babies—at least until the lack of sleep turns everything you say into word salad." He shook his head. "Try to keep it under control, will you?"

"The first floor of this building is a gym," Jules said cheekily. "I promise to shower there at least every other day."

"You think you're joking, but you're not," Simon said. "Take your week with my blessing. And don't forget to get in touch with the temp agency right away."

"On it, boss," Jules said, which always put him in a good mood.

It did not put Vivian in a good mood.

"A week?" she said that night. "That's all he gave you?"

Jules stared at her. "Vivian, remember when Mariel had her baby last August?" she asked. "How long did you give her to come back?"

"Company policy dictates—"

"Yeah, yeah, but how long did you give her? I mean *informally*?"

Vivian sniffed, acting like she didn't remember.

"Also a week. And she was the one who actually gave birth. And she worked until the afternoon she went into labor!" As in her contractions had actually begun at work, and she'd kept sifting through advertising copy until they were six minutes apart. "And then you fired her anyway."

Vivian waved an impatient hand. "That had nothing to do with it. Did you see the copy she produced?"

"I got a week," Jules said. "Let's be grateful, okay?"

Vivian huffed and proceeded to ignore Jules for the next two hours.

Jules tried not to mind. If Vivian actually needed a good reason to act out, being eight months pregnant and counting was probably it. She'd avoided the massive pregnancy crying jags Jules had read about. Irritability in the final trimester seemed like a narrow escape.

Then, at the end of the evening, Jules got an email from the editor of the essay collection she'd submitted to. She gasped loudly.

Vivian looked up from her armchair with a startled expression. "What's wrong?"

"Nothing at all!" Jules hurried toward her chair with her phone extended so Vivian could see the email. As far as Jules was concerned, it contained three of the sweetest words in the English language: *revise and resubmit.*

"Hmm. I see their point. I wouldn't have accepted it right away either."

For the first time, Vivian was reading Jules's essay. They'd moved to the bedroom, changed into PJs, and now Jules was on tenterhooks for Vivian to give her honest feedback.

Just not brutally honest.

"Yeah?" she asked.

"Yes. Your central argument is sound, but they're right about needing more examples as well as contradicting yourself in paragraphs nine and ten. And your language is overblown right here."

"They didn't say that."

"No, I'm saying that."

It wasn't Jules's fault that she loved metaphors. Her seventh-grade English teacher had instilled bad habits in her that she'd never been able to break. "Oh."

"Think of it as a learning experience," Vivian said as if consoling her. "It'll be easier next time."

Jules didn't need consolation. Her article had made it one step closer to publication, and it had nothing to do with Vivian's or Simon's influence. It was based on merit that the editors had seen in Jules's work and *only* her work. That was more precious than all of Harry Winston's jewelry inventory put together.

"Vivian, I was worried they'd reject it outright. It's awesome that I still have a chance. I'm not mad they didn't think it was perfect right away."

Vivian looked mystified.

It figured. Jules repressed a chuckle. "Anything else?"

As it happened, there was a lot else. By the end, Jules's wrists were cramped from typing out Vivian's copious notes, which gave her flashbacks to her time at *Du Jour.* None of her college professors had ever been as exacting, and she'd had plenty who were *really* exacting.

255

She gulped as Vivian wound to a close. Writers needed thick skins, but Vivian had really done a number on her confidence with all that critique. "Um…it's not garbage, right?"

"No." Vivian sounded exasperated. "I told you the argument is sound, and that's the main thing. Did you agree with everything I said?"

"Not all of it," Jules admitted.

"Which parts didn't you agree with?"

"Well, I actually think it was relevant for me to mention Gianni Versace's murder right here. The essay needs some historical context, and they liked that part in their notes."

"It's not directly related to queerness in fashion."

"No, but I think…"

The discussion continued until Vivian was flagging too much to go on. However, when Jules apologized for tiring her, she said, "Do you remember what I told you when we got together? That I like talking to you. Believe me, if I weren't worn out, I'd have plenty more to say."

Jules was feeling pretty worn out herself by now, so falling asleep was fine with her. "Yeah, so would I. I'll start revising tomorrow night after work. I want to get it done ASAP, before…" She touched Vivian's belly.

"Yes." Vivian put her hand over Jules's. With a groan, she arranged herself around her maternity pillow.

When the lights were out, it didn't take Jules long to go to sleep, even as thoughts of revisions danced in her head. One other larger thought circled around them all: the memory of Vivian telling Jules they'd be good together. Not just emotionally.

Jules had asked her how. Vivian had replied, challengingly: *stick around and find out.*

Thank God she had.

CHAPTER 30

ONE WEEK TO GO.

It was a mystery how quickly the last two weeks had flown by. Now Jules was looking into a large canvas Prada tote bag. The thought of packing it up seemed more intimidating somehow than submitting her revised essay yesterday had been.

Her list seemed to go on forever: toiletries, a copy of the birth plan, a bathrobe, and comfy clothes were the essentials. And then there were the luxuries: fluffy towels better than the hospital would provide, a Bluetooth speaker, an essential oil diffuser, and more. A lot more.

By the time she was done, the Prada tote bag had been supplemented by a full Chanel backpack. Jules zipped it up, stretched her back, and looked around the room.

She sat in the middle of the nursery, now fully tricked out by Darius's design firm. They'd done an amazing job. The walls were painted in a gender-neutral pale green with one accent wall covered in wallpaper with baby animals on it. No bees, though. Darius had hung artwork that was mainly soothing, abstract prints in complementary colors.

The one exception was the selfie of Jules and Vivian on the couch blown up to enormous size and given pride of place opposite the crib.

Said crib was handmade in Sweden by artisans who only produced a hundred of them per year, as if to keep bourgeois babies clad in Baby Gap onesies from clamoring at their door and ruining the company image. Jules found it completely ridiculous.

Next to the crib sat a rocking chair that cost well over what Jules brought home in a month, tenderly lit from behind with a real Tiffany lamp. The nursery also featured a hand-painted vintage toy chest, a bassinet that rocked itself and played soothing white noise, and a Fendi stroller.

That didn't even touch on the bureau and closet, packed full of baby clothes and shoes from high-end designers. Jules had no idea why an infant needed Christian Dior booties she'd outgrow in a month, but it wasn't her money.

In Vivian's defense, most of the excess wasn't her idea. She'd adamantly refused a baby shower, but people had sent extravagant gifts anyway. Phillip Lim was personally responsible for a whole series of cashmere sleepsuits and socks.

Nobody had sent anything really practical, of course. It had been up to Jules and Evan, Vivian's assistant, to order the diapers.

Jules looked back at the hospital bag and traced her fingers over the strap. The padding rubbed against the tips, tempting her to squeeze it between her thumb and forefinger. It helped relieve some of her tension.

Vivian's C-section was scheduled for two days from now. The prospect still made Jules nervous as hell.

These days, the thoughts keeping her up at night had nothing to do with work or writing. They were mainly: *operations are dangerous. Recovery takes longer. Vivian's older than most new moms. She'll be okay, right? She's got to be okay.*

The alternative was unthinkable.

"Ready for bed?"

Startled, Jules looked up to see Vivian in the doorway wearing a bathrobe.

She looked worn out to the bone. She'd wiped off her makeup, and her hair was still damp from the shower. Instead of her usual proud stance, she was slumped against the doorway, arms crossed.

How late was it? Jules looked at the darkness outside the window and then at her phone. Damn. Ten thirty had crept up fast.

"Just let me change," Jules said, rising to her feet with a grunt.

Vivian glanced around the room. "It's come together well."

"Right?" Jules walked to Vivian and put her hands on her waist. "How could it not, though, with that high-end construction on a Fendi stroller."

Normally Vivian just rolled her eyes at Jules's jibes. Tonight she put a hand on Jules's shoulder and shook her head, clearly too exhausted to snipe back.

"C'mon." Jules slid her arm around Vivian's shoulders and tugged her back toward the bedroom. "Let's go."

Soon they were ensconced in the giant bed with Jules taking Vivian's hand. She said, "You feeling okay tonight?"

"I've forgotten what okay feels like." Vivian shifted in bed, looking miserable. "My Braxton Hicks contractions kept coming and going. It was fantastic to sit in a board meeting this afternoon while my uterus kept squeezing like a fist. I'm pretty sure Stan wouldn't have been able to empathize."

Wincing, Jules patted her hand.

Vivian continued. "Although they all kept looking at me as if they were afraid I might drop a baby on the carpet any second."

Jules laughed. "It'd serve them right. They can afford the cleaning bill."

"It would have livened things up. Meetings are a lot more fun when you're in charge of them."

A note in her voice grabbed Jules's attention. Jules bit her lip. "Do you miss *Du Jour*?"

Vivian looked off into space and didn't answer. For a moment, Jules thought she wouldn't say anything. But then she replied, "A lot."

Jules swallowed and patted her hand again.

"Don't get me wrong," Vivian said with a sigh. "It was time to move on. Time for a change. And I like my job. But I'm not going to lie—it's not the same." She smiled wryly. "I've been trying very, very hard to stay out of Beatrice LaSalla's hair."

"Good. I've seen her hair. She probably spends a thousand dollars a month to keep it styled like that."

Vivian raised an amused eyebrow. Then the amusement shifted into irritation as she squirmed against the pillows and gave a pained groan. "Have I mentioned I hate this?"

"A few times," Jules said and wrestled with herself before blurting out, "You're doing great. I'm really proud of you. I'd never have the guts to do what you're doing."

"Yes, you would," Vivian said dismissively. "If it came right down to it, you would. Because you can do what you have to do"—she raised an eyebrow—"just like I can."

"Maybe," Jules said. She looked down at Vivian's feet. "Did I ever tell you I had a pregnancy scare when I was in high school?"

"No," Vivian said after a moment.

"Yeah. I was seventeen. I was so terrified. It was a false alarm, but I still wonder what I would have done."

"Not what I did?"

Vivian was referring to the abortion she'd gotten when she was eighteen, right before moving to New York. It had set her free. She'd told Jules she didn't regret it.

So Jules had to tread carefully here. It wouldn't do to sound judgmental, but she wanted to tell the truth. "Like I said, I don't know. It's easy to say I would now. But I was a scared kid and so confused. Who knows what I would have decided?"

"I'm sure your parents would have had something to say about it. They usually do." Vivian tugged the blankets up higher over her belly nearly to her chin.

"I don't know what they would have said either. Some things you don't know until you're actually in the situation." Jules had had ample time to learn that over the past several months. "Thank God we never had to find out."

"Yes. It's worked out better for all concerned." Vivian smirked. "Except maybe your parents. Now, I need to get some sleep."

Easier said than done these days. Jules fully expected Vivian to lie awake all night, especially with the Braxton Hicks contractions she'd mentioned. But to her surprise, Vivian went to sleep quickly.

Grateful for mercies small and large, Jules did the same.

She'd started to dream about Vivian giving birth. Not nightmares. Not usually, anyway, although sometimes she dreamed that something had gone wrong. And even though her subconscious wasn't totally clear on what that something was, she still woke in a cold sweat. But usually she just dreamed that the baby had been born: vague, fleeting impressions of a child in Vivian's arms and the usual weird stuff that dreams had, like a crib floating in midair or a bottomless diaper pail.

Tonight, maybe because of what she and Vivian had discussed, she dreamed about her parents.

"You're going to have to be a good father," her dad said solemnly, laying a hand on Jules's shoulder. "Always make sure the kid has clean socks."

Jules wouldn't be a father, but that didn't seem important right now. She nodded very seriously. "I've got the washing machine all ready."

"Did you clean the lint tray in the dryer?" her mother asked.

"Yes, Mom," Jules said in irritation. "And I have the socks all ready. Lots and lots of socks. You won't believe how many. Here: look."

She turned to point at Sock Mountain behind her, but the ground rocked. An earthquake? Jules staggered away from her parents.

Another shake. Her shoulder. Hot wind was blowing unevenly in her ear. And then there was a groan.

"Julia," Vivian called, a pained note in her voice.

Jules woke up right away to find Vivian shaking her shoulder. The hot wind in Jules's dream turned out to be Vivian's breath in her ear, rapid and unsteady.

"What?" Jules managed.

"Call an ambulance."

That was all Jules needed to scramble right back into the waking world. She was reaching for her phone even as she asked, "What's wrong?"

Then beneath the covers, her left foot brushed over a wet spot.

She sat up and threw the covers back to see liquid spreading over the sheets, turning the gray fabric darker.

Vivian's water had broken.

"Call a fucking ambulance," Vivian repeated, her voice reaching a high pitch that Jules had never heard before. "Now!"

"On it." Jules's fingers could not tremble. Not now of all times. She kept them steady as she dialed 911.

"It's two in the morning," Vivian groaned. "This isn't happening."

"Shh, shh." Jules took hold of her hand and tried not to yelp when Vivian squeezed back brutally. "It's going to be fine."

"Nine one one," a woman's voice said over the phone. "What's your emergency?"

"My girlfriend's going into labor." How could Jules sound so calm when the world was turning upside down? "We need an ambulance."

The operator gathered the usual intel—name, address—before asking, "Now just give me some more information. Is this premature? Is there blood or an unusual amount of pain? We get a lot of calls like this, and it's possible you might be able to bring her to the hospital yourself."

How much pain was an *unusual amount*? "Uh—well—"

"Fuck!" Vivian grabbed her belly and looked at Jules with huge, horrified eyes. "I can feel it—oh Christ, she's on her way out of me!"

"Oh no," Jules said into the phone. She was dizzy. Her hand was aching from how hard Vivian squeezed it. "We definitely need a professional."

CHAPTER 31

As they waited for the ambulance, Jules's recurring, nonsensical thought was *It's too early*. Vivian's natural due date wasn't for a week. Surely the baby wouldn't dare to be off schedule. Nobody did that with Vivian.

It had been—Jules checked—seven minutes. That didn't seem right. Surely they'd been waiting for hours while Vivian puffed, groaned, and writhed.

By now Jules's hand ached from how hard Vivian was squeezing it. She might need to get it amputated.

"Um, operator?" she said. "Any advice on what we should be doing right now?"

"Get towels," the operator instructed via speakerphone. "Remove the bottom half of her clothing, if you haven't already. Make sure the front door is unlocked for the medical crew, if you can't leave her to answer the door."

"Oh right. Shit. Right." Jules unlocked the door with the security app, tugged free from Vivian, and stumbled to the linen closet with her hand tingling. She returned with what felt like a thousand towels in her arms.

She dumped them on the bed, not sure what to do with them next, and wrestled Vivian's pajama bottoms off, followed by her underwear. Then she looked at the exposed flesh beneath. It looked like the photos she'd seen in her studies. That had to be a good sign, right?

"It looks normal," she told Vivian. "Like the pictures, I mean."

Vivian looked up at the ceiling. "Can you see anything? Like the head? Is she coming out?"

"Uh, not yet." Thank God.

"I need to push."

"Wait on that," the operator said. "Did you study breathing techniques? Use those until help arrives."

"I need to push," Vivian repeated as if she hadn't heard.

"No," Jules said quickly, putting her hands on Vivian's knees. "Listen to her. We have to wait for the ambulance."

"I can't! It's like the worst period cramps I've ever had. My pelvis is cracking open."

"No, it isn't." Jules ran soothing hands up and down Vivian's legs. "I guess those weren't Braxton Hicks contractions after all."

"They were regular," Vivian said through her teeth. "They kept getting stronger and happening closer together. How was I supposed to know the difference?"

Jules stared at her. "Vivian, Braxton Hicks contractions literally do none of those things. That was real labor!"

"Well, I'm sorry if I skipped the reading," Vivian spat. "I've been busy."

Oh great. Had Vivian skipped *all* of the reading? Because some stuff was coming up that would be kind of important. It probably wouldn't be helpful for Jules to get out one of her baby books and read aloud to Vivian and the operator what to expect in the next couple of months.

"For God's sake." Vivian glared at Jules as if she could see her thoughts. "I read about the *baby*. Just not labor. I was getting a C-section. Why would I have bothered to— *Ow.*"

"What is it?" Jules asked anxiously.

"*It* is an infant, Julia. What the hell do you think? My lower back is killing me."

"Do you have a heating pad?" the operator asked. "Heat can relieve pain and discomfort."

"So can throwing that phone out of the window," Vivian snapped.

"How far apart are the contractions?"

"J-just a few minutes." Vivian shifted again. Sweat plastered her hair to her forehead. "Do ambulances carry epidurals?"

"No. It sounds like you're getting pretty close to the end of labor anyway. Just wait for the—"

Right at that moment, Jules heard the whoop of a siren and saw the flash of red lights on the other side of her curtains. "Oh, thank God."

Moments later, somebody pounded on the door loudly enough that Jules could hear it on the second floor. Since no baby was actively on its way out of Vivian, Jules left her side and rushed downstairs.

"I unlocked the door!" she yelled as she reached the foyer, realizing that she might just as well have yelled that a flight of stairs ago.

The door swung open. Two uniformed paramedics, a man and woman, stood on the doorstep. The ambulance had parked in the street, its red lights reflecting off the asphalt and streetlight.

"Somebody call about delivering a baby?" the man asked. He carried a hefty red bag in one hand.

"Yes! Thanks so much for coming." Jules waved them in. "She says it feels like it'll happen any second now, but I don't know. We just thought—"

"Better safe than sorry." The woman followed the man inside. "Where is she?"

Jules closed the door. "Follow me. Uh, hopefully we can take her to the hospital? She was supposed to have a C-section in two days. Not that that matters, I guess. You don't really need to know that. I'm babbling."

"Just lead the way," the woman said, and they both followed Jules upstairs.

When the three of them entered the bedroom and Vivian got a look at the two strangers in her house, she closed her legs.

"Sorry, ma'am, but we're going to have to take a look," the woman said. "I know it feels weird, but we're professionals."

Vivian pointed at the man with a shaking finger. "*He* can wait by the door."

The man's eyes widened. "But—"

Vivian's glare had enough acid in it to eat through the floor.

The man took a decorous step back to the door and averted his eyes.

The female paramedic put her hands on Vivian's knees and gently parted her legs. "I was a nurse, and I've worked in a neonatal unit. I've seen this plenty of times before. My name's Holly."

"Why aren't you a nurse anymore?" Vivian managed.

"Burnout," Holly said dryly.

Jules hurried to Vivian's side, sat on the edge of the bed, and took her hand. "It'll be okay. They'll take you to the hospital. I'll be right behind you."

"Um…"

Jules and Vivian both turned to Holly, who was looking between Vivian's legs with a critical eye.

"What?" Vivian said.

"Are you going to check her dilation?" Jules asked.

Holly snapped on a pair of latex gloves. "I don't think I need to. And we'll wait to take you to the hospital. Ma'am, are you ready to push?"

"I've been ready." Vivian grabbed Jules's hand again. "I was holding back, but I don't think I can help it anymore. I hung up on that fucking operator too."

"No more holding back. Randy, radio and tell them to prep the gurney. All right, sweetie: deep breath and push!"

"Don't—call me—sweetie!" Vivian tightened her hold on Jules's hand, braced her heels against the mattress, and bore down with a tremendous groan.

"Oh, my God," Jules said. "Is she—is she really giving birth *right now*? Literally?"

"She really is," Holly confirmed.

Randy stepped back into the bedroom, quickly cleared off a table by the door, and began unpacking the bag he'd brought in. From it he withdrew a clear bulb attached to an oxygen mask. Then he rubbed the table down with what looked like an antibacterial wipe. "Resuscitation area prepped, if required."

Everyone was speaking in a normal tone of voice, and yet it was like they were yelling. Everything was moving too fast, and the red lights were still flashing through the bedroom curtains. None of this seemed real.

Vivian made an agonized sound and clamped down hard on Jules's hand.

Jules looked over to see Holly draping one of the towels over Vivian's legs, giving her some cover.

"First baby?" Holly asked.

"Yes," Jules said, since Vivian's concentration was entirely elsewhere.

"Hmm. Usually labor's not this fast with a first pregnancy."

"She was in labor all day," Jules said. "She just didn't know."

"Oh? Yeah, that happens sometimes. Some women go about their day and don't have any idea."

"Do they all like being talked about in the third person?" Vivian hissed. "Oh Jesus. Julia, do something."

If this were the office, Jules would know exactly what to do: send an email to Chanel, make an appointment with the pedicurist, fetch a cup of coffee. But this was not the office. "Uh, sure—what do you need? Oh, you should drink some water. Let me get—"

"Don't you *dare* leave me!"

"Ow! My hand. I won't leave you. I promise, honey."

Vivian looked like she needed the promise. Her face was bright red from effort, and she kept licking her lips. She had to be thirsty, but apparently Jules wasn't allowed to go on water duty. Her every breath was a groan now.

"So you two are partners?" Holly asked.

It was clearly conversation meant to put them at their ease as if this was a normal evening. Jules still wanted to yell at Holly to fucking focus because this was *not* a normal evening, this was the only thing happening to anybody on planet Earth. Nothing else merited discussion.

"Yes." Vivian closed her eyes and tilted her head to the ceiling. "And we'd—appreciate your—discretion."

"Um, sure." Holly clearly hadn't recognized Vivian, had no idea why discretion would be called for, and didn't seem to care either. "Anyway, that's great. What did you do, artificial insemination?"

"Not exactly," Vivian said through her teeth.

"IVF, then." Holly clucked her tongue. "Yeah, that's a lot harder. But it's all about to be worth it. Just hang in there, Mom."

Randy called from his station by the door. "Is it starting to—"

"*Aaahhh!*" Vivian cried, arching her back and grabbing the sheets with her free hand.

"Yep, it's crowning," Holly said. "He? She?"

"She." Jules knelt on the mattress, wishing she could see through the towel. "Is she okay? Does everything look okay?"

"Everything looks okay," Holly confirmed. "All right, ma'am. Give me another push." She leaned forward.

Jules looked at Vivian to see Vivian looking right back at her with glazed, pained eyes.

The thought came as suddenly as a lightning bolt: *This is it. The last moment. It's just the two of us.*

Within minutes, Jules's life—their life together—would change forever. Where there were two, now there would be three. There was no going back.

Right now, Vivian had fear in her eyes: fear that Jules would choose to leave Vivian and walk away, her life more or less unchanged.

Vivian had faith in Jules's love for her. She'd said so. But right now, in the midst of physical agony and the shock of birth, all bets were clearly off.

"Julia," she choked.

Jules raised Vivian's hand to her mouth and placed a firm, fervent kiss on it. "I'm here," she said against Vivian's whitened knuckles. "I'm right here with you. I'm not going anywhere."

"It hurts." Vivian panted. She never looked away from Jules, her eyes pleading. "I think—she's being—difficult—"

"She just wants to do things on her terms." Jules kissed Vivian's knuckles again. "Reminds me of somebody. You can do this. We can do this together."

"Push," Holly repeated. "You're almost there."

"We can do it," Jules said. "We've got this, Vivian."

Finally, acceptance—belief—flashed across Vivian's face. She closed her eyes, took a deep breath, nodded, and exhaled.

Then she said, "Who's *we*? I don't see anybody else here pushing" in a tone so familiar Jules couldn't stop a laugh.

"So do it." Jules bent down and kissed Vivian's sweaty forehead. *We've got this.* "Show us how it's done."

Vivian set her jaw, braced herself, and growled, "Watch—and learn—"

She bore down and threw her head back.

Holly glanced at Jules wide-eyed. "Uh, wow."

"She's always like this," Jules said. "C'mon, Vivian—push!"

Vivian let loose a howl that would have done a werewolf proud.

"Oh!" Holly leaned in with a huge grin. "Here she comes!"

"Fuck!" Vivian screamed.

"You can do it!" Jules grabbed Vivian's shoulder with her free hand. "You can do it—"

"*I know!*"

Vivian crushed Jules's hand in her own. Pushed down one more time. Gave a groan that sounded like it came from the depths of the earth.

"She's here!" Holly said. "I've got her!"

Vivian slumped back against the bed, mouth wobbling around a silent cry, tears streaming down the sides of her face.

Jules leaned forward, resisting the urge to tear the towel off Vivian's lap so she could see the baby. She couldn't hear anything. Babies were supposed to cry soon after birth, but how soon? She'd done all the reading. She couldn't remember. Was it taking too long? Were the lungs okay? Maybe the baby had inhaled something on the way out. She'd read that sometimes they did that and the doctors had to suction their lungs, but there weren't any doctors, and maybe Holly wouldn't know how to—

A furious squall split the air.

The air rushed right out of Jules's own lungs as she leaned over, gasping in relief.

"Is she okay?" Vivian asked weakly. She raised her head from the pillow and then let it fall back down. "Does she look all right?"

"See for yourself, Mama." Holly stood up, cradling a tiny reddened, crying newborn in her gloved hands. "Unbutton your top so I can lay her on you."

Vivian didn't seem to take that in, so the task fell to Jules, who pretty much ripped her top open. Her right hand hurt too much from Vivian's grip to be graceful, and her left one was trembling. A few satin-covered buttons popped loose.

It'll be a story to tell her later, Jules thought nonsensically, *about how she was born at home, and I was so nervous that I tore Vivian's pajama top.*

Then Holly lay the screaming bundle on Vivian's bared chest between her breasts before draping a clean towel over her. "There now," she said softly. "Skin on skin."

"Should we clamp the umbilical cord?" Randy asked, finally moving away from the door.

"Not yet. We'll wait just another minute."

Jules couldn't look away from Vivian to keep up with the medical details. She'd never look away again. There was no other sight like this in the world.

The baby's wails had reduced to whimpers as she lay on Vivian's chest with only her head visible. Vivian was stroking the top of the towel over the lump beneath.

The baby had the face of someone unimpressed with the world she'd just entered. Her nose scrunched up, and her eyes were squeezed shut. She was still covered in birth goo. Wispy dark hair covered her head.

And she was so tiny. Photos hadn't prepared Jules for how small she'd be, how vulnerable, shielded only by a towel from an enormous world.

One little fist lay curled on Vivian's chest. Holding her breath, Jules reached out and touched it with her fingertip.

The baby's hand twitched in response.

"Oh, my God," Jules whispered.

"Time for the first Apgar score. Respiratory gets a two," Holly said. She donned a stethoscope.

"Is two a bad score?" Vivian asked weakly.

"Nope, totally normal. Let's move the towel so I can check her heartbeat."

Jules and Vivian both held their breath while Holly checked the baby's heartbeat, muscle tone, reflex response, and skin tone and pronounced them all satisfactory before saying, "We'll check again in four minutes. Randy, hand me the clamp for the cord."

Apgar was normal. Lungs were normal. No resuscitation area required. Everyone was breathing just fine—except for Jules, who'd lost her breath the moment she'd seen Vivian in her New Year's Eve gown and hadn't gotten it back since.

"Hey."

Jules twitched out of her reverie and turned to see Holly offering her a pair of scissors. "Would you like to do it?"

Jules's eyes opened wide, and she looked at Vivian, who nodded with a tired smile.

Oh. Oh wow.

No. Not wow. There wasn't a word in the English language for how Jules felt right now. Not a single word to describe this…this…

Jules kissed Vivian's hand again, feeling something close to reverence, something that was definitely relief, and something else that was a hundred other things all at once.

She rose to her feet and, with an astonishingly steady hand, cut the cord.

CHAPTER 32

THE UPSCALE MATERNITY CARE CENTER at Mount Sinai West was something else. It included services like private duty nurses, lactation consultants, and professional photographers for the baby's first day. Vivian had always intended to recover there, so Jules already knew to arrange for a corner private room that came with a view of Central Park.

Right now, at 3:45 a.m., the curtains were drawn, which was just as well since Vivian didn't seem to be in any shape to appreciate the view.

Jules approached the bed, Vivian's two heavy bags in hand, her eyes growing larger all the while.

The lights were off, save for a fluorescent bar humming over the sink, and Vivian was fast asleep. She looked small in her double-sized hospital bed. Her eyes had dark rings beneath them, her hair was a mess, and her belly still rose beneath the blanket. Someone had changed her out of her pajamas into a hospital gown. She had an IV in her arm—Jules nearly panicked until she saw it was just a hydration drip.

"Good morning."

Jules gasped as Dr. Viswanathan, Vivian's stern obstetrician, rose to her feet from the bedside chair.

"H-hi." Jules set the bags down next to the bed. "Sorry. I didn't see you."

A rare smile hovered over Dr. Viswanathan's lips. "I understand you've been preoccupied. It sounds like you had an exciting night."

"That's one word for it." It hadn't slowed down since the birth. Jules had been on the phone with Evan, Vivian's bleary assistant, telling him to cancel everything on Vivian's calendar and make no plans to reschedule. At the last second, she remembered to tell him to schedule the housekeeper to come in and clean up the bedroom. No way would Vivian want to come home to bloody linens.

Now she ran a hand through her hair, which couldn't be much neater than Vivian's. "How is she?"

"Exhausted, as you can see, but fine. The placenta was delivered safely. She came through all of this well, especially for a woman her age with no hospital care during the birth."

"She wouldn't dream of coming through any other way." Jules walked to the bed. Vivian looked so out of it, so unlike herself. Jules longed to touch her cheek, to make sure she was really here and okay.

It wouldn't do to wake her, though. With a sigh, Jules contented herself with brushing her fingertips over the top of Vivian's hair, careful not to tug on any strands. Good enough for now, but the moment couldn't come soon enough when she could hold Vivian tight.

She turned back to Dr. Viswanathan, who was regarding her with a raised eyebrow.

Jules looked defiantly back. She'd been in on this whole situation from the beginning, even if her role had...changed throughout. And she was beyond sick of owing people explanations.

"Is the baby okay?" she asked.

If she wanted explanations, Dr. Viswanathan didn't ask for them. Instead, she straightened out her white lab coat. "She is perfectly well and sleeping in the nursery. I came when called for, of course, but it seems my presence was unnecessary, which is a good thing."

"Yes. Uh, sorry you got woken up for no reason, though."

"This is the reason." Dr. Viswanathan approached Vivian's bedside and checked the beeping machines before giving her chart one more look. "You don't become an obstetrician without preparing for late-night calls. Every child is worth it."

That seemed more sentimental than Dr. Viswanathan usually got, but maybe it was the lateness of the hour or just the reduced lighting in the room that softened the planes of her face. Even the streaks of iron gray in her dark hair seemed less severe. Here in the shadows, she was one woman talking to another, giving reassurances that Jules badly needed.

"Julia?"

Jules whipped back around to see Vivian blinking in confusion at her and then at the IV in her arm.

"Oh," Vivian said. "That's right, I had a..." She shifted in the bed and groaned.

"The word you want is 'baby.'" Jules didn't bother restraining herself this time and rubbed her thumb tenderly over Vivian's cheek, which was soft but with a glimmer of sweat on her jawline. "How are you feeling?"

"I don't know. Awful." Vivian looked vaguely around the room, frowning. "Where is she?"

"Nursery, Doc said," Jules replied.

"Now that Jules is here and you are awake, Vivian, I will go home," Dr. Viswanathan said. She looked a little more distant than she had while talking to Jules.

Jules wondered what Vivian had said to her before conking out.

"You're in fine shape, and the nurses will be able to look after you," Dr. Viswanathan continued. "I'll return later in the day to check on you."

"Yes. Yes, fine," Vivian said as if she was only dimly aware of what her doctor was saying. "Julia, I want the baby."

Jules was already turning to the door before she realized they wouldn't let her wander into the nursery and walk out with a newborn. She pressed the nurse's button on Vivian's bed instead, waving absentmindedly at Dr. Viswanathan as she left.

Then she rubbed Vivian's arm. "Hey. You look good. I mean, all things considered."

"I bet I do." Vivian seemed to be waking up more. "Put a necklace on me and I'll be ready to host the Met benefit."

"That's not until the end of August. I think you've got a little time."

Just then a nurse poked her head in. "You called?"

"She's awake." It was impossible to hide the eagerness in Jules's voice. She didn't bother trying. "Can we see the baby?"

"Sure." The nurse glanced at Vivian's chart. "Carlisle, room 344A. Be right back."

Jules watched her go. Wow. That woman was going to bring back...a baby. The baby Vivian's body had been sheltering for months.

"What time is it?" Vivian asked groggily.

Jules looked at the clock on the wall. "Almost four a.m."

"But it didn't start until two. It…it all happened very fast, didn't it?"

Jules swallowed. Vivian looked composed now—sheer exhaustion must help—but not so long ago, she'd been in frantic pain.

"Yeah," Jules said. "Maybe it's better that way, though?"

"I'll take it over fourteen hours in agony or whatever other women go through. But do you see why I wanted a nice predictable operation?" Vivian rested her head back against the pillows, then her eyes darted again toward the door.

"I'm sure the nurse will be back soon," Jules murmured. She took Vivian's hand.

Then her eyes got hot and wet. Oh great, tears out of nowhere—but tonight could have gone wrong, *really* wrong, and instead she and Vivian were here in a hospital room after… "I'm so glad everything's all right," she choked. "Oh, my God, I'm so glad."

"Don't collapse on me," Vivian warned. "One of us has to have functioning brain cells, and it's not me right now."

"I'm not collapsing." Jules sniffled and dashed her hand across her cheeks. "I can't promise anything about the brain cells."

Before Vivian could respond, they heard the rattling of wheels outside and turned to the door as the nurse steered a bassinet inside.

"She's still asleep," the nurse said softly.

"Let's count our blessings," Vivian murmured. She tried to sit up but then fell back with a groan. "Julia…"

Jules reached in, took Vivian under her arms, and helped hoist her up.

Then the nurse carefully lifted a little red bundle wrapped in a white blanket and gave it to Vivian, who settled it against her breast, visibly holding her breath as she did so. Then the nurse gave them a nod and a smile and silently left the room.

Jules held her breath too as she leaned in for her second glimpse of the child. She definitely looked better after a bath. Someone had given her a little white knit cap with a bow on the front. Her face was still red, her eyes still squeezed shut, and her nose was wrinkled, all of which gave her an unmistakable expression of disgust at the state of the world.

Jules stared at her, and stared, and stared some more.

"She doesn't quite look like a *baby* yet, does she?" Vivian asked, cuddling her daughter closer. "More like…I don't know, a tiny village elder."

"No," Jules heard herself say. "She's beautiful."

Vivian turned to look at her. Her eyes widened. "Julia?"

"Look at that sweet li'l face," Jules said dreamily.

"Oh no," Vivian said, closing her eyes.

"Look at her hand poking out of the blanket right there. Her fingers are so tiny!"

"What did you expect?"

"Aw-w." The dumbest grin ever had to be on Jules's face. "Look at what you did. Isn't she amazing? She's a little person!"

"You're going to be ridiculous about this, aren't you?" Vivian's tone was dry as she tucked the blanket tenderly around the baby.

"Oh, I won't be that bad." Jules's eyes widened. "I think she has my nose!"

"It's a miracle," Vivian said. "I think you need to get some sleep."

"Uh-uh. Never sleeping again." Jules leaned in and rested her head against Vivian's shoulder, the hospital gown rough against her cheek. "She's perfect. So are you. You are both completely perfect."

"Well," Vivian said, "I guess you can stay awake if you're going to talk like that."

Just then the baby wriggled and began to whimper.

"Uh-oh. Hold her for a second. I think I can figure this out." Vivian handed the baby to Jules like it was no big deal, then fiddled with the laces on her gown.

Jules gasped as she felt the baby's weight in her arms. She stared down at her as her whimpering grew louder.

"Right. I did this earlier, and I was half dead." Vivian pulled her gown apart enough to expose a breast. "Let me have her again. Quick."

Jules handed the baby back with shaking arms and watched as her mouth latched on to Vivian's nipple.

A little gasp escaped Vivian's mouth. She said, "God, that's weird. You see other women doing it, but you don't know."

Hypnotized, Jules watched the baby suckle. "What's it like?"

"It's warm. Kind of tingly. I don't think much is coming out yet."

"Yeah, that'll change soon. Look, she knows exactly how to do it! She's totally a genius."

"Totally." Vivian didn't sound as if she were joking at all.

"Gets it from me," Jules added. "Wow. Look at her go."

"Yes," Vivian said softly. Jules spared a moment to glance at her and saw a warm look in her eyes as she watched the baby nurse.

Jules sank down in the chair Dr. Viswanathan had vacated earlier. Together, she and Vivian watched the baby nurse in silence for a while.

Then Vivian said, "Felicity."

"Huh?" Jules blinked, then figured it out. "Oh."

"Her name is Felicity."

Jules's brain, tired as it was, staggered around the name, trying to figure out if it fit or not. It was pretty but seemed fancy for the squirming little bundle at Vivian's breast. "Okay. Why Felicity?"

"I like the double meaning." Vivian stroked her fingertip over the baby's soft cheek. "The first one is 'happiness,' of course. Remember the second one, English major?"

"Um...maybe if I was more with it, I'd—"

"Good fortune." Vivian looked up at Jules with eyes that were tired beyond the telling of it but that were soft too. "In the archaic usage."

Vivian had the most beautiful eyes in the world. No wonder Jules could only manage to reply, "Archaic, yeah. Cool. That's really cool."

Then she looked back at the baby—at Felicity—and felt a big, silly grin stretch her face again. "Hi there, Felicity Carlisle."

"Yes," Vivian whispered to the baby. "Hi."

She and Jules remained in silence for a few moments, savoring the peace. In just a few hours, once New York awoke, the pace would pick up again. More people would have to be contacted, more decisions would have to be made, and more details would have to be painstakingly arranged.

Jules could shield Vivian from some of it, could run interference with Vivian's staff so that she wouldn't need to be troubled any more than necessary—but the mêlée would be on, and there would be no turning it off.

She stroked Felicity's cheek with the very tip of her finger. "Wow. She's so soft." She pulled her hand back, half fearing she'd bruise the kid with even a featherlight touch.

"Mm," Vivian said.

Felicity's suckling ceased, and she gave a tiny sigh as she went back to sleep.

Jules's heart stopped, melted, and then started beating again.

"Hold her for a while?" Vivian's voice had a hopeful, hesitant note in it.

Jules barely heard it because she was already extending two greedy hands for an armful of baby. "Oh, my God," she said as she leaned back in the chair.

It wasn't like she'd never held a baby before—she'd held several—but this was different. So different. "Hey, how heavy was she? Is she?"

"Seven pounds, fourteen ounces," Vivian said as she covered her breast back up. "And she was early. I've decided I'm incredibly lucky."

"You sure are," Jules said and cooed down to Felicity, "She sure is lucky to have the most amazing baby in the whole world, isn't she? Isn't she?"

Felicity yawned and promptly began to emit an unmistakable odor.

"Oh God. Is that—" Vivian began.

"Whoops. Yeah. I'm all over it." Jules carried Felicity to a nearby changing table, where she unwrapped her. "I brought a couple of diapers in your kit."

"They probably have a few lying around here somewhere. It's a hospital."

"Yeah, but we need one right now." Jules whisked it out of the bag. "Relax. It's like riding a bicycle." A nasty, smelly bicycle.

Extra nasty. Jules winced as she checked out the situation. Not all the babysitting in the world had prepared her for meconium. At least this was supposed to pass out of a baby's system over a few days. Holding her breath, she quickly wiped Felicity down and changed her.

Vivian looked impressed.

"I babysat in high school," Jules said, proud that it finally came in handy. "One couple had a toddler and an infant. They were desperate to get out for a few hours a week. I made some pretty good money, but whew, the kids could be exhausting."

"No wonder you were so frightened at seventeen," Vivian said quietly.

Jules's fingers paused as she wrapped Felicity back in her blanket. She'd fussed a little during the diaper change, but now that she was clean and comfortable again, she had apparently decided to forgive Jules and go back to sleep.

"Yeah, I guess," she said. Vivian had been referring to Jules's high school pregnancy scare. She wondered how frightened Vivian had been at eighteen when she'd actually had to get an abortion.

That was a question for later. In the meantime, Jules held Felicity close to her chest again and looked down into her tiny red face with a feeling in her heart too huge to name.

I've known about you since Vivian has, she thought. *I've known you from the start. Welcome home.*

Impulsively, she kissed Felicity's forehead, softer than down, and smiled against her skin.

She heard a soft noise and looked up to see Vivian watching the two of them. Her eyes were suspiciously shiny.

But Vivian blinked, and no tears fell. She cleared her throat. "Ah…well. Have you decided what her middle name's going to be?"

Jules's arms were smarter than the rest of her. They held on to Felicity instead of dropping her in shock. "Have I what?"

Vivian gave her a small wry smile. "Her middle name. Pick it. Or do you think she shouldn't have one?"

Jules slowly sat back down in her chair, close enough that Vivian could reach out and touch either her or Felicity if she wanted to. "You'll let me pick it? Really?"

"I wouldn't let anybody else. It seems to me you have the right." Vivian took a deep breath and looked at Jules with the baby in her arms. "The look on your face with her—I wish you could see it. Yes, you get to choose. Just so you know, I did think about 'Julia' for her middle name, but…"

Julia? Really? Vivian had thought about that?

"But what?" Jules whispered.

Vivian shook her head. "It seems more important that you have a part in this. You can choose 'Julia' yourself if you want, of course."

Jules, her heart aching with joy, looked down at the baby's face. *Felicity Julia Carlisle.*

It was a beautiful name. It was also kind of a mouthful. As much as the idea flattered Jules, the writer in her rebelled. The kid's middle name would already be sandwiched by fancy words with multiple syllables, both heavy on the letter L.

No. It had to be something short, punchy, and with a firmer consonant note.

"June," she said, looking at the baby and testing it out. "Felicity June Carlisle."

After a pause, Vivian said, "Why June? Is that a family name?"

She'd sounded puzzled, not resistant, so Jules felt confident saying, "I just think it sounds good. It's like my name, too—Jules, I mean—and..." She hesitated before admitting, "And a little like your old one. Jenny. Although it's not Jenny, of course," she added hastily.

She glanced up at Vivian, whose face had closed a little. "That's a name I left behind, Julia. Why would we want something that echoes it?"

"You said you want her to work for what she gets," Jules said. She stroked a fingertip over Felicity's forehead. "Jenny Fluharty did that, just like Vivian Carlisle does now. And like I said, it's not really Jenny. But we can give her a little bit of that."

Vivian pressed her lips together, maybe because the lower one seemed to wobble for a second. Then she cleared her throat again. "Felicity June Carlisle." She squinted as if she was trying to imagine how it would look on paper. "Felicity June..."

"See?" Jules said happily. "Sounds good, doesn't it?"

Vivian stuck her tongue in her cheek, frowned again, then nodded decisively. "June it is."

"Hello, Felicity June," Jules said to the baby. "Hello, sweetheart."

At that moment, Vivian's stomach gave a rumble loud enough that it could be labeled a gurgle. She placed her hand on it, and her expression slid into shock. "My God. Suddenly I'm starving."

No wonder. Her body had just worked harder than it ever had. Jules said, "I looked this up too. Chicken noodle soup is good. I packed a cup of instant soup in one of your bags."

"You did?"

"Of course I did. Hold her while I get it ready." Jules handed Felicity back.

Vivian drew her baby close while looking up wide-eyed at Jules.

Then Jules stood up, ready to go to the tote bag. But before she could take a step, Vivian reached out and grabbed her wrist.

Surprised, Jules looked down into her wide, reddened eyes.

Vivian's grip loosened enough that her hand could slide down and take hold of Jules's. Their fingers twined together.

But Vivian didn't say anything. She just kept looking up, searching Jules's face from forehead to chin over and over. Her lips parted as if she were about to speak, but she didn't.

Then just when Jules was starting to feel really self-conscious, Vivian said almost inaudibly, "Thank you."

Jules opened her mouth to respond, but then Vivian closed her eyes, kissed Jules's hand, and said, "Thank you" again. And she kept mumbling it against Jules's skin, her voice hoarse with disbelief. "Thank you. Thank you. Thank you."

Jules didn't know whom Vivian was thanking. It might not even have been her. But she still bent over, her heart pounding hard, her breath coming fast. She kissed Vivian's forehead and then her temple and then her cheek as Vivian kept her own lips pressed hard against Jules's hand while she murmured her gratitude to—or for—the one who loved her best.

EPILOGUE

Three months later

COMING OUT IN STYLE: VIVIAN CARLISLE AND JULES MORETTI TAKE MANHATTAN

Bob Chambers

Modernity Magazine Contributor

The time for our interview is clearly coming to a close. Clouds heavy with waiting rain are gathering over La Grande's outdoor patio as if Vivian Carlisle has summoned them to punctuate our time together.

I take one final look at her. This requires some courage, particularly in Carlisle's case. Everyone tells you not to make eye contact with lionesses, since they'll take it as a challenge.

Carlisle, perhaps mellowed by good food, good wine, and her companion, doesn't gut me with her steak knife.

I call it a win and look over at Moretti with her deceptively mild eyes and easygoing smile. She has an essay forthcoming in a collection about queerness in fashion, and she's twice now been a contributing writer for the entertainment website Vox. *I don't doubt that she's set her sights higher. One underestimates her at their peril, I think.*

"One last question," I say. "Since you officially debuted as a couple at the Carnegie benefit two weeks ago, how have you been handling the media attention?"

Carlisle gives a shrug so magnificently indifferent that I somehow become convinced she is divorcing me.

"I'm less of a public figure now," she says. "What reaction there was has died down quickly. We're happy to enjoy our private life."

I'm sure Beatrice LaSalla's recent antics in Nice have helped in that regard. Du Jour has a new diva at the helm, and she's been attention worthy, to say the least. One notes in particular those leaked emails that make de Sade seem like a monk in comparison. It's the perfect distraction from Carlisle's own life. The timing is so convenient, in fact, that I almost wonder if it's been orchestrated.

I do not ask about this.

Instead, I cheat with one more question, even though I said I'd asked the last one. "Now that you're out, what's next?"

Carlisle raises her eyebrows behind her Versace sunglasses and looks at her girlfriend. "Well, next month we're off to Monaco for a conference, but until then—"

"No fall fashion weeks?" I ask in surprise.

In return, I receive a look from Carlisle that says, Did I say fall fashion weeks?

"Not this year. We're keeping things low-key." Moretti takes Carlisle's hand as if it's the easiest thing in the world instead of like someone who's grabbing a sword by its naked blade. "Right now we're concentrating on the everyday stuff, especially Felicity."

"Especially Felicity," Carlisle agrees, giving Moretti's hand a brief squeeze. She turns back to me.

I open my mouth to thank her for the interview, the meal, and the benevolence of the heavens in not raining out our table.

"I think that's everything," Carlisle says. "You can go now."

"That poor bastard." Jules chuckled as she finished reading the interview aloud.

"He deserved it," Vivian replied.

"He's won a Pulitzer."

"He's a pompous ass who kept trying to talk about himself—how many times did he get 'I' in the article anyway?—with his testicles drawing farther and farther up into his abdomen. You're a better writer."

"Cheers to that."

They clinked their glasses of Cabernet together. Vivian had two hours until Felicity's next feeding, so she'd judged it safe to have a drink. And there was something about sitting on the rooftop on a clear October night that called for a glass of wine.

Jules looked up at the sky. Thanks to light pollution, only the brightest stars were visible. She tried to pick out her lucky one and thank it.

"Simon asked me why we gave the interview to *Modernity* instead of a Koening publication," she said.

Vivian sipped from her glass. "Oh? And what did you say?"

"Just the truth. That it was a nice way to signal that I'm your partner, not your toy. I'm sure Carter Mathson got the message."

"I'm sure Carter Mathson's boss got the message," Vivian said dryly.

After a decent pause, Jules said, "He told me you look good. Simon, I mean."

"I ought to with what I'm paying my trainer and nutritionist." Vivian's casual tone belied the purse of her lips when she finished speaking.

Jules waited.

"So you and Evan have scheduled my lunch with him?" Vivian asked.

"Next week. Just half an hour."

"That's plenty of time."

Thirty minutes didn't sound like plenty of time to Jules, but it was a start, anyway. It had been weird to schedule something for Simon as his assistant while working with her girlfriend's own assistant. Jules had still been delighted to do it. They wouldn't be going on double dates with Simon and Maxwell anytime soon, but détente was in view.

Amazing how having kids could make people reassess their relationships and priorities.

Speaking of which, Jules looked at the wireless video baby monitor that sat hissing with static on the table between her and Vivian's chairs. She exhaled in relief to see that Felicity still slept peacefully in her crib.

Everyone said that babies grew fast, but Jules still hadn't been prepared for the acceleration from newborn to three months. Felicity had started off as a loaf of bread in a white blanket, and now she was a proper armful who could swipe at Jules's face and say things like "ah-goo."

Felicity had just started to laugh too. There was no more heart-melting sound in the cosmos. It turned Jules into a puddle.

Vivian pretended to be cooler about it, but she wasn't fooling anybody. Especially now, when she leaned in toward the baby monitor, her eyebrows anxiously raised. "Everything okay?"

"Yeah, she's asleep. I'm sure Zahra's off somewhere, giving prayers of thanks."

That was mostly facetious. Felicity was a good baby—at least so their live-in nanny had assured them. Nevertheless, Zahra seemed like a gift from the universe. Even with her presence, Jules and Vivian ended each day exhausted and wondering where the time had gone. It was so easy to let time slip by.

Not tonight, though. Tonight Jules had vowed they'd spend the evening together, having a stay-at-home date after she got home from work. It was a pretty simple date. Relaxing evening on the roof and glass of wine: check.

She looked at Vivian's elegant profile, specifically the faint blush that the red wine had brought to her cheeks.

Vivian glanced over, saw her looking, and blushed a little more. Her lips twitched.

Time for date night, part two.

"Something on your mind?" Vivian asked.

"Who, me?" Jules asked innocently. She tilted her head to the side and gave Vivian her most winning smile. "I'm just thinking about how much you mean to me."

"It's either sex or you're going to ask me to talk about feelings."

"And how hot you are."

"Oh, thank God."

"Only if you're up for it," Jules said quickly. "It's just that you said this morning maybe tonight we could, and I was thinking…"

Vivian gave Jules a slow, wicked smile, and Jules's stomach began to melt.

"Yay," she finished weakly. Who could blame her for being incoherent? She and Vivian had only had sex twice since Felicity's birth. It was completely understandable, but Jules's hunger for Vivian had begun as an all-consuming thing and wouldn't be sated anytime soon.

"'Yay'?" Vivian said. "You have a wealth of imagination, and that's the best you can do?"

"You've got a point." Jules considered that. "Hey, Vivian?"

"Hmm?"

"I'm going to fuck you cross-eyed," Jules said.

Vivian stiffened. Her breath caught.

"I'm going to spread you and take everything I want," Jules said. "I'm going to make you forget your name."

"Oh?" Vivian whispered, closing her eyes.

"And if you're not careful," Jules said, "I'm going to do it right here on the roof." She took Vivian's hand and squeezed it. "Is that better?"

"Let's go," Vivian rasped. "Now."

"Let's." Jules let go of her and held the roof door open. She brushed her hand against the small of Vivian's back as she passed and watched the resulting shiver with delight.

They'd be lucky if they made it to the bedroom without stopping to feel each other up. Which they probably shouldn't do with Zahra in the house somewhere.

If they *did* make it to the bedroom, though, they'd be home free. Zahra knew it was date night. They wouldn't be disturbed. Felicity could be bottle-fed if necessary.

Luckily, they got to the bedroom without incident. It was a near thing, since the back of Vivian's neck was red and her hands trembled. She wouldn't want slow and careful, not tonight, now that she was feeling better, after doing it just twice in over three months.

The door shut behind them. Vivian locked it, and before she could say anything else, Jules was on her.

They kissed, then kissed again until Vivian groaned and pushed Jules away just enough that she could start unbuttoning her own blouse.

Jules tore off her own shirt, but as soon as she got another look at Vivian with her blouse open, she decided that the rest of her clothes could wait. She pressed Vivian back against the door the second Vivian kicked off her shoes.

Jules tangled her fingers in Vivian's hair and tilted her head back, and Vivian slid her arms around Jules's waist, tugging her even closer. During the first time they'd done this after Felicity's birth, they'd both been stunned by the way the space just evaporated between them, now that the bump wasn't there for the first time ever.

Jules had been ready to take it slow and gentle anyway, but the novelty had helped—the way they could lie so closely together, Vivian's legs around Jules's waist and Jules's arms around Vivian's shoulders with nothing in between. They'd both reveled in the closeness, had taken their time savoring it, drawing it out.

Not tonight, though. Tonight, Jules gave Vivian another hard kiss and then dropped to her knees and rubbed her face against Vivian through her skirt.

Vivian's hips jerked forward, and she gasped before grabbing Jules's hair.

The smell of her made Jules groan. She slid her hand beneath Vivian's skirt, let her palms rub up and down her thighs, moving the skirt up just a little higher each time until she could rub her thumbs against Vivian's underwear. *Mm.* Silk.

So her thumbs teased Vivian through her panties, and her mouth and nose teased Vivian through her skirt, and Vivian's head rested against the doorway as she panted for it.

Finally, when Vivian had begun to wriggle, Jules pushed the skirt all the way up to her waist. Vivian let go of Jules's hair so she could hold it up while Jules leaned in and mouthed at her through her underwear. Which was exquisite.

"This is new," Jules murmured as she placed tiny, gentle kisses all up and down, clit to slit, through the pale green silk and lace, so soft and warm against her lips and tongue. "Did you get these just for tonight? For me?" She slid her hands up and down Vivian's thighs again in time with her kisses.

"Uh—" Vivian gulped. "Uh, yes, I, um—"

Aw-w. "You want it?" Jules whispered and exhaled hotly against the wetness that seeped through the silk. "You ready for it?" She licked roughly and Vivian gasped. "You going to give it to me?"

"G-give you—" Already Vivian could barely talk.

"Give me this." Jules slid her hand up her thigh and cradled Vivian through her underwear.

Vivian bucked her hips forward.

"My favorite thing." Jules licked again and even scraped her teeth.

Vivian cried out and rose up on her toes, shoving frantically against Jules's mouth.

"Give it to me," Jules said.

"Yes!" Vivian whimpered. "Oh! Yes—"

It wouldn't take much to bring her off against the door just like this. But Jules didn't want that, not after such a long wait. She stood up, leaned in, and kissed Vivian so hungrily that by the time they parted, Vivian's breaths were all ending in tiny cries.

She was beyond ready. Jules tugged her to the bed, pressed her back down on the mattress, and yanked off her panties to spread her open. Vivian threw one leg over her shoulder.

"It's mine," Jules whispered. "It's mine," and she buried her face in the wet that was so wet that she knew Vivian had been waiting all day for this, just like Jules had, and had tried her damnedest to pretend otherwise. In retaliation, Jules licked again and again, even rougher than before.

Vivian keened, arched up, and grabbed Jules's hair once more.

"Oh Jesus, yes, Vivian," Jules whispered against her, licking and sucking.

Vivian was writhing now, hissing, panting through her nose.

"I'm taking it, I've got to have it, it's mine."

"Take it...t-take—" Vivian sobbed for air. Her leg trembled where it hooked over Jules's shoulder. "Yours, take, oh *please*—"

Jules spread her wider, sunk two thumbs in, leaned in and fluttered her tongue against Vivian's clit.

287

Vivian let go of Jules's hair, slapped both hands over her mouth, and screamed.

Oh yes. Fast. Fast and good, judging by the way Vivian's legs were shaking.

Jules wiped her mouth, stood up, and lay down next to her.

Vivian covered her eyes with her hand, still gasping. "Oh, my God," she whimpered.

"You okay?" Jules asked, just to make sure.

"Uh…huh." Vivian licked her lips.

Jules looked down at her, eating up the sight of her messy hair, red-cheeked face, and heaving chest. Incredible. Fantastic. Still so new and so astonishing.

"Oh," Vivian finally managed, "I'll…for you. Just give me a second."

"It's okay. Take your time," Jules said and grinned.

It was a rare night, and Jules kissed Vivian. She snuggled up too, putting an arm over Vivian's waist.

Vivian's breath slowed as she returned to herself. Then she sighed, turned her head toward Jules, looked right into her eyes, and gave Jules her most wicked smile.

"I've been thinking, Julia," she said.

Jules's skin prickled hotly all over.

"You've been very patient. I know you'd like to do this more often."

"I don't want to pressure—"

"And there's something I'd like to give you. A present."

"A present?" It came out of Jules as a hopeful squeak. Mortifying.

Vivian didn't seem deterred. "I know there's something you've been wanting."

The list of things that Jules wanted from Vivian could, if written down, wrap around the entire house. "What is it?"

"Sit up," Vivian said softly, "and watch me."

Jules sat up slowly, eyes widening by the second.

Vivian wriggled out of her wrinkled skirt and tossed it to the floor. And then she parted her legs. And reached down between them.

And arched into her own touch.

"Oh, my God," Jules said, which was a miracle, since someone had just sucked all the oxygen out of the room.

"Watch me," Vivian whispered as though Jules could do anything else. And trying not to faint, Jules watched.

Vivian was red and swollen now, slick and wet and no doubt extra sensitive, so her fingertips slid up, down, and around so lightly that it almost looked like she wasn't touching herself at all. Delicate and gentle, just the way she liked it. She hadn't begun to pant or anything, but her breathing was starting to get a little deeper a little more quickly.

She spread her legs to give Jules a better look. She parted her labia wider with the fingers of her left hand and stroked and dipped between them with her right—swirled her index finger just around the edges of her clit and sighed, "Mm" through her nose as she closed her eyes.

"This is how you do it?" Jules asked hoarsely. "This is how you do it when you're thinking about me?"

Vivian opened her eyes again, warm and hazy with desire. "When I'm not in a hurry," she said huskily.

"When—" Jules swallowed before she could choke. "When are you in a hurry?"

"I haven't been in a while," Vivian admitted, rubbing her clit again. She shivered.

Jules couldn't decide which to watch, Vivian's fingers or her face. She settled on the face just for the moment because Vivian was still whispering.

"But before...before we ever made love..." She batted her lashes long and slow and gave Jules a sweet smile. "Well, I don't want to bore you. You probably don't want to hear about it."

"I will give you everything I own if you tell me."

Vivian laughed softly and slipped one finger inside herself.

Jules groaned. *Fuck.*

"After you kissed me." Vivian arched her hips. "So many times after you kissed me. Before I went to sleep. Then I did it slowly, just the way I like it best."

Shortly after they'd begun their relationship before they'd had sex, Jules had wondered if Vivian ever touched herself and if she ever did it while thinking about Jules. Then she'd made herself stop thinking about it before it drove her out of her mind.

"But sometimes you didn't do it slowly?" she asked.

"Yes." Vivian never turned her eyes away from Jules. "Sometimes, I couldn't wait. I'd go to my room and shut the door. I wouldn't even get undressed."

Jules had to close her eyes and breathe deeply to keep from hyperventilating.

"And once I didn't even make it to the bed. I leaned against the door, just like you had me tonight."

Jules moaned, unable to open her eyes because if she did—

"I knew by then that you'd be so good to me, Julia. I knew the moment I said yes, you'd—ah—"

Jules's eyes flew open at the whimper in her voice.

Vivian had buried two fingers inside herself and was thrusting gently. "But it wasn't enough just to think about it. I had to know. I had to feel it for myself."

It was all over then. Jules slid right off the bed and bent toward Vivian again. She'd be too sensitive for Jules to eat her up as she had a few minutes ago, but Jules could no more be a passive bystander than she could wear an Altuzarra suit with flip-flops.

She began kissing the inside of Vivian's thighs, adding just that extra bit of stimulation while Vivian touched herself.

"Julia!" Vivian groaned.

"Keep talking," Jules growled. She nipped the inside of Vivian's thigh. "Tell me everything."

"It was so good." Vivian's legs began to tremble again. "I'd known it would be good, but I didn't know how much." She slid her fingers halfway out. Jules nudged the knuckles with her nose, and Vivian slid them back in with a groan. "Oh, my God, the first time you made me come, I didn't even have my shirt all the way off."

"So beautiful," Jules gasped, then reared up and began kissing Vivian's belly. It wasn't completely flat again, but it was warm and smooth. "You were so beautiful, I wanted to eat you up, make you mine. I never wanted anything like that with anybody else before." She bit as if to prove her point.

Vivian groaned, pulled her fingers out, and rubbed them against Jules's lips. "Take off your pants," she managed to say.

Yes, ma'am. Jules pulled away just long enough to yank her pants and panties off, tossing them onto the carpet. Then she leaped back onto the mattress and lay on top of Vivian, holding herself up by her elbows.

Vivian wrapped her legs around Jules's waist and then her arms around Jules's shoulders, and they twined together.

Jules rubbed her sticky face against Vivian's, Vivian combed her sticky fingers through Jules's hair, and it was best like this, when they wanted so much but could give so much too.

"I heard myself begging you." Vivian sounded drunk with it. "I'd never begged before, but I thought I'd die if you stopped. I didn't recognize myself."

Jules groaned against her shoulder. "I love you. I'm the luckiest person alive to be here with you, to have you like this, me and nobody else."

"Spread your legs. Get on my thigh."

Oh hell yes. Jules was throbbing so much that it seemed like the space between her legs had taken on a life of its own. She obeyed Vivian, straddling her firm thigh.

Vivian's skin was smooth and warm against Jules's soaked flesh. It coaxed a groan out of Jules's chest that was so deep, it hurt a little. Helplessly, Jules rocked back and forth against her thigh, the pressure licking its way through her whole body.

"Oh yes." Vivian grabbed Jules's ass and helped her move, encouraging her to go faster and press harder. "Yes. That's right."

"F-fuck!" Jules looked up into Vivian's eyes to see Vivian looking right back at her.

Vivian's gaze devoured Jules, possessing her as fully as Jules longed to possess Vivian in return.

"Give it to me, Julia," she breathed. "Give me what I want the most."

It only took one more thrust against that firm, smooth thigh before Jules was coating Vivian's leg with her come, trying not to scream in Vivian's ear.

"Excellent," Vivian purred while Jules barely managed not to collapse on top of her with her full weight.

Jules said into the pillow, "Um, yeah. Um, God. Um…"

Vivian laughed, stroking her palms up and down Jules's back. "Well," she said, "if I remember correctly, I now own all of your earthly possessions. Yes?"

"Sure," Jules mumbled. "Enjoy the espadrilles."

"Pass." Vivian sighed in contentment as she patted Jules's ass. It felt great. "They're out of season."

Jules rolled off Vivian and cuddled up next to her again. She lay her head on Vivian's shoulder. Delicious lassitude curled through her, but if she dozed off, Vivian would never let her hear the end of it.

She kissed Vivian's throat. "That was amazing. Thank you."

Instead of her usual smug reply, Vivian rubbed a hand over Jules's back again, rumpling her blouse. She said nothing.

By now, Jules knew Vivian's silences well. This felt like a significant one. She waited.

"I've got one more present for you," Vivian said eventually.

That woke Jules up, all right. Whatever this present was, it was clearly more serious than a roll in the hay. "Oh yeah?"

"It's something you wanted to know. I've been meaning to tell you for a while." Vivian inhaled deeply through her nose. "Tonight just seems like the night, I guess."

Was Vivian trying to kill her with suspense? "Okay, so what is it?"

"When we got together in London, you asked me how long I'd had feelings for you. I told you I didn't know. But I do know. Down to the minute."

Jules propped herself up on her elbow. She had to get a good look at Vivian's face, which was still flushed from sex but contemplative now, maybe a little apprehensive.

Did Jules seriously get to know about this? Her heart began to race as if they'd started making love all over again. "When?"

Vivian seemed to wrestle with herself for another moment before she smiled in wry concession. "In London after Christmas. Do you remember? I'd had a nightmare, and I couldn't sleep. I came downstairs, and there you were, curled up and asleep in an armchair."

Jules's breath caught. Yes, she remembered. The way she'd woken up to see Vivian standing over her. The shock on Vivian's face.

"The armchair?" she asked.

"You had your tablet in your lap." Vivian looked into Jules's eyes. "I saw you were reading a pregnancy book. I realized you were up in the middle of the night trying to help me, and I thought about how the last few days had just felt all wrong without you there. And then I just…knew."

She stopped and swallowed hard while Jules stared at her, afraid she was about to clam up. But she kept going. "And you said you'd come to me when I hadn't forced you to. I realized how much you mattered to me. I knew I had to keep you with me—I just didn't know how. Even after New Year's, when I knew how you felt, I didn't know what I should do."

"Oh, Vivian," Jules whispered.

Vivian didn't seem sentimental about her confession. In fact, she actually glared at Jules. "I dithered for months because of you," Vivian said, "and I never dither. It shows a lack of character—but obviously something had to be done. And then during London Fashion Week…"

Vivian bit her lip and looked unhappy for a second, no doubt remembering the moment Jules had finally let loose on her.

Best not to dwell on that. Jules quickly kissed her. "You made me totally happy during Fashion Week. I mean, at the end."

Vivian sighed. "Anyway, I knew it was time. And then I…" Her voice trailed off, and she obviously didn't know what to say next.

"And then you decided we should be celibate," Jules said. She stroked her fingertips over Vivian's thigh. "That was your best idea ever."

"Ha, ha," Vivian said. She touched Jules's shoulder and tugged.

It was a summons Jules was only too happy to obey. She lowered herself back into Vivian's arms and tucked her head beneath Vivian's chin.

"Thanks for telling me that," she murmured.

"Felicity's sleeping a few doors down from the bedroom we share. It seemed relevant."

Vivian's careless tone didn't deceive Jules for a second. She didn't know what specifically had prompted Vivian to tell her this tonight. She might never know. Vivian Carlisle would never run out of mysteries, that was for sure.

And that was okay. Jules fully intended to spend the rest of her life solving as many as she could.

———————

"Buh."

"Exactly."

"Ah-blub."

"I agree completely."

Felicity's next noise was a raspberry, so Jules simply nodded and bounced her.

"We'll be back in a couple of hours," Vivian told Zahra. "Ben will pick us up at the park and take us to Harvest Kitchen at eleven for brunch."

"Enjoy." Zahra smiled and touched Felicity on her button nose. "Have a good time with your moms, cutie."

Felicity cooed.

"Okay, sweetie. Go to Mommy." Jules handed Felicity to Vivian.

Felicity promptly tried to grab Vivian's nose. She missed.

"And that's why I've stopped wearing dangle earrings," Vivian grumbled, but she kissed Felicity's chubby cheek.

Jules opened the door and picked up the folded stroller so she could carry it down the carriage house steps. She was getting to be a real pro at this. As Vivian followed with Felicity, Jules unfolded the stroller, snapped the wheels and handlebars in place, and positioned the straps so Vivian could put Felicity into the seat.

"Do you think her hat is warm enough?" Vivian asked. "It's a pretty thin knit, and it's cold out."

"It's just past ten." Jules buckled Felicity securely into the padded straps and tugged on them to test the give. "It'll warm up."

Vivian fastened the diaper bag to the stroller handle. "If you say so. Ready?"

"Let's go."

They set off down the sidewalk toward Central Park, Jules pushing the heavily laden stroller. It was a decent workout for her arms. They were looking pretty toned lately.

The stroller had two cupholders, both of which carried thermoses of coffee. Vivian took one. "It's a beautiful day."

She was right. The sky was blue, and there wasn't a cloud in it. The leaves were beginning to change into their fall colors, although they wouldn't peak for another week or two.

Jules's lungs ached pleasantly as she took in a deep breath of crisp autumn air.

Just then a strong breeze hit them, and Felicity began to whimper.

Vivian quickly leaned in to see her. "I told you she needed a warmer hat."

"Yeah, yeah, yeah." Jules could admit when she was wrong. "I put a spare one in the bag."

"You did?" Vivian opened the bag and began to rummage through it.

"Yes. It's by the… Oh, you found it."

Vivian pulled out the little fleece cap and stared at it. Then she shot Jules a pointed glare.

"What? It'll be super cute on her," Jules protested.

Vivian took the mustard-colored cap and leaned in toward Felicity. She asked, "Mama certainly has some bad opinions about colors, doesn't she?"

Felicity stopped whimpering as soon as the cap was on.

"See?" Jules said. "She likes it. Kid has good taste."

After one more critical look, Vivian straightened up and returned to Jules's side. "Julia, you know I've never cared for yellow."

"So I've heard." As they began to walk again, Jules nudged Vivian gently with her elbow. "But you care for me."

Vivian snorted but didn't deny it and even looped her arm through Jules's as Jules pushed the stroller.

They approached the end of the block. Across the street, Central Park waited with its myriad paths and landmarks. At this time of day, the grass would still be wet with dew, the earth dark and damp. In spite of their solitude, Vivian's voice was quiet when she said, "I do more than care for you. I love you. You know that."

Jules blinked. Suddenly, Central Park looked blurry across the street and she had a lump in her throat.

She turned to Vivian, who said nothing about her tears but gave her a small, affectionate smile.

Conversations had been had. Plans had been made. Lawyers had been consulted. The words "adoption" and "second parent" had appeared on numerous documents. And yet, after all the paperwork and legalese, nothing ever made Jules feel as much a part of her own family as moments like this.

"Yes." Her voice was thick, but nothing was going to stop the smile she gave Vivian, wider and more brilliant. "I do know that."

"Smart girl." Vivian squeezed her arm. "I always thought you were more than just a pretty face."

"Yeah?"

"Oh yes. Given enough time, you might even convince me that yellow's not so bad after all."

Jules gave her a dubious look.

"Or not," Vivian conceded.

The street was quiet. Nobody was looking. "Or not," Jules agreed and leaned in, kissing her gently.

One thing was certain in this life: loving Vivian Carlisle would never, ever go out of style.

OTHER BOOKS FROM
YLVA PUBLISHING

www.ylva-publishing.com

THE X INGREDIENT
Roslyn Sinclair

ISBN: 978-3-96324-271-7
Length: 285 pages (103,000 words)

Top Atlanta lawyer, icy Diana Parker, is driven and ruthless, and stuck in a failing marriage. Her new assistant, Laurie, seems all wrong for the job. Yet something seems to be pulling them into a secret, thrilling dance that's far too dangerous for a boss and employee.

How can they resist the irresistible?

A smart, sexy lesbian romance about daring to face the truth about who you are.

THE AWKWARD TRUTH
Lee Winter

ISBN: 978-3-96324-583-1
Length: 289 pages (102,000 words)

Ice queen lawyer Felicity runs on pure ambition. When her media mogul boss asks her to solve a mystery at a Bronx pet charity, she's on it.

She can't help noticing gorgeous soft-butch vet Dr. Cooper and her adorable dog. But Felicity's determined not to be distracted even if that might be exactly what she needs.

This funny opposites-attract lesbian romance digs up the awkward truth about what really matters in life.

JUST FOR SHOW
Jae

ISBN: 978-3-95533-980-7
Length: 293 pages (103,000 words)

When Claire, an overachieving psychologist with OCD tendencies, hires Lana, an impulsive, out-of-work actress for a fake relationship, she figures the worst she'll have to endure are the messes Lana leaves around. It's only for a few months anyway. And it's not as if she'll enjoy all those fake kisses and loving looks. Right?

A lesbian romance where role-playing has never been so irresistible.

A ROLL IN THE HAY
Lola Keeley

ISBN: 978-3-96324-355-4
Length: 185 pages (66,000 words)

Veterinarian Tess has quit the city and her cheating girlfriend for a new life in a Scottish village. On day one, she has a run-in with stuck-up Lady Karlson who tries to boss Tess around as if she owns the whole town… which she sort of does. But could there be something more to the constant, rising tension between the warring pair?

An enemies-to-lovers lesbian romance about making your own path.

ABOUT ROSLYN SINCLAIR

Roslyn Sinclair was born in the southern USA, but she's now enjoying the Northeast and its beautiful fall weather—not so much the colder winters! She loves to travel and has gotten writing inspiration everywhere from Kansas City to Beijing. Roslyn lives with her wife and a cat who, while old and cantankerous, is nevertheless a very good boy.

CONNECT WITH ROSLYN
Website: www.roslynsinclair.com
Facebook: www.facebook.com/roslyn.sinclair.338
Twitter: @writingroslyn
Instagram: www.instagram.com/roslyn_writes
E-Mail: roslynwrites@gmail.com

Above All Things
© 2022 by Roslyn Sinclair

ISBN: 978-3-96324-648-7

Available in e-book and paperback formats.

Published by Ylva Publishing, legal entity of Ylva Verlag, e.Kfr.

Ylva Verlag, e.Kfr.
Owner: Astrid Ohletz
Am Kirschgarten 2
65830 Kriftel
Germany

www.ylva-publishing.com

First edition: 2022

Credits
Edited by Lee Winter and Julie Klein
Cover Design and Print Layout by Streetlight Graphics

CPSIA information can be obtained
at www.ICGtesting.com
Printed in the USA
LVHW042150300522
720037LV00002B/207